THE RAINBOW ABYSS

Barbara Hambly

Grafton

An Imprint of HarperCollins*Publishers*

Grafton
An Imprint of HarperCollins*Publishers*
77–85 Fulham Palace Road,
Hammersmith, London W6 8JB

Special overseas edition 1991
This edition published by Grafton 1992
9 8 7 6 5 4 3 2 1

First published in Great Britain by
Grafton Books 1991

ISBN 0 586 21300 7

Set in Times

Printed in Great Britain by
HarperCollinsManufacturing Glasgow

Barbara Hambly is the author of many highly successful fantasy novels, including *The Darwath Trilogy*, *Dragonsbane* and her series of tales about the mercenaries Sun Wolf and Star Hawk. She has also written a vampire tale, *Immortal Blood*, two Star Trek novels and the novelization of the television series *Beauty and the Beast*.

As well as a Masters degree in medieval history, she holds a black belt in karate.

By the same author

The Darwath Trilogy:
The Time of the Dark
The Walls of Air
The Armies of Daylight

Dragonsbane
The Ladies of Mandrigyn
The Witches of Wenshar
The Dark Hand of Magic
The Silent Tower
The Silicon Mage
Immortal Blood

For Mary Ann

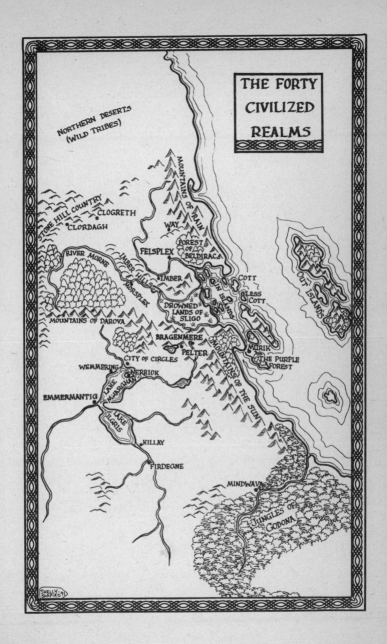

ONE

"IT MAY NOT HAPPEN HERE."

"That's what they said about the Plague."

Shavus Ciarnin, Archmage of the Order of the Morkensik Wizards, flashed an irritated look at his old friend's pupil—Rhion the Brown merely pushed his spectacles a little more firmly into place on the bridge of his nose with one pudgy forefinger and returned the glare calmly. Old Jaldis the Blind brushed a tendril of milk-white hair from the tattered blanket that wrapped his thin shoulders and moved a little closer to the brown wall of chimney bricks which was the tiny attic's only source of heat. "So they did," he observed mildly. "I do not see how it *can* happen here . . . or how it could have happened at all. But this lack of understanding on my part does not alter the fact that it *has* happened there . . ."

"Don't be a fool," Ciarnin snapped irritably. His scarred, sun-darkened face seemed to darken still further, cold blue eyes appearing very light in their deep sockets. "Magic can't just cease to exist! Magic *is*! It's an element, like the light of the sun, like the air we breathe! Men could no more stop it from existing than they could keep the sun from rising by shaking their fists at it."

"To our knowledge," the blind mage replied in his curiously sweet, toneless voice.

Huddled in his threadbare cloak at his master's feet—the room only boasted two chairs—Rhion could barely recall what Jaldis' true voice had been like. He'd only heard it upon one occasion, when he was sixteen, a few months before the old king's troops had arrested Lord Henak, Jaldis' then-patron, and torn out Jaldis' tongue and eyes to keep him from witching them while they'd brought the traitor earl and his court mage to trial in the High City of Nerriok. The only reason they hadn't cut off the wizard's hands as well was because they'd feared he'd die of gangrene before judgment could be passed.

For the eleven years since his acquittal, Jaldis had spoken by means of a curved rosewood box which hung strapped to his chest, a sounding-chamber filled with intricate mechanisms of silver, reed, and gut, even as he saw—after a fashion and with head-splitting concentration—by means of a pair of massive spectacles wrought of opal, crystal, and gold. Charging the left lens with spells of seeing had been Rhion's first attempt at major magic, and he still remembered the shuddering surge of joy he'd felt when he'd seen the lattices of the crystal's inner structure shift and change, seen life stir deep in the opals' pale, fiery wells. The sense of release had been almost like the physical breaking-open of some locked core of bone deep in his chest, the realization that all those dreams, all those longings, all the strange madnesses which had whispered in his mind since childhood had been real . . .

He remembered, too, the week of vomiting and delirium which had followed, for of course he'd been far too young to attempt anything like the power needed for such spells. He'd tried desperately to keep his illness hidden—it had been his parents' first clue to their only son's abilities, and he'd come back to consciousness to the news that they had published, in all the temples of the Forty Realms, the notices of his death.

Though he'd never told Jaldis, Rhion's own extreme short-sightedness dated from the casting of those spells.

"And yet you must admit, Shavus," that thin, buzzing drone went on, "that there are places in this world where there is no air—in the depths of oceans and rivers—and no light, in caves and crevices . . . indeed, for half the turning of the day there is no light anywhere. And there are places, as we all know, where magic does not exist."

"Bah," the Archmage grunted, and the back of his cracked and much-mended chair creaked with the uneasy movement of his shoulders. The attic room above the Black Pig Inn, which had served Jaldis and Rhion as lodgings for the last two and a half years, was unheated, save for the warmth which radiated from the bricks of the kitchen chimney. On snowy midwinter evenings like this one it saved them from freezing to death, but when the turgid warmth of the low-plains summers held the city of Felsplex in its grip, the room was unspeakable. There was no fireplace in the room itself, nor any kind of candle or brazier—the landlord having an almost hysterical fear of fire—but, despite the fact that the windows were closed against the bitter cold by heavy wooden shutters, the lack of light posed little problem for wizards. Though the three men—young, middle-aged, and old—sat in complete darkness, Rhion could see the Archmage's square, ugly face and coarse shock of iron-gray hair as easily as if the room were flooded with daylight. And he saw how the pale eyes shifted at the mention of such things. "Any fool knows about those."

"But this is more than the Chambers of Silence," Jaldis went on, "that lords build into the dungeons of their palaces to hold a wizard's power in check—more than the *pheelas* root that numbs our skills, more than the spells of silence, the fields of silence, that a powerful mage can weave to cripple his mageborn foes." Behind sunken and shriveled eyelids ruined muscles moved, as if his destroyed gaze could still encompass the gray-haired old ex-soldier opposite him and the short, sturdy young man at his feet. From the top of a stack of books beside his chair, Jaldis' opal spectacles seemed to review the room with a bulging, asymmetrical gaze, and the old man's hand, deft and shapely before arthritis had deformed it, stroked subconsciously at the talismans of power which festooned the rosewood soundbox like queer and glittering seaweed upon a rock.

"I am speaking of a world, a universe, where magic does not exist at all, and has not existed for many years."

"And I'm saying such a thing's preposterous," Shavus retorted. "What you *think* you heard . . . what you *might* have seen . . ." He shook his head again, angry and dismissive, but Rhion saw the heavy, corded hand fidget uncomfortably with the snagged brown wool of his robe.

"I know what it is that I felt." Jaldis' thin face hardened with a flash of angry pride, though the monotonous voice of the soundbox did not alter. "I have opened a Dark Well and through it have seen into the Void which lies between all the infinite number of universes of which the Cosmos is made! And in that Void . . ." The sweet, shrill tones sank. "In that Void I heard a voice crying out of a world where magic had once existed, but now exists no more."

"Jaldis, old friend . . ." Shavus leaned forward placatingly, causing the ruinous chair to emit an alarming creak. "I'm not saying you didn't see it, didn't hear it. But I am asking how, if magic has ceased to exist in some other universe, someone there could make his voice heard in the Void? I've studied the Void as well, you know. I've opened Dark Wells into it, to try to glimpse something of how the Cosmos is formed . . ."

"I'm glad someone has," Rhion remarked, folding his arms around his knees and huddling a little more deeply into his faded black cloak. "The other night when Jaldis asked me to get a message to you about this was the first I'd even *heard* of the things."

"Which is as it should be," the Archmage snapped irritably. "It is not a branch of knowledge for the young—or the light-minded."

He turned back to face the blind man, bundled like a drying skeleton in cloak and quilts which all but hid the tattered brown robes of the foremost Order of Wizards in the world. His tough, seamed face softened. "Old friend, in all my studies of the Void, in all my communications across it and through it, I've never encountered a world where magic in some form didn't exist. I'm not denying that you heard something. But one piece of hearsay is damn little grounds to risk the hideous danger of crossing the Void itself, as you're asking me to do . . ."

"Not asking, Shavus," the old man said softly. "Begging. Someone must go there. Someone must help them. Don't you see that . . ."

Heavy footsteps on the narrow wooden spiral of the stairs made the whole building shudder. The Black Pig rose four floors above the common rooms and kitchens, a rickety inverted ziggurat of ever-protruding balconies and upper floors seemingly supported by a mystifying web of clotheslines and makeshift bridges over the streets and by the surrounding buildings against which it leaned. Rhion frequently wondered what would happen if any of the overcrowded tenements, taverns, countinghouses or gimcrack temples of unpronounceable foreign gods that made up the river quays quarter of Felsplex were to disappear. Beyond a doubt the entire district would come crashing down like a house of cards.

It was the landlord. Rhion recognized the tread. Pulling his cloak tighter about him, he got to his feet and navigated delicately among the few pieces of furniture which cluttered even that tiny chamber, summoning a blue-burning shred of magelight to flicker like will-o'-the-wisp above his head. The wavery gleam only served to make the room appear dingier, its moving shadows outlining with pitiless emphasis the cracks in the plaster of the walls, the stained beams from which bunches of winter mallow and stork grass hung drying, the chipped cups and water-vessels, and the precious books and scrolls arranged neatly along the table's rear edge. Darkness would have been less depressing, but Rhion had long ago learned that those who were not mageborn found wizards' ability to see without light disproportionately unnerving.

"Lady to see you," the landlord grunted, scratching his crotch.

"Are you—er—a wizard?"

Rhion was awfully tired of the question and of the dubious look that invariably accompanied it. He'd grown his beard as soon as he was old enough to do so, but the short-clipped, scruffy brown tangle evidently did nothing to dispel the boyishness of his face nor the way his wide-set blue eyes were magnified by the lenses of his spectacles. Short, unobtrusive, and of the compact, sturdy build which slips so easily into chubbiness, even without a wizard's ability to move unobserved he would have been the last person anyone noticed in a crowd.

The lady who was waiting for him in the smallest of the inn's private parlors had obviously been expecting someone a little more impressive.

He considered responding with *Are you—er—a lady?* but suppressed the impulse. He and Jaldis needed the rent. Instead he smiled genially and said, "We come in all shapes and sizes, mistress. Would you trust me more if I had horns and a tail?"

She let out an unsteady titter and her eyes, above a concealing veil of purple-embroidered silk, strayed to the hem of his robe as if she really expected to see the jointed tail of a scorpion-grim peeking out.

Inwardly, Rhion sighed. *Gold pieces to barleycorns she wants a love-potion . . .*

"And how may I serve you?" he asked, still with a smile and the reflection that asking the question in his capacity as wizard was an improvement upon doing so in the capacity of bar-boy, a position he'd occasionally filled at the Black Pig when things got bad. *If my father could see me now . . .*

She leaned forward, her little purple-gloved hands clenched upon the scrubbed oak tabletop. "There is . . . a man."

Rhion sat down on the opposite side of the table, folded his hands, and nodded encouragingly. Above the edge of the veil, her eyes were dark, enormous, and painted with green kohl and powdered gold; her cloak was lined with marten fur. From his days of loitering in the most fashionable scent shops in the City of Circles, he could price her perfume to within a few royals, and it wasn't cheap.

She went on, softly and simply as a child, "He must love me or I shall die."

"And he doesn't."

The delicate brows above those immense eyes puckered tragically. "He doesn't know I'm alive. He is fickle, frivolous . . . his affections turn on a whim. Give me something that will draw him to me, something that will make him love me . . ."

Rhion had never, personally, been able to fathom why human beings persisted in craving the love of people who didn't know they were alive, but this was far from the first time he'd encountered the phenomenon, or used the proceeds to put food on the table.

"Look," he said gently. "Are you sure he's the kind of man you want? If he's that fickle, that frivolous . . . A love-potion won't change what a person is. Only—and only temporarily—whom they want."

"That is enough," she breathed, and clasped her hands at

her breast as if to contain the throbbing of her heart. Her cloak, falling back a little, showed strand upon strand of filigreed silver beads at her throat, gleaming against a ground of ribbon and featherwork like a field of summer flowers. "If only I can have the chance to win his regard, I know I can make him love me. If once I hold him in my arms, I know he will come back." She swayed forward and clutched his hand, as if fearing he would rise to his towering five-feet-five and denounce her as a strumpet. "Oh, name your price!"

They always said, *Name your price*, but Rhion had learned over the years what the going rate on love-philters was and had also learned that the rich especially would be screaming for the magistrates if the sum quoted were so much as a dequin above it.

He fetched candles from the mantelpiece, noting automatically as he passed the door of the common room the two chair bearers and the linkboy, drinking wine from boiled-leather cups beside that room's enormous hearth. Unlike the attics, the commons and the private parlors downstairs were pleasantly warm, redolent of beer and woodsmoke, sweat, onion stew, and the sawdust that strewed the floor. Judging by their clothes, the chair bearers were hired men, probably ex-slaves who'd bought themselves free and gone into business, for of course his client, no matter how rich she was, would have used hired bearers to bring her here, rather than her own household slaves.

No lady of respectable family would let her own servants know about coming to a place like the Black Pig, let alone to visit a wizard. People did visit wizards, of course, and pay for their services, in spite of the fulminations of every priest of every god in the landscape, the same way his father had visited the more expensive prostitutes and his mother had visited those skilled in the dyeing of hair. They just didn't talk about it. As he brought the tapers back to the table, he was aware of the way his client clutched her cloak about her

and of the apprehension in the doelike eyes gazing at him
from above the veil. She flinched when he sat down again,
drawing as far from him as the high-backed chair would allow; and when he said, "Take off your glove," her painted
eyelids made as great a play as if he'd asked her to remove
her dress.

From a pocket in his robe he took a twist of paper containing the herbal powder that was the basis of all love-
philters, a supply of which he kept made up beforehand.
From another pocket he drew the piece of red chalk he always carried and a goose-feather. He explained, "For a love-
potion to work, it has to carry the . . . the scent, the essence,
of your flesh."

"I know." Her voice sank to a whisper. "They said you
. . . you would mix it upon my naked body."

Before he could stop himself Rhion said, "Well, generally
we do, but this table's awfully hard and the fire's gone
down . . ."

"I would not mind the cold." Her eyes smoldered, and
Rhion bit his tongue in exasperation, both at himself for making the joke and at her for not realizing it *was* one.

"A hand will be fine."

She removed her glove and offered her soft little palm,
scented with attar of roses. Rhion turned her hand over and
poured a quantity of the powder on the back. "If you'll keep
silent now," he remembered to say. He'd never had a client
yet, male or female, who, if not silenced beforehand, didn't
feel compelled to relate the details of the affair while he was
trying to concentrate on the spells.

She let out her breath, looking a little disappointed.

He took the woman's thumb and little finger gently in his
own two hands, which rested on the table on either side of
hers. Closing his eyes, he slowed his breathing and stilled
his thoughts, calling up and focusing the power that rose
from within himself like the slow expansion of a single can-

dle's light gradually illuminating some enormous, darkened room. This was the part of spell-weaving that he loved and the part that made him most uneasy at times like this, the most vulnerable in the presence of these representatives of the mundane world for whom wizardry was a matter of rumor and whisper and dread.

Though his eyes were shut, he could see the woman's hand still, lying between his own. The green-gold powder sparkled against the creamy flesh in the candles' limpid light. In time, eyes still shut, he moved his hands, making the correct passes in the air above the powder, drawing with the thin, glimmery air-traces that only a wizard could see the runes of binding, the symbols of oneness, that imbued the dried rose petals and shamrock leaves with the essences of the woman's well-cared-for flesh. His mind blended with the scents of the powdered sandalwood and salts, the smell of her perfume, the warmth of her hand, and the perfect shape of those cowlike brown eyes. He heard the high, delicate sweetness of her voice in his mind as a lover would hear it, finding its childish accents endearing rather than annoying, seeing in those wonderful eyes heart-touching innocence rather than—as was his private opinion—self-centered stupidity.

You must love them when you weave the spells, Jaldis had said to him years ago . . . *Seven? Six? . . .* when he had taught him the spells for the drawing of the heart. *Love them for their own sake, as a true lover does, whatever your private self may think. See charm in their imperfections, as the shadows of flowers mottle a sunlit wall. You must understand what beauty is before you can wake desire for it in another mind.*

It had taken him a long time to learn that, he recalled. Months of watching flowing water and the shadows of flowers. He still wasn't sure he understood.

Opening his eyes, he gently brushed the table before him

with the goose-feather, then tipped the woman's hand so that the powder spilled off. Delicately he feathered the last residue from her skin, then with the chalk drew a small Circle of Power around the grains, and closed his eyes again. With the feather, with his fingers, with his mind, he shaped in the air above it the runes necessary for the spell, calling down the constellations of power and the clusters of invisible realities related to each archetypical sign.

The Cup, the rune of the heart, filled with clear water and utterly mutable, ruled by the Moon and the tides. The sixth rune, of caring and giving and duality, of two voices blending in harmony, and of the warmth closed in between two hands. The fifteenth, ugly and dark, the rune of obsession that chains the will and blurs the senses, sculpting reality to what one wishes it to be. And all the while the woman sat across from him, gazing with those huge, affrighted eyes, or glancing nervously back into the lights and laughter of the common room as if she feared that among the dock workers and fishwives gathered there she'd see one of her fashionable friends, someone who'd recognize her and tell. Rhion was not a particularly strong wizard, and after ten and a half years of study he'd come to understand that, even if he attained the level of learning Jaldis and Shavus had, he'd probably still never have their terrible strength. But he did weave a very pretty lovespell, though he said it himself.

"Sprinkle this into his cup or his food, if you can," he said later, handing her the ensorcelled powder done up in a twist of cheap yellow paper. "If you can't get access to his food, sprinkle it on his clothing, or his bed."

"And it will bring him to me?" She raised those childlike eyes to his. Standing with her on the threshold of the common room, Rhion was uneasily conscious of the way the chair men were watching him, as if they suspected him of laying witcheries on this woman to draw her back to his bed some night against her will. "It will make him love me?"

"It will bring him to you," Rhion said wearily, pushing his spectacles up more firmly onto the bridge of his nose. "He will desire you for a few hours, a few days, and forget about the others in the intensity of his desire. But unless you can win his real love, his genuine affection and care—unless you can be someone that he *can* love—it won't last. It never does. There is no counterfeit for love, and over love, magic has no power."

But in her sparkling eyes he saw she wasn't listening.

Rhion climbed the stairs again feeling tired and rather old. His sense of alienation from the nonmageborn world hadn't been lessened by an encounter with the landlord, a massive man with a stubbled chin and the broken nose of a prize-fighter, who had intercepted him on his way through the kitchen and relieved him of half the silver royals the woman had paid. "For use of the room," he'd growled, and Rhion hadn't argued. It had been difficult enough finding anyone willing to rent to wizards in the first place.

Jaldis was still sitting, wrapped in cloak and blankets, in his wobbly chair near the chimney wall. The sharp point of his chin was sunk on his breast so that his short-trimmed silver beard touched the soundbox at his chest. At the creak of Rhion's foot upon the floorboards he raised his head, his long white hair catching the wan glimmer of the witchlight that his pupil called into being among the slanting rafters overhead. The talismans dangling from the soundbox clinked and glittered faintly with the movement: pendants wrought of silver and crystal, discs of animal bone, scraps of parchment enclosed in glass or gold and the single great golden sun-cross which Shavus had made for him, symbol of the living strength of magic and its eternal renewal—objects imbued with power by all the wizards who had given him them, so that the magic which set the box's delicate chords and whistles vibrating would not fail when Jaldis' own strength became exhausted by other spells.

"Shavus is gone?"

The old man nodded. "I had hoped that I could prevail upon him to help me," he said softly, the whisper of the instrument like the sigh of harpstrings when the wind passes through. "But he sees nothing . . . nothing."

"I'm not sure my own vision of the subject is noticeably more acute." Rhion turned up the sleeves of his brown robe and those of the rough-knitted pullover he wore beneath it and began to clear the tiny coffee cups the three wizards had drunk from earlier in the evening. The dreamy velvet bitterness of the coffee and the sweet pungence of cinnamon still flavored the air, mingling with the astringent scent of the overhead herbs and the smoke that seeped from the bricks of the chimney wall. "You're saying it's possible to . . . to *cross* this Void you're talking about? To go to other . . ." He hesitated. "Other universes?"

"Not only possible," the old man murmured, "but necessary."

Rhion paused in the act of dipping wash-water from the half-empty bucket, placed near the chimney bricks to keep it from freezing, and cocked an eyebrow at his mentor. "Necessary . . . but not safe."

"No." The word was no more than a drawn-out buzz of strings, a vibrating inflection of weariness and defeat. "Not safe."

Rhion was silent, unable to picture a world so incomprehensibly separated from that which he knew.

In the ten years he had followed Jaldis, learning from him the whole tangled complex of facts and lists, spells and metaphysics, meditation and mental technique that constituted what the mundane world called "magic", Rhion had known the old man kept certain secrets, certain knowledge, to himself. In the books and scrolls Jaldis had so painfully collected over the years Rhion had found references to things he did not understand, things Jaldis sometimes explained and sometimes evaded on the grounds that his student had not been studying long enough . . .

But the night before last—when the old man had stumbled, exhausted, from the tiny chamber hidden under the eaves in which he had been closeted since the early winter sundown and had whispered to him to bring the Archmage—had been the first time that Rhion had heard of the Dark Well, the Void, or other universes besides the one he knew.

Frightened by his master's ghastly pallor and ragged breathing, Rhion had called the Archwizard's name again and again into the strongest of Jaldis' several scrying-crystals, until at last Shavus had answered. That night had been the night of the winter solstice, when all wizards were taking advantage of the additional power generated by the balance point of sun and stars to work deeper and stronger spells than were ordinarily possible, and Shavus had been less than pleased at the interruption. But he had come, with such speed that Rhion guessed he had not stopped for rest anywhere on the snow-covered roads between his house in the forest of Beldirac and the gates of Felsplex.

"Why 'necessary'?" he asked, spreading out a rough towel and setting the cups to dry. "Yes, if there's a world where magic has ceased to exist it should be investigated . . ."

"It must be investigated without delay." With sudden energy Jaldis rose to his feet, his hand finding at once the crutches which leaned against the side of his chair. In addition to blinding him and cutting out his tongue, all those years ago, the old king's soldiers had hamstrung him as well. Rhion hurried to help him, knowing he was still far from recovered from his fatigue, but leaning on the long sticks of bog-oak with their padding of leather and rags, the blind mage seemed suddenly flooded with a driven energy. Mummified in blankets, he had appeared fragile, almost tiny;

standing up, he was half a head taller than his pupil. When they had first met, he had been taller still.

"*He* won't see the urgency of it, the importance of it," the blind man went on, turning to limp toward the tiny door nearly hidden in the shadows of the far wall. "But *you* must."

He paused, his crippled hand on the rough wooden latch, turning back to Rhion as if the sunken eyepits still had sight, as if the dark, haughty gaze he had once had was still his to compel, to command. "Someone must go to that world to learn *why* magic failed there. If it was something that men did . . ."

"Could they have?" Rhion felt suddenly loath to have him open that cracked plank door, dreading what might lie beyond for reasons he did not himself understand.

Some of the furious lines of concentration and will eased, leaving Jaldis' features sunken and old. "I do not know." He pushed open the door, and, limping on his crutches, hobbled through, Rhion following unwillingly, wiping the wash water from his hands, the ribbon of ghostlight trailing in their wake like will-o'-the-wisp.

This second room, no more than a triangular nook of waste space under the steeply slanting roof, had never been intended for anything but storage. During their first year of residence at the Black Pig, Rhion had spent many nights surreptitiously shifting decades' accumulation of mouse-infested junk to other sections of the attics to make of this closet an inner sanctum, a meditation chamber, a workplace of the deeper and more secret magics that comprised the true heart of the calling that was their life. It was unlighted and unbearably stuffy, and though, like their dwelling-room, ringed about with spells against the roaches and mice to be found everywhere else in the inn, it still had the dirty, musty smell of these vermin and of dry rot and smoke. From barely head-high by the door, the ceiling beams slanted sharply to the floor, forming the hypotenuse of a triangle scarcely twelve feet across the base.

In this place Jaldis—and Rhion, when he could—worked in the deepest meditations that were the foundation of the wizard's metaphysical arts, sinking the mind into silence and stretching out the senses, scrying through fire and water, crystal, and the fine-spun fabric of the wind, to study the shape and balance and pulsebeat of the world. Here in the inky silence they practiced the magics of illusion and light, not for their own sake but for what they could teach about the nature of the mind. Here Rhion meditated and studied the nature of the runes which were the foundation of the magic as the Morkensik Order practiced it; the making of the hundreds of sigils that were built of them, and the greater, more complex seals that called together from a swirling chaos of probabilities the loci of power and likelihood, bridging the gap between the will and something more. Here Rhion practiced patiently and slowly all those spells which Jaldis had taught him over the years, memorizing their forms and painstakingly exercising the slender powers that were his, until he could call trickles of water up the slanted side of a dish, bring forth illusions of flowers and jewels, make a talisman of gold which would rob poison of its virulence, or cause dustdevils to swirl all around the shut and windless room.

And in this place, Rhion saw now, Jaldis had drawn Circles of Power on the floor, circles which occupied almost the whole of that tiny chamber: circles in chalk and silver-dust, in springwater and in blood, crossed and interwoven with rings and spirals of pure, glimmering light that only wizards could see, drawn in the air above the worn and splintery floorboards or sinking down into them, visible a few inches into their depth like light submerged in water . . . stars and crescents and the sun-cross of power, all feeding the energies of air and life and the turning earth into holding the circle intact.

And in the center of that circle was darkness, a column of shadow that even Rhion's dark-sighted eyes could not pierce: a darkness which filled him with uneasy horror.

"It took me three days to call it into being." The voice of the box was no more than a thread of sweetness in the terrible silence of that tiny room. "With the strength that magic can call from the solstice's power I sent my mind deep into that Well, seeking to learn something of the nature of magic, the nature of the Cosmos that divides universe from universe in an infinity of colors and dark."

Staring into the darkness, Rhion barely heard him. It seemed to draw him, as some men are drawn with terrible vertigo to the edge of a precipice. Staring into it, he thought he saw movement there, strange iridescences as if blackness had been refracted into shuddering rainbows of something other than color, anomalous stirrings that trailed lightless fire.

Behind him, Jaldis' voice went on. "I caught glimpses of things I do not understand, of worlds whose natures and substructures are incomprehensible to me: ships that whirled flashing between stars; clouds of terrible and free-floating power, drifting eternally in the abyss. And somewhere in that chaos I heard a voice crying out, 'Magic is dead . . . magic is dead. If any can hear us there where magic thrives, magic is dead here, dead . . . magic is dead. It has been gone for two hundred years.' "

Rhion looked back at him, seeing in the soft blue glow of the witchlight the desperate tension in the old man's withered face, the mingled grief and eagerness, as if he heard again that thin voice crying. "Over and over it called, and I called back, 'I hear you! I will help you!' " His hand trembled on the crutches; his voice would have, too, had the forces of law left him with one. "I do not know whether they heard me or not."

With a sigh he turned away, as if he could no longer bear to stand so close to the place where he had heard those terrible pleas. Slowly he limped from the room, Rhion following thankfully at his heels. The witchlight drifted after them; looking back over his shoulder as he closed the door, Rhion could see that even the soft clarity of that light could not pierce the dreadful shadow held prisoned within the ensorcelled rings.

"He might have been speaking of some kind of—of field effect, the kind of thing you'd get with a spell of silence and a talismanic resonator."

"No." Jaldis shook his head as he sank once more back into his chair by the chimney wall, gathering his patched blankets about his rawboned frame. Among the rafters, the wind groaned, the whole building shuddering faintly, like a horse twitching flies from its skin. In the silence that followed, Rhion could hear the dry skitter of ice fragments, blown like sand across the tiles overhead. "He would not have spoken so, calling into the Void for help, were there any hope of help within his own world."

Below them, the inn's guests were preparing for bed. Muffled voices and the scrape of furniture came dimly through the floor, a woman's laugh. Had he concentrated, as wizards were trained to do, Rhion could have pinpointed and identified the inhabitants of every room.

"Men hate magic, Rhion," Jaldis continued very softly, his twisted hands rubbing his shoulders for warmth. The witchlight that had rippled like a sheet of blown silk in the darkness was growing small and dim—it caught a final gleam on Jaldis' sun-cross talisman, on the gold lettering of a book's worn spine and the staring, ironic crystal rounds of the spectacles still balanced beside his chair. "They hate magic and hate those of us born with the ability to work it. That woman who paid you tonight, she too will hate you in her heart, for you can do something which she cannot. If magic has perished in some other world—in an entire world, an entire universe—we must learn why. I must go on seeking, go on scrying in the Well no matter what the cost to me, to you, to anyone. I must convince Shavus to help me, to go to that world in spite of all the peril of crossing the Void.

"Don't you see?" He turned desperately toward Rhion with his sunken eyelids, his closed and scar-torn lips, wreckage left by the hatred of magic which only magic could now relieve. "If men found some way to cause this to happen, how long will it be before those in our world, in this world, learn to do so, too, and destroy magic here forever?"

TWO

RHION WOKE WITH A START, FROM A CONFUSION OF UNEASY dreams.

He was back in the Old Bridge Market in the City of Circles: a plump little dandy in a red velvet doublet whose buttons flashed with rubies and to whose carefully dressed brown curls clung the scent of cloves. Blue and yellow awnings flapped in the bright spring sunlight around the ancient bridge-temple of Bran Rhu. The air was thick with the smell of lilies and the stink of the river's sewage below. Rhion was thumbing through the old pieces of broken books piled in a used-paper seller's barrow: fragments of romances and hymnals, their illuminations faded and yellowed like dessicated leaves; scrolls of religion and philosophy with their glue cracking along the joins; old household receipt books; and the accounts of forgotten military campaigns. The lowest of kitchen slaves would come by occasionally to buy the stuff by the bagful for kindling and would look at that modishly dressed youth with curiosity and suspicion in their eyes. Rhion, even as he examined the incomprehensible glyphs of a red and green accordion-fold book from the unknown south, tried to formulate in his mind some fashionable motive—mockery, or aesthetics, or something of the kind—should one of his fashionable friends see him and laugh . . .

A shadow had fallen over him. "Are you hunting for secrets?" Jaldis asked.

And turning, Rhion saw him for the first time.

But this time—he had dreamed this scene before—Jaldis looked as he did now. His face was thin and gray under the stringy web of his beard, his white hair no thicker than spider-floss in the sunlit breeze. The threadbare blankets and worn black cloak which wrapped him parted to reveal the voice-box strapped to his breast, and its silvery drone was all the voice that Rhion heard.

No! he thought, his mind clutching at the receding shreds of the deep, musical tones which had originally framed those words. *No, he's not like that! He wasn't like that, not then! His hair and beard were still mostly brown, he still had his eyes then, dark and luminous and kind . . .*

But his mind could reconstruct neither the image of him as he had been, nor the sound of his voice.

As he had indeed done on that day of glassy sunlight and intoxicating flower-scents so many years ago, Jaldis reached into the paper seller's barrow and brought out a book.

But instead of the few pages of star lore and mathematics that it had actually been, it was a book with black covers, covered with dust and sticky with cobweb. The air around it seemed to quiver fitfully, half-visible spirals of light shuddering like a heat dance, and when Rhion opened it, what he held in his hands was not a book at all. Only darkness lay contained in those black covers, a darkness which dropped away into a hole of inky nothing between his hands. As he stared at it in horror, the Abyss exploded upward around him, like water gushing up from a spring; a darkness filled with colors that should not have been colors, gouging a hollow in air and light and in all sane things as if the world which he knew had merely been painted on paper, now touched to destroying flame. Airless beyond comprehension, cold as he had never understood cold could be, the darkness opened around him like the unfurling petals of a sable rose, dragging him down into it, swallowing him . . .

He was falling. His cry was silent.

Then he found himself in a place he had never seen before. He stood at the edge of a meadow with a forest at his back and a small hill rising before him, crowned with three ancient stones. Two had fallen and lay nearly buried in the thick, calf-deep grass; the third still reared its worn head against the azure well of the summer night. It was close to midnight, he thought—the air was laden with the peep of frogs, crinkled with the trilling of crickets, and summer constellations unrolled in a glittering banner beyond the black spikes of the surrounding pines.

The thick sweetness caught at his throat as he waded through the grass, up the hill to the stones. His feet hewed a dark swathe through the dew that glittered in the starlight, a shadowed track leading back into the coagulated gloom beneath the trees. Looking over his shoulder, he felt a kind of panic, a terror of pursuit . . . fear of being traced here, captured, taken . . . Taken where? The thought of it turned him cold but he could conjure nothing, no reason for that hideous dread.

But if he could reach the stones, he'd be safe. If he could reach them by midnight, he could escape . . .

Escape?

Jaldis. His mind groped for bearings in the disorientation of the dream. *Where's Jaldis in all this? He can't run, he's crippled. He won't be able to get away from them . . .*

Who?

The thought of capture turned him sick.

He sprang up on one fallen stone. Around him in the starlight the grass of the meadow lay like a silken lake, cut by the single dark line of his tracks. Overhead the sky was a glowing well of blue, an inverted morning-glory sewn with light. Raising his arms, he called down the power of the wheeling stars to him, calling strength and hope of flight . . .

But as he turned he saw all around him in the encircling

woods the terrible glitter of silver and steel, the closing ring of eyes . . .

He jolted from sleep like a man falling from a height. His heart was pounding with panic, and for one terrible second he knew that he had not escaped. Waking had only postponed the knowledge of what would happen to him next . . . but only momentarily. They would capture him and . . . and . . .

But it was only darkness.

Only a dream.

Only a dream, Rhion thought, breathless, trying to slow his heart and still his panic. The cold killing lust of the hunters, the poisoned fog of impersonal hate . . .

But those did not fade from his mind. They grew stronger than before, and he realized that those, at least, were real.

Rhion dropped his hand from beneath the covers to where he had left his spectacles on the floor by the bed. His wizard's sight let him see as well in darkness as in light, but without his spectacles what he saw, day or night, was only a blur. The metal rims were icy against his temples and for a moment the warmth of his flesh misted the thick, curved glass. The room was freezing, for it was the last hour or two of the long winter night, when the heat of the banked fires in the kitchen far below no longer warmed the chimney. Beside him, curled tight for warmth beneath their few blankets and both their shabby cloaks, Jaldis still slept; around them, the little room was as tidy, as orderly, as it had been when they had gone to bed. On the shelf above the bed Jaldis' opal spectacles stared unwinkingly into darkness; the rosewood soundbox rested like a sleeping turtle in its sparkling nest of talismans and tangle of leather straps.

But there was danger.

And it was coming closer.

Closing his eyes, Rhion slowed the panic from his breathing and listened deeply, fully, as Jaldis had taught him years ago and as he had practiced daily in meditation, stretching his senses to the somnolent city outside.

He became immediately aware of the crunch of many booted feet, the clamor of mob rage. At the same moment the urgent tug of fear redoubled, and he understood then that it was coming to him from one of the wizard's marks he had made in the streets surrounding the inn.

In none of the Forty Realms was it considered a crime to kill a wizard. In fact the cults of the gods Bran Rhu, Agon, Kithrak, and Thismé considered such an activity an act of merit and likely to win either the god's favor or promotion to a higher plane of spiritual being, depending on the cult, and Rhion had been a wizard long enough and had talked to enough of his professional colleagues on the subject, to have a healthy wariness about settling down to sleep.

For this reason, within the first week of moving into the Black Pig Inn, Rhion had drawn wizard's marks—barely visible signs imbued with a trace of his personal power—on housewalls, fountain railings, and doorposts in a loose ring, perhaps half a mile wide with the Black Pig at its center, marks that would awaken and whisper to him if passed by a large number of people with that particular species of determined, impersonal hatred in their hearts.

It was far from a perfect warning system, of course. Wizard's marks had to be renewed periodically—Rhion's more frequently than Jaldis' would have to be, because of Rhion's lesser strength—and were by no means accurate in what stirred them to life. Time after time Rhion had been called from his meditations, from sleep, or from consultations with clients by bar fights, matrimonial disputes, and, on one occasion, by an angry mob of local fishwives out to storm the house of a particularly unpopular moneylender. At this hour of the night—or morning, for dawn was at most two hours away—it was more likely that the problem was some kind of drunken brawl.

But still, Rhion slipped from beneath the covers and, breathless with cold, hastily pulled on his robe over the knitted pullover and hose he'd worn to bed and laced up his boots. His father had been a man with a motto for every occasion—"Better to be safe than sorry," had been one of his favorites. Having seen just how sorry it was possible to become, Rhion was willing to opt for an uncomfortable safety every time.

The cold in the attic was breathtaking, and Rhion hadn't the heart to take his cloak from the top of the piles of blankets over Jaldis. Moving swiftly, his breath a trail of white behind him, he unbolted and slipped through the crazy door, pausing long enough to work the bolt back into place by magic behind him in case someone tried to break in while Jaldis was still lost in his exhausted slumber. The staircase, which rose like a flue through the inn, was warmer, and Rhion concentrated on whispering the words of a generalized sleep-spell as he hurried down the elliptical spiral of the steps, not sure whether he was getting the spell right or whether it was working. It was one he hadn't practiced lately, and half his mind was on the danger that had—he was almost certain now—shaped the fears of his dream.

In the huge kitchen, low-ceilinged, shuttered, silent, and dark but for the feeble glow of the banked embers on the hearth, Rhion pulled the landlord's heavy green cloak from its peg and slung it around his shoulders. Outside the noise was clearer—definitely armed and angry men, definitely headed this way.

He paused on the threshold, panting, to collect his thoughts. It still took him a long and meticulous time to work any kind of spell, though he practiced diligently, and Jaldis told him that speed and mental deftness would come with time. Against the rising shiver in his breast, the inner clamor of *There isn't* time *for this . . . !* he closed his eyes, calmed his breathing, and reaching out with all the senses of wizardry, realized that the mark the mob had passed was the one he'd put on the side of a little shrine of Shilmarglinda, goddess of grain, over on the corner of Sow Lane.

Clutching the landlord's cloak about him, he ducked and wove through alleyways choked with half-frozen garbage and no wider than the span of his arms. As he ran he shoved resolutely from his mind all the thousand questions trying to heave to its surface like porridge on the boil, questions like *Who's behind this?* and *Where the hell can we go? The landlord'll never bolt the door against them* . . . Instead he concentrated on forming a spell to cloak him against the notice of people who might very well know him for the wizard's apprentice. Unlike the sleep-spells at the inn, tossed hastily about him like a sower's seeds, this one had better keep him from being recognized or he stood in grave danger of having to choose between a very severe beating—if nothing worse— and some defensive action that might trigger further mob violence. In situations like this it was axiomatic that the wizard—or the wizard's friends and acquaintances—could never really win.

The mob had spilled into Suet Lane. It was nearly fifty strong, though its core of two dozen men in the dark-blue livery of some town nobleman's household bravos was being added to all the time by the kind of tavern idlers and day laborers who could always be counted upon to join an affray. Rhion recognized two of the magistrate's constables among them and a couple of lesser officials of the local Temple of Kithrak, the war-god whose cult was strong in Felsplex. One of these was yelling something about servants of evil and insulters of the names of the gods, and Rhion had a sinking certainty about whose honor this assemblage was in.

Nevertheless he fell into step with one of the local wastrels, a little female stevedore he'd seen drinking frequently in the Black Pig. Hoping his spell of Who-Me? would hold, he asked, "What's going on?"

The woman barely glanced at him. A torch in one hand, an ax-handle in the other, she appeared to be—and, by the workings of the spell, in fact was—momentarily absorbed in keeping an eye on the thickly quilted back of the liveried bravo in front of her. If later challenged to describe the man who had spoken to her, she would have been able only to arrive at a vague recollection of someone about her husband's height and build. "Gonna kill them witch scum," she grunted, and spat through gaps in her teeth into the frozen sewage underfoot.

The word she used for "kill" was *fruge*, a verb which had application only to animals, almost a technical term except that it was used so commonly. It denoted a killing which meant nothing and which demanded no explanations—a self-evident axiom. One never asked why someone would *fruge* a rat, or a cow for beef. One did it because that was what one did with rats and cows.

"Yeah?" Rhion said in the local slang, and wiped his nose on his sleeve. "What'd the bastards do this time?"

"Sold a love-potion to that whore wife of Tepack the moneylender so's she could drag her husband's partner's innocent son into bed with her." His companion nodded toward the solid core of liverymen, like a knot of lead poured into a wooden club to make of it a killing weapon. "Only sixteen, he is, and his daddy—Lord Pruul—says he's gonna *fruge* them wizards, since Tepack's not gonna let anyone say a word against his wife . . ."

But Rhion was already gone, holding the landlord's cloak-hem up out of the mud and thinking, *Real smart, Rhion. Didn't think to ask if the bint was married, did we?*

But of course the question would only have elicited a lie. Perhaps a lie that the woman herself believed. He was familiar with Lord Pruul's son, having sold that raped and innocent victim enough lover-philters and clap-cures to stock

a pharmacy over the past thirty months. *Dammit, we really
did need the money . . .*

He ducked into the doorway of one of the huge, gray-
timbered tenement blocks that made up the neighborhood,
pressed his hands to the door to work back the bolt by magic,
then darted through the downstairs hall where beggars slept
in rags and garbage. Cutting through the filth in the yard
behind the place, he was able to reach the junction of Suet
Lane, Goat Lane, and Cod Alley before the mob did, only a
few hundred feet from the Black Pig. Amid the towering
walls of tenement houses, wineshops, and the vast bulk of
the St. Plomelgus Baths, the little square was like a deep
cistern full of shadow, only the tiny brick-and-iron shrine of
St. Plomelgus—a demi-god of the Thismé cult—catching the
wan starlight on the iron spikes of its roof.

His hands shaking with panic, Rhion forced his mind to
calm as he drew the sigils for a spell of misleading on the
shrine itself, the corner of the baths, the corner timbers of a
tenement house. The Lady, the Fool, the Dancer at the Heart
of the World . . . runes twined together, calling into themselves and radiating forth, in their proper combination, the
certainty that one turned right instead of left, that Goat Lane
was in fact the street which led to the Black Pig; a line of
light stretched across the mouth of Cod Alley, glowing visible for a moment, then sinking back into the air. To throw
a little twist on things Rhion added a spell of argumenta-
tiveness to the governing Seals upon the shrine, then, as
torchlight flickered over the stiff lead saint in her pigeon-
desecrated niche and voices echoed against the high walls,
he gathered his cloak around him and fled.

Jaldis was already dressed, patiently, with twisted fingers,
lacing his boots. He raised his head inquiringly as Rhion
fumbled the latch open with his mind from the other side.

"Lord Pruul's men," Rhion gasped, crossing immediately to the table and beginning to shove things into his pock-

ets—packets of herbs, precious bits of bronze and gold and rare woods for the making of talismans, scrying-crystals, and bread. "That woman I sold a philter to earlier tonight was the wife of his business-partner. She used it to seduce his son, though from what I know of Pruul Junior I wonder that she needed to bother."

Jaldis slipped into the leather harness that bound the voice-box to his breast, found his spectacles without groping for them, and hooked them onto his face. The talismans on the voice-box clinked with fragile music as he erected his crutches and climbed to his feet. "My books . . ."

Rhion turned to view the row of volumes along the back of the table, the stacks on the floor beside the chimney wall, the little bin of scrolls beside his master's customary chair, and cursed. It was appalling how much impedimenta they'd picked up in two and a half years here. They'd come to Felsplex with twenty-one books of various shapes and sizes—grimoires, demonaries, herbals laboriously copied from volumes in Shavus' little library in that stone house in the forest—and in the years they'd been here they had, at great pain and expense, acquired a dozen more. Precious volumes, some of them irreplaceable. While court mage for the traitor Lord Henak, Jaldis had collected a library of nearly a hundred volumes of magic and wisdom over the years, added to what had been passed on to him by his own master. The High King's men had burned them all. Rhion had heard Jaldis say that he regretted that loss more than he did the loss of his eyes.

He cursed again, feeling already exhausted and defeated, and cast a quick glance at the window that he already knew would be their means of egress. The shouts of the mob were audible through the walls, furious and frustrated as they wandered helplessly in the maze of twisting streets. If he'd had time to cast a more elaborate spell . . .

Swiftly he tore the blanket from the bed. "It's going to be

close,'' he warned, and crossed to the window at a run. Once the shutter was thrown back, the cold was brutal, making his eyes water and his numbed fingers ache, even with both gloves and writing-mitts on his hands. The wind had died down; the sky was iron-black above the slanting jumble of tiled roofs. Most were too steep to hold snow, but moisture had frozen on them and they'd be slick and treacherous. Rhion thought about negotiating them with forty or fifty pounds of unwieldy paper on his back, not to mention trying to guide a blind man on crutches, and shuddered.

"We can't take all of them." The words cut like a wire noose—Jaldis loved those books like children, and there were several that Rhion had not yet studied. But he knew as surely as he knew his name that if he tried it, they would both fall to their deaths. "I'm sorry. We just . . ."

A spasm of sorrow contorted the old man's face. "Then you choose." The arthritic hands passed, trembling, along the volumes on the table, touching them as he would have touched the faces of people he loved. "For they will be yours now longer than they will be mine."

"Don't say that!" Rhion spread the blanket on the bed and dove back toward the table, steeling himself against the agony of decision and thinking desperately, *That spell won't hold them long* . . . "We're going to get out of here just fine . . . Can you call fog?"

"In a moment." Jaldis remained beside the table, head bowed, hands touching this book or that as Rhion worked hurriedly around him . . . *Dammit, that one's got the Summoning of Elementals in it! I hadn't learned that yet* . . .

Shavus will have it, he told himself firmly. But the book seemed to cling to his hand like a child he was trying to abandon in the woods. *Hell, Jaldis was searching for that Book of Circles when I met him* . . .

"Jaldis . . ." With the window open the noise of the mob

came to them quite clearly. It was growing louder again. They must have gotten their bearings.

"In a moment. You're leaving *these*?"

"Yes. Come *ON* . . . !" He piled the fifteen or so books that he could not possibly bear to let slip from their possession in the center of the blanket, threw in some spare clothing and food, and tied the corners, then bent and pulled from beneath the bed a long, cleated plank—the gangway, in fact, of one of the hayboats that came to the quays from upriver in spring. He'd appropriated it two years ago when he'd first mapped out this route of escape, foreseeing the possibility of just this event, even as he'd made wizard's marks that would glow at a word on the various chimneys, turrets, and crudely carved roof-tree gargoyles—designed to frighten goblins and grims, these decorated every roof in the city—along their chosen route . . .

But the thought of actually doing it still turned him queasy.

At that time he'd practiced manhandling the plank down the roof tiles to the gap where the alley separated them from the next building. But that had been two summers ago, when the steeply sloped tiles were dry. Black ice cracked under the soles of his boots, and the wind froze his face, his heart hammering so hard it nearly sickened him. Eastward across the pitchy jumble of roof trees and gargoyles, his mageborn eyes could make out, like a dirty fault-scar in the wilderness of grimy plaster and half-timbering, the line of the river. The noise of the mob was louder, down in Cod Alley now, certainly—there was no note in it of the baffled fury of a mob confronted with a locked door.

Of course the landlord would let them in. His only request would be that they not break anything downstairs. "He'll probably sell them drinks on their way up," Rhion muttered savagely, as he struggled back through the window again.

Jaldis was still standing beside the table, head bowed and long white hair hanging down over his face as he passed his hands lightly across the covers of each of the rejected books in turn. For an instant, watching him, Rhion's heart constricted with grief—it was as if the old man was memorizing one last time the touch of the bindings, the whisper of the things within that now would be destroyed. But the building was already shaking with the pounding of fists upon the doors, of feet upon the stairs . . .

He pulled the blanket-wrapped bundle onto his back, tangling it with the landlord's green cloak, and girded up his robe through his belt. "Now," he said, as gently as he could through the hammering urgency of panic, and took Jaldis by the arm. He saw the old man's forehead pucker with the agony of concentration as he called the spells of sight into his opal spectacles.

"Did you call the fog?" Rhion whispered as he eased himself out the window again, praying with all that was in him that the weight of the books on his back wouldn't overbalance him on the slippery roof.

Jaldis, leaning out the window to take his pupil's steadying arms, shook his head. He was using all his strength, all his attention, to see. He could seldom operate both eyes and voice at the same time, much less call unseasonable weather conditions like fog in winter, even when he was rested—certainly not in the exhausted aftermath of working with the Dark Well.

Instead he had been saying good-bye to his books. Scared as he was, Rhion could not feel anger. The *Grand Demonary* had been given Jaldis by his own old master Xiranthe, Archmage of the Morkensik Order for forty years, who had gotten it from hers—it was one of the few which had escaped the High King's men. The collection of the wizard Ymrir's personal notes had been copied nearly a hundred years ago and was the best redaction of those notes either of them knew about, the least corrupted . . .

But, Rhion thought despairingly as he started to ease his

way down the steep tiles, with the old man's tall weight on one shoulder and the shifting, awkward sack of books on his back, *we surely could have used that fog*.

The flight from Felsplex was a nightmare that in later years Rhion would look back upon with a kind of wonder, amazed that he'd been scared enough even to think about trying it. Wind had started up by the time they'd crossed the gangway, blowing from the north and arctically cold. Rhion could smell sleet on it but knew that neither he nor Jaldis could spare the concentration needed to turn the storm aside. With the books overbalancing him, he didn't have the leverage to pull the gangway across after them, but had to tip it over into the deserted alley below.

Then came the slithery agony of edging along the slanted roofs, easing their way around gables and ornamental turrets, clinging to gargoyles and rain gutters slick with ice and rotten with age and neglect. For the most part, the buildings in this crowded riverside quarter were close enough together, with their projecting upper stories and jutting eaves, to make leaping over the gaps a relatively easy matter, in theory at least. But theory did not take into account the hellish cold and slippery footing, the yawning blackness of forty- and fifty-foot drops to the cobblestones below, nor the storm gusts that came whipping unexpectedly around the corners of those tall black roof trees to pluck at their clothes and claw their faces.

The coming storm had killed whatever dawnlight had been rising. Rhion hoped it would also discourage their pursuit, but he could still hear the angry voices in the streets below as the men fanned out through the whole district, torches leaping in the charcoal shadows of those twisting chasms, curses echoing against the crowding walls. One of the first things Jaldis had taught him, ten years ago—and he'd been studying it on his own even before that—was to read the weather; he could tell that the sleet wouldn't hit soon enough to drive Lord Pruul's bravos indoors. It would only soak and freeze him and Jaldis once they got clear of the town . . . if they could manage to do so without breaking their necks.

Thanks a lot, he muttered, addressing the gods Rehobag and Pnisarquas, Lords of the Storm. According to the Bereine theologians who strolled in the pillared basilicas of Nerriok, Rehobag and Pnisarquas were only aspects of the Lord Darova, the Open Sky, God of the Blue Gaze, the Lord Who Created Himself . . . a god notoriously antithetical to wizardry and all its works. *It figures.*

Rhion was trembling with exhaustion by the time they reached their goal: a tenement by the river whose five-storey bulk jutted out on pilings over the dark waters, a tenement whose inhabitants, like all those of the riverside community, routinely fished off crooked platforms that clung like swallows' nests to the building's side, connected by a thready tangle of ladder no more substantial than spiderweb and straw. As he helped the exhausted Jaldis down that suspended deathtrap of sticks and rope, Rhion thanked whatever gods listened to wizards that the river was deep enough at Felsplex not to have frozen, and that the intense cold had damped the smell of it here under the pilings where every privy in the district emptied.

There were several boats tied among the piers beneath the tenement, where a single lantern hanging from a crossbeam threw hard yellow scales of light on the oily water. Rhion's gloves had been torn to pieces by the scramble over the roofs, and his hands were so stiff they would barely close around the oars. At this season the water was low. Had it been spring, he did not think he would have had the strength to row against the current.

"I don't see any smoke," he commented after a time, as they approached the city's water gate with its thick portcullis—half-raised now like a dog's snarl—where the river ran out westwards into the flat open country beyond, dirty-white

and mud-brown beneath a livid sky. Wind tore at his face,
the first sleet snagging in his beard. It was, he knew, nearly
impossible for even a mage of Jaldis' powers to turn a storm
aside when it was this close. But he knew, too, that they'd
have to try, or they'd never make the upstream market town
of Imber alive.

Jaldis, sitting huddled in the boat's prow under his own
cloak and Rhion's, his hood drawn up over his face, did not
raise his head. White hairs flicked from beneath the edge of
the hood, like snow blowing from the crest of a roof; muffled
by the cloaks that covered it, the voice of the box was nearly
inaudible. "That few books would not make much smoke,"
he said softly. "They would cast them into the kitchen stove
. . . it will easily accommodate so small a number. No . . ."
And he sighed, a soundless, aching breath of regret. "My
great sorrow is that they will have destroyed the Well."

"The Dark Well?" Bending his aching back to the oars,
Rhion tried to remember what it was about the Dark Well
that had frightened him so badly, why the very name of the
thing made his scalp creep. But he could remember nothing,
other than standing and looking into the eldritch, shifting
colors of blackness . . . that terrible hollow . . . A vague
impression tugged at his mind that perhaps he had dreamed
something . . .

And then it was gone.

But, grieved as he could see Jaldis was at the loss, he
himself could work up very little in the way of regret.

"The Dark Well," the old man again echoed. "They will
wipe out the lines that bound it, trample away the symbols
that gave it power, that held it in place. It will vanish, and
all its secrets with it. Those who cried out to me from its
depths . . ."

"You'll be able to create another one, in time," Rhion
said, manufacturing as cheerful a tone as he could. "As soon
as we get to Imber and find someplace to stay . . ." He tried

to recall if he'd pocketed their money in their haste to get out, and couldn't. "You'll be able to find them again, and help them."

"No, my son," Jaldis softly said, and shook his head. "No . . . If someone has found a way to destroy magic, to end it, make it cease to exist, in an entire universe—it is *we* who may need *their* help."

THREE

BUT IT WAS TO BE A LONG TIME BEFORE JALDIS THE BLIND
and his pupil found the peace and security necessary for the
weaving of another Dark Well.

It took them two days to reach Imber, a good-sized market
town twenty-five miles upriver from Felsplex, built around
the temple complex of Ptorag, God of Grain. In most of the
Forty Realms Ptorag's worship had been supplanted by that
of Shilmarglinda—the north-desert deity of all the fruits of
the earth—but in Imber it was still strong and the cult owned
most of the vineyards lining the hill slopes above the river.
Rhion, having ascertained that he *had*, in fact, dropped the
little velvet pouch which Tepack the Moneylender's wife had
given him—brainless trollop!—into the blanket's load of
books and spare clothes, figured resignedly that if worst came
to worst he could always seek employment corking and seal-
ing bottles when the vintage was laid down toward winter's
end.

"But on the other hand," he added, extending numb hands
toward the small brazier of coals which the landlady of the
Red Grape Inn had sent up to their miniscule—though extremely costly—chamber, "if everyone in this town is as
calm about wizards as the innkeeper here, I can probably
find work as an accountant. That would make my father
proud." He grinned a little as he said it, his beard crackling
with ice, and began gingerly unwrapping the frozen rags he'd

37

tied around his hands. They hadn't the money to remain more than a night or two at this inn, and he'd have to sell the tiny amount of gold they kept for talismanic work in order to obtain permanent lodgings; but, for the moment, Rhion was glad to have found a warm room out of the wind, with prospects of food.

He flexed his fingers in the glow exuded by the little copper dish of coals. "Here, let me see your hands . . ." In the river-bank cave where they'd spent part of yesterday morning, sheltering from the worst of the sleet, he'd cut strips from the hem of their former landlord's cloak—which was too long for him anyway—to wrap around Jaldis' arthritic fingers and his own. He'd hauled stones up from the river-bank and had been able to call sufficient spells to them to heat them up so that their radiant warmth had kept him and his master from freezing to death, but the effort had exhausted him; Jaldis had worked for nearly two hours, drawing and redrawing the figures of power in the air, before he had been able to turn the sleet storm aside. After that the old man had collapsed and slept; when they'd pushed on later in the day and all through the next southward along the banks of the frozen stream, he had the strength to say very little.

Or perhaps, Rhion thought now, stealing a worried glance at his master's face, the delicate cords of gut and silver wire, the tiny vibrating whistles and membranes within the voice-box itself, had simply frozen fast.

Now the old man said softly, as Rhion chaffed his crippled fingers in a basin of cold water, "I am sorry, my son."

"Sorry?" Rhion looked up at him in genuine surprise. Outside the windows, the short winter day had ended in slate-colored gloom. In the kitchen directly beneath their room, the innkeeper's husband was singing a midwinter carol as he prepared supper for the Red Grape's few guests: roast lamb with rosemary for those wealthy enough to pay for it, lentils and mutton-fat for itinerant mages out of work. "*I* was the one who sold that silly woman a love-potion without asking if she was married or whom she was going to use it on." Gently he removed the two cloaks and the blanket from Jaldis' shoulders and laid them over the backs of the room's various chairs and table to dry. While it was possible to dry clothes, as it was to heat rooms, with magic, under ordinary circumstances it took far more energy than it was worth. In the long run it was cheaper to pay for coal.

For a moment he stood looking down at Jaldis' sunken cheeks and scarred eyelids, gray as fishbelly with fatigue and with long weeks indoors at the Black Pig. He remembered as from a dream how his white teeth had flashed in a smile, how his voice had boomed with laughter, the day of their first meeting on the bridge. Down to the ends of his long white braids, he had seemed to crackle with energy, with life and delight . . . with magic. And Rhion had known, as unquestioningly as if he had recognized his own face in a mirror, that that was what he wanted, and had always wanted, to be.

Quietly, he added, "I'm sorry about the books."

The hard, arthritic grip closed with its surprising strength upon his hand. "It was not your business to ask her if she would use the philter to commit adultery," Jaldis said. "No more than it is the business of a stationer to ask of a man buying paper and ink if he plans to use them to betray a friend's trust. Magic is only magic, Rhion."

The sparse white eyebrows drew down over the bridge of his nose, the thin face filled with urgency, willing him to understand. "It is neither evil nor good, it is neither health nor a sickness. It is only what it is—like a knife, or a man's life, or a new name for God. We cannot begin to judge what will be done with any of these things, for we ourselves can only hold opinions, and we cannot be sure that the information we are given on any of these is complete or correct.

"It is enough that we do no harm, as our vows enjoin us;

that we do not presume to decide things for which there is no proof.'' The crooked, clawlike fingers tightened; as the blind face looked up into his, Rhion had the sensation that through those deformed hands the old man could feel, not only his bones and flesh and the warmth of his blood, but the soul within him, reading it like a handful of colored silk ribbons braided into some elaborate code, feeling the texture of his thoughts as he would feel the petals of a flower, the grit of granite, or the cold strength of steel.

"I am only sorry," Jaldis went on, "that having promised you the wisdom of the universe, the knowledge of balance and truth, I have caused you to leave your family and the world that would have made you comfortable, and then have given you only this: dream weaving, philter brewing, and casting horoscopes and luck-charms, the toys of magic rather than its substance. It is not magic, Rhion . . ."

Rhion was silent, remembering the soul-deep shiver he had felt when he had first understood the true name of light, the name by which fire is summoned—the true reality of what true reality is. The moment in meditation when all the component parts of the world fell suddenly together, showing that there was, in fact, sense to what happened . . . He remembered, too, all that long and gaudy parade of nobles, burghers, farmers, and slaves who had come to him and Jaldis over the past ten years, asking for what they thought was magic: medicines or luck-charms or to have their fortunes read. And every one, he reflected, had taught him a little more about what men dreamed.

"No," he said, squeezing those crippled old fingers in return. "But it sure beats working for a living."

And Jaldis laughed, sniffing through his high-bridged nose. Laughter was the one sound that it was impossible for the voice-box to make.

Acting on the advice of the innkeeper's husband, a little brown sparrow of a man whom he instinctively trusted, Rhion sought out the best of the local pawnbrokers the following day and sold the little gold and silver he and Jaldis possessed. With the proceeds, again on their landlord's advice, he found a widow who owned a garden farm a few hundred yards down the road outside Imber's gates, who had a room to rent.

"Now, I don't mind myself that you're witchylike," she said, pouring the milk bucket she carried into setting pans—Rhion had found her in the dairy behind the small, half-timbered box of the farmhouse. She turned to face him, tucking hard brown hands into the armpits of her quilted coat for warmth. She was a young woman of about Rhion's own twenty-seven years, though her face was leathery with out-door work. Under the close-fitting cap widows wore in the low countries of the Fel Valley her braids were bright yellow; she wore a blue ribbon around her neck with a green spirit-bead upon it and a little fragment of mirror glass to scare away grims. "It's just that I don't want no trouble, see."

"We'll try to keep the orgies down to four or five a week," Rhion replied gravely, and then added, "joking . . . joking . . ." as her eyebrows dove down into a worried frown. "It's just myself and my old master; we may have clients coming from time to time but I promise you we're well behaved." *And one of these days I'll even learn to have some sense about what I say.*

She grinned, showing a gap where childbearing had cost her a tooth. "Well, as to that, if the magistrates ask why I rented to such folk, I can always say you put a Word on me, can't I? I've sold milk and greens to the wizards in the town enough to know they don't cut up children, no matter what my granny said. But, not meaning it personal, I've got a girl—three she'll be come Agonsfire Night—and I'd appreciate it if you'd stay clear of her. Just for the sake of what the neighbors say."

For God's sake, your daughter's honor is safe with me . . . "Of course," said Rhion, bowing with hand over heart.

"Are there wizards in Imber?" he asked Jaldis later, as the two men carried their meager possessions across the town square and down the cobbled lane to the western gate. The snow that had been drifting down all last night had ceased, leaving the sky overhead a high, nebulous roof of pewter. Farmers had set up their barrows under the wide arcade surrounding the market square, and housewives in yellows and greens, and the dark-dressed household slaves of the rich, were picking over bundles of beans and yams and prodding the rabbits and chickens which hung dead by their feet like grotesque tassels from hooks on the beams overhead. The square itself was a palimpsest of tracks in the churned-up snow, and now and then a mule litter or sedan chair would pass, carrying a rich man on his way to one of the town's gymnasia or baths, or a brown-robed priest of the great temple of Ptorag, archaic gold amulets flashing and temple secretaries trotting obediently in his wake.

"They are Selarnists." Jaldis' voice was incapable of expression, but by the pause before his reply and by the way he held his shoulders, he might have been identifying them as a species of roach. "A small House of them, I believe."

"Oh," Rhion said. He had met few members of the Selarnist Order of wizardry in his years of apprenticeship with Jaldis, mostly because members of the White Order, as it was called, tended to live cloistered in Houses wherever the local authorities would let them, shunning contact with politics, the public, and members of other Orders alike.

"Worthy enough mages, I suppose," the old man went on, the voice of the soundbox smooth and strong now that he had rested, the rhythm of his arms and back as he limped along steady and sure. "And their methods of teaching are, on the whole, sound." When he had taught Rhion to observe insects he had found several good things to say about the lowlier members of the grasshopper tribe as well. "But one must admit that their Order's studies have become considerably corrupted and filled with errors since first they split away from the Morkensiks, six hundred years ago.''

They passed a school, thickly attended now that it was winter, boys and girls crowded eight to a bench and peering over one another's shoulders at the hornbooks they had to share. Warmth blew out of the open store front in which it was being held, pleasant on Rhion's face as he walked along under his blanketful of books. It was astounding how much easier they were to carry on the relatively level surface of the street, the packed and slippery snow underfoot notwithstanding. Jaldis, too, had insisted upon splitting the load with him, and though Rhion watched him carefully, the old man seemed strong and fit enough.

"You could do worse than go to the Selarnists for some teaching while we are here," Jaldis added as he and his pupil turned down the length of Westgate Lane, past the towering walls of the temple complex, beyond which the soft groaning of horns and of the bronze sounding-bowls could be heard, accompanying chanted prayers in languages few people understood anymore. "Though they tend to put too much emphasis on breath-control and physical orientation, they could teach you far more of the finer nuances of herbalism than I."

"If they're Selarnists they might not want to teach a Morkensik their secrets," Rhion pointed out, shifting his burden from one aching shoulder to the other. His muscles hadn't recovered yet from the scramble across the roofs or from the hours of rowing up the white-banked black silence of the river with the sleet stinging his face. "But it's worth a try. There's still a whole lot I don't understand about herbal metaphysics . . ."

"Much of it is practice, my son."

"True. But in any case, if the priests who rule this town let a whole Houseful of *them* stay here, they won't have any objections to the two of us."

And indeed, it was not the priests of Ptorag who were

responsible, two days later, for having Rhion and Jaldis thrown out of town.

It was a morning warmer than the preceding week had been, warm enough that the river had begun to thaw. Clouds hung low over the hill country to the south, and a faint mist turned the air to pearl as Rhion crossed the farmyard from helping their landlady with the milking, and found Jaldis sitting at the little table under their room's wide window, arranging his books by touch.

When Rhion had first become Jaldis' student, he had known nothing of wizardry—only the desperate sense of the magic within his veins, and the insistent, terrifying, disorienting need to learn to use that ability, the need to know that he was not insane for wanting to. But he had assumed, meeting Jaldis, that magic was something one learned, like accounting. When one was done learning, one was a bookkeeper.

It had come as both a shock to him and, once the shock was over, a delight, that magic was a learning, a pursuit—that one never finished learning magic. The learning had been longer, a deep foundation against whose painstaking meticulousness he had rebelled more than once in screaming boredom: for the first year and a half he hadn't realized Jaldis had been teaching him anything. All the old man did was command the boy to do things like prepare the floors of rooms where magic was done, ritually cleansing every corner and ritually laying wards on every door, window, pot, knife, and vessel, and in betweentimes simply enjoined him to observe insects and plants, clouds and stars and rain . . . It was only after he had amassed years' worth of information, of tiny detail—until he could tell at a glance the seed of the amaranth from that of the millet—that it came to him how necessary all this information was to the weaving of spells that could change poison to harmless sap, or steer the cumuli by altering the temperature of the air beneath them.

For Jaldis, he knew, learning had never stopped. There were always new plants to study, whole new families of them from the jungles of the south or the bare rock plains of the north and west; spells that had been woven, and written, and lost again; unknown properties of gems or salts or different types of animal blood. He'd seen Jaldis bouncing up and down like a schoolboy one afternoon when they'd visited Shavus at his queer stone house in the forest of Beldirac, and the Archmage had shown off a century-old scroll containing fifty or sixty alterations to spells which strengthened or lessened their effects, depending on the position of certain stars. Rhion had spent a month copying it out—it was one of the books that had been left in the attic.

"I meant to ask you," Rhion said, untucking the folds of his robe from his wide leather belt. "Was there a reason you couldn't summon fog to cover us, when we were getting out of Felsplex? Did working with the Dark Well hurt you that much? Or was there just not enough time?"

"The Dark Well . . . tired me, yes." Jaldis half turned in his chair. "It saps power, drinks it . . ." The diffuse white light that came through the window's oiled parchment panes lent a matte yellow-gray tone to his lined face, making him look tired and ill. He'd been wearing his spectacles to accustom himself to his new surroundings; they lay now on the table beside his hand, and the air was permeated with the bittersweet pungence of lime and rue he'd burned to relieve the headache that was the result.

"That was one reason why it so grieved me that the Well was destroyed—that we had to leave it and that men, in fear, will rub out the Circles of Power which hold its darkness in place. It will be some time before I regain the strength to undertake the making of another."

The longer, the better, as far as I'm concerned, Rhion thought, a little guiltily.

"At the equinox, perhaps," Jaldis went on, turning back

to the ordering of his books with crooked, groping hands. "The turning of the spring, when I can use the momentum of the forces of the stars to help me. The evening star will be in transit then, too, which should help—there are spells which call down its power at such times which I must teach you. It is imperative . . ." He broke off, and shook his head, a quick, small gesture, dismissing the preoccupation which, Rhion knew, had been gnawing at him all through their flight.

Then he looked up again, a small, closed smile flexing the scarred corners of his lips. "But as for the fog . . . I could not work two spells at once, Rhion. Not two spells as dissimilar as weather-spinning and summoning."

"Summoning?" Rhion perched one flank on the corner of the table and frowned. "Summoning what?"

"Summoning the books back to us." And his smile widened as if he could see his pupil's expression of startled, enlightened delight. "Have I never shown you the sigils to draw, the spells to weave, to convince an object that its proper place is in your possession?"

"I didn't even know such spells existed, but tell me more." He drew up another chair. Compared to the Black Pig, the room was hopelessly primitive—damply cold, so that both of them wore their cloaks and kept their blankets wrapped around them most of the time, the beds only platforms built of planks and covered with straw, and the whole place smelling of the barnyard onto which it looked. Rhion suspected from the stains on the scoured stone floor that the thatch would leak come spring. But it was clean, and the landlady was liberal in her interpretation of the word *board*.

"I thought the books were burned."

Jaldis sighed, and nodded. "And indeed, they probably were." The sweet voice was incapable of tone, but his eyebrows drew down in a faint twinge of pain, like a man who speaks of friends rumored dead in some catastrophe. Then he shook his head, gestured the thoughts aside with the two fingers still mobile upon his right hand.

"But in the event that some of them were not, in the event that they were thrown into the midden, or cast out the window, the spells I laid upon them—if my strength was sufficient at that point for any spell to work—would cause them to be found by someone who would see in them a source of income, and not an insult to whatever god he was taught to revere. And the spells—if they had worked thus far—would lead that woman or man to sell them to a dealer, perhaps, who might be journeying to Imber when the roads clear in summer, or to an antiquarian, or a seller of used paper, who would in turn, if chances so fell out, display them along with his other wares at a time when you or I or someone who knows us would be passing his shop. That is the reason I never neglect to examine the wares of old paper dealers— one reason of many. Here . . ." He reached with one stiff claw and drew the *Grimoire of Weygarth* to him, opening its crumbling leather covers to stroke the parchment within. Across the faded illuminations of the title page his finger traced a dim line of blue-white light that flickered like a live thing in the pallid gloom, then seemed to sink into the page itself, like a colored ribbon laid upon water.

"It is a spell like other sigils of summoning, but comprised of the Lost Rune, and that of the Dancer, accompanied by the words . . ."

Three shadows passed the soft brightness of the windows and Rhion touched Jaldis' wrist in warning. A moment later there was a faint, polite scratching at the rough plank door.

The man who stood on the threshold was middle-aged, the woman elderly. Both were clothed in the white wool robes, the long white cloaks, and the simple wooden beads of the Selarnist Order of wizardry. Rhion's landlady stood in the background, her skirt still tucked up from work and her muddy boots showing beneath it, her hands shoved for warmth into her sleeves.

The male wizard inclined his head. "Are you Jaldis the Blind and his pupil Rhion?"

"I'm Rhion, yes. Come in." He stepped back from the door, but neither of the two visitors made any move to follow him inside. A moment later he heard the scrape of Jaldis' chair legs on the stone, and then the almost soundless tap of crutches and rustle of robes.

"I am Chelfrednig of Imber, and this in Niane. We understand that you have come to stay in Imber."

"For a time," Rhion said, hiking his cloak a little higher over his shoulder. He mistrusted the man's tone, the cool distance of his manner. It was something he recognized, the attitude that said, *Don't blame ME for what's going to happen. It's nothing personal . . .*

"It's nothing personal . . ."

"Fine." Rhion lifted a hand amicably. "At this short an acquaintance I have nothing personal against you, either. Now that we've established that . . ."

"We understand that yesterday you sold a good-luck charm to a slave named Benno, who works at the shrine of Mhorvianne."

"He didn't tell me his name," he said, more cautious still, "but yes, I did make a talisman of good fortune for a man who came here, and by the way he dressed I figured him for a lower servant or a slave."

With a quickness that reminded Rhion irresistibly of carnival-show sleight of hand, Chelfrednig produced a round billet of elderwood, roughly the size of a double-weight copper penny, from his sleeve and held it out. Rhion did not touch it. Upon it he recognized his own elaborately interwoven seals, spelled to attract circumstances of pleasantness and peace, of good feeling and fortunate coincidence. As he had explained to the man who had come to them yesterday, no magic could turn aside true misfortune, just as no magic could bring the thundering strokes of great luck that change a person's life—and he didn't think his first client in Imber had wanted to believe him. But as far as it went, the little emblem was good for a few extra rolls of dice, for a capricious master's change of mood when a slave had broken a dish, or for an extra jog at the memory about a pot left on the stove. And what more, Rhion thought, could you do for a slave?

With his forefinger he pushed his spectacles a little more firmly up onto the bridge of his nose, and waited.

"We of our House," Chelfrednig said sententiously, "have striven over the years to achieve a harmony with the authorities of this town, the priests of Ptorag, the local magistrates, and the Earl of Way's governor. We believe we have convinced them that those born with the powers of wizardry, if properly instructed and disciplined, are not monsters, nor are they traitors to the gods and to humankind; that we do not hold orgies at the turning points of the universe and do not slit children's throats to make magic with their blood. And we have done this by keeping ourselves to ourselves, and by refraining from meddling with the lives of anyone in this town."

"That's very nice," said Rhion grimly. "Who pays your rent?"

"Investments," the White Mage replied, with a dismissive gesture of one gloved hand. "But the fact remains that our living depends upon the sufferance of the local authorities. And this . . ." He took Rhion's hand in his, and placed the talisman in the plump palm. ". . . we cannot have."

Rhion heard Jaldis come up behind him; a swift glance back showed him the cold flash of daylight on the opal-and-crystal spectacles that the old man had donned.

"You cannot deny us our right," the old man said, "to make a living."

"Ah." Under a long flow of herb-scented beard, Chelfrednig's mouth flexed in a small, tolerant smile. "I had forgotten that when the Morkensiks split off from the Selarnist Order they conveniently dropped the portion of the Oath not to concern oneself in the affairs of humankind . . ."

"It was the Selarnists who split off from the Morkensiks," retorted Jaldis, with a frown of anger and what would have been a deadly edge to his voice, had it been capable of anything except a sweet, buzzing monotone. "And the Oath was and always has been, to do no harm . . ."

"Be that as it may." The Selarnist's tone was clear: *What is the point,* it asked, *of bandying words with a heretic?* "We cannot, alas, deny you what you consider to be your right to 'make a living,' as you say; but we can deny you your freedom to do so in this town. Now, you are welcome to stay in our House for a time if poverty is a problem . . ."

"So that you can tell me what I can and cannot do?" Jaldis demanded. "So that you can sequester my books, and my crystals, and the implements of my art, in your own library, for the good of the magistrates of this town?" And Rhion saw Chelfrednig's eyes shift. "Thank you," the old man went on stiffly, "but we will earn our bread in some other fashion while we are here, and study as we please."

"I am afraid," Chelfrednig said, "that that is not an option open to you either. The guilds in Imber are quite strict about wizards entering businesses or trades. Quite understandably, seeing how an unscrupulous mage—one not bound by *proper* rules—could take an unfair advantage of lesser men."

Hesitantly, the landlady said, "I'm sorry. But you see, I sell most of my greens to them, and milk . . ." Her bright, worried eyes went nervously from Jaldis' face to Rhion's, torn between her liking for them, her need for money, her sense of justice, and her fear that, as wizards, they would cause a scene of the kind she could barely guess at and draw down still more trouble upon her head.

"Right . . ." Rhion muttered furiously, and Jaldis placed a staying hand upon his shoulder from behind, and inclined his head.

"Very well," he said. "My good woman . . ." He turned his disconcertingly insectile gaze upon her, and she shrank back in spite of herself. "My sincerest apologies for the trouble we may have caused you, and . . ." With a very slight motion of his head he indicated the two Selarnists, ". . . my apologies to you on behalf of all wizardry, that these persons considered it incumbent upon themselves to interfere in your life." He turned to face Chelfrednig fully. "We shall be gone by sunset. Is that sufficient?"

"Noon would be better," the old woman with the ashstaff said, speaking for the first time, "if you want to come to shelter before night."

"That," replied Jaldis chillingly, "is our business. I bid you good day."

They were on the road again by noon. "The nerve of them!" Rhion fumed, picking his way cautiously along the most solidly frozen and least cut-up side of the main highroad that led from Imber south through the hills toward the steep-sided Valley of the Morne, and so on to the Mountains of the Sun, and to Nerriok beyond. "I mean, it's not like we were Hand-Prickers or Earth-witches selling cut-rate horoscopes and conversations with your dead ancestors on the street corners, you know! We're Morkensiks! We were the original founding line of wizardry . . . !" His foot slipped where a cartwheel earlier in the day had sliced through the snow and into the frozen clay beneath. He caught himself on the walking staff he'd cut, and put out a hand to guide Jaldis around the place.

Beyond the brown hedges and drainage cuts that hemmed in the road the fields lay empty under the silence of winter. Even this short a distance from the town walls the hedges were overgrown, the ditches silting up, and sedges prickling thick and black through the blanket of dirty snow. The road itself was narrow and unkept; for a long time the township of Imber had been disregarding the corvee laws of its titular liege, the Earl of Way. At least, thought Rhion, hunching deeper into the hood of his cloak and scanning the deserted and overgrown fields nervously, if they were attacked by bandits out here, or in the stony hills or the wilderness of the Drowned Lands that lay beyond, they had the option of fighting back without concern about future retaliation against wizardry in general.

To most people, he knew, a wizard was a wizard was a wizard—as had been the case with himself before he'd become Jaldis' pupil—a mysterious figure in a long robe who acted from unknown motives and held strange and dangerous powers. And from that standpoint, he supposed, Chelfrednig's argument was correct: his sale of potions would contradict what the Selarnists had been laboriously working to convince the town authorities was the nature of wizardry. *Though it was only their opinion of what it should be, dammit!* And thus, though he and Jaldis could have summoned lightning from the sky to blast Lord Pruul's liverymen and their volunteer helpers out of existence, or even have caused the stairs at the Black Pig to collapse under their weight long enough to have given them time to make a getaway, in the long run it would mean more trouble for other wizards they knew, who would have suffered the retaliation.

It was, in fact, the reason that Jaldis had left the house where he had lived for so many years in Nerriok—that tall, narrow house on one of the dozen tiny islands that made up the city, where Rhion had first learned the nature of magic and had first seen what it was to be a mage. When the old High King had died and his brother had briefly taken the scepter, the brother had hated wizards due to some bad financial dealings with an Ebiatic mage who, in Rhion's opinion, should have known better. As a result all mages, from respected masters of the Great Art like Jaldis down to the

Figure-Flingers throwing painted bones on the street corners, had been banished from the city and the realm, to earn what livings they could in places like the Black Pig.

The old High King's brother had died at the turning of autumn, of dysentery contracted while besieging the stronghold of a rebellious vassal in the Clogreth Hills in the west. On the night of the winter solstice, even as Jaldis had been listening in the Dark Well to the clamor of voices crying of the death of magic, the High King's daughter had been crowned in the great Temple of Darova in Nerriok, and had received the homage of all the lords of the Forty Civilized Realms.

It was, Jaldis had said quietly, time to return home.

Night fell early. Owing to the rucked and muddy condition of the winter roads and to Jaldis' lameness, the two wizards were far from the inn which even in summertime lay a good day's journey from Imber's gates. They pressed on long after it grew fully dark. Throughout the day the cloud cover had been thinning under the creeping dryness of the north wind; rags of moonlight filtering through the bare trees which pressed ever more closely about the road through the hills eventually showed Rhion the inn itself, perched on a little rise where the road up from the Drowned Lands divided to run northwards to Imber, and to Felsplex in the east.

Snow lay heavy on the bare hilltops above the road and among the trees that grew thick as a bear pelt about their feet. Against its luminous pallor, the inn's gray stone walls bulked heavy and dark. Every shutter was fastened, every door bolted; every stall in the snow-blanketed stableyard was empty and smelled of fox-mess and field mice, and the tracks of deer and rabbits were a scribbled message all about the walls: *Not at Home*.

Rhion swore fluently for a short while, then walked with what caution he could muster—a city boy born and raised, he had little woodcraft—all around the inn and its outbuildings, sniffing, listening, searching with the hyperacute senses of a wizard for the least sign of danger. But all he heard was the scurrying of mice across bare wooden floors, and the chewing of beetles in the walls. Coming nearer, he found some evidence that a small troop of horses—maybe the mounts of bandits—had occupied the stables a week or so ago, but had been gone before the fall of the snow. No smoke curled from the chimneys, no track broke the snow crust around the woodpile outside the kitchen door.

"There was sickness, I think," Jaldis said sometime later, pressing his hands to the stones of the chimney breast in the dark and deserted common room. "It is hard to read. So many griefs and joys, so much talk and laughter have seeped their way into the stones here. But I feel most recently bad news from somewhere, early in the autumn . . . fresh apples. They had just picked the apples, the smell of them was strong in the room. Ullana . . . Ullata . . . some name like that. Ullata is sick, they said."

He shook his head, the white strands floating around his thin face rimmed with the new-coined brightness of the fire Rhion had kindled in the hearth. The warm light turned the rosewood voice-box the color of claret, and flickered in the talismans that hung from it, dancing chips of green and gold and red. He had put his spectacles away, and wore instead, as he frequently did when he went abroad, a linen bandage over the collapsed and sunken lids of his empty eyes.

"Ullata is sick . . . and so we have to go."

Rhion looked up from adjusting massive iron firedogs meant to uphold wood enough to heat the enormous room. "Maybe Ullata was going to leave them some money." Behind the blaze, tiny in the midst of all that acreage of blackened hearth bricks, a torture chamber ensemble of spits, hooks, and pot-chains loured in the shadows of the huge chimney. "At least Ullata didn't get sick before they cut the winter's wood."

Nevertheless, when he straightened up again he placed his

own hands to the stone of the overmantle, and sent his mind feeling its way through the tight-crossed, gritty fibers of the granite, touching the voices, the images, and the fragments of other days which permeated the stone. The inn had stood for hundreds of years: he glimpsed a red-haired woman washing a new-born baby on the hearth and weeping bitterly, silently, as she worked; saw a young man sitting with his back to the iron firedogs, every window open into the heart-shaking magic of summer evening, greedily reading a scroll stretched between his up-cocked knees; saw an old man shelling peas and talking to a blond-haired child whose brown eyes were filled with a hungry wonder and the shadows of strange destinies. But he had not Jaldis' fineness of perception. He could not separate ancient from recent—all these people might well have been dead for centuries—nor could he make out words. Only the smells of smoke and beer and roasting meats came to him, the echoes of bawdy songs and the clink of the little iron tavern puzzles that hung silent now in a neat row from spikes driven into the chimney's stones.

The widow woman had given them bread and cheese for the journey, as well as most of Rhion's money back; there were yams, dried beans, and sweet dried apples from the trees along the inn's west wall to be found in the cellar. After a meal of these, while Jaldis sat with his opal spectacles on his nose and his scrying-crystal—a chunk of spell-woven quartz the color of bitterroot tea—between his palms, Rhion put on his cloak once more and left the inn to make another circuit of it and draw wizard's marks upon the surrounding trees.

As he came back across the moonlit stillness of the yard, he noticed a gleam like a fleck of quicksilver near the door-handle, and, looking more closely, saw that a silver nail had been driven into the heavy oak. Thoughtfully, he picked his way over the slippery drifts to the nearest of the shuttered windows. Silver nails had been driven into the sills of them all—tiny, almost like pinheads, for the metal was expensive.

The inn's protection had doubtless owed more to its roaring fires and the lamps in their iron sconces which had ringed the yard and to the noise of its customers and the smells of their massed bodies and blood. But standing in the snow that lay glittering like marble all around the inn, listening to the forest silence pressing so close about its walls, Rhion remembered that in waste places at night there were more things to be feared than human prejudice and human spite.

He hated the thought of risking the only thing that stood between him and starvation. Nevertheless, he swept the crusted snow from the bench beside the door, and sat on it to draw from his pocket the little velvet bag of coins. There were seven or eight silver royals among the copper. *Minted in Felsplex,* he reflected dourly, biting one. *God knows if it's even as pure as it's stamped.* His father, one of the wealthiest bankers in the City of Circles, had always held the Felsplex municipal council's fiscal policies in utter contempt, and having seen them at medium-close range for two and a half years now Rhion couldn't blame him. However, it was all the silver they had, even if it was less pure than the buttons of some doublets Rhion had worn back when he was still his father's son.

''Alas for lost opportunities,'' he sighed to himself, and went to work laying small words of Ward on each silver coin. Then he buried them in the snow—with suitable, and invisible, marks over each so he could find them in the morning—in a loose ring around the inn, and drew a tenuous thread of spells from coin to coin, forming the protection of a Circle of Silver.

And thus it was that in the dead of night he was awakened by the chittering whisper of attacking grims.

FOUR

HE CAME AWAKE AT ONCE OUT OF A FAR DEEPER SLEEP THAN he'd meant to allow himself. By the dull ochre of the banked firelight he could just make out Jaldis, seated on a bench beside the shuttered window, listening with bowed head. Pulling his blankets tightly around his shoulders Rhion sat up, for it was the deep of night, and even here beside the common room fireplace the chill was like iron.

"Did the Circle hold?" He groped for his spectacles, finding them by memory, muttering a curse as the lenses misted from the warmth of his flesh.

Jaldis, still deep in his meditative listening, shook his head.

"Damn inflationist idiots on the municipal council passing off silver-washed copper . . ."

"They're going by," the voice of the box hummed. "They come from all directions, but they all go in one direction, and that is not here. They cross over the Circle on their way . . ."

Even through the heavy shutters, Rhion heard a woman scream.

He was on his feet and heading for the door almost before he could think—he and Jaldis both had been sleeping booted and clothed. He had his hands on the heavy door bolt before he remembered that grims frequently counterfeited the voices of women and children crying for help, to trick victims into opening shutters and doors and breaking what field of power

57

the silver nails might generate. He thought the scream sounded genuine, but still . . .

"*Alseigodath, amresith*, Children of the Dusky Air . . ." he muttered, collecting the first of the demon-spells Jaldis had long ago had him memorize and hoping he could call accurately to mind the long catalogue of the names of demons and grims and the strange pain-spells that held such creatures in check. He caught up his walking staff and flung the door open as a second scream cut the air. Hearing it, he knew it was no grim that made that sound.

Calling up within him all the power that he could, he ran.

Foul with ice and half-melted snow, the road dipped beyond the inn's little hill to the thicker woods and broken jumble of ground that was the first frontier of the Drowned Lands of Sligo. In this season the pools and marshes which six hundred years ago had filled in the upper end of the Morne Valley were frozen, black cattails and the twisted stems of sunken oak and hornbeam protruding like skeleton fingers from the gray sheet of starlit ice. But with the recent thaw, even the shallow ponds were treacherous. Rhion's foot broke through what had appeared to be solid ice in the roadside ditch as he scrambled across, soaking him to the knees in freezing water.

Far off, amid the tangled bog-hummocks and leafless willows, he could see a flickering greenish light.

There were hundreds of them, thick as flies above a midden in summer. As he whispered the words of the spells within his mind he could smell them, queer and cold and bodiless; see them through their own ghastly weavings of semivisibility and shifting forms. Like the intermittent hallucinations of migraine, grims flitted through the bare boughs of maple and ash, skeletal forms with huge eyes and dangling feet, strange organs heaving luminously through transparent skin, eyes and faces and limbs, human and bestial, materializing one moment, then vanishing or becoming, hideously something else. A thing came loping out of the black under-brush beside him in the form of a huge black dog, to snap and tear at his legs with teeth suddenly solid and real; Rhion struck at it, his staff ablaze with blue-white witchfire, and the creature screamed at him with a human face and went gibbering back into the dark.

As he had suspected, they were driving the women toward the frozen sloughs.

Through snow-clotted fern and bracken, it was easy to trace the rucked hoof-tracks of her panicked horse; far off he could hear it neighing with terror. They were out on pond ice already, though, from the high ground where he stood, Rhion could see the rider fighting to rein back to safer foot-ing. He scrambled down the scarp bank, black tangles of wild ivy and vine snagging his feet like rabbit snares under the snow, swinging his flaming staff at the grims when they came too close. Their claws raked at his face and his hands—*If they get my specs off me I'm a dead man,* he thought detachedly—shrieking like the soulless damned, while ahead of him clouds of them blew like poisoned green smoke around the frantic dark forms wheeling in the starlight.

They were far out on the ice, the horse's hooves skidding and slipping, and underfoot Rhion felt the ice buckle and crack. The Drowned Lands were a maze of fen and swamp and pond, deep even this far inland, in these sweet marshes, two days' journey from the salt marshes where the heart of the realm of Sligo had lain. By the bulrushes that fringed the gray glimmer of ice, Rhion guessed this pond was deep. Ahead of him he saw by the noxious ur-light the face of the rider, a girl of no more than seventeen, taut and scared as she tried to force her mount back into the driving swarms of eyes and claws that lay between her and the safety of the shore. Fingers like thorn-branches snagged and lifted a huge cloud of pale hair; another grim tore the long, full train of her riding skirt, and she lashed at it with her quirt, clinging to the rein as the terrified horse twisted out of control.

Then the ice cracked beneath them and they plunged, forehooves-first, into the heaving brown water beneath.

Rhion flung up his staff and cried *"ALSEIGODATH!* Children of the Dark Air . . . !"* in a voice of power, the trained, booming shout completely unlike his normal light tenor, and the grims, screaming with laughter as they swirled around their struggling victims, scattered in all directions in a vicious, glittering cloud. Summoning about him the essences, the true names, of silver and fire and burning sunlight, Rhion strode forward, blazing and flashing and crying out the tale of the demon lists he had memorized over the years, the true names of as many as these flickering, amorphous things as had been gathered by wizards of the past, weaving them into a net of illusion and power and ruin.

And he tried not to show—and indeed, tried not to feel— his surprise that they did retreat, since as far as anyone could tell the power of the grims increased the more of them there were.

The girl sprang from the saddle as soon as the grims whirled back, tearing off her jacket and throwing it around the head of the terrified horse. Its forelegs were still trapped in the ice and its frantic pitching threatened to drop them through what remained; she caught the bit, trying to drag the animal free, and Rhion, still shouting the names of power and pain and light, ran to her and caught the bridle on the other side.

"*Malsleiga, Brekkat, Ykklath*—say when . . ." he panted. "*Rinancor* and *Tch'war, Flennegant the Pig-Faced* . . ."

"Now!"

Both hauling in unison, they pulled the terrified beast's forefeet clear, ice-water showering everywhere and soaking them both to the skin. The horse tried to bolt, demons still eddying around their heads like flaming leaves in a whirlwind, and through that hellish storm Rhion and the girl managed to drag it across the sagging floe. Only when they reached the more solid packs among the reed-beds did the wickering ring thin, swirling away like blown smoke into the darkness and melting into cruel, luminous laughter among the silent trees.

"Thank you," the girl gasped, brushing back her tangled hair with a hand that shook. Even etiolated by starshine, Rhion could see it was mingled brown and fair, the color of burned sugar, where it wasn't soaked dark with marsh water. Her cap had been torn away, but its gemmed pins remained, flashing coldly in the streaming mess like phosphorous in seaweed.

". . . *Filkedne the Black, Qu'a'htchat* . . . What the hell were you doing riding alone in the woods at night?! You could have been killed out there!"

The gratitude in those huge gray eyes turned to anger, and for a moment he thought of a very young hawk, bating against a clumsy hand. "I wanted a little exercise!" she snapped sarcastically. "And nobody had *ever* told me about grims haunting the wild places at night, so I thought I'd be *perfectly* safe!" She jerked the rein from his hand. "And since it's such a lovely night and I've had such a wonderful time so far I think I'll just . . ."

Rhion realized that his question had included an unspoken, *Are you stupid or something?* and blushed. "I'm sorry," he said quietly, catching back the girl's hand, his breath drifting in a silvery cloud around his head. "That was a stupid thing to say. What's wrong, and can I help?" The girl's face had been cut by a claw or tail-stinger—the wound was already beginning to puff. His own face was torn and welted, his robe, like the girl's dark-red riding dress, soaked and dragging with water. "I'm Rhion the Brown . . ."

"Tallisett . . . Tally . . ." She swung around at the sound of a man's voice shouting in terror, far off in the woods, the neighing of terrified horses and laughter like the sparkle of corrosive dust. The fear returning to her eyes as she looked swiftly back at him made her suddenly seem very young, despite the fact that she stood a good two inches taller than he.

"It's my sister's child," she said, trying to keep her husky young voice steady. With a sudden move, she pulled the jacket from the horse's head and drew it on, shivering at the touch of the sodden wool. "They've taken her." She caught the stirrup preparatory to mounting again.

"Wait . . ." Rhion caught her elbow, pointy and delicate in his grip. "We'll get my master."

"Why didn't you push on and take shelter in the inn, by the way?" he asked a few minutes later, as the two of them half strode, half ran up the frozen slush of the road back toward the deserted public house, their breath puffing in silver clouds with exertion, the exhausted and shivering bay gelding stumbling between them. "You do know there's an inn here . . ."

"A peddler we met this afternoon coming from Imber said it was shut up and barred. We hadn't been able to get fresh litter mules at the last inn and when we knew we couldn't get a change here, either, we decided to make camp. We lit fires all around the camp . . ."

"That doesn't always work if there's a lot of them."

Tally had tucked up her heavy skirts through her belt to run—because of her height her stride was long, though unlike so many tall girls she was not gawky, but moved as gracefully as a dancer. Heavy silver earrings swung in the tangle of her hair, gleaming coldly in the ragged blue witch-glow; her boots, the wool of her dress, and the many strands of barrel-shaped amber beads around her neck proclaimed her a rich man's child. Her hand in its buckskin glove, gripping the horse's cheekstrap, though slender, was as large as a man's.

"How many were you?"

"A dozen. One of the grooms rode with me to search. We had torches, but they fell into the snow when the horses got spooked . . . What was that you shouted at them?"

The magelight that shivered and flickered above their heads as they walked would have left her in no doubt as to what he was. But there was no apprehension in her wide, inquiring eyes. Probably, Rhion thought wryly, because no woman is ever really afraid of a man who's shorter than she is.

"Their names—or names that might have been theirs. There are lists of them, different lists for different parts of the country, lists that have been accumulated, handed down, passed on by other wizards who in one way or another have gotten some specific grim or demon in their power long enough to get it to rat on some of its fellows."

"Is that easy to do?"

"Oh, yes. They're all cowards, and half of them hate each other anyway—they feel no loyalty to anything as we understand loyalty. Since you weave spells with a thing's true name, the name of its soul, grims will generally retreat if they know you know their names. Because they don't have true bodies, you can put a *hell* of a pain-spell on a demon . . . Were you hurt?"

She shook her head. The dark blood gleamed where it was drying on her temple, and Rhion made a mental note to apply a poultice later. The uneasy feather of witchfire threw fluttering shadows over the gray trunks of the maples along the roadbed and made the snow flash like salt rime where it squeaked beneath their boots. Far off in the darkness, the dreadful slips of light still wavered, and the night was rank— to Rhion's hypertrained nostrils at least—with the nauseating ammonia muskiness of the grims' smell. Blood dripped to the snow from the horse's torn flanks and bitten hocks—they must have driven it here and there through the woods, laughing and egging one another on, delighting in its fear and in

Tally's anger, trying to get it to throw her so they could chase her through the dark.

Jaldis was waiting for them in the open door of the inn, witchlight streaming out around him. As if they had discussed the matter—which they hadn't—they led the horse inside as a matter of course, and it stood, head down and shivering, while Rhion rubbed its coat dry and Jaldis listened, nodding, opal spectacles flashing weirdly in the firelight, while Tally told him of her niece's disappearance.

"What is her name?" the old man asked at length, and the girl glanced, startled, from the closed, scar-crusted mouth to the soundbox upon his chest.

But she only said, "Elucida. She's three. I still don't understand how they can have taken her. Damson—my sister—and I put a mirror over her cot and a silver chain around it in a circle . . ."

"Beyond a doubt they lured her forth in her sleep," the wizard replied, stroking the gold sun-cross talisman thoughtfully. "She crossed the silver herself, to where they could come to her. Unlike the water-goblins, they seek to frighten, not to kill, though it does not matter to them if the victim dies in the process. But goblins haunt these marshes, and if they can find a way to get her through the ice they will. My cloak, Rhion . . ."

Rhion slung a rug over the horse's back and fetched his master's cloak, while Jaldis dug in the purse at his belt and produced his scrying-crystal, whose long, irregular facets he angled to the fire's light. The reflection of the blaze, which had been built up high, glanced sharply off the brown quartz and repeated itself endlessly in the chips of crystal worked into his spectacle-lenses, and echoed in the girl Tally's worried gray eyes.

Softly, as if following his thoughts without his conscious volition, the box murmured, "Elucida, Damson's child . . . Little Elucida, daughter of daylight . . ."

Tally glanced over at Rhion, as if for help or guidance. Rhion signed to her with his fingers that all would be well. As he stepped over close to her she breathed, "We have to hurry. She was only wearing a nightdress, she'll freeze . . ." Her own clothes were steaming in the warmth of the fire, bullion embroidery sparkling faintly under the mudstains, the crisscrossed maze of ribbonwork on the sleeves discolored and sodden, save for here and there, where creases had protected and now revealed startling squares and slips of bronze and blue.

"It'll be all right," Rhion said softly. "It'll be all right."

The gesture of Jaldis' fingers, the movement of his head, were clear as a murmured, *Ah*! He made a pass or two above the crystal with his crippled hand, the tracing of runes too quick, too subliminal, for Rhion to identify them all. "Now," he said, reaching for his crutches and rising from the bench beside the fire. "Let us go."

From the inn doorway they faced out into the dark. Something swift and glowing flickered by just beyond the outstreaming bar of magelight—Rhion couldn't be sure, but he thought it was only a marsh-fae, tiny and naked and curious about all the hullabaloo. Around them, the blue-white glow of witchlight softened and dimmed until it was little brighter than the ghostly powder of starlight on the snow. "Look out across the trees, both of you," said the old mage softly. "Can you see light?"

The starlight was unsteady, the woods thick and wild, a tangle of bare black willow, of ash and maple and laurel thickets. The earthquake which six centuries ago had sunk the Drowned Lands and thrown down the walls of every city from Nerriok to Killay had left the Morne Valley a jagged ruin of fault scarps and banks, broken ground difficult to navigate even where it was not studded with potholes and ponds.

Rhion shook his head. "No."

"And now?"

Far off, a gleam of blue witchlight flickered bright among the knotted trees. "Yes . . ."

"Then come."

They found the little girl where the grims had abandoned her when they'd grown bored with driving her here and there in the haunted woods. With the self-preservative instincts of a little animal she'd crawled into a hollow log; over this log, Rhion saw as they came nearer, Jaldis with his scrying-crystal had called a glowing column of magelight, a moving rope of disembodied, unearthly brightness, whose light made the snow all around glitter as if strewn with diamonds. Rhion had brought extra blankets; Tally snatched them from his hands and fell to her knees, wrapping the half-conscious child in them, her face solemn, as if she worked to save the life of a kitten found drowning in a stream.

"She's alive . . ."

Rhion knelt in the snow beside her and felt the baby's hands and cheeks. Cold as the silken skin was, he felt blood moving beneath. Gently he called the spells of healing and warmth, and the aversion of ills. The child herself was thin and small, not pretty, but with a porcelain-doll delicacy and a soft tangle of blond-brown hair ridiculously like that of her young aunt.

"She'll be all right," he murmured, the words half-embodying the charm in themselves, both promise and invocation as his fingers traced the signs of Summer Queen and Sun, the signs of health and longevity and light, on the forehead, the cheeks, and across the energy-paths of the child's face and neck which governed lungs and skin. It seemed incredible to him, touching that skin which in its texture, its softness, and its newness was so absolutely unlike anything else of the mortal earth, that something so small could have those same paths of energy that traced the adult body, perfect in miniature, like a baby's fingernails or the veins of the tiniest leaf.

Holding the child cradled to her shoulder Tally looked across at him as they knelt side-by-side in the slush, their faces mottled by tree-latticed starlight and darkness. She drew in her breath to speak, to thank him . . . But by the soft glow of the flickering witchlight their eyes met, and silence fell between them, a silence in which Rhion was conscious of the almost-unheard sibilance of her breath, of the way her dust-colored hair stuck in dark strings to the hollows of her cheekbones, of the small, upright line of puzzlement between her brows as her eyes looked into his . . .

Clumsy with sudden haste he got to his feet. "Jaldis will . . . will be able to help if she's taken any hurt."

A moment later he realized he should probably help Tally, overburdened with the child as she was, to her feet. But she had already risen, not noticing or not thinking anything of this omission. "She's all right, I think. Thank you," she added shyly.

The two wizards walked with her back to the campsite on the southward road. Jaldis moved along behind on his crutches, the witchlight that wavered in rippling sheets all around them flashing coldly off the bulging spectacle-lenses and dancing like strange blue fire on the mud and snow of the roadbanks. Rhion and Tally, walking ahead, traded off carrying the child Elucida and leading the horse. "How did you become a wizard?" Tally asked as they passed beneath the black shadows of a grove of naked elms, and Rhion laughed and shook his head.

"Have you got till spring?"

"No, really. I mean, everybody talks about wizards as if the first thing a wizard has to do is spit on Darova's altar—and then everybody turns around and goes to wizards for spells and horoscopes and things. And the wizards I've met at . . . at my father's house . . ." She hesitated there. Rhion saw her hand steal to the amber beads she wore, which announced her to all the world as a marriageable virgin of truly substantial dowry, and wondered if somebody had told her—as his parents had repeatedly told his sister—not to reveal her father's name to chance-met strangers for fear of being carried away for ransom.

She recovered quickly and went on, "The wizards I've met at my father's house have all seemed—well, very decent, if a little strange. And you didn't have to come out to help me." She reached out, and touched the puffy red welt on the side of his face, left by a grim's stinging tail. "So I just wondered . . . Why you did it? Become a mage, I mean. Because I refuse to believe, as the philosophers say, that wizards were born without souls and have to become what they are."

Rhion sighed. "I don't know if I was born without a soul, because, if I was, I wouldn't know what really having one feels like." He glanced back over his shoulder, at Jaldis stumping sturdily along behind the exhausted horse. "But yes . . . We have to become what we are."

It was something he'd never been able to explain to anyone not mageborn. He remembered, back in the days when he was still one of the most fashionable young dandies who hung around the perfume shops and flower boutiques, standing with several of his friends watching a pack of children tormenting an old Earth-witch who'd set up shop on a blanket on the steps of one of the great downtown baths. The children had been throwing dung and rotten vegetables at her, chanting obscene songs. Furious as the old woman was, she had borne it in silence, and Rhion knew instinctively that she dared not do anything that would cause the children to run to their parents crying, *The lady hurt us* . . . And his friends had joked about why anyone would want to be a witch in the first place.

And he, Rhion, had been silent.

Because even then he had known.

Very softly, he said, "You reach a point where you can't live a lie anymore. Where the pain of not—not using what you *know* you have, of not reaching out to take that power—becomes so intolerable that you don't care what happens to you afterward. It's like sex . . .''

Oh, great! he thought in the next instant, *Go ahead and shock this poor virgin . . .*

But the great gray eyes were not shocked.

"When I was a little boy," he went on, his voice still low, as if he spoke to himself, "I used to see pictures in the fire. Simple things, like my mother putting her make-up on, or my friends eating breakfast . . . One day my parents went to the shrine of St. Beldriss, and I mentioned to my nurse that I'd seen in the fire that a wheel had come off a cart in the narrow streets around the shrine and caused a hell of a traffic jam and that they'd be late coming back. She beat me." His eyebrows flinched together over the round lenses of his spectacles. "She said that nobody saw things in the fire, that it was just daydreams that were no good for little boys. She told me not to say anything about it to my mother, but of course I did, and Mother punished me for lying."

He still remembered the dark of the attic closet where he'd been locked, the furtive, terrible scurryings of the rats he knew lurked just behind the walls. It was not something he would ever have done to a child of four. He remembered other things as well.

"For years I convinced myself she was right—that I had lied. And I tried so damn hard to be good."

There was a silence, in which their feet squeaked a little in the packed snow and mud of the road. The child Elucida slept, a warm, muffled burden against Rhion's chest, beneath his patched black wool cloak. The last of the grims had faded back into the earth and trees where they lurked in daylight, and the frozen swamps, the sheets of gray ice, and the dirty piebald snow, all broken with the iron stems of naked shrub and willow, seemed to have lain locked in that sleeping enchantment since the beginnings of time.

"What were you doing traveling at this time of year, anyway?" Rhion asked after a little time, looking back across at the tall girl who strode at his side.

Tally seemed to shake herself out of some private reverie and smiled ironically across at him. "We were going to Imber to meet Damson's husband. He has property near there and interest in shipping . . . he says." She hesitated, as if debating whether to say more, her hands tucked into her armpits for warmth. A small tired line, the wry foot track of a passing thought, flicked into existence at the corner of her mouth and then as quickly fled.

"And a mistress, too?"

Her gray eyes slid sidelong at him, then away. The bitter dimple reappeared, all the comment necessary.

"And you?"

"I wanted to get away. I like to travel." They came within sight of the camp, five or six pavilions at the top of a steep bank, twenty feet high above the swerve of the road where it ran across a dilapidated stone bridge. Even in the icy night, the smell of blood, both fresh and nauseatingly stale, breathed from the round little stone hut on the nearer end of the bridge, where offerings to the guardian troll had been left. The thing's tracks were visible in the trampled snow, shambling along the bank of the marsh which the causeway spanned and so into the rocks of the glen. Lamps in the red and orange tents high on the bank turned them into glowing treasure-boxes in the bitter darkness, and Rhion could hear voices and glimpse the flash of steel by the jittery flare of torches.

He revised his estimate of the girl's social position upward. A wealthy merchant or banker could have bought those great amber beads and the silver bullion that stitched her breast and sleeves, but a camp like that meant old nobility, at least.

On the threshold of the bridge Tally halted and took her sleeping niece from Rhion's arms. Elucida murmured a little and cuddled deeper into her aunt's breast. For a moment Rhion saw Tally's face, as she turned to look down at the child, filled with a solemn tenderness, the deep, protective affection that had sent her out into the woods herself when she could have detailed grooms and liverymen to the task.

She looked up again and shrugged, her breath a misty vapor as she spoke. "When I'm married, I won't be able to journey," she said.

"Is that going to be soon?" he inquired, not nearly lightly enough.

"I suppose. Father needs an alliance, you see." Her voice was trying hard to be matter-of-fact. She glanced at Jaldis, surrounded by the nimbus of the witchfire that protected them, then back at Rhion, small and battered with his scratched face and his round-lensed spectacles and his rough ashwood walking staff gripped in one mended glove. Behind her, the lights and voices of the camp rose like a wall of color, warmth, and security within call.

"My father is the Duke of Mere," she said quietly. "So it isn't a question of what I want, really. Just when. And who."

Shaking back the filthy strings of her oak-blond hair, she turned a little too quickly and hurried across the bridge, back to her father's servants and troops. But after a step or two, almost against some inner inclination, she turned back, still holding the child cradled on one hip like a peasant woman, the rein of the exhausted horse hooked through her arm. Her face was a pale oval in the frosty gloom.

"Rhion . . . You will . . . Will you ever be coming to Bragenmere? Father . . . he's a scholar, you know. And he does invite wizards to Court."

Then as if fearing she'd said too much, she turned swiftly away and hastened across the bridge, her boots leaving deep tracks in the crusted muck of snow and dirt. For a few moments Rhion stood watching the spangled dusk of her hair and the moving white blob of the horse's off hind stocking blur with the dark of the ascending road. Then torches and colored lanterns came streaming out of the camp and down the path to greet her and to take her back among them again.

"Dinar of Mere may be a scholar," Jaldis' soft, artificial voice buzzed from the freezing dark behind him, "but as for the wizards he invites to his Court . . . ! Ebiatics trying to transmute lead into gold and call the wind by means of silver machines; Blood-Mages stinking like troll huts with demons and grims squeaking in their hair like lice . . . Why, his court mage for years, when he was still land-baron of the Prinag marshes before he overthrew the house of the White Bragen-meres and married the old duke's daughter, was a foul old Hand-Pricker who could barely talk for the spell-threads laced through his lips and tongue. Go to Bragenmere indeed!"

Looking back, Rhion saw that the old man, though draped in the heavy black cloak and surcoat that marked them both as members of the most ancient of the Orders of Wizardry, was shivering in the cold, all the talismans of power at his breast twinkling in the witchlight and his pale face lined with the strain of using his spectacles to see. Rhion walked back to him and said quietly, "Let's go back to the inn."

The witchlight faded from above their heads. They turned away, an old cripple and a young pauper, bearded, scruffy, and insignificant in the leaden darkness before the winter's dawn. But looking over his shoulder, Rhion could see, on the edge of the camp, a plump little woman in a dress scin-tillant with opals and featherwork come running out to embrace Tally and the sleeping child, and lead them toward the largest of the lighted pavilions. And he saw how Tally turned to look out into the darkness, and it seemed to him for a moment that their eyes met.

FIVE

FOR A LONG TIME AFTER JALDIS SLEPT RHION SAT AWAKE BY the fire, staring into its silken heart and listening to the silence of the deserted inn.

And thinking.

You reach the point where you can't live a lie anymore, he had said. And, *I tried so damn hard to be good.*

He had never spoken to a nonwizard about wizardry like that. On the whole, those who were not mageborn—those not born with the strange sleeping fire in their veins, their hearts, the marrow of their bones—found it impossible to comprehend why those who were would subject themselves to such stringent teaching and disciplines in order to achieve a state of virtual outlawry, the state of *beldin nar*—literally, to be dead souls, whose deaths were no more a matter for vengeance than the desecration of a dog's carcass.

Yet he had said it to her, knowing she would understand.

And saying it, he had remembered afresh how much it had hurt to wonder and pretend and fake being something everyone thought he should be; to live in the subconscious hope that it wasn't true or that, if it was true, he could keep people from guessing.

On the whole, to those nonmageborn acquaintances who evinced a genuine interest in the subject—and there had been some among their patrons and clients from the court at Nerriok—he had explained his initiation into wizardry in terms of teaching, education, and eagerness to learn. To them he had recounted how he'd cooked and cleaned and run errands, fetching and carrying up and down all those long rickety stairways of the tall, narrow house in Nerriok, even in the days when they could afford a servant; made a good story of all the tedium of ritually cleansing crucibles and implements in the attic workshop, censing and sweeping the sanctum where the meditation was done, and washing the vessels before and after. That they would understand, at least in part. But never all.

All those first years he'd been reading, absorbing almost without knowing it, all the infinite, tiny gradations of lore necessary to wizardry, gradually becoming aware, through conversation with Jaldis, with Shavus, and with other mages of the Order who stayed with them of the interweavings of all things in the physical world, the metaphysical, and the strange shadowland of ghosts and faes and grims that lay between them—learning how all things were balanced and how no alteration of the fabric of the world could be made without somehow affecting the rest of the universe, sometimes in rather unexpected fashions.

After the spells of imbuing Jaldis' crystal spectacle-lenses had nearly cost him his own eyesight, Rhion had taken the concept of precautions and Limitations very seriously indeed. He had not worked a spell for a long while after that, and had been careful to make the Circles of Power and Protection absolutely correct, to study carefully the Words of Ward and Guard. Simply the study of these had taken him nearly three years of painstaking memorization, during which time he had also studied all those things that his father had never bothered to have him taught: the structure and nature of plants, and how to tell them from one another by sight and touch and smell; the names of every plant, every bird, every beast and fae and spirit and insect and stone, and how they differed from one another; and how each was its own creation, with its own secret name.

Such things were not necessary to accounting—things not only beyond a banker's ken, but beyond even one's imaginings.

And somewhere in those first few years he had learned the thing that he'd never been able to explain to even the most sympathetic of hearers: that magic was not something one did; it was something you were, ingrained in the deepest marrow of the soul. He remembered one of the local tavern girls in Nerriok, with whom he'd had a cozy, if casual, affair, asking why Jaldis hadn't quit being a wizard after he'd been blinded. "Would have made me quit quick enough, let me tell you," she'd said, shaking her tousled head.

Rhion had simply said, "He's stubborn," and had left it at that.

But the truth was that you couldn't quit, the same way he realized that it was almost impossible not to become a wizard, if you were born with the power to do so. You couldn't not be what you were.

On the whole, that was something only other mages understood.

Tally . . .

The fire had sunk low; the burning log collapsed on itself with a noise like rustling silk, and Rhion fetched the poker to rearrange the blaze. The renewed flare of saffron light lent a deceptive color to Jaldis' sleeping face, an illusion of health and strength.

Jaldis. For ten and a half years, teacher and father and friend. It had taken Rhion over a year to realize that Jaldis was also one of the most prominent of the Morkensik wizards, renowned throughout the Order for the depth of his wisdom and the strength of his spells.

He had taught Rhion thoroughly, patiently, and from the ground up, riding easily through the petulance, temper-tantrums, and fits of impatience and sarcasm that the older Rhion still blushed to think about. As a rich man's son, he had been less than an ideal pupil. "What the hell does *that* have to do with magic?" had been his constant refrain—sitting by the fire, Rhion could still hear himself, like a stubborn child refusing to see what the alphabet has to do with being a poet of world renown. And Jaldis would always say gently, "Do you have anything else you're doing today?"

Personally, Rhion would have taken a stick to that plump and spoiled youth.

To philosophers, the metaphysical division of essence and accidents—of true inner nature and the chance combination of individual differences—was a matter of theoretical debate; to magicians it was the very heart of spells. It was easy, Jaldis had pointed out, to change accidents—easier still to simply change the perceptions of the beholder. But to change the essence—truly to alter a poisonous solution into harmless plant-sap, to transform the physical structure of gangrene into inert scab-tissue—required greater power. And anything above that, far more power still.

And so from metaphysics he had gone on to study the nature of power.

Jaldis had taken him to the places where the paths of power moved over the earth, deep silvery tracks pulsing invisibly in the ground: "leys" the mages called them, "witchpaths," "dragon-tracks" . . . straight lines between nodes and crossings at ancient shrines and artificial hills, marked sometimes by ponds and shrines. On these lines, spells worked more quickly, more efficaciously. Scrying was easier, particularly at certain seasons of the year. Everything related to everything, and the balances of power were constantly shifting: the pull of the moon and the tides, the waxing and waning of the days, the presence or absence in the heavens of certain stars—all these had their effects, to be learned and dealt with.

And like the earth, and the heavens over the earth, the human body was traced with leys of its own, paths that could be used to promote healing, or create illusion, or draw or repel the mind and heart. Animals, birds, insects, fish, every tree and blade of grass—all these had their paths. In his deep meditations on summer nights Rhion had often seen the faint silver threads of energy glowing along the veins of weeds and flowers, the tiny balls of seeds within their pods shining like miniscule pearls; looking into crystals, he had seen the leys shimmering there, utterly different from those of plant and animal life, but there nevertheless, whispering strange logics of their own.

All of this Jaldis had taught him, forcing him to memorize, to meditate, to strengthen his skills while building the colossal foundation of magic itself. And all the while magic was opening before him like a gigantic rose, drawing him in to deeper and ever deeper magics hidden within its heart.

He learned the runes, the twenty-six signs capable of drawing down constellations of power, clusters of coincidence, to themselves, and how these runes could be combined into sigils and seals, to affect possibility and chance. He learned the art of talisman making, how to imbue an inanimate object with a field of altered probability or to cause it to have an effect upon the mind or body or perceptions of those it touched; learned which metals, which minerals, which materials would hold power, and which would shed it like a duck's feather shedding water.

He learned Limitations and which spells were dangerous to work because of strange and unexpected effects—there were spells which would turn a man's entire body into a field of blazing good fortune, so that luck would inevitably fall his way, but which were never used because the side effect was that the man would go mad; other spells of protection that, at certain seasons of the year which could never be accurately predicted, would call upon their wielder every grim and demon for miles around, attacking and attacking in a biting cloud; or spells that transformed ugliness into astonishing physical beauty, but which brought with them unspeakable dreams.

He learned also Illusion, the wizard's stock-in-trade: how to make a man or woman believe that a cup was made of gold and gems, instead of cheap wood, and how to make them continue in that belief for hours or days; how to make them believe that the cup was filled with wine when it contained only water, and to make them not only taste the wine but get drunk on it, though it took a very clever wizard to engineer a convincing hangover the following morning; how to make a guard fall asleep, or believe that someone entering the room was a dog or a kitten, or someone else he knew and who had legitimate business there; the spells of Who-Me? and Look-Over-There that Rhion had used in dealing with the Felsplex mob.

It had all been like playing in a field of flowers.

He had learned, too, that simply knowing a spell, or having learned it once, was not enough. There were many who called themselves wizards who thought that it was, but usually these did not survive. Shavus had taught him, by the rough-and-ready expedient of chasing him around the room, beating him with a stick, that certain spells must become second nature, so that they may be cast accurately in an emergency, or when the mind is clouded with panic or sleep or—sometimes—poison or drugs.

And he had learned the Magic of Ill.

Jaldis had been unwilling for many years to teach him the spells to cause pain to another human being, spells to pierce certain portions of the brain like slivers of glass, spells to inflame the joints and the bowels with agony, spells which could, if wielded by a mighty enough mage, suffocate a man or rip his organs within him. "They are the obverse of healing spells," he had said, "the dark side of our ability to shift the small workings of the body, and they must be used only in the gravest, the direst emergencies. There have been wizards who have allowed themselves to be beaten to death, rather than work such spells upon their killers.''

''Why?'' Rhion had asked, remembering the wold woman sitting on her blanket, with a smear of dog turd on her cheek. He'd been in his early twenties then, and still in the stick phase of his education, nursing a dozen bruises under his robe. ''I mean, if it's a choice of your life or theirs . . .''

''It isn't simply your life,'' Jaldis had said quietly. That had been at Shavus' house. The big old warrior-mage and the two apprentices he'd had at that time, fair-haired brother and sister from Clordhagh who bickered constantly and affectionately, had been sitting at the scrubbed oak table with them, the dark book of those spells lying on the table between. ''For the mageborn, for such as we, the world is an infinity of divisions . . . it is not so for everyone. Even for us, Shavus, if you found that a fox had come into your hencoop and killed your chickens, and if the following evening you sighted a fox in the woods, would you not *fruge* it immediately, without asking whether it was the one who had done the damage?''

''Aye,'' the big man growled. ''If it wasn't the one had done it before, it's only a matter of time till it *does*.''

''Precisely,'' the sweet, buzzing voice said, that was all the King's men had left him with. ''And so it is with humankind, and wizards. They may use our services, but they will never truly trust us. They fear our powers over them—our powers to deceive them, if you will; our powers to make them act against their wills, or under the compulsion of illusion or threat. It takes very little to rouse them against us. Rumor of a wizard having used his powers to advance his own speculations in trade against other merchants', or to seduce a woman he wanted, is enough for all wizards in a town, or a Realm, to be driven out of their homes, deprived of their power with the *pheelas* root and executed, shot from ambush . . . Only from people's fear.''

They will use our services, Rhion thought, staring into the heart of the fire on the inn's great hearth, *but they will never truly trust us . . .*

He recalled how Tally had hesitated to mention that her father was one of the richest, the most powerful, lords of the Forty Realms. Had that been because her father, as a usurper, had enemies who would not hesitate to kidnap her if they found her alone? Or had it been reflex caution against those whom every priest of every god declared excommunicate, creatures other than human?

Yet he remembered how she had turned to look out into the darkness; remembered the way their eyes had met.

Not that there was any possibility of anything existing between the Duke of Mere's daughter and himself, he hastened to add. Even had he not been a mage, even had he remained his father's douce and respectable son and inherited the biggest countinghouse in the City of Circles, he could no more have . . . His mind shied from the first phrase that sprang to it, and he hastily substituted, *have spoken seriously* . . . He could no more have spoken seriously to Tallisett of Mere than he could have spoken seriously to the High Queen of Nerriok.

And rising stiffly from his seat beside the chimney breast, he mended the fire a final time and stood for a moment listening, extending his senses out into the stillness of the woods beyond the gray stone walls for any sign, any hint of danger. Hearing none, he lay down in his blankets by the hearthstones, took off his spectacles, and fell asleep.

SIX

IN THE END, JALDIS AND RHION DID NOT GO TO NERRIOK after all. The morning after their hunt for the grim-harrowed child, Jaldis slept long and heavily and woke weak with fever. Their little stock of medicinal herbs had been one of the things left behind in the attic of the Black Pig; Rhion hunted patiently through the snowy thickets and roadbanks for elf-dock and borage to take down the old man's fever and clear the congestion he feared was growing in his lungs. But the winter woods kept their secrets, and when he returned to the inn, well after noon, he found his teacher no better and dared not leave him again.

He was up with Jaldis, trying to work healing spells without the wherewithal to aid the physical body, for most of the following night.

"Look, I need to get you to some help," Rhion said to him, during one of the intervals in which the fever had been reduced by means of a spell which had left Rhion himself feeling ill and shaky. He took from the pouch at his belt his own scrying-crystal, a lump of yellowed quartz half the size of his fist, and held it to the wan light from the single window he'd unshuttered when daylight came. "I'm going to try to contact the Ladies of the Moon. They're the closest place we can take you."

Jaldis sighed, and his groping hand touched the voice-box long enough for it to whisper the word, ". . . corrupt . . ."

81

But the shake of his head was only of regret, not refusal, and Rhion settled himself into a corner of the old kitchen with his crystal to work.

He chose the kitchen hearth—which he suspected had been the main hearth of the original inn—because at that point a minor ley crossed through the building. Though he couldn't yet, like Jaldis, simply close his eyes and hear the silvery traces of energy like thin music in the air, he had had the suspicion that the inn was built upon a ley, and a brief test with a pendulum-stone confirmed it. He guessed it was the one connecting the Holy Hill beyond Imber with one of the now-inundated shrines of the ancient city of Sligo. Cradling the crystal in his hands with its largest facet angled to the pallid window-light, he slipped into meditation, and after a few minutes saw, as if reflected in a mirror from over his shoulder and a great distance away, the Gray Lady's face.

He had never met the Lady of the Drowned Lands, though he had heard of her, from Jaldis, Shavus, and travelers who had passed through the fogbound mazes of swamp and lake and cranberry bog that tangled the Valley of the Morne. She looked puzzled, to see in her scrying-mirror a stranger's face; but when Rhion explained to her who he was and that Jaldis the Blind was ill and in need at the old inn on the Imber road, she said immediately, "Of course. The Cock in Britches . . ." Her wide mouth flexed in a smile. "Once the God of Bridges, though I think the sign has a rooster on it these days. There are Marshmen who serve us living near there. I shall send them to fetch you here."

In the days before the earthquake the city of Sligo, built on a cluster of granite hills where the Morne estuary narrowed to its valley between the hills of Fel and the great granite spine of the Mountains of the Sun, had been among the richest of the Forty Realms, rivaling the inland wealth of Nerriok and ruling most of the In Islands and wide stretches of valley farmland along the great river's shores. Now all that remained of those fertile farmsteads were the marshy hay meadows and lowland pasturage for the thick-wooled, black-faced sheep, isolated oases among the sweet marshes and salt marshes, thick miles-long beds of angelica and cattail, bog-oak and willow, a thousand crisscrossing water channels where the tall reeds met, rustling overhead, and redbirds and water-goblins dwelled as if the place had been theirs from the foundations of the world. For the rest, Mhorvianne the Merciful, Goddess of Waters, had claimed her own. But whether An, the Moon as she was worshipped in Sligo of old—in Nerriok they worshipped Sioghis, Moon-God of the southern lands—was in fact merely an aspect of Mhorvianne as some said, no one these days knew.

As for the Lady of the Moon, some said she ruled the Marshmen by ancestral right, descended as she was from the Archpriestesses of the ancient shrine; some, that she held sway over them by means of her enchantments. Others claimed that she and her Ladies traded their magic for food-stuffs and wool—still others claimed they traded their bodies as well.

Crouched uneasily beside Jaldis' head in the stern of the long canoe, watching the black silhouette of the Marshman on the prow, poling with uncanny silence through the dense, fog-locked silence of the salt marsh, Rhion understood why no one could say anything for certain about the Drowned Lands. To enter here was to enter a whispering, sunken labyrinth, where the bulrushes and water weeds grew thick and the footing was uncertain—where the water was never open water, the land never dry land. Hummocks of maple, willow, and moss-dripping salt-oak loomed like matte gray ghosts through wreaths of coiling fog. Now and then, nearly obliterated by tall stands of reeds and almost indistinguishable from the root snags of dead or dying trees, the moss-clotted tips of stone spires and gables could be discerned, rising up through the brown waters, the decaying remains of the buildings sunk deep underneath.

The Marshmen themselves were a silent folk, wiry and small, impossible to track and difficult to speak to even when they consented to be seen. They used the Common Speech intelligibly enough, though with a strange, lilting inflection, but Rhion had to invoke the Spell of Tongues, the magic of hearing words mind to mind, to comprehend what they whispered to one another in their own dialect. Eyes green as angelica or the uncertain hazel which was no identifiable color—the color of the sea where it ran to the salt marsh's edge—peered watchfully from beneath loose thatches of thick brown hair at the two wizards. Often during the three-day journey, by sled across the frozen sweet marshes, and down here among the brown reed beds of the salt, Rhion had felt the sensation of those strangely colored eyes watching him from somewhere just out of sight.

It was a land of strange superstitions, Jaldis had told him, and beliefs which elsewhere had long since died out. Wrapped in the gray-green plaid of the native blankets, Rhion could see the curling line of blue tattoo marks on the boatman's hands and ears, and could count half a dozen little "dollies" woven of feathers and straw dangling from the lantern on the canoe's long prow.

"Rhion . . ." The voice of the sounding-box was soft as a single viol string, bowed in an empty room. The fog down here in the salt marshes was raw and thick, especially now that night had fallen; in spite of the blankets in which the Marshmen had wrapped him, Jaldis' breathing sounded bad.

"They will try to take the books," he murmured, as Rhion bent down close to him to hear. Rhion cast a quick glance up at the Marshman on the prow, then at the bundles of volumes stacked behind Jaldis' head: books containing the secrets of the Dark Well, the means to look behind the very curtains of Reality; scrolls of demon-spells, and the Magic of Ill.

Like twists of driftwood wrapped in rags, the cold fingers tightened urgently over Rhion's hands. "The Ladies are greedy for knowledge, stealing it where they can from other mages, other Orders. Do not let them do this . . ." The voice of the box paused, while Jaldis bent all his attention on stifling a cough, the sound of it deep and muffled with phlegm. He turned his head, feverish again and in pain, as he had been throughout the journey despite all that Rhion could do. "Do not . . . whatever they may offer. Whatever they may do."

A drift of salt air stirred the clammy fogs, shifting them like the shredded remains of a rotted gray curtain. Blurs of daffodil-yellow light wavered in the mists. Before them Rhion descried the huge, dim bulk of a domed island, dark masses of trees rising from the waters like a cliff. Below them was a floating platform, designed to rise and fall with the seasonal level of the marshes and the inundations of the tides. Just beyond the circle of the lamplight which surrounded it, marsh-faes skimmed like silver dragonflies above the mist-curled surface of the fen. Looking up at the island, Rhion could see where the long roots of trees and dangling, winter-black vines gripped the ancient blocks of hewn stone walls just visible above the waters; everything seemed thick with moss and slimy with dripping weed.

On the platform itself stood four women, dressed not in the robes of any order of wizardry, but like the Marshwomen themselves, in belted wool tunics of dull plaids or checks, or brightened by crewelwork flowers. The Gray Lady he recognized. Even if he had not seen her in the scrying-stone three days ago, he would have known at first sight of her that she was, like Jaldis, a mage.

"Welcome," she said, stepping forward. "You are most welcome to the Islands of the Moon."

When communicating through scrying-crystal, a wizard's appearance was not the same to another wizard as it was in the flesh; Rhion noted that the Lady was older than she had appeared in the crystal's depths. Certainly ten years older than he, if not more, her square, homey face was framed in heavy streams of malt-brown hair. There were blue tattoos on her ears, and her hands were knotted and strong from bread bowl, distaff, and loom. The ladies behind her were clearly as used as she to manual tasks, for they lifted Jaldis from his bed in the canoe as easily and deftly as if he had lain on a couch and carried him up the zigzagging wooden stair.

Another lady stepped forward to take the books . . . "I'll get those," Rhion said and shouldered once again the heavy sack. Deeply as he regretted the volumes left behind in Felsplex, he had become very grateful he hadn't let the impulse to take them all overcome his better judgment.

"As you will," the Gray Lady said, and he thought he detected a deep-hid flicker of ironic amusement in her hazel eyes.

Like all the Ladies' dwellings on what had been the tips of Sligo's hills, the house they had prepared for Jaldis had once been a palace, now fallen into deep decay. Vine and morning-glory from ancient gardens had run riot in centuries of neglect, and the heavy pillars, wider at the top than the bottom, were sheathed thick with cloaks of vegetation that, in several rooms, had begun to part the stones themselves. The walls of the sleeping chamber were still intact, but the windows, glazed with random bits of glass like pieces of a puzzle, were nearly obscured under a thick brown jungle of creepers, an open latticework in the leafless winter, but promising to be an impenetrable petaled curtain in summer months. Throughout the night, as he sat up with the Gray Lady at Jaldis' bedside, the faint scrape and rustle of that living cloak blended with the Lady's murmured healing-spells and the bubble of the kettle whose healing steams filled the room with the scents of elfdock and false dandelion; in the morning, their shadows made a dim harlequin of the pearly fog-light where it fell upon Jaldis' pillow.

"He should rest better now." The Lady ran her strong brown fingers through her hair, and shook out the cloudy mane of it as she and Rhion stood together in the villa's ruined porch. Through the milky fog, the glow of the community ovens, not ten yards away amid the overgrown riot of laurel and thorny bougainvillea around what had been a shrine, was no more than a saffron blur, like a yellow pinch of raveled wool, though the fragrance of baking bread hung upon the wet air like a hymn. Beneath it, Rhion smelled damp earth, water, and the sea; beyond the matted vines that enclosed the tiny chamber of the porch, the marsh was utterly silent, save for the isolated notes of stone chimes stirred by a breath of wind. It seemed to Rhion that they were cut off in that shadowy ruin—from the Forty Realms, from his life, and from the future and the past.

"You should get some rest yourself," she added. She deftly separated and braided the streams of her hair, and her hazel glance took in the grayness of his face, the blue-brown smudges of fatigue more visible when he removed his spectacles to rub his eyes. "You look all-in." Her voice was low and very sweet, like the music of a rosewood flute heard across water in the night. At times last night, Rhion had not recognized the spells she wove, but had had the impression that the voice was an integral part of them, a lullaby to soothe weary flesh, a bribe to tempt the wavering soul to remain.

"It was just that I'd been working healing-spells without the medicines to go with them," he said, shaking his head. "I didn't have much sleep on the way here. Thank you . . ." He yawned hugely. The queasiness which sometimes assailed him after he had overstretched his powers was fading, and he felt slightly lightheaded and ravenous for sweets.

"You did well with the spells alone. I've seen men much worse in like case."

Rhion smiled a little. "I don't think that was my efforts so much as just that Jaldis is too stubborn to let illness get the better of him. I did try to find some herbs—you can usually find borage if you look long enough—but in the winter it's hard."

"Perhaps while you're here you'd like to speak to some of our healers, and see the scrolls and herbals we have in our library." She gestured out into the impenetrable wall of fog, toward what Rhion had originally taken for the dim shape of a hillock of willow and vine. Now, looking again, he saw the outline of what had been a pillared porch, a few crumbling steps, and the primrose trapezoid of an uneven window, lighted from within.

"Our library goes back to the days of Sligo's glory, though much of it was lost in the earthquake and the floods that came after. We add to it what we can."

The words, *Yeah, I was warned about that*, were on his lips, but he clipped them back. The Gray Lady was his host and might very well have saved Jaldis' life last night. Moreover, in spite of Jaldis' warnings, after a night of working at her side, of seeing her patient care and her willingness to perform even the most menial of healing chores, he found himself greatly inclined to like the woman.

"Come." She took his hand and led him to the buckled terrazzo steps. "Channa—the cook—will get you bread and honey . . . Or shall I have one of the girls bring it to you here?" For she saw him hesitate and glanced back into the slaty gloom of the house, where Jaldis lay helpless with his books piled in the corner near his bed.

"What did he mean," she asked, his hand still prisoned in those warm, rough peasant fingers, stained with silver and herbs, "when he spoke in his delirium of the Dark Well?"

Rhion had taken the voice-box from him, seeing the sudden intentness of the Lady's eyes, but not before the old man, clinging to it in fevered dreams, had stammered brokenly of the Well, of the Void, and of voices crying out to him from the iridescent dark. After Rhion had removed it, Jaldis had groped urgently amid the patched linen sheets, his movements more and more frantic, though he had not uttered a sound. Even in his delirium, his pride had flinched from the broken, humiliating bleatings of a mute; in ten and a half years of traveling with him, Rhion had never heard him break that silence.

Now the Lady was watching him again, with sharp interest in her face. "The most ancient scrolls in the Library make mention of something called a Well of Seeing," she continued. "It was said to 'grant sight into other worlds and other times.' Not 'other lands' . . . the glyph is very clear. 'Other worlds.' "

"I . . . I don't . . ." Rhion stammered, wanting to avoid the clear, water-colored gaze and unable to look away. "He found reference to it in some notes he'd inherited from another wizard in Felsplex. He was searching through them when the mob broke into the inn. We got out with our lives, but the notes were destroyed." The story sounded lame and thin even to him. He cursed the exhaustion that seemed suddenly to weight his tongue and clog his brain, as if the inventive portion of his mind had taken the equivalent of *pheelas* root and subsided into numbed oblivion.

The Lady leaned one broad shoulder against the marble hip of a caryatid nearly hidden within the vines beside her, and her hand, still enclosing Rhion's, had that same quality that Jaldis' sometimes did, as if through her grip she could read the bones within his flesh and plumb the shallow, sparkling shoals of his soul. "You escaped with your lives—and with the books?"

"With what we could seize." He felt a kind of confusion creeping over him, his mind distracted by the question of whether it would be worse to avoid her eyes or to try to hold that clear, tawny gaze . . . wanting to will himself to meet her eyes but obliquely aware that if he did she could read his heart. And through it all her sweet alto voice drew at his concentration as it had drawn back Jaldis' wavering will to live.

"The books, but not the notes, that so filled his fevered dreams?"

"I . . . That is . . ." He knew he should make some reply but could not frame anything even remotely believable. He felt tangled, enmeshed in his own evasions, between the strength of her hand and the strength of her gaze and the gentle, drawing sweetness of her voice. To lie seemed, not useless, but unspeakably trivial, like a child lying about the size of a fish it has seen. She waited quietly, watching him, as if they had been there together, with her watching and waiting for the truth, since the foundation stones of time were laid . . .

For an instant it seemed as if that were, in fact, the case— a moment later it flashed through his mind, *Nonsense, if we'd been here since the beginning of time we'd have felt the earthquake* . . . and somehow that gave him the last foundering grasp of logic needed for him to look away from her eyes. He found he was panting, his face clammy with sweat in the raw dampness of the morning. Desperately he fixed his thoughts on Jaldis' buzzing voice: *They are greedy for knowledge . . . greedy for knowledge* . . . the gentle coaxing did not seem to him like greed, but that, he understood now, was part of the spell.

He pulled his hand from her grasp and it came easily—he had to catch himself against the caryatid opposite the one she leaned upon, as if she had drawn him off balance physically as well as in his mind.

After a moment that flute-soft voice said, "I see. A thing of great power . . . a thing to be kept hidden at all costs."

Face still averted, Rhion managed to whisper, "I don't know about that."

There was silence, filled with the scents of water and fog, but he felt her mind still bent upon his, surrounded by the implacable strength of her spells.

He took a deep breath. "Please let me go."

Her fingers, firm as the fingers of the caryatids would be, but warm and vibrant, touched his brow, feeling the perspiration that wet his skin. "You work very hard for a man who claims nothing to protect." But she was teasing him now. Instead of the heart-dragging beauty of her spells, her voice was light, like a healer's magic flute playing children's songs for joy.

He looked around at her again and saw only a sturdy brown-haired woman with one braid plaited and the other still undone upon her shoulder, and a smile, half mocking, half affectionate, in her eyes. Abstractedly he identified the crewelwork flowers on her homespun gown as marigold, lobelia, thistle and iris; a thin strand of blue spirit-beads circled her throat.

"Go back and sit with him," she said gently. "I'll send someone over with bread and honey—and I promise you I won't dose it to question you further or to send you to sleep." And she smiled again at his blush. "You may sleep, if you will. No one will trouble you."

Rhion wasn't sure he could believe her on that score—he'd been badly shaken by the spells she'd cast—but as he stumbled back into the dimness of the house, he reflected that he probably didn't have much choice in the matter. He stood for a moment in the doorway of Jaldis' room, looking at the cracked black-and-white mosaic of the ancient tile floor, the frescoes of birds and dancers on the walls, faded now to cloudy shapes, like music heard too far away to distinguish the tune. His body hurt for sleep, and more than that for food, particularly sweets; he knew, too, that any circle or spell of protection he might lay around the books stacked in the corner beyond the bed would be, at this point, no more potent than the chalk scribbles around the bed itself, smudged by feet and bereft of their power.

Propped upon pillows, Jaldis lay in the narrow bed of cottonwood poles, deeply asleep, a vessel of gently steaming water on either side. For some time Rhion stood looking down at the ruined face, too exhausted to feel much beyond a tremendous sadness for which he could find no name.

In time he picked up Jaldis' cloak and mashed it into a rude pillow and, wrapping himself in his own cloak, lay down in front of the books on the floor. He slept almost at once and dreamed of starlight and witchfire and snow-clad silence, all reflected in shy gray eyes.

Jaldis mended slowly. The Gray Lady and the other Ladies of the Moon whom Rhion quickly came to know well nursed the old man by turns, not only with the healing spells and herb-lore for which they were famed throughout the eastern realms, but with a patient diligence and unstinting sympathy that, he suspected, had more to do with healing than all the medicines in the world. After that first morning, the Gray Lady made no further effort to question him regarding the Dark Well, though Rhion would generally volunteer to sit with his master at night, when his fever rose and he sometimes spoke in his dreams.

"You did rightly," Jaldis said, when Rhion told him about why he had taken the voice-box from him that night. "It is not well that the Witches of the Moon learn the secrets of the Morkensik Order." His voice was a fragile thread; his hand stroked restlessly at the silky curve of the dark red wood, toyed with the glittering flotsam of talismans among the faded quilts.

"I don't think she learned any secrets." Rhion glanced across at the books, still heaped in their corner with his discarded blankets and the empty bowl from his breakfast. In spite of the Gray Lady's assurances, he'd been a little dubious about the breakfast; much as it was his instinct to like her, he wouldn't have put it past her to dose his porridge with *pheelas* root; and several times in the course of the morning, he'd summoned a little fleck of ball lightning to the ends of his fingers, just to make sure he still could.

"But you were speaking of things you had seen—of boats with metal wings that flew through the sky, of carts that moved without horses. Of magic things without magic."

"Magic things without magic," the blind wizard echoed and his powerful chest rose and fell with his sigh. "Things that can be used by anyone, for good or ill, for whatever purposes they choose, without the training or restraint of wizardry. And the wizards themselves, born with magic in their bones, in their hearts, in their veins, even as we were born, for whom no expression of such power is possible. Wizards who are taught to forget; who, if they cannot forget, go slowly insane."

Rhion was silent, remembering his own days of slow insanity.

"They are calling to us, Rhion," that soft, mechanical drone murmured. "We must find them again, somehow. We must go and help. For their sakes, and for our own." Then the arthritic claws slipped from the silky wood, and Jaldis drifted back into his dreams.

In those days Rhion had to contend with dreams of his own.

The first time he summoned Tally's image in his scrying-crystal he told himself that it was simply to ascertain that she and her sister and her sister's baby did, in fact, reach Imber in safety. The crystal had shown him the image of Tally, very properly attired in a rust-colored gown stitched with silver and sardonyx, sitting quietly in a corner of a painted marble hall while the short, plump woman who must be her sister argued in polite hatred with a colorless young man in gray.

Though the crystal, used in this fashion, was silent, he could read frigid spite and contempt in every line of the young man's slender body, while all the jewels on the plump woman's sleeve fluttered in the burning lamplight with the trembling of her stoppered rage. Tally was looking away into the noncommittal middle distance of an unwilling witness forcing herself neither to see nor hear, but her hands, all but concealed under the pheasant feathers which trimmed her oversleeves, were balled into white-knuckled fists.

After that he told himself—for a time, at least—that he only wanted to make sure that this wretchedness, whatever it was, had passed. That she was all right. That she was happy.

And sometimes she was. When riding she was, in the brown frozen landscape of the Imber hills. He could see it in her face, and in the way she laughed with her favorite maid—a tall girl like herself, but full-breasted and bold—and the chief of her honor guard, a broad-chested and rather stupid-looking young demigod who flirted with both girls and everything else moderately presentable who came his way in skirts. She was happy with her dogs, a leggy, endlessly-circling pack of red and gold bird-hunters whose ears she would comb and whose paws she would search for thorns. Alone she was happy, curled up with a silken quilt about her beside a bronze fire-dish in her bedroom, playing her porcelain flute with two dogs asleep at her feet, the huge branch of cheap kitchen candles flaring like a halo behind her head and turning her hair to a halo of treacle and gold.

But more than once he saw her, white-lipped and silent, at table with her sister and the fair young man who must be her sister's husband, while servants displayed herbed savories and frumentaries on painted platters for their approval, delicacies which Tally was clearly barely able to touch. On one such occasion, during yet another mannered, vicious quarrel, he saw her quietly leave the dining room and return to her chair a few minutes later, chalky and trembling, having clearly just vomited her heart out in the nearest anteroom. Once—though the image was unclear owing to the fact that the room they were in had long ago been ensorcelled to prevent scrying—he saw her and her sister holding one another tight, like two victims of shipwreck tossed on a single plank in rough waters, weeping by candlelight.

And with passionate despair he thought *Damn him! Damn him for doing that to you . . . !*

In time he quit watching, and put the scrying-stone away as he would have put away an addictive drug.

But like a drug it murmured to him when he was alone.

Rhion had always known that such behavior was against the ethics of wizardry and never called up her image without a pang of guilt. Among the first things that Jaldis had told him, when he had taught him to use a crystal, and later to prepare one for use, was that the powers of a scryer were not to be used for private pleasure or for private gain.

"It is not only that the evil done by one wizard redounds upon all wizards," the blind man had said, putting aside his opal spectacles and rubbing the pain from his temples. "Not only that we are not perceived as being separate individuals, good and evil, but only as wizards, without distinction and without discrimination. But spying, peeping, prying is in itself a dirty habit, and worse for a wizard who can do it so much more efficiently. What would you think, Rhion, of a mage who uses this power to look into the bathing chambers of every brothel in the city, just for the sight of women's breasts?"

Rhion, being at the time seventeen, had promptly answered, "That he's saving himself some money," and had had to wait another six months before being instructed in the scrying-crystal's use.

But it was, in fact, a conclusion that Rhion himself had come to as a tiny child, the first time he'd called a friend's

image in the nursery fire and seen that friend being placed
on the chamber pot by her nurse. It had embarrassed him so
thoroughly he'd been very careful about calling images after
that.

But abstaining now from its use didn't help. He found that
quasi-knowledge of Tally—knowing what her favorite jewels
were, her favorite dresses and how she braided her hair,
knowing that she liked to play the flute or the mandolin when
she was alone, and that she loved her little niece with the
delighted affection of a child—was not the same as being
her friend. All he knew was that she was in pain and that
he could not help. And would never be able to help.

In his hopelessness and uncertainty, Rhion turned, as he
had always turned, back to the study of magic.

The library on the Island of the Moon dated back to the
days before the earthquake, a small building all but buried
under thickets of laurel and vine. At least a third of its score
of tiny rooms had fallen into utter desuetude, the saplings
that had sprouted in the earthquake's cracks now grown to
massive trees, whose roots clambered over the broken blocks
like rough-scaled, gray serpents and whose branches were
in many places the only roof. From these rooms the books
had been moved, to crowd the other chambers, both above
the ground and in the unflooded levels of the damp clay-
smelling vaults below; the whole place, like the islands themselves, was a maze and a warren, shaggy with moss and
choked with ancient knowledge and half-forgotten things.

Here Rhion read and studied through the rainy days of the
marshlands winter and sometimes throughout the night: herb-
lore and earth-lore and the deep magics of the moon and
tides; the legends of the old realm of Sligo, going back two
thousand years; of the islands that had sunk in the earthquake; and tales of discredited gods. Here the Lady acted as
his teacher and guide, for she had been the Scribe of the

place before her ascension to her current status, and if there were chambers whose thresholds he was forbidden to cross, or volumes he was forbidden to open, it was never mentioned to him.

"We add to it what we can, year by year," the Lady said, setting down two cups of egg-posset on the table near the firebasket's warming saffron glow. She shook back the loose stream of brown hair from her shoulders. "Even in the old days, it was one of the great repositories of knowledge and the beauty of letters, the joy of tales for their own sake. Many of the volumes destroyed in the floods existed nowhere else, even in their own day. And now we know of them only through notes in the ancient catalogues and a quote or two in some commentator's work."

It was late at night, and the library was silent, the black fog that pressed the irregular glass windows smothering even the glowworm spots of light from the kitchen and the nearby baths. Rhion looked up from the smooth, red-and-black bowl of the cup to the Lady's face, the strong, archaic features serene with the calm of those marble faces that clustered everywhere beneath the wild grape and wisteria or gazed half-submerged from the waters of the marsh.

"The treatises of philosophers," she went on softly, "the histories of old border-wars, tallies of spell-fragments that do not work, even . . . For who can say when we will find another fragmentary work that completes them, and broadens our knowledge of what can be done with the will, and the energies sent down to Earth by the gods?"

And who can say, Rhion thought, remembering Jaldis' warnings, *who will have access to those spells a year from now, or two years, or ten? Who can say one of the Ladies won't take it into her head to become a Hand-Pricker or a Blood-Mage and feel free to transmit whatever knowledge she gleans here to them?* He remembered what Jaldis had told him of the uses to which the Ebiatics had put the knowledge of demon-calling, when they had learned it; remembered Shavus' accounts of wizards who had not the training that the Morkensiks gave in balance and restraint.

Do no harm, Jaldis had said. But six years of brewing love-potions had taught him that the definition of "harm," even by those without thaumaturgical power, was an appallingly elastic thing.

He started to raise the posset to his lips, the sweetness of honey within it like the reminiscence of summer flowers, then hesitated, and glanced over at the Gray Lady again.

She smiled, reading the wariness in his eyes, and said, "Would you like to see me drink it first? Out of both cups, in case I'd switched them . . ."

And he grinned at the absurdity of the position. "I'll trust you."

Her wide mouth quirked, and there was a glint in her tawny eyes. "Or hadn't you heard we also have a reputation for dosing passersby with aphrodisiacs as well?"

Rhion laughed and shook his head. In the topaz glow of the brazier she had a strange beauty, the light heightening the strength of her cheekbones and catching carnelian threads in her eyelashes and hair. "*Now* you have me worried."

"That Jaldis would disapprove?"

"That I'd burn my fingers playing with fire." He raised the cup to her in a solemn toast, and sipped the sweet mull of eggs, honey, and wine within.

As the winter wore on, he found in the Gray Lady's company a respite from his thoughts of Tally, from the sense of futility that overwhelmed him at even the thought, these days, of having a nonmageborn friend. That she was fond of him he knew, as he was increasingly of her; now and then it crossed his mind to let her seduce him, but fear always held him back. He did not believe, as the garbled tales told, that the Ladies of the Moon lured lovers to their beds with spells and later sacrificed them to their Goddess at a certain season of the year; but he hadn't forgotten the spells she'd laid upon his mind to try to draw from him the secrets contained in Jaldis' books.

But her company was good. With her he practiced the art of maintaining several spells at once under conditions of duress: he would try to turn aside the acorns she hurled at him while he concentrated on holding various household objects suspended by spells in the air, and they would laugh like children when the cook's chairs, buckets, and baskets went crashing to the kitchen floor or when she scored a fair hit between his eyes. She also showed him the secret ways of the marshes, leading him across the sunken root-lines that connected the innumerable hummocks of salt-oak, cypress, and willow when the tide was low. The watery labyrinths of the Drowned Lands changed from season to season with the rains that brought down water from upcountry and from hour to hour with the rhythm of the tides. When the waters were high, the twenty or so ancient hilltops, with their ruined shrines and overgrown villas, were cut off from one another and from the hummocks that had grown up all around, rooted to the immemorial muck beneath or to the half-submerged roofs of ancient palaces. But there were times when they could cross between them on foot, picking their way carefully over the sunken trunks and roof-trees, to hunt the rare herbs of the marshes or to find skunk-cabbages by the heat of them under the snow in the sweet marshes and, later, violets by their scent.

At such times she seemed to him like a creature of the marshes herself, born of the silent waters and fog; when she spoke of the ancient days of Sligo, she spoke as if she remembered them herself, of what the ancient kings and wizards had said and done, of how they lived and how they died, as if she had been there and seen what they wore, where they stood, and whether their eyes had been brown or blue.

Some nights they would sit out, shivering in a Marshman's

canoe that she handled as easily as Tally had handled her horse, watching the water-goblins play around candles set floating in bowls. "Does anyone know what they are?" Rhion asked on one such night, in the wind-breath murmur that wizards learn, scarcely louder than the lapping of the incoming tide against the boat's tanned skin. "I mean, yes, they're goblins . . . but what *are* goblins?" He pushed up his spectacles and glanced sidelong at her, seeing how the bobbing brightness of the candle intermittently gilded the end of her snub nose. "Like faes, they don't seem to have physical bodies . . . Are they a kind of fae? Do they sleep? Do they nest in the ground or in the trees, the way grims seem to do? Why do they take food, if they have no bodies to nourish? Why do they steal children and drown them? Why are they afraid of mirrors?" They'd had to cover the one on the boat's prow before the goblins would come to the candle, though the straw luck-dollies still dangled, like mis-shapen corpses on the gallows, from the bowsprit. "Is there any work of the ancient wizards in the library that says?"

She shook her head. "There are some that ask the same questions you ask, but none that gives an answer. Curious in itself—they are in their way much more an enigma than the grims, whose names at least can be known. The Marshmen think they fear mirrors because they can't stand the sight of their own faces, but look . . . You can see they aren't afraid of one another. And they really aren't that ugly, if you get close to them . . ."

"Well, I wouldn't want my sister to marry one."

She laughed at that, but she was right . . . outlined in the flickering candle glow the goblins were queer looking, with their huge, luminous eyes and froglike mouths, but the trans-lucent, gelid forms did not shift, as the grims did; and if their limbs were numerous and strange, at least they remained constant.

"I think it may have something to do with the glass itself,

or the quicksilver backing," the Gray Lady went on softly, as the long, thready hands reached up from the water to snatch at the flame. "You know you can put spells on fernseed and scatter it behind you to keep them from dogging your steps in the forest . . ."

"I've heard poppyseed works, too. At least, according to the scroll I read in the library last week, it can be spelled to confuse human pursuit."

"I've tried to follow them a dozen times in a boat or across the root-lines on foot—twice I've tried swimming after them. But they always vanish, and it's dangerous, swimming down underwater among the pondweed and the roots."

On the whole, Jaldis seemed to regard the spells which the Lady taught Rhion as little better than the pishogue of Earthwitches, but approved of his learning the lore of the marshes and the Moon. "To be a wizard is to learn," he said, looking up from the tray of herbs he was sorting by scent and touch. He was able to sit up now, wrapped in the thick woolen blankets the Ladies wove, beside the green bronze firebaskets in his sunny stone room. On the afternoons of rare pale sunlight he would sometimes sit outside on the crumbling terrace that fronted their house, overlooking the silken brown waters of the marsh. For weeks now they had been remaking their supply of medicines and thaumaturgical powders, Rhion hunting them in the marshes as he learned a little of the mazes of islets, Jaldis ensorcelling them to enhance their healing powers.

"Though I don't suppose," the old man added, "they let you have access to the inner rooms of the library, or the inner secrets of their power." He rubbed the bandage that covered the empty sockets of his eyes. Etsinda, the chief weaver of the island, had knitted gray mitts specially for his bent and crippled hands, easy to draw on and keeping the useless fingers covered and warm.

"I haven't been told to stay out of any room."

"I doubt they would need to tell you," Jaldis replied, with a faint smile. "You would simply never notice the doors of those rooms, though you might pass them every day; or if you did notice them, your mind would immediately become distracted by some other book or scroll, and you would forget immediately your intention to pass that threshold till another day."

Rhion blinked, startled at the subtlety of such a spell . . . but now that he thought about it, he could easily believe the Gray Lady capable of such illusion.

"Beware of her, my son," the blind man said softly. "Some of their knowledge is corrupt, and inaccurate, being gleaned from all manner of sources. But like us, they are wizards, too."

And being wizards, Rhion knew perfectly well that the Gray Lady had never given up her intention of getting hold of Jaldis' books.

On their second night in Sligo, Rhion had set out, shaking with apprehension and clutching a line of thread to guide him back to firm ground, across one of the tangled root-lines to another islet, carrying Jaldis' books once more on his back. He'd used thread to guide him because he feared to leave wizard's marks, guessing that the Lady would have a way of reading later where they had been. The ragged remains of his old landlord's cloak had been ensorcelled with every sigil of preservation and concealment he and Jaldis had had the strength to imbue, and the hollow oak where he hid the wrapped volumes he had surrounded with the subtlest of his spells of warning and guard.

As often as possible he checked this secret cache, by scrying-crystal and in person, whenever he could—at least, he thought, the Lady could not call his image in a crystal, something no mage could do except for direct communication. The islet where he had hidden the books, far up the snag-lines from the Island of the Moon, was perhaps three-quarters of a mile long and no more than fifty yards across, thickly wooded and tangled with sedges and laurel, cranberry and honeysuckle, in places treacherous with potholes where vines growing between the overarching willow-roots gave the appearance to the unwary of solid ground. Several times such potholes gave way under his feet as he crossed the root-lines at low tide, and he narrowly avoided plunging through into the shadowy waters beneath. Now and then, on his surreptitious investigations of the islet, he discovered evidence that someone had been searching that island and others around it, though the books themselves remained, as far as he could tell, undisturbed.

Then one evening during the first of the winter thaws, as he sat reading in the dark library after the failing of the short winter daylight, something—a sound, he thought at the time, though later he could not recall exactly what it had been—made him look up in time to see the Gray Lady glide noiselessly between two of the massive king-pillars. Her homespun woolen cloak hood was drawn up over her face, and, moreover, she was wreathed in a haze of spells, which would have covered her from any but the sharpest eyes. She held a book cradled in her arms; though he only glimpsed it briefly, he thought that it was the red-bound *Lesser Demonary* which had been among the books in the secret cache.

Rhion froze, stilling his breath. The Lady passed without glancing his way through a lopsided doorway and down four steps into another of the library's tiny chambers. Without so much as a rustle of robes, Rhion gathered his cloak about him and slipped out into the raw iron gloom outside.

Jaldis was deep asleep already in the big stone room with its black-and-white floors. Taking his scrying-crystal from his pocket Rhion angled a facet to the light of the room's bronze fire bowl, calling the image of the hollow oak. But the image was unclear; he seemed to see a tree that looked something like it, but the surroundings were wrong—he had only a general impression of vines and reeds, as if fog hid the place. But the night, a rare thing for winters in Sligo, was clear, with the promise of coming rain.

"Damn her!" He shoved the crystal back and was tucking his robe up into his belt as he strode from the room. "How the hell did she know where to look? If they're taking them to copy one at a time . . ."

There were half a dozen boats tied to the jetty when Rhion scrambled down the long ladder—the platform floated low on the slack tide. He took the one with the lightest draught, knowing he'd probably have to haul it over shoals and snags— he still had not acquired much of an instinct for the tides. The sluggish waters whispered around the prow as he poled away, skirting the wide beds of reeds, sedges, the silken puckers of the water's inky surface that marked submerged snags, and the moss-crusted stone spires raised like dripping skeleton fingers from the deep. Once he saw something glowing pass under his boat and felt a tentative tug at the pole—he cut down sharply at it, and the tugging ceased. There was a mirror on the bowsprit and half a dozen woven straw dollies and god-hands; Jaldis called it all superstitious nonsense, but Rhion found himself hoping his master was wrong.

There would be grims, too, on the wooded isles, lurking and whistling in the trees. For no reason, he heard Tally's low, husky voice: *Since it's such a lovely night and I've had a wonderful time so far . . .*

And grinned.

His grin faded. As deliberately as he would turn from a painful sight, he pushed the image of her thin, elfin face from his mind and forced himself to pursue that line of thought no further. As soon as spring cleared the roads, he and Jaldis would return to Nerriok, the City of Bridges. With luck he'd never see the Duke of Mere's young daughter again.

The boat's shallow keel scraped on snags and bars as he

tried to negotiate the twisting channels through house-high beds of dripping reeds; twice he had to pull the little craft up over root mats, his feet sinking to his boot calves in icy ooze. *Thank God it's winter, and night,* he thought, bending his back to the pole as he tried to force a passage through jungles of blackened cattail. *In summer the midges would eat you alive. You can't hold spells that make them think you're made of garlic all day.*

At last he hit the long, sunken ford that led to the islet of the books. He left the boat, keeping the long pole for balance, and made his way gingerly along the dripping, snake-like strands of exposed roots, hearing the water lap and gurgle, black and shining as obsidian beneath his feet. These sunken hummocks, treacherous with slime, wound for miles through this part of the marsh, the islets widening and rising from them like knots in a string.

Even if the Ladies had seen me coming this way, he wondered, *how the hell would they have known which islet I went to? They're all pretty much alike. They can't have searched every tree . . .*

A flash of bluish light behind him caught his eye, and he swung around, remembering the goblins. Clouds like stealthy assassins were already putting pillows over the pale face of the baby moon; he smelled the sea and rain. In the growing darkness, a lantern would have burst upon his eyes like an explosion.

But it was only a half-dozen marsh-faes, fragile, naked sprites darting away in every direction from something which had startled them in a reed bed. A fox, perhaps.

But there were no birds as yet in the winter-still marshes. No prey and no predators.

As if he had turned a page in a book and seen it written there in full, Rhion realized, *The Ladies. They're following me now.*

He could have hit himself over the head with the boat-pole. *Idiot!* he cursed himself, *numbskull, dupe, goon! If the Gray Lady didn't want to be seen by you in the library, do you think you'd have been able to glimpse her, even if she walked up and hit you over the head with the silly book?* He remembered the subtleness of the Archpriestess' magic, the coercion which had operated, not through force, but through the slightest of whispered illusions.

He wondered now how he could possibly have been so sure that the book in her arms was the *Lesser Demonary*—at that distance there had been nothing but its size and shape to go on. But she'd known that, if he thought she had it, he'd run immediately to the cache to check . . .

I'll strangle the bitch.

Oh, yeah, he thought a moment later with a grin at both his own outrage and at his thoughts of vengeance. *Fat chance. You'd spend the rest of your life hopping from lily-pad to lily-pad catching flies with your tongue.*

Though there might be some advantage, he reflected, looking around him at the dripping desolation of snags and roots, *to being a frog in these circumstances.*

His mouth set in a grim smile and he turned with elaborate casualness back along the snag toward the eyots and reed beds in the whispering dark. *Well, my lady, if you want to go wading tonight, we'll go wading. I've got a pocketful of poppyseed and I'll use it just as soon as I've got you well and truly pointed in the wrong direction. We'll see who spends a soggier night.*

Balancing himself with the pole with great and gingerly care he began to work his way up the snag-line, crossing the islet where the books were hidden and angling away along another ford towards the murkiest and wettest part of the marsh.

And in very short order, as he should have known he would, he got lost.

SEVEN

VERY NICE, RHION, HE THOUGHT, SURVEYING THE SHUDDER-ing brown waters of the marsh through a haze of wind-thrashed rain that had already rendered his spectacles opaque with spatterings. *Have we got any other clever ideas? Like maybe drowning yourself to really throw them off the track?*

He'd long ago shaken off his pursuers. With the spell-entangled poppyseed he had woven a wide pocket of disorientation, of subtle confusion, and a tendency to poor guesses and errors of judgment; in two other places he had left spell-lines of invisible brightness to tangle and turn the feet. Unfortunately, unfamiliar with the Limitations inherent in these spells and even more unfamiliar with the terrain of the marshes themselves, he was beginning to suspect that he had inadvertently stumbled back through his own spell-fields himself. He certainly seemed to have missed his way in circling back to his boat, or else the tide had begun to come in, changing the water levels around all the islets and altering or obliterating his bearing marks. It was astonishing how even six inches of water altered the appearance of a snag or root and its relationship with the shore. He'd taken as a guide mark the lights of another islet where the Priestesses of the Moon had occupied an old summer palace, but uncannily those lights seemed to have moved . . .

Then it had begun to rain. Rhion had already fallen through a pothole, soaking him to the waist in muddy water and tearing boot leather and the flesh of his calves on the splintery wood of a submerged branch—he had spent a panicked, agonizing half-hour in extricating himself. The cold had begun to sap his energy, making it harder still to concentrate.

And the tide was now very definitely coming in.

Emerging from the black curtains of a reed bed Rhion found that his bearing light had unaccountably shifted again. It was only when he heard laughter, thin and dry as ripping silk, seeming to drift from nowhere in the pitchy blackness all around him, that he realized that the light he had been following had been conjured by grims to lead him still further astray.

Maybe at this point drowning myself would be simpler after all.

He turned back to see grims swarming the reeds behind him like cold, glowing lice in a beggar's hair, and their pallid skeleton shapes twisted around the willow knees of the hummock he'd just quitted as he waded back to it along the submerged and slimy roots. At his approach the wraiths opened cold-burning mouths to hiss and bite, and backed away, still hissing, as he summoned a furious blaze of witchfire to the end of his boat pole and swung at them; their shrieks of laughter shivered in the streaming darkness after they had slipped out of sight into the trunks of the trees. Scrambling and slipping over the roots, Rhion reflected that coming back to the islet had done him damn little good—by the feel of the slime on the trunks the place would be chin-deep in three hours.

In the distance he thought he could hear women's voices calling out to him, but could not be sure—it might very well be the grims. Panting and shivering, he scrambled as high up the willow roots as he could, but the reed beds hemmed him in with a wall of whispering black. He called out, but gusts of wind clashed in the sedges, and the rattle of rain on the waters all around him drowned out his shouts; the wind cut through his wet clothing, chilling him to the bone, and the voices faded.

Rhion had begun to feel a little frightened. He could sense deeper cold coming in on the heels of the rain, cold enough to frost hard, even this close to the sea. His clothes were soaked and his leg throbbed, and he knew he had to find shelter before morning. He did not know how deep into the marshes he was, but he guessed, from the grims' propensity for leading travelers astray, that he was miles from the nearest habitation—even if he called a bright blaze of witchlight, he wasn't sure the Ladies, if they were searching, would follow it. They, too, would be familiar with the ways of the grims.

He fished his scrying-crystal from his pocket and squinted at it in the pelting rain. Even calling witchlight over his head to create the needed reflection in its surface, he had to hold it inches from the end of his nose to see anything—a gust of wind blew rain into his eyes, and he edged around towards the lee side of the willow . . .

Beneath his feet the tangle of heather and vines gave downward with a sodden, splintery crack. Rhion yelped and clutched at the roots as he fell past them, but the whole footing caved in around him, dropping him down into blackness and freezing water. Bark tore at his palms as he grabbed the willow knees; with a hard jerk, he broke his fall, dangling by his hands in pitch blackness, the rain falling on his face and the coal-black water lapping and gurgling around his armpits and chin.

And below the water, a faint glow of blue passed through the blackness, and cold fingers closed around his ankles and pulled.

"Dammit!" Rhion yelled, genuinely frightened now. "You scum-eating . . . Celfriagnogast, dammit . . . CEL-FRIAGNOGAST . . ." He yelled one of the few words of power known to be effective against water-goblins, but other hands gripped his feet, tugging and scratching; he felt things pick and tear at his robe, felt stirring in the black waters all around him.

Don't panic, he thought desperately, *if you panic you can't make it work . . .*

It was perhaps one of the hardest things he'd done, to calm his mind and enter the mental state where magic can be made, to draw power from within himself, to repeat the words of power, the illusions of light and pain. The goblin fingers slacked—keeping the magic in his mind he kicked viciously at the underwater things, and felt them slither away with a few final, angry bites. His hands clawed at the roots and vines over his head, feeling them shift and sag with the swaying of his weight . . .

Lady of the Moon, please don't let the grims come back to chew my hands . . .

Somewhere above him, distant across the water, he heard a voice crying, "RHION!"

"*HERE!!!*" he bellowed, squirming as carefully as he could to readjust his hold on the vines; gingerly, painfully, he pulled himself up through the crackling, soggy mess into the air again. Rain lashed at his face and whipped the head-high reeds all around the islet into a churning sea of invisible movement; he flung upwards the illusion of a ball of witch-fire, climbing like a carnival rocket to burst in the black air.

"Rhion . . . !"

"Over here, Rhion!" cried another mocking voice from somewhere in the reeds, imitating words and thoughts with the uncanny mimicry of the Children of the Dusky Air.

"Rhion my love . . ."

"Here, my darling . . ."

"This way, beautiful princess . . ." A scattered coruscation of lights flared, small and blue and cold, among the impenetrable sedges, sparkling in the pelting rain.

Cursing at the grims, Rhion groped for the boat pole which

he'd let fall—it was seven feet long and hadn't dropped through the roots into oblivion, which was more than could be said of his scrying-crystal—and, using it to probe the muck in front of him, he waded out through the reeds again.

The bobbing yellow glow of lanternlight swung out over the pounded water; behind it, he made out a shallow punt and a cloaked figure poling, bent under the downpour. Rhion flung up a bright glow of magelight all around him—the grims hissed and shrieked with laughter, and the figure on the prow of the punt straightened up, slashing at the air with her open hands.

"Go!" The flute-sweet voice was no longer rosewood, but jade, or what music would be if diamonds could be wrought to create it, hard and sparkling and blazing with a dreadful power. "Get thee gone, Alseigodath, Children of the Second Creation . . . Go!" And her voice scaled up into a drawn-out cry, cold and strong and flaming with power, shaping words Rhion did not understand. Through the darkness he could see her face, knowing it for hers, though the features were unclear, reflecting a lightless glory like levin fire on silver. Her long hair swirled in the rain. The laughter in the darkness around them turned to cries of terror; Rhion felt the air thrum, as if under the beating of a holocaust of wings.

Then there was only the driving silence of the rain and the dark woman in the sodden cloak poling her boat toward him, shading her eyes to peer past the lantern's light.

"Are you all right?"

"I feel like a drowned mole, but other than that . . . Is there a way to get on one of those things without tipping you over?"

"Lie flat over the gunwales and turn . . . There!" She bent and caught a handful of sodden robe, pulling him up amidships with a soggy splash. Rhion saw that the punt was little better than a narrow raft, and already half-full of rain. Stoically, his drenched robe dragging at his every joint, he found the small bucket and began to bail while the Lady poled around the edge of the reed bed, and out across the black waters again.

It wasn't until they reached an island that promised a core of solid rock that either one spoke, except to exchange information about the water level in the punt, or instructions regarding its beaching among the clustering snags. The Lady led the way up a short path to what had been a hilltop shrine, its airy pillared walls now blocked in with rough-mortared stone. Inside, a small quantity of dry wood and sea coal were heaped upon a crude hearth; beside them lay dry blankets.

"There are a number of such places, refuges for lost travelers," the Gray Lady said, wringing out her wet hair as Rhion kindled fire on the hearth. "There are spells laid on them of summoning those who are cold and frightened—we were hoping you'd come to one eventually. Rhion, I'm sorry! I'm so sorry. We never thought you'd see us, much less . . ."

"Much less try to lead you astray in your own back garden?" He grinned up at her, shaking the rainwater out of his tangled curls. "I admit it takes a special kind of stupidity to try a trick like that." He fumbled in his pocket for his spectacles, all blotted and smeared with the greasiness of being wrapped in soaked wool—he wondered how he'd ever get them clean and dry and simply gave up on it, replacing them where they had been.

Her breath escaped her in a soft laugh, half with amusement at his self-mockery and half with relief. "We were worried about you . . ." With a simple natural modesty she gathered a blanket to her and, turning her back on him, pulled off her sodden dress and the shift underneath, letting them fall with a wet *splat* on the marble floor. While her back was turned Rhion likewise stripped off his robes, wrapping himself in a blanket and sitting down before the coin-bright newness of the fire to pick apart the torn ruin of his boot.

"Let me see that . . . We meant to trick you into moving the books to a new place—a place we'd be watching, of course—but never that you'd come to harm." She reached over to her wet clothes and disentangled her belt-pouch from the mess, drawing out several small packets of herbs wrapped securely in waxed cloth. "We didn't even know we'd been seen until we ran into your spells of misdirection . . ."

"Well, they must have been pretty good, since I walked back through them and got lost myself," Rhion sighed. "At least, I'd like to think that was what happened and not that I just got lost like any other fool who goes wading around the marshes at night . . . Ow! If that cut didn't get sufficiently washed in three hours of wading I don't know what it *would* take to get it clean . . ."

"That should hold till we get back in the morning." She bent over the bandaging of the makeshift poultice, murmuring herbwife spells; at the touch of her fingers, Rhion felt the pain lessen. Reaction was stealing over him, with the warmth of the little stone room and the fatigue that follows prolonged exertion in the cold. He leaned back against the wall and listened to the low, sweet voice as he would have listened to the rain, without trying to disentangle the spells she wove, only hearing in them the sounds of healing and of peace. He found himself wondering what her name had been and whether, if she had been born in some inland village or hill march, she would have found apprenticeship to some Earth-witch and eventually have become a village healer . . .

Or would the call of the Goddess have brought her to this place, wherever she had been born?

What would have happened to him, he wondered, had he been born a farmer's son a hundred miles from the nearest city, with no way to learn of wizardry and magic, no way to meet Jaldis. Or was it like the summoning spells on the books, he wondered. But then who was the summoner, and whom the summoned?

In the firelight, without his spectacles, her face seemed younger but very tired, the face of the girl she had been.

And if she had been born the daughter of a Duke?

Father needs an alliance . . . It isn't a question of what I want . . .

But that was something of which he could not bear to think.

She raised her head, her eyes seeming darker, like blue amber, mingled browns and russets and treacle golds. "The books would have been returned, you know," she said. There was apology in her voice.

She moved around to sit beside him, the rough stone wall poking them both in the back. "You would not even have known they'd been taken, read, the major spells copied . . ." An expression almost like pain drew at the corners of her generous mouth, and her broad brow darkened.

"The Goddess enjoins us to welcome sojourners in need, to help them. I know that what I have done is not the act of a host." She sighed, and passed a hand across her face, shaking aside the wet trail of hair from the blanket where it lay across her shoulder.

"But you have told us how you live and what became of Jaldis' other books in Felsplex. You've seen the books in our Library—old and crumbling, some of them, and some of them the only copies left of certain volumes, certain spells, certain knowledge . . . And of some books we know only their names, know only that they existed once. Paper is only paper, Rhion. Flesh is only flesh."

Profiled in the amber nimbus of the fire her face was tired, and infinitely sad. Perhaps it was that which broke the wall of his mistrust: the hunger, the sadness, and the yearning that were his own birthright of wizardry. The fire burned out of its first leaping brightness and settled down to a steady, crackling warmth, the rain's drumming eased as the sea-wind carried the somber clouds west to the stony uplands of Way, and their talk turned to other things. He had not forgotten the cold, bright power of her voice as she drove the grims away, nor the dreadful strength of the spells she had cast upon his mind—but he perceived that the power she held was only a part of her, and that at heart, within, she was very like himself.

In the warmth and pleasant weariness as they sat together he put his arm around her shoulders, and later, when she turned to him, he did not turn away.

Rhion was the Gray Lady's lover until the equinox of spring. He never did quite trust her where the books were concerned, but he liked her enormously, both as a lover and as a friend. In an odd way he felt safer, sensing that she was not a woman to weave the secrets of a man's bed and body into spells of coercion; there were magics, too, that wizards used in the bedroom which nonwizards—the tavern girls in Felsplex, or the Marshmen—found unnerving.

It would have been different, had he not known that Tally could never be his.

He knew that the Lady had had other lovers. Indeed, two of the children who sometimes accompanied the Marshfolk to the Islands had her square face and snub nose, and he had heard Channa the cook speak matter-of-factly of "the Lady's husband." But it wasn't until shortly before the equinox that he saw this man, a slender, gray-haired Marshman with a deeply lined face and twinkling eyes, when he came to the Islands to speak to her about the forthcoming spring rites.

"The chieftain of the Marshfolk is always the Lady's husband," Jaldis explained on one of the rare clear evenings when he and Rhion sat on the ruinous stone terrace along the water, observing the movement of the stars. The Moon had not yet risen—sprinkled with diamond fire, the huge arch of darkness seemed hard and shatteringly deep. "I'm told sometimes another man—or occasionally a woman—will ask to take the husband's place in the rites, but it's usually the Lady's husband . . . Have they asked you to preside over their rites at the turning of spring?"

The old man spoke without taking his concentration from the silver astrolabe he held, sighting above the lacy clouds of trees on the next island for the first appearance of the star called the Red Pilgrim. But there was, in spite of his efforts to conceal it, an edge to his voice. Across the marshes, the ducklike quacking of the first wood frogs could he heard; farther upriver, Rhion knew, in the wet meadows the sheep would be starting to lamb. The old man had only shaken his head when Rhion had told him about the Lady, but Rhion was aware these days that Jaldis was keeping a rather close eye on the hidden books. As soon as he'd been strong enough to go there himself Jaldis had marked the place with his own seals and, Rhion knew, had fallen into the habit of checking on them often.

This stung him a little, though he perfectly understood the concern. He didn't *think* the Gray Lady would—or could— use magic on him without his knowledge, but that conviction in itself, he was well aware, might have been induced by some spell more subtle than he could fathom. That she was stronger than he, he had always known.

He sighed and propped his spectacles back into place with his forefinger, keeping his attention on identifying the positions of various changeable stars. "They asked me if I'd attend, but they didn't say anything about presiding. Wouldn't the Lady herself do that?"

"Male magic and female work differently in their system," the old man replied, "as I'm sure you know. Here, see? The Pilgrim star is in twenty degrees of ascension, in the constellation of the Child." Since both of them knew that a quarrel would be based, at heart, in completely irrational feelings, neither was willing to step over the tacitly drawn lines. Thus many of their conversations had an oddly informational quality these days, something Rhion guessed would pass in time, when they left Sligo.

"Talismans of protection seem to be influenced by this

position, those made while that star is in ascendance having a greater efficacy, especially against poison, though conversely poisons, too, brewed in conjunction with death-spells, have greater strength . . . Very curious.''

He turned to regard his student, pinpricks of starlight twinkling deep within the bulging plates of jewels which hid what remained of his eyes. ''Certainly men and women are trained in different techniques. They generally have a man to preside over the rites.''

''Is it something you don't advise?''

''There is no reason why you shouldn't attend.'' The old man flicked back a spider-floss strand of his hair, and cocked his head like a bird. ''You'll find it interesting. The principles of magic *per se* have become deeply corrupted here and mixed with what was, originally, a religious cult, as I'm sure you've seen. The equinox rites clearly have their roots in what elsewhere came to be celebrated as the Carnival of Mhorvianne—the powers evoked at the turning of the four balance-points of the celestial year they attribute to the favor of their goddess rather than to the strength of their own wizardry and the nature of the cosmos itself. But it is never an ill thing to witness the raising of power, nor the shapes taken by the human soul.''

Still, it was with an irrational sense of disharmony, almost of guilt, that Rhion made his way in company with the Ladies and nearly all the folk of the marshes along the curved, gray beach of the Holy Isle at sunset of the equinox eve. Jaldis had remained behind in the main cluster of the islands, perhaps the only man in the lands of Sligo to do so, in order to work his own conjurations, calling the powers generated by the stars' balance to strengthen the spells on their medicinal herbs.

Without a word being said, Rhion knew that what Jaldis had really wanted to do was weave another Dark Well and search in its depths for the wizards who had begged their help, but he knew also that the old man was not about to do such a thing where there was a risk of having his secrets discovered, particularly by those whom he considered little better than Earth-witches. Jaldis was certainly capable of imbuing herbs with healing-spells unassisted—such was his power that he could probably have cured the plague with common grass—and, in any case, he would never have given Rhion an ultimatum of any sort.

Nevertheless, Rhion knew the old man hadn't liked being left alone.

In many ways it had been an uneasy winter.

Jaldis was right about one thing. The rituals practiced by the Ladies of the Moon were those of a religious cult rather than of wizardry, cluttered with curious practices having no apparent bearing on magic as Rhion understood it.

They were profoundly unnerving nevertheless.

The sun sank over the green-brown wall of the sweet marshes. Shadows flowed forth across the murky tangle of sawgrass and salt-oak that lay in long, uneven crescents seaward of the Holy Isle as the Marshmen began to assemble in the sacred place. The flotilla of canoes had left the Ladies' islands in the black dark long before dawn—at one time, Rhion guessed, soon after the days of the earthquake, this islet had been the last point of land facing out over the sea. From the crumbling double circle of menhirs on the beach, twin lines of unshaped standing stones extended out into the brack brown waters of the marsh, their heads gradually vanishing beneath the surface like the Sea-God's silent armies; a cloud-streaked mauve twilight lay upon the black, decaying shapes like a smoky shroud. When darkness was fully on them, the tapping of a drum began, and the men and women of the Marshfolk took hands, forming long winding chains that wove between the stones of circle and lines, looped far out onto the beach and into the waters and so back again, treading in the sand and the water the ancient shapes of the Holy Maze which had been passed down the years. Chill salt wind stirred their tangled hair and coarse garments, shredded the torch smoke and carried over the desolation the single, hoarse cry of a bird; Rhion, seated alone on a small boulder just above the tide line, drew his cloak about him and shivered. The lines of the dancers passed by him unseeing, though the stars that came to shine through the wispy clouds gleamed silver in their open eyes.

The dance began, and ended, and began again, now walking, now hastening, now bending down with long, shuddering ripples that passed through the lines like waves of the sea or the turning of a serpent's tail. Though torches ringed the stone circle thrust upright in the sand, the dancers carried none—as the darkness deepened their forms seemed more and more like the passing of a spirit host, lost between the realms of the living and the dead. The music was oddly random, strange knockings and dronings broken by shrill bird cries, and yet, through it all, moved a rhythm that eluded the seekings of Rhion's mathematical mind. More than ever, he had the sense of visiting a world that was half-invisible half the time, a world where things appeared to make little sense and yet moved to patterns unguessable—where things that seemed common were lambent with power. In other parts of the Forty Realms tonight was the Carnival of Masks, the feast of Mhorvianne the Merciful, the rite of forgiveness. Here, it seemed, atonement involved something beyond a sheltered remorse.

The night drew on. The sea's whisper was hardly louder than the dragging of hundreds of feet through the heavy gray sand. Soft wind herded the clouds westward and the stars turned their courses unimpeded above the headless stones. The tide of the equinox lifted and stirred in Rhion's blood.

Beside the altar in the midst of the ring of stones and torchflame the presiding mage raised his arms to the sky— an old Hand-Pricker from up the marshes who looked ancient enough to be Jaldis' grandfather. It was close to midnight; Rhion felt it in his bones. He could feel, too, the spiral whisper of magic that floated now like a glowing mist all around the holy place. Magic rose from the dancers, from the sea, from the maze they had trodden into the sand, and from the ley that crossed through the island and plunged down the lane of stones to drown itself in the waters of the marsh; magic closed tighter and tighter about the altar-stone like the wool winding on a distaff, like the twisting ropes of a catapult's spring. In a high, shaky voice the mage was chanting the words of the raising and concentration of power, and the lines of the dancers changed their pattern and drew the circles smaller yet, giving him the power they raised.

Though Rhion had not seen her approach, the Lady stepped forward out of darkness into the bloody glare. He saw that she wore the garments of the bygone priestesses of An, red as the anemones that grew in the sweet marshes in spring, sewn with plates of pierced gold. Her face was painted white and black after the ancient fashion, framed in the smoky rivers of her hair; she wore the old diadem of the priest-queens on her head, the white moon jewel, the flowers and the bones. And to the altar her husband came, as the husbands of the Lady of Sligo had come for centuries past, naked to the waist with his silvery hair unbound and his twinkling eyes solemn.

He stretched himself upon the stone and a priest and priestess came forward—the priestess, Rhion noticed distractedly, was Channa the cook—taking knives of meteor iron that the Lady gave them, the blades glinting blue in the starlight. At a word from the Lady, the torches were quenched in the sand, but the dancers continued to turn and weave along the maze's invisible tracks in the darkness, silent as wind. Even the music had stilled, but it seemed to Rhion that he could hear, along with the hiss of their feet in the heavy sand, the beating of the blood in their veins. The old Hand-Pricker stretched forth his hands to the stars. The priest and priestess moved to either side of the man who lay upon the altar. The blades glinted as they were raised—then they bent and cut the victim's throat.

Rhion shuddered, looking away as the Lady stepped forward, her crimson gown a darkness now broken only by the white shapes of dangling bones. He'd seen that the cuts were carefully made, slitting the veins, not severing the arteries or the windpipe. Still, even allowing for the added power that the turning of the equinox midnight gave to healing magic, it would take a tremendously strong spell at this point to save the victim's life. Thin, icy wind streamed up from the salt marshes of the east, carrying to his nostrils the sweet, metallic repulsiveness of the blood; the dancers' feet swished in the sand, starlight flashing on the sweat of their faces, the curled tips of the waves, their feet weaving and re-weaving the maze between sea and earth.

A flute awakened, crying wild and sad and alone; somewhere a tiny drum trembled with a skittery beat in the torchless dark. When Rhion looked back the altar was empty. Priest and priestess, Lady and mage and victim, were gone. The air seemed to sing with the aftermath of magic, drawn from the turning of the heavens, dispersed along the leys to the four corners of the sleeping world like a shuddering silver heartbeat and called back from them again. A dark thread of blood ran down the side of the stone, gleaming black in the starlight.

But whether the Lady's husband had walked away alive, or had been carried off dead—which as he later learned frequently did happen in these rites—Rhion did not hear for many days.

Spring rains had started a few weeks previously, turning the waters of the marsh to sheets of hammered steel and transforming all the familiar channels as the water level rose. Waking early, to meditate on the old stone terrace or walk to the library to study, Rhion heard among the reeds the cries of the returning birds.

One day shortly after the rite at the standing stones, Jaldis announced that enough dry weather lay ahead to permit them to take the road once again.

"It will be good," he said simply, "to be home."

Nerriok, Rhion thought, the green City of Bridges, walled with golden sandstone upon its island in the midst of ring after ring of *crinas*, floating eyots of dredged silt and withe anchored by roots to the bottom of Lake Mharghan and thick with trees and flowers—corrupt, sprawling, and unbelievably colorful, with its markets heavy with the perfumes of melons and bread and flowers, its majestic temples and marble baths, its periodic riots among the students of different schools of philosophy and its huge concourses of foreigners that turned certain quarters into strange bazaars of the East or grubby, sprawling barbarian villages . . .

The noise, the smells, and the excitement of the place came back on him in a wave of strange nostalgia—libraries, playhouses, poetry, music, and the meeting of minds . . .

And at the same time he thought about the shaggy green silences of the marshes of Sligo and the faint speech of wind chimes on foggy mornings mingling with the cawing of crows.

He pushed his spectacles more firmly up onto the bridge of his nose, and said, "The Gray Lady has asked me to stay on here as Scribe."

Jaldis said nothing. His bent and crippled fingers turned over and over the seal-hair brush he'd been wielding, to write talismanic signs on a luck-charm. The breeze off the marsh, sniffing like a little dog across the terrace upon which Rhion had found him sitting, stirred the cream-colored parchment under its weighting of river stones. Cool sunlight flooded a cloud-patched sky overhead and glanced across Jaldis' spectacles. The vines that cloaked their crumbling old house had begun to put out leaves. Within a month the Drowned Lands would be a jungle of whispering green.

The brush made a little silvery *tinck* as it was set down on the pitted limestone table-top. "Perhaps you should."

Rhion shook his head. "I couldn't leave you alone."

He made his face as noncommittal as his voice. When Jaldis was wearing his spectacles it was difficult to tell whether he was using them to see or not.

"You'll have to one day, you know." The set of the old man's back, the way he tilted his head up at Rhion as if he could see, were calm and matter-of-fact. "I do not want that it should come to it, that you would begin to wish me dead."

"I won't."

Jaldis drew in his breath as if he would speak, but let it out again, and the rosewood box upon his chest only murmured, like the drawn-out trickle of the marsh winds, "Oh, my son . . ."

Rhion reached down and took his hands. In a way he knew that Jaldis was right. Unsettling as the sojourn here had been, at heart they had both known that Rhion's affair with the Lady, like his other relations with the tavern girls and flower sellers of Nerriok and Felsplex, was not something that would alter his life, or change what lay between them. Yet somewhere in the course of the winter something had changed. Learning the mazes of the marshes, studying the scrolls left by ancient wizards, meditating on the healing spells the Lady had taught him, Rhion had realized—or, more accurately, had come to believe within himself—that he could be a wizard away from Jaldis' teaching.

But now was not the time. For one thing, Jaldis needed him. In the misted silver light he could see the marks of the winter's hardship on that lined and weary face: *How could he even REACH Nerriok if I stayed behind?*

And there were other things.

"You're my teacher," he said quietly. "My friend. Ten years ago when I was going insane trying to—to crush out the fire inside me—you told me that it was possible to have that fire, to hold it and keep it, not as a secret that I had to hide but as a way I could make my living and as a glory, a joy in itself. You told me that dreams were not insanity. Just for that, if you'd done nothing for me from that moment on, I'd still owe you . . ."

"You owe me nothing!" The crippled fingers tightened fiercely over the soft, stubby ones in their grasp. "Owe—it's a filthy word! We are not permitted to marry, but we need sons and daughters, Rhion, to whom we can pass our knowledge. To whom we can pass what we are. Not children of the blood, but children of the fire." There was long silence, broken by the far-off mewling of gulls.

"Ah," Rhion replied, as if he had at last understood some great piece of wisdom. "I see. So you really *enjoyed* spending all those hours getting migraines teaching me to scry through a crystal. It gave you heartfelt fulfillment, that time I lit the attic on fire back in Nerriok . . ."

The scarred ruin of Jaldis' mouth flexed, the closest he could ever come to a laugh, and he pulled his hands free of his adopted son's. "You are an impertinent boy," he said.

"Besides," Rhion added with a grin. "Every time I think you've taught me all about magic, either I bollix something up and you have to remind me I need five hundred times more practice, or you pull out some obscure spell that you've forgotten to tell me about, like the come-back spells on the books. I'm not about to let you get away till I'm damn sure I've got it all, which should be in about another thirty years. So I'll just go inside and start packing . . ."

The crippled fingers, startlingly strong from eleven years of supporting his weight on the crutch handles, caught at his wrists once more. It never failed to surprise Rhion how accurate the old man's awareness was of where things were.

"You will have to leave me one day, you know," he repeated, refusing to be put off, as he had always refused to be put off by his pupil's elusive clowning. "One day you will need to seek your own path, to establish yourself. Don't give that up for the sake of looking after me.''

Rhion looked about him in silence. Under a cloak of weeds, the marble pavement was pitted and broken; beyond it stood the library, the huge stone blocks of its walls being forced apart by the roots of trees. All around them, ancient marble faces peeped like ghosts from the foliage that wound this island in a flowering shroud. Gulls circled overhead, and distantly he heard a bittern's harsh cry. Chilly spots of sunlight flashed in the reed beds and on the brown waters beyond. A silence of peace lay upon the lands, and everywhere, like the murmuring of the waters, he could breathe the whispering scent of magic.

He made himself grin again, so that the lightness would carry into his voice. ''When I find a path I want to tread by myself, I'll tell you.'' Turning quickly, he went inside.

Later he sought the Gray Lady at her loom. By the way she raised her eyes to his face when he came in he saw that she read what his answer to Jaldis had been, and thus his answer to her. Even when he had gone to seek his master on the terrace, Rhion had not been clear as to what his decision would be.

''I can't leave him,'' he said quietly, sitting down on the bench beside her. ''Not now. Not yet. He was hurt enough by my—I don't know, deserting him, I suppose, for you, or even seeming to. It sounds silly . . .''

She smiled, shook her head, and laid the shuttle by. ''All fathers want their sons to grow to manhood and walk alone,'' she said. ''But they are all sure they know best about the direction in which their sons should walk.''

Under his scrubby beard Rhion's mouth twisted at the sudden memory of his own father's constant moan about the ways of modern youth. But the thought inevitably brought back that sweaty red face trembling with anger above its tight embroidered collar. *You are dead to me as from today. My son is dead. My son is dead . . .*

And so, Rhion thought, he was.

After his ejection from the family home, he had scried for sight of his father in the fire of the cellar where he and Jaldis had been sheltering. He had seen him in tears, alone, locked in his counting room where not even Rhion's mother would find him. He had never sought for sight of him again.

"I'm sorry." He sighed, and looked up at the Gray Lady's face, then around at the little stone chamber, a round room like a dovecote built onto the back of what had been a temple, its hearth where the altar had been. Through a doorway he could see the gray pine poles and white curtains of the bed where they had lain. "I would have liked to stay longer."

Even as he said it he felt guilty, as if he had said to Jaldis, *I'd rather study with the Lady than with you. I'd rather sleep in the Lady's arms than look after a lame old man. I'd rather stay in a place where they have hundreds of books, than follow after a cripple who's down to his last dozen . . .*

And a voice still deeper within added, *I'd rather be a man than a boy.*

But right now, to Jaldis, lame and blind and set adrift, it all came to the same thing: *I'm leaving you.*

And that, he could not say.

She smiled and shook her head. "Never be sorry when the Goddess leads you somewhere by the hand. She's usually very clear about what will be best for us—it's just that sometimes we think we know more about it than She does. I will miss you, Rhion." She drew him to her and kissed him on the lips, the warm, brief kiss of friendship. Wan sunlight, falling through the open window beside the angular black skeleton of the loom, picked out the crow's-feet around her hazel eyes, and the first threads of gray at the part of her smooth-braided hair.

"We see time like wanderers in a maze," she said. "She sees it from the top. I'll have Channa put up some supplies to take on the road. But I wouldn't advise you to go to Nerriok. The queen has lately come under the influence of the priests of Agon, the Eclipsed Sun. Like most of the sun cults, they are intolerant and jealous of wizards' powers. My advice, if as you say you have done a favor for a member of the ducal house, is to go to Bragenmere instead.''

They reached Bragenmere in four days. Their speed on the road was greatly assisted by the half-week of dry weather Jaldis had foreseen and by the two small donkeys and the Marshman servant the Lady had lent them for the trip. Able to carry blankets and foodstuffs as well as Jaldis' books—which Jaldis tested with spells the first night on the road, as soon as he thought Rhion was asleep, to make absolutely sure that the Gray Lady had not handled them—the two wizards were thus able to avoid spending what little cash remained to them on inns. They reached Bragenmere with enough in hand to rent two small but clean rooms—one upstairs and one down—in one of the hundreds of little courts of which that dry upland city consisted, a court which was owned, ironically enough, by the local Temple of Darova, a god whose disapproval had gotten them thrown out of more than one town in their time.

Rhion fell easily back into the role of housewife, sweeping out their new dwelling place and scouting the nearest markets and fountains. They were lucky in that, though Shuttlefly Court itself didn't possess a fountain, which was one reason the rents there were cheap, it backed onto the Laundry of Fortunate Sheets, also owned by the Temple of Darova, which operated a small banking house and a very large bordello in the neighborhood as well. The laundry master was willing to sell surplus fountain water after sundown and all the 'used' they cared to carry away for bathing and dishwashing purposes. Bragenmere, perched on the high, arid knees of the Mountains of the Sun, was watered by a number of springs, two very fine stone aqueducts, and the Kairn River's sluggish marshes below the Lower Town's walls, all of which had been sufficient for its population back in the days when it had only been a trading town for the upcountry hunters and shepherds. Since the increase of the weaving trade under the patronage of the Dukes of Mere, the city, capital of this realm, had grown vastly, and as was the way of things in any city of the Forty Realms, the great public baths and temple fountains, and the water-gardens of the Duke, the nobility, and the wealthy, tended to get larger shares than any number of the poor.

The other occupants of the court were mostly weavers, with the exception of the usual two or three dramshops to be found in every court in the city, a pawnbroker, who was also subsidized by the Temple of Darova, seven free-lance prostitutes and an embroiderer who hadn't been able to afford the higher rents of Thimble Lane a dozen yards to the east. There was a school at one corner, thinly attended since most of the neighborhood children spent their days on the loom. The schoolmistress, a sturdy gray-haired woman with a voice like a war gong, descended upon Jaldis and Rhion the first day and informed them in no uncertain terms that they were not to interfere with any of her pupils, several of whom had already pelted Rhion with goat dung on his way back from the market. Three nights later the woman was back to purchase a remedy for a headache as if neither the pelting nor the confrontation had ever taken place.

Ah, what it is, Rhion thought, watching her departing back dart furtively from shadow to shadow of the cottonwood posts supporting the court's rudely thatched arcade, *to be a working mage again.*

The business of actually earning one's living by wizardry, he had long ago discovered, was transacted mostly in the first two or three hours after sunset. It was the time when people—like Mistress Prymannie—had the impression they would not be seen. This was an advantage as spring warmed to summer and the dust kicked up from the unpaved court frequently made the downstairs kitchen unlivable. There were spells that would draw down dust out of the air and collect it in the corners, but these tended to vary so much with weather, with the phases of the moon and the ascensions and declensions of various stars that they were never really effective. In his reading and study, Rhion was constantly on the lookout for others that worked better and wondered if the Gray Lady would have given him a good one if he'd thought to ask. Even in a city as relatively friendly to wizards as Bragenmere, few people would be seen openly going to a mage's door in the daytime.

Thus he was startled one afternoon, while sitting in the kitchen roughing out calculations for a talisman that might work in attracting wealth their way, by a knock on the door. Jaldis was upstairs reading, for the light was better there and it was easier to make his spectacles work. Rhion got to his feet and walked the length of the corridorlike adobe room, thinking, *Not the local magistrates telling us to move on. Please, Darova, give us a break for once. After all, we're paying our rent . . .*

He opened the door.

Framed against the bright spring sun of the court outside, her taffy-colored hair braided back under a virgin's stiffened gauze cap, was Tally.

She blinked into the dimness of the kitchen, her eyes clearly not used to the splintery blue shade under the courtyard arcade, much less to the unmitigated gloom of the kitchen itself.

She said, "Excuse me—I have heard that you're a . . . a wizard? I want . . . I want to purchase a potion, to win the love of a man."

EIGHT

RHION COULDN'T HELP HIMSELF. "IS IT FOR YOU?"

"Of course!" But the quickness of her reply, and the hot blush that suddenly suffused her cheeks, told their own story and the relief that went through him almost made him laugh. "That is . . ." she began, and peered suddenly into the shadows of the room. *"Rhion?"* And recognizing him, she smiled.

He thought, quite clearly, as if warning someone else against inevitable tragedy: *Don't do this.* But it was already done.

"Come in." He stepped back to let her pass, then hurried before her to the plank table—one he'd scrounged in one of the many rubbish stores of the district—to shove aside the books and papers that strewed its stained and battered surface. "Don't tell me your governess lets you come to this part of town," he added as he did so. "If I were your father, I'd sack her."

"My governess thinks I'm in the mews helping Fleance with the young hawks . . ." She gazed around her as she spoke: at the rough-hewn rafters from which every herb they could buy or gather in the Kairn Marshes hung drying; at the round little beehive of a tiled stove; at the plank shelf of dishes, the cool red-and-black-work done in the Drowned Lands. "Don't you have a crocodile? A stuffed one, I mean, hanging from the rafters? Wizards are supposed to."

"Wizards do if they can afford them," Rhion replied with a grin. "The ones you see in spell-weavers' shops aren't stuffed but drying, and when they're properly dried you cut them up and store them for potions and mummify the skin in camphor oil, for talismanic work. But the baby crocs are tremendously expensive and you have to import them from Mindwava. Jaldis and I are still working on cheaper things like saffron seed and glass and getting a decent crucible." He leaned against the corner of the table and scratched a corner of his scruffy beard, realizing he hadn't trimmed it lately and wishing he had. She walked around the bare little room, looking at the herbs and books and cheap clay pots with their careful labels in frank wonder and delight. He remembered the grace with which she moved, surprising in a girl so tall, but he'd almost forgotten the husky, boyish alto of her voice.

"Does it have to be?" She turned back to him, her gray eyes shadowed. "A love-potion, that is. I mean, does it have to be for . . . Could someone get one that would work for two other people?"

When she had come in, Rhion had seen, as well as the smile that stopped his heart, the purplish prints of sleeplessness in the tender flesh around the eyes and the puffy spoor of last night's tears.

He sighed, wishing he didn't have to be the one to tell her. "A love-potion won't save your sister from unhappiness, Tally."

Her mouth flinched, but she didn't ask him how he knew. Perhaps she expected that, as a wizard, he simply would know.

"They don't last," he went on, as gently as he could. "Even if you were to give her husband several in succession, in time the effects would wear away. And if he hates her now, what do you think he'll feel after a few weeks, or a few months, of being impelled by his own body, by needs he doesn't understand, to make love to her?''

She was silent, digesting that. It was clearly something she hadn't thought of. Rhion remembered she was a virgin—remembered what it had been like to be seventeen.

At length she said, ''I don't think . . . that is . . . He isn't indifferent. At least Damson says . . .'' She hesitated, an inexperienced and well-bred girl sorting hastily through all the precepts of good breeding for what it was and was not proper to say. She took a deep breath, and plunged in. ''Damson says—and I think she's right—that Esrex isn't indifferent to her. If he was, he wouldn't be trying to hurt her, he wouldn't be flaunting his mistresses the way he does. But he's very proud, and very bitter. He sees in her the daughter of the man who took the realm away from his grandfather—our grandfather, because his aunt is my mother—the man who humbled his family. And he's spiteful. Loving her could change that, couldn't it?''

The anxious look in her gray eyes, after her tomboy incisiveness and the courage she'd shown in the snowbound woods, went to his heart. Her voice was almost timid as she asked, ''Are they really not permanent?''

''Love isn't permanent, Tally,'' Rhion said quietly. ''It renews itself, from day to day—sometimes from hour to hour. And lust and longing, which create their own illusions—and illusion is what the potions really arouse—are more evanescent still. I'm sorry . . .''

She shook her head quickly, as if to say, *Not your fault,* her eyes not meeting his. For a time she leaned half-perched upon the corner of the cluttered table, head bowed beneath the drying jungle of mallows and milkwort overhead, looking down at her hands in her lap. But when she spoke again she raised her gaze to his.

''It's his pride, you see,'' she said. ''Damson has always loved him, from the time he was sixteen and she was twenty;

I think they . . . they slept together . . . in spite of the fact that he always blamed Father for the fact that he—Esrex—isn't Duke of Mere now. But he never wanted to marry her for that reason. Then he found out she was behind his family forcing him to do so—and right after that she miscarried of his son. He hasn't been near her since. But if he could just be drawn back to her, even for a little while . . . if she could just bear him a son.''

Was that her wishful thinking, he wondered, or her sister's? Running an idle finger along the worn grain of the table corner on which he perched, Rhion remembered the chilly-eyed young man he'd seen in the scrying-crystal. Good-looking in his way—though Rhion had long since given up trying to decide what kind of looks drew men and women to one another—lace-gloved hands fastidiously turning bunches of expensive winter flowers, his face expressionless as a cat's. His power over Damson had been clear in the way she'd flinch from his words, in the way her eyes would follow him when he'd stalk from the room.

"You think it would help?"

Something stiffened in her shoulders as she tucked a strand of seed-colored hair defiantly back under her cap. "It might."

And so it might, he thought. With loving and hating, one never knew. But too many people had come to him and Jaldis over the years, asking for magic to fix their lives. He knew of no spell which could not be twisted out of its purpose by fate, no potion which would for better or for worse change a human soul's inner essence. No sigil he'd made had ever altered the words that rose automatically to a person's lips when they weren't thinking.

Yet people kept acting as if someday the laws of magic would spontaneously change and spells would do all these things.

He felt suddenly very old. "Does your sister know you've come?''

Tallisett shook her head. "Damson says wizards make most of their money blackmailing the people who come to them for love-potions or potency drugs or abortions . . ."

"Damn!" Rhion smote his forehead with the heel of his hand. "So *that's* what we've been doing wrong! I *knew* there had to be a better way to make money out of this . . . Ow!" She'd come around the table in a stride and smacked him hard on the shoulder, but she was laughing as she did so.

"No," he added gently, shaking his head. "That's part of the oath of our order. Secrecy, as physicians must swear it."

Tally frowned. "But there was a wizard just a few years ago who was doing that over in Way . . ."

"So he was probably a Blood-Mage or an Ebiatic or one of the cheapjack astrologers you get on the street-corners . . ."

She shook her head, baffled, like most people completely ignorant of the differences between the orders of wizardry. "All I know is that they burned him for it, and before they burned him he confessed to having blackmailed hundreds of people. He'd get the women to sleep with him and the men to kill or beat up people who disagreed with him . . . and anyway," she added, as Rhion groaned at the retelling of those hoary rumors, those accusations which had been leveled at every wielder of magic who had ever lived, "Esrex belongs to the Cult of Agon. If he ever thought there was wizardry involved between him and Damson he'd probably stay away from her for good, out of fear of what they'd say."

"And you're willing to risk that for her without her knowledge?" He cocked an eyebrow at her, and pushed up his spectacles again. Her color heightened.

"He'd never find out . . ." But he could see that, even as she said the words, she was aware of how childish they sounded. She looked down again, for a few moments concentrating on picking precisely identical quantities of gauze undersleeve to puff out between the embroidered ribbons of her oversleeve. "She loves him, you see," she said at length, not meeting his eye. "I don't see how she could, after all the cruel things he's said to her—he really is a spiteful little prig. But she does. If she didn't . . . If she didn't need his approval the way she does . . ."

"And if we didn't all have to eat to stay alive," Rhion sighed, "think how much money we'd save at the market." Her profile, half averted, was like a line of alabaster behind the stiffened wing of her cap; the pearl that hung from the cap's point was less smooth than the forehead beneath it. He felt a certain amount of sympathy for Damson's impossible position.

The silence lengthened. Outside in the courtyard a couple of drunks were arguing in front of the Skull and Bones, and even through the weight of the adobe wall he could hear the steady beat of the looms in the chambers next door. The air smelled thickly of dust and lanolin, of the pigs foraging in the court and of acrid soap being boiled a few courts over in Lye Alley. He remembered the way Tally had jerked the wet leather of the reins from his hand, the defiant flash of her gray eyes in the gibbous reflected ghostlight of the grims. He remembered how she had charged without a second thought to seek for her sister's child.

"If I don't help you," he said, not asking it as a question, "you'll look for someone who will."

She didn't look at him but he saw her mouth flinch again.

"Tally," he sighed softly, "don't do it. Leave her free to choose her own road."

She raised her eyes then, like a child's, hoping, not that authority would relent, but that the world was in fact not constituted as it was. The stiffness went out of her back with the release of her breath. "Damn you." Her small voice was utterly without rancor, a friend's casual railery at a friend. "Are you always right about things?"

"No," he told her sadly, for he wanted to be able to help

her, wanted to free her from the grinding pressure of misery he had seen in the crystal. "But this time I'm afraid I am."

Dammit, he thought, *all those weeks in the Drowned Lands wondering if there were some way I could make her happy, and it turns out it's this.*

"There are ways to do it, yes. But really and truly, it's against our ethics to make a love-spell or any other kind of spell for someone who isn't present and consenting. Can you see why that is?"

And she nodded, not liking it, but seeing. She didn't, like many girls of that age, say, *This is different . . .* If she thought it, it was not for long.

"I'm sorry. I'm truly sorry."

"It's all right." She sighed again, and produced a crooked smile for him, manufacturing cheer in her voice as he had so recently manufactured it for Jaldis. "If she weren't so afraid of word getting back to Esrex . . . or of being blackmailed . . ." She shook her head, chasing the thought away. "He's trying very hard to curry favor with the priests of Agon, you see. Though the gods only know why anyone would want to belong to that cult. But I'll think of something."

She straightened her shoulders and smiled a little more convincingly. In that single gesture, he saw all the burnished self-confidence of one of those children of fortune who have not yet known defeat. Rhion had been acquainted with a lot of them, having gone to school with the offspring of the wealthy bankers and traders and merchant senators of the City of Circles. At one time he had been one himself. He still remembered what it had felt like.

She turned to go.

"Wait . . ." Pulling himself out of his reverie, he twisted around to grub in the debris on the table for the bits of parchment he'd purchased with the proceeds of his last toadstone. "Just a minute . . ."

Half closing his eyes, he dipped down within himself, calling forth the meditative light of magic. After a moment, he drew a standard sigil comprised of the second, ninth, and eighteenth runes—the first such seal he could think of at short notice—and threw in the Lost Rune for good measure, rolled it up in a small piece of cured lambskin, at ten or twelve dequins the square foot, and bound it with a slip of punched copper. "Carry this when you leave. It'll keep people from looking at you, or recognizing you if they do see you, provided you keep quiet and don't call attention to yourself. All right?"

She hesitated, holding it as if she feared it would somehow contaminate her soul by touch. Then she slipped it into her skirt pocket. "All right. Thank you." She meant the charm, he could tell, as he walked her the length of the shadowy room. But when he opened the door she turned back in the mottled tabby light of the arcade's thatched roof, and said, "Thank you," again, meaning something more.

Then she was gone.

He climbed the ladder to the floor above and recounted to Jaldis all that had passed, not omitting that he had called Tallisett's image in his scrying-crystal while they were in the Drowned Lands, "to make sure she and her sister got to Imber all right," and so knew the poor state of Damson's marriage.

"It's a bad business," Jaldis sighed, shaking his head. Because of the strong spring heat, worse in the upper room, he'd braided and clubbed his white hair, and his head with its narrow features and close-trimmed beard strongly resembled that of a bird, thrusting up from the loose folds of his brown cowl. Before him on the table lay his spectacles, surrounded by half a dozen fragments of flawed crystal the color of dirty water, the best they could afford.

"Not that Dinar Prinagos wasn't perfectly right to overthrow his liege lord and keep Alvus' ineffectual idiot of a son from inheriting,'' the old man went on, fingering each fragment in turn: reading, Rhion knew, every shear and shadow in the brittle lattices of their structure, judging how much use, if any, they would be. Every flaw meant a Limitation, or a variation of whatever spell the future talismans would hold; every shadow, a break in the energy paths of the crystal's heart which would have to be laboriously accounted for.

"There's bad blood in the White Bragenmeres, and I'm told Esrex, for all he's a fop, is a dangerous young man to cross. A Solarist, he used to be, denying all the gods and magic as well. But he switched over to the Cult of Agon when it became clear that the High Queen favored them."

The blind man shook his head, the lines of his face deepening. To a great extent he seemed to have recovered from his illness, and even the journey up from Sligo seemed to have left him little the worse. But listening to his voice as he spoke of Tally's father, Rhion found himself comparing its tone and strength with his recollections of how it had been before the flight from Felsplex—before the strain of opening and using the Dark Well. *It draws energy,* Jaldis had said . . .

Lately he had caught himself watching Jaldis closely, mentally comparing with recollections and repeatedly reassuring himself, *Yes, he looks the same . . . his movement hasn't slowed down any . . . there's been no real change* and wondering if he was just imagining that the old man seemed slower and more halt, wondering whether his hands had always looked so thin . . .

"I'm not sure which is worse," Jaldis continued, oblivious to the uneasy scrutiny. "The Solarists and their heresies or the Cult of Agon with its secrets, its spies that take every piece of information they hear back to the priests of the Veiled God. No one even knows who half its members are, though they're supposed to be legion. You were well to send the girl away, poor chit. You don't think she'll go to a Hand-Pricker, do you, or to that poisonous old Ebiatic, Malnuthe, over in the Shambles?''

"I don't think so,'' Rhion said. The window was shuttered with a pair of dried and splintery jalousie shades; sitting in the embrasure of the thick adobe wall, he was able to peer through a couple of the missing louvers into the blindingly bright sunlight of the square. With the ending of the spring rains, the lush weeds and thorn-bushes growing all around the courtyard arcade were turning brown. The mountains that towered over Bragenmere were taking on their wolfish summer hues: by August the sheep and cattle ranges would be coarse brown velvet, the pine trees blackish tangles in the rock clefts that marked the springs. Children too young to be working the looms were playing knucklebones in the dust, their voices rising shrilly to Rhion's ears; across the square, one of the whores lay on her balcony, a damp towel spread over her face and her hair, nearly the color of the summer hills, spread out to bleach in the sun.

"I think she understands now why it isn't a good thing to make a decision like that for someone else, no matter what *she* thinks should be done.''

"We can but hope. Listen, Rhion . . .'' The old man set aside his crystals and half-turned in his twig-work chair. "I have been making calculations. It is my belief that a Dark Well could be wrought in the cellar beneath the kitchen here.''

Rhion tried not to shiver at the thought of Jaldis' tampering once more with the Void. "That little hole? It's so small you'd have to climb back up to the kitchen if you wanted to scratch . . .''

"Not if we removed the shelves there—they are probably rotted in any case—and cleared the wood-stores up into the kitchen.'' He leaned forward, the talismans dangling from the voice-box clinking with the dry silvery sound of moving wind. "Rhion, it is six weeks until the summer solstice. The solstice or the equinoxes are the only time that the wizards in that other universe—the wizards without magic—might just be able to raise enough power to reach through the Void and contact us here. Even if we can get only an image, a glimpse of their world, something to guide our search in the blackness of eternity, we will know at least in which direction to look the next time we search, and the next . . ."

Something flicked through Rhion's mind and was gone, like movement glimpsed from the tail of the eye. Something evil and cold, something . . . A dream? Night sky and standing stones . . . ?

Turning his mind from his vague fear of what danger Tally might run herself into he said, "Yes, but . . . how likely is it they'll still be calling? By the time of the solstice, it'll have been six months. That's a long time. Anything can happen in six months."

Jaldis smiled, sweet and wise in spite of the ruin of scars. "My son," he said quietly, "they may have been calling into darkness for six years. And to help them in their isolation— to learn what robbed their world of its magic, to prevent such a thing from coming to pass here, I would listen for six, or for sixty."

Not children of the blood, Jaldis had said . . . *children of the fire.* As he had been.

"I have sent for Shavus Ciarnin," the blind man went on, turning back to the table and picking up the bits of crystal, placing them one by one in a crude little painted clay pot he'd padded with bits of fleece. "We must have his help, his power, to find this world. We need his power to contact those wizards in that other universe, to tell them what they must know in order to guide us across . . ."

"*US?*" Rhion swung sharply from the window. "Wait a minute, I think that box of yours has developed a flaw, old friend. I thought I heard you say the word *us.*"

"I can scarcely ask Shavus to undertake a journey I am not willing to make myself."

"The hell you can't," Rhion retorted. "That world has no magic. What's going to happen to that voice box and those spectacles when you get there?"

"Nothing," the old man replied serenely. "The spells that imbue them and the talismans that give them power were wrought here and should hold their magic no matter what."

"You care to bet your life on that hypothesis?"

"I would," he said soberly, "if it would help."

"Look," Rhion said in subconscious imitation of his father at his most reasonable. "I'm willing to go with Shavus . . ." And he shivered as he said it. ". . . though I'm not thrilled about leaving you here alone and even less enthusiastic about traveling with the Archmage for any length of time. But I'm not going to let you go. Besides," he added more calmly, for his light, quirky voice had risen with his fears, "Shavus will need someone on this end to guide him back, if what you say is true."

"You have reason," the old man conceded. "And the less power there is there, the more there will be needed from here. But even so . . ."

From the kitchen downstairs came the swift, hard rapping of someone knocking at their door. Rhion flung open the jalousies and leaned out over the bleached gray thatch of the arcade. "COMING!" he bellowed.

We've got to stop living in slums and hovels, he thought, as he clambered down the rude pole ladder to the kitchen below. *I'm starting to lose all my manners.* His father, of course, had had a slave—a Cotrian from the In Islands, for he did not believe northerners could be trained—whose sole job it was to sit in the little alcove off the vestibule and answer the door, so there had been none of this yelling out the windows business. He still remembered the blue-and-white flowered tiles of the alcove's floor and the man's matching blue tunic. *Now, if I put a wizard's mark on the door that said, 'I'm coming' in a low, polite voice . . .*

But Shavus and Jaldis had known wizards who had done things of the kind. Aside from the difficulty of any long-distance spell of speaking—and fifty feet *was* a long distance for such a spell—the usual result was to fuel the fires of public uneasiness about wizards in general and add to their reputation of uncanniness and danger. Wizards who used their powers in such a fashion frequently found themselves being shot with poisoned darts from ambush or having their houses burned above their heads.

Of course, Rhion thought wryly, hurrying down the length of the shadowy kitchen and glancing unconsciously up at the place in the rafters where Tally had expected to see a stuffed crocodile, *wizards who* don't *use their powers thus are just as likely to have the goon squads after them, armed with weapons on which Spells of Silence have been laid, so how much odds does it make?*

He opened the door, smiling as he recalled the obsequious grace of old Minervum back home, who could make of the act a favor, a privilege, or an insult at will . . .

A very grubby fourteen-year-old girl stood there, clad in shabby silk obviously stolen from a much older and wealthier woman, combs of steel and tortoiseshell gleaming at careless random in the dirty snarl of her hair. In her arms she held a huge black book.

"My Mom says a customer brung this in," she said, with a jerk of her head back toward the pawnshop a little further up the court. "She says she can't sell the thing 'ceptin' for kindling paper, but you witches might want to buy it. It's thirty dequins."

It was the *Book of Circles* that Jaldis had put a come-back spell on, in the attic of the Black Pig.

NINE

"RHION!" THE SHARP RATTLE OF PEBBLES STRIKING THE JAL-
ousies startled him from sleep. The room was suffused with
the moonstone pallor of very early morning, the window at
the far end a blurred screen of silver-shot grisaille, the air
tender. The voice had been human, a hissing attempt to com-
bine a whisper with a shout, not the buzzing tones of Jaldis'
box.

And indeed, all that was visible of Jaldis was a hunched
twist of bone and white hair beneath the single sheet of the
other cot, rising and falling with the slow, steady rhythm of
sleep.

Rhion rolled hastily to his feet and, clutching his own
bedsheet about him and fumbling his spectacles onto his
face, hurried to the window. Outside, Shuttlefly Court was
drowned in shadows still, though the sky overhead was the
color of peaches, the hills beyond the roofs like something
wrought of lavender glass.

Tally was down in the square, standing up in her mare's
stirrups with trails of sugar-brown hair floating mermaidlike
from under her cap.

"Could you really hit my window from down there?"
Rhion asked softly, as—decently robed and scratching at his
beard—he let her in downstairs a few moments later.

"Of course. Can't you?"

"I couldn't hit it from inside the room with the shutters

143

closed. You shouldn't have brought your horse. You rarely see good horseflesh in this part of the city. People will notice . . .''

"I left the charm you gave me tucked under the saddle blanket." She dropped into one of the rickety kitchen chairs and disengaged a small bag from the voluminous pocket of her green riding-habit. "I brought coffee."

"Dinar of Prinagos has just won my unqualified support against the perfidious White Bragenmeres under any circumstances, at any time, in thought, word, deed, spell, and incantation." Rhion tweaked open the bag and, holding it cradled in his hands, inhaled deeply and lovingly. Their small stock of coffee—copiously adulterated with dried acorns— was another of the things left behind in Felsplex. Beans like these they had not been able to afford since their days in Nerriok, when they'd been patronized by nobles of the court.

"I also brought all the little doings," she added, getting up to fetch cups from the shelf while Rhion set the sack down and went to dip water into the kettle from the big—and now mostly empty—jar in the corner. "A grinder and a strainer and sugar and cinnamon . . ."

"Will you marry me?" The jest was out of his mouth before he could stop it, and she looked around swiftly, their eyes meeting, and for one flashing second it wasn't a jest.

"Forget I said that," he apologized quickly, which only made it worse. She looked away and he saw the color rise to the roots of her hair. He knew he should say something, make some other light remark to cover his own confusion and hers, but the air between them teemed with unsaid words, with possibilities unthinkable, like tinder which a spark would set ablaze.

The women he had loved had all been affairs of affection, begun in the knowledge that, as a wizard, he was legally a dead man with no position in the laws of any of the Forty Realms—unable to marry, unable to hold property, unable to enter business or trade or to sign a binding contract. And yet looking at this girl . . .

She took a deep breath after far too long, set down the cups on the table, and stammered, "Will . . . I suppose the talisman you gave me *will* keep people from noticing a full-grown horse?"

"I'm not sure," he said, gladly accepting the offer of a straight line. "It might keep them from noticing half of it but then the rest would be awfully conspicuous."

She giggled, her painful blush fading; to the relief of both, the moment passed in laughter.

"Where'd you learn to make coffee like this?" she asked a few minutes later, when he poured the inky, bittersweet liquid into the bottoms of the two red-and-black Sligo cups which were much too large for the tiny quantity to be consumed. "If wizardry ever quits paying, you really *will* be welcome in my father's service."

"What do you mean, if wizardry ever quits paying?" Rhion demanded in mock indignation. "For one thing, as you may have noticed, wizardry *doesn't* pay, and for another, making good coffee *is* wizardry. Why do you think I've been apprenticed to Jaldis for ten years? Because I like climbing over slippery roofs in the snow? No," he added, fishing in another lidded pot for yesterday's bread and putting it and the small jar of honey on the table between them. "It's just one of those things rich young men are supposed to learn, like dancing."

"I know." Tally gravely spooned enough honey onto her bread to satiate a regiment of bees. "My deportment master used to crack me over the elbow with his stick if I didn't curve my arm properly when I weighed out the sugar or added the cinnamon. My brother Syron has to put up with all that now." She held the spoon high above the bread for the sheer joy of watching that lucid amber curtain flow to its destiny. "Were you a rich young man?"

"Once upon a time." Rhion smiled, remembering the ruby doublet buttons which he'd cut off to buy the opals and gold for Jaldis' spectacles. Somewhere in the maze of courts, a rooster crowed. The mare nickered outside their door, the sound loud in the thin cool of morning. Other than that, the square was silent. Even Mistress Prymannie had not come out to unshutter her schoolroom. The rich smells of coffee and cinnamon mingled with the faintly prickly velvetiness of dust, the steamy whiff from the laundry in the next street, the odor of privies and stale cheap cooking, a strange, slubbed tapestry of fustian and silk.

"Well," Rhion went on more briskly, "did you just come to see me because your father's cook can't make a decent cup of coffee, or . . ."

"My father's cook makes a perfectly good cup of coffee and would demand that you be beheaded for treasonable utterances if he heard you say different. But," she went on, "I've figured out what to do about Damson. And she's agreed."

"I'll have to talk to her about that," he warned, and Tally nodded.

"You will." She set down her coffee, cradling the round smoothness of the cup in her hands. Something about her matter-of-factness—or perhaps the gesture of warming her hands in the steam of the cup—reminded Rhion strongly of his sister, and he felt a curious pang when he realized that he still thought of her as a girl of fifteen . . . *She must be married long ago, with children . . .*

"There's a disused pavilion at the end of the kitchen gardens of Father's palace," Tally was saying. "You can reach it through a postern in Halberd Alley. Damson will be there tonight, masked and hooded and the whole thing. I've told her you don't know who she is . . ."

"Thank God she didn't see us when we rescued her daughter."

She ducked her head shyly, then looked back at him again with her gray eyes bright. "I thought that, yes. The house is right on the palace wall. If you didn't know it was actually connected to the palace, you couldn't tell it by looking. It really could be anywhere. That should lay to rest her fears about being blackmailed or about word of it getting back to Esrex. I told her that I told you that she was a rich merchant's wife and I was her maid, so remember to treat us that way, all right?"

"Sure thing, lambchop," he leered in his slangiest street dialect, and she laughed and shoved him playfully. For all her usual gravity there was a sparkle of humor in her eyes, lurking like a wildflower in a bed of well-bred tuberoses, and he suspected she spent a good deal of her time, as he did, explaining *Joke . . . that was a joke . . .*

Regretfully, he gave her his hand. "I think you'd better be getting back. They really *will* be wondering where you are . . ."

"I told them I was going hawking in the marshes," she said, standing up and shaking out her long green skirt. "And I really am, though it'll be awfully late by the time I get there. I told Marc—Marc of Erralswan, the Captain of the Palace Guard, who's supposed to be meeting me and my waiting lady Amalie there—that I had some business to attend to in the kennels and that we'd be late. Amalie will cover for me. She's getting the hawks and will tell them at the mews . . ."

"You're full of tales today, aren't you?" he teased, as they passed beneath the suspended thickets of drying herbs towards the door. "First you're posing as your sister's maid, now you're playing cross questions with your escort . . ."

"Well . . ." When she averted her face that way she looked like a very dignified ten-year-old caught raiding the jam. "Didn't you do that?"

She put her hand to her cap, a modest little thing his sister would have called paltry. He'd seen the wealthy virgins of

Bragenmere sporting cap wings that would have lifted them out of the saddle if they'd ridden at any speed, had some of the wearers not been a solid half-hundredweight heavier than they should have been, that is. But not Tally. She was too thin, if anything, with scarcely more breast than a gawky boy. The light of the open door, strong now that the sun was slanting down over the tiled roofs, cast a gauzy crescent against her cheek and made the amber of her necklaces glow like the honey that still dabbled the plates on the table behind them.

He smiled again. "All the time."

Catching his eye, Tally laughed again, brightness passing across her face like spring sunlight in the Drowned Lands, breathtaking, fragile, and swiftly dimmed. "I don't like to," she sighed. "There'd be a hideous to-do if I was found out."

"To put it mildly, yes."

Across the square beyond her shoulder, boys and girls were arriving to school, loitering outside in their clumsy wool and serge clothing or chasing stray chickens in the weeds. Knowing from his own schooldays how easily anything other than lessons will hold a child's attention, Rhion drew about himself and the girl, and about the mare standing with reins hitched to the cottonwood post, a thin, numinous aura of Look-Over-There.

Tally's mouth, well-shaped without being either full or soft, tightened, the dimple beside it flexing again into a tired line. "It's just that . . . They want so much of you, you know?" Her gesture failed, half-made. "And I want . . ." She shook her head, scanning his face helplessly, not sure, in fact, what it was that she did want.

"To be alone?" The incessant grind of his father's demands seemed to echo along the corridors of his mind—learn this, help me with that, meet all the right men and be sure to be friends with their sons . . . And his mother's hands forever straightening the already-perfect set of his sleeves, her fussy disappointment in him pursuing him wherever he went.

"Sometimes." Her face softened again. "And sometimes . . ." She broke off once more, her eyes on his, and he understood, and she knew he understood. It had to do with music, some of it, and some of it with silence, but there was no clear word for what it was that she sought. His hand moved instinctively to touch hers, but he thought twice and closed his fist instead.

She turned quickly from him. "I'll come for you after dark."

And Rhion, reaching out with mind and magic, nudged the schoolmistress into a bustling fit of self-importance, so that she fussed the last of her pupils into the building and got them seated, distracting their minds from the sight of Tally mounting her mare and reining away across the court.

As Tally had promised, the pavilion near the kitchen gardens could have been any small house in the Upper City, with its modestly slanted roof of red tiles and its pale stucco bleached silver by the light of the bright spring stars. After the eternal mists of the Drowned Lands, the dry, hard brightness of the air in the Mountains of the Sun made everything seem slightly unreal, like a child's drawing; every weed stem growing along the alley walls and every pothole and broken brick in the road were distinct, even in this wan and shadowy light. The air was redolent with the flower and vegetable markets a few streets away, with the smells of the Duke's extensive stables, and with dust and garbage. Here at the back of the palace complex, the walls lacked the intricate ornamental brickwork, the tiled niches, and the marble statuary that characterized its front, and Rhion guessed as they climbed the tiled steps from the little pavilion's hall that the place had been built originally to house some married stablemaster or chief cook and his bride.

The light of the single candle in Tally's hand darted fitfully over painted rafters and bright frescoes on the walls and glinted on the spectacles hidden deep within the shadows of Jaldis' concealing hood. "Can we get ourselves seated before she comes into the room?" Rhion whispered. "That way, with luck, she won't see him standing up at all to know he's crippled."

Tally nodded. They were all cloaked and hooded like conspirators in a cheap street-corner melodrama—Jaldis had shifted his voice-box up onto his back, so that its smooth roundness, combined with a deliberately assumed crouch, gave the impression that he was hunchbacked; in place of his crutches he leaned on a long staff, and upon Rhion's arm.

"Good idea . . . Drat this mask—it won't stay tied . . ." She set her candle on a pine hall stand to tangle with the ties of her mask, and Rhion had to stop himself from reaching to help her. Under her cloak he saw she wore the plain, black frock and short petticoat of a serving-maid, her ankles slender as willow switches above sensible shoes. "There. The light's pretty low in there; I don't think there's much danger of her recognizing either of you, once you get your mask on."

She was right about that, anyway, Rhion thought when he and Jaldis entered the room. A single candle in a crude brass holder provided all the illumination—if such it could be called—available; the candle, moreover, placed not on the oak table in the center of the room but on a sideboard, where its feeble glow would leave everyone's faces in deepest shadow. "Why do they always have the lights so low they won't be recognized?" wondered Rhion aloud, helping Jaldis to his chair at one end of the table and moving the candle to the far end of the sideboard so that its light was almost directly behind him, leaving nothing visible of his face but a black shadow within his hood. "Don't they realize wizards can see in the dark?"

He took his own seat and removed his spectacles, putting on the scarlet mask he'd bought for three dequins with some of the money Tally had advanced them and pulling up his hood again. Carnival had been over a month ago—in the slop shops of the Lower Town masks were cheap this time of year. His back was to the candle, his face toward the door, which at this distance was only a muzzy line of shadow on the wall. *Good God,* he thought suddenly, *what do I do if I can't tell Tally and Damson apart at this distance . . . ?*

But the concern was set at rest a moment later, as the hall door opened and he saw two nebulous figures framed in the darkness. He'd momentarily forgotten: one form, lithe and freemoving and graceful, was a good seven inches taller than the other.

"Mistress . . ." Rhion deepened and hoarsened his voice as much as he could and half rose to his feet to bow. Jaldis, to nonmageborn eyes a black form almost invisible in the dark, merely inclined his head.

"My maid has told you what I want?" Damson groped around for the chair back in order to sit—as far as visibility went, her identity, Rhion thought, would be safe from *this* potential blackmailer, anyway. Without his spectacles, at a distance of three feet only the fact that the boiled leather mask covering her face was silvered let him know she was masked at all. He could make out the blurred shape of lips where a cut-out had been made for speech, but couldn't have taken oath whether they were long and squared, like Tally's, or round and pouty—only that they were darkened with a considerable quantity of rouge. A dark shawl the size of a bedsheet concealed her hair. She wore a cloak over her dress, and the only way he knew there was any kind of decoration on either covering was when an occasional sequin or gem would catch the candle's light and flash in the dark like a purple star.

"A philter, she said," Rhion replied. "To win the love of a man."

Damson leaned forward. Her scent was patchouli with a heavy dollop of ambergris and touches of lily and spikenard. Any wizard, trained as all were in the identification of herbs by scent, could have picked it out from among hundreds. That was another thing they never thought about. "These are his." From beneath the all-enveloping cloak she pushed a silken scarf containing a big knot of ivory-fair hair-combings, and a rolled-up linen shirt. The scarf itself was worked with a pattern of red pomegranates, the house badge of the Prinagos.

Nice disguise, Sis.

"I want him to be drawn to me, to love me . . ."

"You understand," Rhion said, "that such a philter will only work for a short time? And that afterward, because of being drawn to your bed, he may be angry with you? May even hate you?"

"No." The plump woman shook her head so that the amethysts flashed in the silk of her shawl. "He thinks he hated me before, but I made him love me. He's only a boy—I know what his needs are, better than those callow hussies . . . Better than he does himself. He needs *me*, though his pride won't let him admit it . . . And in any case, what he thinks doesn't matter. If I can bear his son, he'll not be able to have me put aside."

Tally's head turned sharply; Rhion heard the catch of her breath. "Did he say that?"

"Of course he did," Damson snapped, not looking back over her shoulder at her sister, keeping her eyes on the two wizards before her like a duellist watching circling foes. "Why do you think I agreed to this in the first place? I can't let him go—*I won't let him go!* He's *mine*. I'll be whatever he wants me to be—he'll see that, once I've got him back."

"If this is true," Rhion explained patiently, "it won't be

because of the philter. If what you say is true, he may very well go on loving you afterward—or he may not. A spell such as the one I'll weave for you has only a limited, and a very specific, action, namely, a surge of unreasoning desire for you so powerful it would take an extremely strong-willed man to resist. But it cannot affect what he will feel about this desire, or about you, once its effect has passed."

"But it *will* bring him to my bed?"

Rhion sighed. He sometimes wondered why he bothered with the warning—they almost never listened. Inevitably they brushed it aside with, *But it WILL work, won't it?*

"Unless he's a very strong-willed man, or unless he has some kind of counterspell from a stronger wizard than I . . . Yes."

"That is enough, then." She sat back a little and there was a self-satisfied note in her crisp, high-pitched voice. "It's all that matters. I'll make him need me, once I'm past his silly pride—once he sees that he *does* need me. It's only his pride that makes him spiteful, anyway."

Rhion was silent. Loving and hating were so close, two sides of a coin whose name was Need. He wondered if Esrex' hate and cruelty had been weapons of defense rather than offense, a final bastion to protect himself, not only against the demands of the daughter of his enemy, but against his own lust for one whose family had already taken away from him all that he had. In that case the breaking of this last bastion of his personal integrity wasn't likely to make him any more pleasant . . .

But he didn't know and he couldn't know. And, as Jaldis had said, it was none of his business to judge.

For a moment he smelled sawdust and stale beer and looked again into cowlike brown eyes above a sequinned veil; and behind the woman at the Black Pig he saw clustered like a spectral regiment all those other encounters in darkened kitchens and inn parlors and the faces of every other man or woman who'd ever asked him to use his powers to get them between somebody else's sheets.

It all had so little to do with magic, with what magic actually was.

And Tally had asked for his help.

He held out his hand for hers. "As you wish, my lady."

"One other thing . . ." Her hand held back from his, as if fearing to touch. It was a very round, delicate little hand, all four stubby fingers and the thumb tightly ringed in elaborate confections of opal, ruby, and pearl whose design could have been recognized like a signature. "Another tincture, or powder, or spell that will guarantee that I conceive and bear a son."

In for a lamb, in for a sheep . . . Somebody might as well get some good out of this . . .

Again, Rhion inclined his head.

Of the two spells, the love-philter was by far the easiest. Rhion heaped the standard base-powder on Damson's scented hand, then feathered it onto the shirt which had been laid down like a table-cloth for him to work on, and around them wove the circles of power and need. The Gray Lady had taught him many variant spells of this kind, different mixes of ingredients, and he'd calculated which to use tonight to take into account the phase of the moon—which was four days past the third quarter—and the position of the rising stars. Having observed Damson in the crystal he knew what she looked like and was able to weave into the spells a specific hunger for that plump white body and no other, a thirst unquenchable save by the scent of her mouse-brown hair. Esrex was young, Tally had said, barely twenty—impecunious, unpleasant, bitter, and proud, but male and young. With them, he wove spells of luck and hope and the image of Damson in her husband Esrex' arms.

Jaldis, in silence save for a little cracked humming in his broken throat, wove the stronger geas, the more difficult one, a spell of conception, and, more importantly, to prevent miscarriage, accident, or the spontaneous shedding of the child in the first few fragile weeks. They had guessed that Damson would request such a tincture and had come prepared for it, remembering that she had miscarried at least one child already. With luck, the Duke's elder daughter would be able to keep her husband returning to her bed for several weeks. Unless the young man himself had become sterile, that should suffice.

And during the whole proceedings, Damson sat with her plump hands folded, the steel grip of her will almost palpable in the leaden gloom. She would have that young man, bring him to heel from his spiteful strayings! Now and then the jewels on her fingers would flash as they tightened, her protuberant gray eyes would shift behind the eyeholes of the silver mask. She was wondering, Rhion supposed, whether either of the wizards she'd hired would guess who she really was.

Only after Damson had gone, leaving behind her a fat pouch of coin, and Tally was leading them down the stairs to the postern gate once more, did Rhion relax, pulling the mask off and shaking the sweat out of his tousled brown curls, and putting his spectacles back on.

"That was well done," Jaldis murmured softly, his arthritic grip tight upon Rhion's sleeve. The night had turned cold, as spring nights did in these dry highlands; the smells of lotus and jasmine from the Duke's vast water gardens breathed through the window lattices, like subtle colors in the creamy dark. "As good a love-spell as any I ever cast."

"Great." Rhion sighed, and flexed the crick from his chubby fingers. "Just the reputation I always sought. The pimp's delight, provided my clients' husbands don't kill me." The memory of all those other love-spells, the sour sense of having prostituted himself, still clung like the redolent musk of Damson's perfume. "Why do they call them love-spells, anyway?" he added bitterly. "It isn't love, you know."

"Maybe because some people can't tell the difference." Tally slid back the postern bolts, and stood her candle in the near-by niche of the little gate god to open the door. "Or if they suspect there's a difference, they don't want to know."

In the candle's reflected light her gray eyes were troubled and sad. Without his spectacles, he wouldn't have been able to see her face during the conjuration, even had she not been masked; now he saw that she had been thinking about what she'd been watching. She'd gotten what she'd gone after—all of her life, he guessed, she had been Damson's champion: riding into the woods to save her child; seeking out what means she could to alleviate her heartbreak at Esrex' cruelty; and submerging her own thoughts in the necessity of fixing her sister's life. Clearly the steely self-will of Damson's words had troubled her deeply.

In her face, as she looked mutely at him in the shadows of the gateway, were questions deeper than could be asked here on the threshold of departure, the questions of a girl who has begun to realize that love was not what she thought it was, and magic was not what she thought it was . . . perhaps nothing was what she thought it was.

"Or maybe," she added, nearly inaudibly, "they think it really *is* love. Rhion . . ." There was sudden pleading in her voice for reassurance, for forgiveness, and for help against a revelation she would rather not have seen.

He couldn't answer. More than anything in the world he wanted to go somewhere quiet with her, talk to her, and share with her what he had seen of the muddled affairs of the human heart—and to have her reassurance against his own bitter confusion of mind. To get to know her.

But it was out of the question.

Their eyes held. The silence rang palpable as a tapped chime.

Then, aware that it was madness—cruelty to her and stupidity of the most suicidal kind to him—he left Jaldis leaning
upon his staff, and gently taking Tally's hands, brushed her
lips with his.

Her fingers crushed desperately over his, trembling and
urgent, and for an instant he felt not only her body, but her
spirit sway toward his, like a young almond tree in the wind's
embrace. In the limpid glow of the candle, he saw tears silver
her eyes; in the eyes themselves, dilate with the night, he saw
the reflection of his own desire, his own knowledge that this
should never be.

It should end here, he thought, with what little sanity was
left to him. *In all propriety—in all sanity—we should never
meet again.*

But he knew even then that they would.

Turning quickly she fled from him, brushing past Jaldis
and vanishing up the stairs in a swirl of black fustian and a
shuddering smoke-stream of tawny unhooded hair.

Quietly Rhion closed the postern gate behind them and
used his spells to shoot the bolt on the palace side. Taking
Jaldis' arm, he led the way back down the alley, making once
more for their rooms in the Old Town.

If he had still been the only son of the banking house of
Drethet, he thought, guiding Jaldis carefully along the wall
where the pavement was unbroken and the footing better, he
could have said, *Can I meet you one day in the marshes to
go hawking?* He could have put on a mask of red leather and
pheasant feathers and ridden in his sedan chair up to the
palace on carnival night, to dance with her at least. He
guessed she was a good dancer, as he himself had been once
upon a time. He could have heard her voice, if nothing else;
touched her hand . . . Gone to the market to buy the finest
porcelain flute purchasable, or a scatterbrained red hunter
pup that would please her . . .

Academically he had known when he made the decision

to become Jaldis' pupil what he was giving up. His family—
the love he bore for his sister and his friends—all rights under
law, among them the right to marry and by implication the
right to fall in love with honest women, let alone the daughters of Dukes. And his blood, the blood of a wizard born,
did not question the decision.

After a long time Jaldis' sweet, thready voice, still muffled
by the cloak, broke the silence. ''There is enough silver in
the bag she gave us,'' it said quietly, ''to allow you to get
drunk, you know.''

Rhion sighed. He had never spoken to Jaldis about Tallisett, but it did not surprise him that the old man had guessed.
''I'd only have to sober up again,'' he said resignedly. ''I
might as well stay . . .''

From somewhere off to their right—an alley, a doorway, a
window, a balcony—came the vicious slap of a crossbow
firing. Something sliced at the back of Rhion's neck, not even
hurting in that first shocked second. In his grip Jaldis' body
jarred and sagged, and turning his head Rhion saw, with a
kind of numbed immobility of thought, a small arrow standing in his master's shoulder, blood welling forth stickily and
copiously under the cloak.

Without thinking he ducked, dragging them both back as
a second bolt slammed into the marbly stucco of the palace
wall which had showed up their forms so clearly in the dark.
Metal glinted in the shadows of a second-storey porch across
the alley. In darkness that would have hidden them from other
eyes, he saw a man and a woman, street-warriors, thugs by
their dress, dodge back out of sight, crossbows and arrows
in their hands. At the same moment half a dozen ruffians
burst from the doorway beneath the balcony's shadow.

''Ambush!'' Rhion yelled, and flung the first illusion he
could call to mind—that hackneyed old stand-by, an explod-
ing ball of fire—at their pursuers, and, flinging one arm
bodily around Jaldis, staff and all, took to his heels.

He knew the arrow was poisoned. *Pheelas*-root would temporarily rob or weaken a wizard's power while leaving the rest of his mind clear, but it was expensive and hard to get. Most assassins contented themselves with cheaper alternatives, either a heavy soporific like toadwort or poppy or an outright, fast-acting poison like datura. If the poison didn't kill the wizard quickly, at least most of his concentration— if he were still conscious at all—would go into counteracting the deadly effects, leaving the assassins free to continue the assault with swords, ax-handles, chains, or whatever other hardware came to hand.

All this flashed through Rhion's mind in seconds as he half-dragged, half-carried Jaldis toward the refuge of the nearest alley. *I can't let them corner me . . .*

He collected his mind enough to fling behind him a spell of faulty aim and another one, a second later, of mechanical failure, though he was fairly certain the crossbows had been counterspelled . . . a suspicion which was confirmed by the bolt that splintered against the corner of the alley wall as he ducked around it.

Jaldis stumbled and slumped, and Rhion felt the last consciousness go out of the old man. He thrust him behind him into the shadows of a porch and caught up his staff, turning in time to strike aside the jab of the nearest sword. His father had never believed in weaponry training for the sons of the merchant class, and Rhion had been far too lazy, and far too much of a dandy, to oppose him in this opinion. It was Shavus the Archmage who, during his first year with Jaldis, had beaten into him the rudiments of self-defense. He swept the sword-thrust aside and reversed the staff to jab and sweep at the man coming at him from the other direction, straddling Jaldis' fallen body and trying frantically to call to mind some spell—any spell—to help him.

But it takes a trained warrior to fight unthinkingly. Backed almost to the wall, slashing with his stick at the five swords which surrounded him in a hedge of steel, Rhion could call few options to mind. A wall of fire in the circumstances wouldn't work—they were too close—and with Jaldis down an explosion of white light would not buy him enough time to get the old man on his feet and drag him away.

Desperately, he flung a spell of pain at them, the tearing and spasming of the organs of their bodies, but it took a powerful mage to do real damage in a short time. One of the men swore sharply, and he saw blood begin to trickle from the woman assassin's mouth, but her eyes hardened to an iron fury and she redoubled her attack. He'd now put them in a position of having to kill him to end the pain—and they knew it.

The Magic of Ill sapped his concentration, too. A sword-blade, slicing through the longer guard of the staff, cut his arm before he could catch its wielder on the side of the head; he had to whirl to block on the other side, ducking and weaving and hoping none of them had a projectile. If he didn't have to carry Jaldis, he might just be able to escape, he thought . . . if he wasn't defending a corpse already . . .

One of the men stepped back from the fray and unshipped a weighted chain from his belt. It lashed out at Rhion like the tongue of a hellish frog, and he was only barely able to avoid having his weapon pulled from his hand. As he turned to block another sword cut, the chain snaked out like an iron whip and crashed across his ankles, dropping him to his knees. He struck back hopelessly, knowing he was finished . . .

And the assassin lunging down at him cried out suddenly and turned, cutting at the two men who had appeared, seemingly out of nowhere, in the alley behind them.

The newcomers were both big men and clearly trained to arms. The shorter of the two, a black-and-red ribbonwork doublet bulging over shoulders like a bull, drove his blade through the woman assassin's chest and shoved her aside like a straw training dummy; the other man, wearing a soldier's short crimson tunic, pulled off one of the two men bearing down on Rhion, and Rhion struck upward at the remaining one, catching him in the solar plexus with the end of his staff and sending him crashing against the wall. In the dark of the alley there was a momentary confusion of struggling shapes. Then the assailants collected their wounded and fled, vanishing around the corner or swarming over the nearest wall, leaving behind only a few splashes of blood in the dirt, vegetable parings, and mucky straw of the porch.

Rhion, still crouched gasping over Jaldis' body, realized dimly that blood was streaming from a cut on his own arm, hot against the cold of suddenly opened flesh. The back of his neck burned where the arrow barbs had slit it, and he felt sick and faint. The man in the ribbonwork doublet came swiftly to him, calling back over his shoulder "Don't bother, Marc!" to his companion, who had started to go in pursuit.

Rhion pulled his arm away from his savior's investigating hand, and shook his head. "Jaldis . . ." he managed to say, turning his master over and feeling at the lined, slack face.

Jaldis still lived. Rhion felt quickly at the veins in his throat to make double sure, then fumbled at the arrow still in the old man's shoulder. Waves of faintness were sweeping him, his vision narrowing to a tunnel of gray at the end of which stood the arrow, like a signpost on some strange dream path rising out of the little mound of blood-soaked brown wool.

"Poison . . ."

"Easy," the big-shouldered man said, kneeling at his side.

Again Rhion shook off his help, forcing his racing heart to slow with an effort of will, collecting a spell of healing around himself. His hands were shaking as he pulled his knife from his belt and slashed Jaldis' cloak and robe to reveal the blue-veined white flesh, smeared with the dark welling of blood. Marc, the soldier, had come back, much the younger of their two rescuers, tall, handsome, and good-natured, if rather stupid-looking. He wore the crimson cloak, tunic, and gilded leather cuirass of the Duke of Bragenmere's guards, and Rhion remembered where he'd seen him before: in the crystal last winter, hunting with Tally on the Imber hills. *Marc,* Tally had said. *Marc of Erralswan.* He was carrying a small bronze lantern, and its light splashed over the porch behind them. Rhion realized for the first time that it was—by the straw and oat-grains everywhere on the pavement—the rear porch of the Duke's stables.

The older man was helping him pull aside Jaldis' gore-soaked robes. He paused at the sight of the rosewood sound-box with its tangle of talismans glittering in the lantern-glow and looked across at Rhion with surprise in his handsome, fleshy face. "You are wizards," he said.

Rhion nodded, and raised a shaky hand to straighten his spectacles. "But don't worry," he dead-panned. "Even wizards don't turn around and put curses on people who've saved their lives."

"Don't they?" The man's teeth were very white against his healthy tan when he grinned; his black hair, carefully curled and smelling of expensive pomade in spite of the sweat that dripped from its ends, still retained a milk-white narcissus or two from an aftersupper crown. "Aren't they like other men after all, then? Marc, call a couple of the guards and get these two inside. Call Ranley, too . . . my personal physician," he explained, as Marc, leaving the lantern, disappeared through a postern into the stables themselves.

He held out a warm, strong hand to Rhion, thick with jeweled rings. "I am Dinar Prinagos, Duke of Mere."

TEN

IN HIS SUBSEQUENT ACCOUNT OF THE AMBUSH RHION OMIT-
ted mentioning to the Duke just what he and his master had
been doing in Halberd Alley at that time of night. He said
only that they had been returning from an errand in the Upper
Town, and the Duke, a man of great courtesy, did not ask
further. Rhion wasn't sure how much either Tally or her sister
had confided in their father; but, remembering his dealings
with his own father, he guessed it hadn't been much.

While the Duke listened gravely, his face crossed by the
swift, purposeful shadows in the guest room's mellow lamplight, his physician—a perfectly orthodox, black-robed little
representative of Alucca, God of Healing—removed the arrowhead from Jaldis' shoulder, and an assistant bound up
Rhion's slashed arm.

"And you have no idea who might have wanted to slay
you?" If he did not, Rhion reflected, use the word "murder"—since technically it was not murder to kill a wizard—
at least the word he did use was one that applied equally to
man as well as beast.

Rhion shook his head. On the guest room's narrow bed
Jaldis was slowly returning to consciousness, white hair
spread out over the pillow and voice-box lying under one
frail hand. Though too weak to use it, he had refused to be
parted from it. For years he had lived in fear of losing either
it or his spectacles, mostly, Rhion suspected, because he

163

doubted he had enough strength to create replacements. Under the bandages, his naked flesh looked almost transparent, sunk against knobby bones like damp silk draped across a pile of sticks. Though the tall windows were open upon a small garden court, the room, airy and small, smelled of herbed steams and of the medicines the physician had given to counteract the effects of the foxglove he had smelled on the arrowhead, odors which did not quite mask the smell of blood.

"Marc," the Duke said, half-turning in his chair of silvered poplarwood. The young Captain stepped over from the door where he'd stood. "Send some of your men out to the houses of Lorbiek the Blood-Mage, and Malnuthe the Black—that Ebiatic who lives in the Shambles—and May the Bone-Thrower down in the Kairnside shanties, and let them know what happened. It's frequently the case," he added to Rhion, as the young soldier departed on his errand in a dramatic swirl of crimson cloak, "that when people take it into their heads to murder wizards, they attack several at roughly the same time, wanting to make a sweep of it, you know. It's happened before, I'm sorry to say."

Rhion nodded. In their first month in Felsplex they'd gotten a warning from another Morkensik wizard in the town that a mob was out to *fruge* wizards, but nothing had come of it. As far as he knew the woman who'd given them the warning hadn't contacted either the local Hand-Pricker or the Earth-witch who operated in the same quarter.

"Believe me," the Duke went on, "I'm truly sorry such a thing came to pass in my realm. I believe—I've always believed—that, as long as they use their powers for good and as long as they don't interfere with other men's affairs, wizards have every right to live and study free of interference."

Rhion scratched at a corner of his beard. "I'd be lying if I said I didn't agree with you."

The Duke's eyes twinkled appreciatively. "You may have

heard that I'm a scholar," he said. "Or a dilettante, at any rate, who'd like to be a scholar and who can now afford to surround himself with scholars . . ."

"No," Rhion said quietly. "No—'scholar,' unqualified, was the word I heard used, actually."

And to his surprise the Duke blushed with pleasure. "Well, whether it's true or not it's good of you to say so." He wore a dandy's elaborately ribboned doublet and a broad necklace of goldwork and rubies that must have cost the price of a small house, but his weapons—dagger and short sword— were by a smith whose name and price Rhion recognized at a glance, a man whose fame stemmed not from ornamentation.

"In any case," the Duke went on, "I know enough to know that learning, and the structure of the universe, rather than spells and cantrips, is the true study of wizards, and I also know that a man would be a fool to pass up the chance to taste a little of that knowledge. If any person threatens you again, or you have cause to believe yourself in danger—or if you learn who is responsible for the attack upon you to-night—let me know, and believe me, I will do for you all that I can."

Rhion nodded again. He had his own suspicions about who had been responsible for the attack, but it would hardly do to suggest to the man who had just saved their lives that his own daughter had hired assassins in order to prevent blackmail about a love-philter to get her errant husband to sleep with her—particularly if the father was the one who'd selected the husband in the first place. And besides, as he had told Tallisett, like physicians, the Morkensiks were sworn to secrecy by their vows.

So Rhion contented himself with their being carried home in a couple of sedan chairs by the Duke's slaves, escorted by Marc of Erralswan and a handful of guards.

By the time they got to Shuttlefly Court, it was close to

dawn. Most of the prostitutes who hung around the Baths of Mhorvianne on Thimble Street had gone, and the mazes of little courts that made up the Old Town were silent and dark. Rhion followed Marc and the two guards who supported Jaldis up the rough ladder to the upper floor and made sure the old man was comfortable in his bed. He had amplified the physician's tinctures with spells of healing, though he could tell the man's remedies to strengthen the heart and cleanse the blood were sound. Jaldis already seemed better, though far too ill to speak.

He himself was shaking with fatigue and the chilled aftermath of shock as he descended once more to the stuffy darkness of the kitchen to see his escort to the door. His arm hurt damnably, and the remains of the poultice they'd put on the back of his neck where the arrow barbs had cut stung as if they'd laid a burning iron in the flesh. As the bearer slaves—eight big, strapping men with the brown complexions of southerners—were picking up the litter poles to go and the guards were exchanging a few final remarks with one of Rhion's fair neighbors who happened to be coming home from work at that hour, Marc of Erralswan paused in the patchy, dust-smelling darkness of the arcade and, leaning down to Rhion, whispered, "The Duke mentioned love-spells . . . Do you deal in them? There's a girl at Court, one of the Duchess' waiting maids . . . I realize you're probably tired now, but if I came back tomorrow evening do you think you could . . . ?"

After bidding him a polite good-night Rhion laughed, with genuine amusement only slightly tinged by exhausted hysteria, all the way back up the stairs.

The Duke was as good as his word. A messenger arrived the following day, his stiff politeness speaking volumes for his personal opinion of those his master chose to patronize, inquiring after Jaldis' health and asking him to dinner at the palace the following week, so that the Duke might better apologize for the ignorance of his subjects. "And might demonstrate his protection, to anyone who is interested, while he's about it," Jaldis mused, who was well enough to sit up in bed, his shoulder bandaged and a sheet over his knees.

"Well," Rhion commented, perched tailor-fashion on the other bed with the remains of his master's breakfast tray, "he also sent this." He bounced in his hand the small leather sack which had accompanied the message. It jingled with the comfortable sweetness characteristic of the nobler metals. "So you can afford to get yourself a new robe. I wonder why we didn't think of hiring assassins to beat us up before?"

"Possibly," his master returned disapprovingly, "because in most cities, passing strangers, once they knew who and what we were, would have been likelier to participate in the fray on the side of the assassins."

The dinner was an intimate one, the company comprised of the Duke, his pale, fair-haired Duchess and one of her ladies, Ranley the physician who, like his master, was genuinely interested in the metaphysical underpinnings of the visible world, Tallisett, and Syron, the Duke's thirteen-year-old son and heir. "You must excuse the absence of my older daughter and her husband," his Grace said, seating Jaldis on the spindle-legged chair at his side and himself placing the supper crown of red anemones on his brow. "Her husband, my nephew Lord Esrex, is indisposed tonight, and she has remained with him in his rooms to bear him company."

"And on the whole," Tally murmured as she passed behind Rhion on her way to her own seat beside her brother, "that's probably just as well."

Musicians played through supper, preceding each course with a trilling fanfare; afterward the talk went late. The Duchess, who despite her gracious efforts to seem interested had begun to wear the frozen-faced expression that comes of stifling yawns before the fish course was finished, departed with her lady and her son as soon as the slaves had carried out the finger bowls on the heels of the last sorbets. "My poor darling." The Duke smiled, when the crimson door curtains had fallen softly shut after them and the pad of their slippered feet had faded on the white honeycomb of the hallway tiles. "She is an educated woman and not at all prejudiced, but her tastes run very much to poetry and political philosophy, not to the mathematics of planetary movement or variations in the forms of snails and fish. And Syron, of course, isn't interested in anything he can't either ride or make come after him with a sword. I suppose at his age it's natural; all I can do is try to teach him, if not my interest in, at least my tolerance for powers and abilities he can not himself possess."

"Oh, I don't know," Rhion said. He'd had a long discussion with the boy on the subject of the general irksomeness of dancing lessons, and Syron had expressed undisguised astonishment that a wizard's apprentice had ever been subjected to anything so mundane. "He did ask me if it were possible to lay spells on a dog to drive away fleas, so it shows he's thinking."

"Is it?" Tally asked curiously. "Possible, I mean. Because my dogs suffer something cruel in the summer."

"Of course," Rhion said, "The problem is that for the spell to last more than a few days, you have to shave the dog and write the runes on its skin, and even then they don't work for more than a couple of weeks."

"Oh, the poor things!" Tally laughed, evidently picturing her own red and gold bird-hunters naked and crisscrossed with magical signs.

"Why is that?" the Duke inquired, leaning forward as a slave entered with brazier, grinder, and pot, and the room was slowly filled with the languorous scent of coffee. "I mean, how does a spell like that work and why can't it be made to work indefinitely?"

And while the Duke himself poured out the aromatic liquid into tiny cups, and Jaldis explained the problems inherent in causing fleas to believe that a certain dog was actually made of copper, Rhion's eyes met Tally's across the table in an unspoken comment on the Duke's cook's coffee, and they both had to look aside to keep from giggling.

After that, Jaldis was asked to dine at the palace fairly frequently—as often, Rhion guessed, as the Duke was not required to entertain nobles who might have objected to the presence of wizards at his board or members of the various priesthoods who most certainly would have done so. A nobleman who was seen too often in the presence of mages frequently came under suspicion of using the wizards' powers to oppress his subjects or spy upon his neighbors, just as a businessman was usually suspected of using wizardry to ruin his rivals, or a shopkeeper, to cheat his customers. And the Duke, tolerant man that he was, was still a usurper, a man who had overthrown his liege lord, no matter how many years ago it had been and how badly that liege had misgoverned. He had to be careful what people said.

But in private, he did not conceal his interest in Jaldis' company, and what had started as an intellectual patronage blossomed into genuine friendship as the summer advanced. Hardly a week went by that a messenger did not arrive at Shuttlefly Court with a gift: food from the Duke's table, game birds, fatted beef, or the sweet-fleshed orange fruits of the south; coffee; sometimes lamb and rabbit skins beautifully cured for the making of talismans, or small gifts of silver and gold.

In gratitude for this, on the last night of April, the night of Summerfire, Jaldis did what he had not done since he'd been court mage to the ill-fated Lord Henak in Wemmering—he agreed to use his magic to enliven the Duke's Summerfire masking.

To Rhion's surprise and delight, Jaldis abruptly taught him

a whole new series of spells of whose very existence he had previously been ignorant, and together the two of them spent three days manufacturing and ensorcelling a powder of nitre, crushed herbs, pulverized bone, and silver, which the servants of the Duke then dusted over every tree and shrub in the palace's garden.

"What'll it do?" Tally asked, pacing at Rhion's side down the graveled path that skirted one of the garden's canals.

Rhion laughed. Morning sunlight filtered warm on their faces through the overhanging lime trees; the small lawns that lay between copses of willow and myrtle and jacaranda glittered with quick-burning dew. Tally had offered to guide him through the maze of pools to the small grotto that marked the garden's farthest corner, and on all sides they were surrounded by the bustle of the upcoming fête. Slaves were stringing garlands around the cornices of the little gazebos and shrines, pulling the ubiquitous, spiky leaves of dandelions from the miniature lawns, plucking pondweed from among the miles of waterlilies and setting up tables for buffets or platforms for musicians. Others—with a disgruntled air and suspicious care—were dusting the faintly musty-smelling powder over rosebush, laurel, and linden tree that made up the intricate knots of foliage at the crossings of the shaded paths.

"Theoretically," he said, "it'll glow. It's one of those silly, useless spells that someone came up with and handed down, something only a court wizard out to delight the heart of his patron would think up in the first place. I'll show you . . ."

Tally led the way down a twisting path that turned from the ponds, leading through a myrtle grove and around the side of an artificial hill crowned with gum trees. A tiny pavilion had been built out of one of the hill's sides, its domed roof half-covered with mounded earth which supported full-grown trees and dangling curtains of flowering vine. Doves fluttered, cooing, from beneath the eaves as they entered, and far in the back, where the marble walls gave way to rock, cool even in the summer heat, a fountain whispered its secrets to the dark.

On a bench of green porphyry and bronze that stood near the fountain's rim Rhion set down the satchel he'd been carrying, and took from it the things he'd prepared the night before: long slips of beaten silver inscribed with traced runes; three milky lumps of rose quartz the size of his thumb; candles; chalk; and half a dozen tubes of glass in which, capped with red wax, tiny rolls of parchment and leather could be seen.

"This," he said, "is a talismanic resonator—or it will be, when I've got it assembled." He knelt beside the bench, and Tally sat on the fountain's rim, pulling off her big straw gardening hat and letting her hair hang down in a big sloppy fawn-colored braid, like a child's.

"After the feast," Rhion went on, "your father's going to announce the masking. Everyone goes outside, to find the terrace dark. The maskers are assembled just below the terrace steps, and under the terrace itself, in that huge room where they keep the orange trees during the winter, is Jaldis, weaving a spell—and it's not a very complicated one—that will make this particular combination of bone and silver glow in the dark."

His hands worked while he spoke, quickly weaving the thin strapwork of ensorcelled metal into the proper patterns around the quartz. He paused, taking off his spectacles to concentrate, his mind summoning the runes, the constellations of power his master had taught him; Tally was silent, observing with grave interest. For a time there was no sound but the gentle plashing of the fountain; even the stirring in the main gardens was left far behind.

At length Rhion went on. "The trumpeters strike up a fanfare, which I'll be able to hear even this far from the terrace. Jaldis speaks the word of power, I set the talismanic resonator into life, the resonator creates a field from the original spell, and in that field the stuff will glow all night. And everyone goes home saying how clever your father is.''

Tally leaned across to pick up and examine one of the glass tubes, turning the little talisman over in her long fingers. ''Why the resonator? I mean, couldn't Jaldis just put a spell on the powder?''

''He could, but it wouldn't cover anywhere near all the garden, and it probably wouldn't last all night. A talismanic resonator expands the area covered by a specific spell, and can be used to lengthen its effects as well, provided it's got talismans of power to keep it going . . . these things.'' He took the crystal tube from her hand, and with his other fingers gestured to the other talismans—not only tubes of glass and crystal, but little round discs of bone bound in gold, or slips of carved ashwood inscribed with sigils of power.

''Resonators,'' Rhion continued, ''draw one *hell* of a lot of power to keep up a field, even for a piddling little spell like this one.'' He sketched a small circle of power in silvered chalk on the flat top of the bench, closing in the strange little tangle of silver and stone. ''That's why it isn't practical politics, for instance, to keep a building illuminated all night—or even a ball of witchlight burning all night—with one.''

''Oh,'' Tally said, disappointed. ''Pooh. And I thought I'd just devised a new source of illumination . . .''

''It's been tried. Also, with some spells—and light's one of them—you get pockets in the field. In a house, for instance, illuminated with a ball of witchlight and a resonator, you might get places where someone would get lost, for no reason at all, on the kitchen stairway or on the way down the hall; or places where everyone would get furiously angry at nothing; or drop and break everything they touched. Or the pocket might draw every ant in the city to it . . . or every streetwalker. You never know.'' He set the talismans around the initial circle of power, and was silent for a time, weaving the spirals of power to include them in the greater spell.

"Why is that?'' Tally asked, when he straightened up again.

He readjusted his spectacles. "No one really knows. My guess—and Jaldis' theory—is that it's because of the impurities in the materials. A wizard's always at the mercy of the materials he has to work with. The resonator magnifies even the smallest flaws of a crystal, or the slightest traces of copper or lead in silver. Which is the reason wizards have to work with as pure materials as possible . . .''

"Is that the story, then?'' a thin, rather cold voice queried from the grotto's vine-curtained entrance. Looking up, Rhion saw the slim gray shape of Lord Esrex framed against the silken light.

He had met the youthful scion of the White Bragenmeres two or three times since the first dinner with the Duke, a slender young man not much taller than himself and perhaps six years younger, always exquisitely garbed in the height of fashion, with the coldest gray eyes he had ever seen.

Rhion's feelings about him had been mixed; knowing how wretched Esrex had made Tally over the previous winter, he had been inclined to dislike him, but sensed in him also the conflict of pride and his desire for his enemy's daughter. Mingled with this had been a kind of guilt at having been instrumental in breaking that pride—probably all that Esrex had left.

The sympathy hadn't survived their initial encounter. Esrex, coldly handsome in spite of a hairline already promising to betray him, had shown to Rhion and to Jaldis nothing but an impersonal and cutting contempt, and Rhion had observed that he treated the palace slaves—and such lesser members of the court whose lineages were not equal to his— in the same fashion. Rhion had been a little curious, up to that time, about Esrex' allegiance to the egalitarian cult of Agon, but guessed that it, too, was merely a tool.

Esrex stood now with his arm possessively around the waist of the plump little Lady Damson, whose unwontedly loose-fitting gown and smug, secret sparkle told their own tale. She said nothing, only eyed Rhion warily from the pillared porch. Rhion wondered whether it was because she guessed that he might have been the wizard who had woven the love-philter—if the assassins hadn't lied and said they'd accomplished their task—or because she was afraid, if she got too close to a mage, she'd miscarry. His beard might be recognizable—his voice almost certainly would be, if she were at all observant.

In any case her bulging eyes followed her young husband apprehensively as he descended the shallow rock-cut steps into the grotto, stepping daintily in his embroidered satin slippers with their ridiculously long, curled toes.

He stopped before the bench, and stood looking down at the resonator in contempt. "Pure silver," he commented.

"I'd appreciate it if you didn't touch it," Rhion said politely, standing up and regarding the young dandy with a wary eye. "Once the spells are in place, if the circles are crossed or broken the whole thing has to be done again."

"Is that so?"

Rhion could have bitten out his tongue with annoyance the next moment, because Esrex tucked the bouquet he carried into his belt, and, his eyes holding Rhion's in deliberate challenge, slowly removed his glove, wet his forefinger with his neat little pink tongue, and drew a line exactly bisecting the circle of power and two of the talismanic spirals, all with a slow relish of one who knows he may commit outrage with impunity because he is who he is.

"It would be a shame if Uncle's fête were a failure."

"I'm sure your aunt would think so," Rhion replied steadily, holding back the desire to slap that lipless little mouth.

Tally, who had no worries about ending up *fruged* in an alley, pushed her brother-in-law aside angrily. "Esrex, what a pill you are," she said scornfully, and he turned and regarded her like an adult contemplating the fury of a child—not an easy matter considering she topped him by an inch.

"My dear cousin," he said, holding his smudged finger to the soft harlequin sunlight that came through the vines. "Are you still so naive that you haven't guessed the real reason wizards insist on pure materials? And always, you notice, silver and gold? How much silver did your father hand that blind old mendicant—if he *is* really blind—to sprinkle into his trees? He says that was what it was for, at least."

Tally opened her mouth in angry denial, but Rhion only folded his arms and said, "Oh, probably about as much as he grants you for your monthly allowance."

Esrex' face blotched up an ugly red. "He does not *grant* me anything that isn't mine by right, witch . . ."

Rhion widened his blue eyes at him, and put a hand to his heart. "Oh, I understand that. It's a tremendous shame."

The young man's hand lashed furiously out, the white kid of the glove he held slashing across Rhion's cheek with a slap like wet cloth. Rhion flinched, then bowed even more deeply. "Ah. I see. That must make it less of a shame."

The red stains on those shallow cheekbones faded, leaving him almost yellow with impotent wrath. "You are a godless little cheat," he whispered, "and your master a whore." And turning, he stalked back toward the steps where his diminutive lady stood. The long toes of his embroidered satin slippers wobbled back and forth as he walked; it was nothing for Rhion to reach out with his mind and catch one of them underneath the other. Esrex went down with an undignified squawk, striking both bony shins on the edge of the worn stone step and tearing his white silk stockings like a clumsy schoolchild. He scrambled up as swiftly as he could, shins bleeding and eyes flaming, to meet Rhion's innocent, bespectacled gaze.

For a moment they stood there in silent impasse, Esrex almost trembling with anger, Rhion with his head inclined in solemn respect. Then furiously the younger man turned away, lashing his way through the curtain of vines and striding off across the lawn in the sunlight beyond.

"That was foolish of me," Rhion said quietly. He took a rag from his pocket, and began to wipe up the violated chalklines. "Now I'll be stuck here for the rest of the day guarding the thing."

"Tally," Damson said in her high, rather squeaky voice, "you'd better come away."

"He won't be here tonight," Tally said, disregarding her. "The cult of Agon has their own rite tonight. That's where he'll be."

"*Tally* . . ." Damson's eyes flicked nervously from her sister to the sturdy little form in the patched brown robe. "Come with me. Please. Esrex didn't mean any harm—not really. You know how prejudiced he is, and he is under a good deal of strain."

"Are you saying his 'prejudice' is an excuse for . . ."

"Tally, *please*!"

Tally hesitated for a long moment, her fine-boned face held deliberately expressionless, and Rhion guessed that things were not as they had been between the sisters. Then with a quick graceful stride she gathered her skirts and sprang up the steps. And as the two sisters crossed the lawn outside together, Rhion heard Damson's high, clipped tones floating back on the balmy stillness: "It doesn't do for you to be unattended with such a man. You know what they say about wizards seducing young girls with love-spells . . ."

Rhion sighed and shook his head. "A love-spell," he muttered to himself, digging his chalk out of his pocket again, "under the circumstances, is about the last thing I need."

* * *

The fête itself was a dazzling success. In addition to the masking and allegorical dances, there was a carousel dance of gaily caparisoned horses in which, Rhion later heard, Marc of Erralswan distinguished himself sufficiently to win the hearts and eventually the corset ribbons of several of the young ladies of the court. At the first chime of the trumpets Rhion lighted the candles of the fire circle which activated the resonator and, in the night's windless stillness, heard, like the drift of sea-roar, the gasp of admiration and delight from the assembled guests. Coming out of the grotto a few moments later, he saw the whole of the enormous garden with every tree and leaf and grass blade outlined in a fine powder of bluish light, as if the Milky Way, stretched like a banner overhead, had been gently shaken to release a carpet of diamond dust upon the world beneath. Even the lily pads and the waxy yellow blooms upon the water were touched with light, and the glowing shapes of the trees were repeated, like the magic echo of a song, in the still sable mirrors of pool, fountain, and canal.

A beautiful spell, he thought, leaning against the mottled bark of a sycamore trunk to watch the weaving of colored lights on the far-off terrace that signaled the masque. Tally would have been standing in one of the places of honor. She would have seen that first moment when the brightness began to spread, like dye in water, to the far ends of the velvet dark.

But later, when strollers passed the lightless, leafy bulk of the grotto hill, he overheard a woman mutter what a shocking thing it was that the Duke had caused magic to be used on a night originally consecrated to the Sun God, and a man grumble, "Well, you know what they say about wizards. I only hope his Grace weighted out the silver he gave them to work the trick and made sure they used it all as they said."

* * *

Esrex' insinuations came back to his mind a few days later as he and Jaldis were on their way up from the Old Town toward the palace on its rise, where the Duke had asked them to supper. They had spent the afternoon in the making of talismans from a crystal the Duke had sent them and the gold melted down from several of his coins, reveling in the ease with which power flowed into the unflawed materials.

"Why gold?" he asked now, as they passed through Thimble Lane where all the tailors and embroiderers were putting up their shutters in the gathering gloom and the lights of lamps made great ochre squares of warmth in the liquid blue dark. "I mean, why do certain materials—gold, silver, and gemstones—hold magic that way? What is it about them that makes them better than copper or tin?"

The old man shook his head. "To learn that," he said quietly, "is every wizard's dream. To understand, not only how magic works, but why. What it is . . ."

He sighed heavily, limping along on his crutches a half-pace ahead of Rhion, turning to lead the way up a narrow street and along an alley short cut that led to the great market square from which the main avenue to the palace rose. He wore his crystalline spectacles, but Rhion knew he wasn't using them to see with now and probably wouldn't do so all evening—they were worn as he sometimes wore a linen bandage, to conceal in politeness the ruin of his eyes from the other guests at supper. For the first several weeks in Bragenmere he had had Rhion take him up and down every street and every alleyway in the Old Town and the New, memorizing turnings, memorizing smells, learning to turn left just after the plashing of the fountain of Kithrak, if he wanted to reach the Joyful Buns Bakery, or that the slant of the ground immediately beyond the warm, steamy scents of the Pomegranate Bathhouse would lead him down twenty-five of his own limping steps to the herbalist from whom he bought ammonia and rue.

"We read the lists made by other wizards of what the metaphysical properties are of every herb, every metal, every jewel and fabric and wood and beast," he went on. "We know that, if one is making a staff for the working of magic, ash is the best wood to use and elm will disperse the power in all directions—cloud and sully it as well. We know that silver will hold impressions of spells, demons, and ghosts. We know that lead is impervious to nearly all magic, that tortoise-shell is necessary in any spell involving learning or memory but that no talisman inscribed upon it will work. We know that sigils inked with the feathers of a swan or a goose will be more powerful, and of a crow, less so, unless the spells be of mischief and chaos—we know that brushes or pens made of the feathers of a pheasant or a wren, or of grasses or reeds, are likely to produce spells less efficacious, more apt to have untoward results. We know that talismans will hold their power longer if they are wrapped in silk and stored in wood, and at that, certain kinds of wood. But why this all should be . . ." He shook his head.

"Could it have something to do with the energy tracks or the energy fields of the body?" Rhion asked. They had left the crowded tenements of the Old Town, and the walls on either side of the narrow streets were now those which enclosed the houses of the rich, pale pink or yellow sandstone ornamented with bright-colored tile or marble friezes and bas-reliefs white as meringues. Beyond the spikes which topped them and the blue or yellow tiles of the roofs, the heads of trees, willow and jacaranda and eucalyptus, reared like feathered clouds against the fading mauve of the sky. "I mean that there's something in the energy of a goose or a swan, that's more in tune with certain types of spells than a crow, for instance . . ."

"There is that theory," his master replied. "But it only leads back to the question of why. Energy travels in straight paths and collects in circles; certain types of energy are drawn to certain runes . . . but why, Rhion, *is* energy in the first place? Why is it humans who possess magic, and not the tortoises or elephants or crocodiles themselves? Or do they, and we are simply ignorant of what manner of magic it is?''

Rhion was silent. Trained as he had been in bookkeeping, he had a mathematician's delight in numbers and sometimes had a vague sense of seeing some kind of mathematical patterns in magic . . . only to have it dissolve when he looked more closely, like faces glimpsed in shadows on water. And the questions still remained.

''It is our business to ask why,'' Jaldis went on quietly, ''and our need. Not only to understand how to make magic work, but to understand why it works. We see its outer rules—the laws of its balance, that power must be paid for somewhere—Limitations, and the summoning of things by their true names. But we do not see its heart.''

''Yet it must have one. Everywhere we see the signs that point to it—or point to something . . .''

Far off, to their left and behind them, the nightly crescendo of market carts was in full swing around the big squares, where provisions, forbidden in the daytime on account of noise and traffic in the narrow streets, were being brought in. Now and then a slave would hurry by them as they made their way along the gently sloping alley, for the night was still early. From the top of a wall, a cat's green eyes gleamed.

''That is what I sought in the Dark Well,'' the old man continued softly, the talismans of his voice-box rattling with the rhythm of his hobbling stride. ''A glimpse of the structure of the Void and the structure of universes that drift within it, hoping that seeing, I might understand.''

''And did you?''

The old man smiled a little and shook his head.

''And the universe without magic?''

''Yes . . .'' The murmur of the box was no more than a drawn-out sigh. ''And its very existence, perhaps, will tell me more. Perhaps it is not an uncommon thing for entire worlds to lose their magic, for the magic to draw away, to depart as light departs with the falling of the night, or water with the ebb of the tide. Since we do not know what magic *is*, any more than we know what light *is*, we cannot tell.''

''But if you *had* seen,'' Rhion said worriedly, ''if you *had* learned . . . Would you then have been able to . . . to summon and dismiss *magic*? *All* magic?''

Jaldis' reply was so quiet that Rhion did not know whether he had spoken with the box at all, or whether he only heard the words in his mind. ''I do not know.''

Emerging from the alley into a wider street, they found themselves face to face with a massive building, a gateway whose black basalt doorposts were unornamented and whose shut iron-sheathed doors were unrelieved by the smallest of decorative patterns, even the rivets pounded flush and soldered. The gray granite pylons which flanked it were windowless, bare of the marble, tile, or ornamental stone courses that made gay the houses of the neighborhood—bare even of stucco, so that the fine-hewn blocks that formed it faced the street with a hard, unblinking stare, like a skull disdaining the frivolous lingerie of flesh.

Even in the warmth of the summer evening, the place seemed to radiate cold—cold, and shadow, and the mingled smells of incense and blood.

Their way took them across the street and to the lane that led up the hill on the other side. But as Rhion and Jaldis moved onto the cobbled pavement, a man-sized slit opened in the featureless doors, and a figure draped and veiled in black stepped out and raised a black-gloved hand.

''Cross back over, witches,'' it said, and its voice, thin and cold and bodiless, might have been man's or woman's, a blurred harsh tone like scraped steel. ''This is Agon's temple. The footfalls of devils are a pollution on the doorstep of the Veiled God.''

"I'm sure they must be," Rhion replied, halting in the middle of the way. Against the black of the doors, the priest was rendered nearly invisible by the inky wool robes and the sable veils that fell from the top of a tall conical headdress to cover face, shoulders, and breast. Unlike the houses of this area, the temple had no lamps outside its door, and the whole street was very dark. Had he not been mageborn, Rhion would have been nearly unable to see anything. "And it must take up all your time, making judgment calls about who's fit to walk how close to the doors—do you have a scale? Five feet for lepers, six and a half for beggars, a yard for slaves . . . ?"

"Do not jest with the servant of the Eclipsed Sun, witch!" warned the voice. "You should be ashamed to parade the streets like whores, and the Duke should take shame for permitting it. As for lepers, beggars, and slaves, Agon has a welcome for them, as he has for all who serve him, who are not the children and spawn of illusion. Now cross back over and go on your way!"

Rhion drew in his breath to speak again but the door behind the priest opened again, and two other forms stepped out—definitely men, this time, both tall and heavily muscled in spite of the massive potbelly sported by one of them. They wore the short tunics and heavy boots of common laborers and, over their heads, close-fitting black masks that covered them down to the chins. The masks had eye slits and mouth slits, as well, for the potbellied man used his to spit on Rhion's face.

Jaldis' hand tightened hard over Rhion's arm. Rhion bowed with exaggerated respect to the priest and his two devotees. "Nice argument," he said pleasantly. "Very convincing. It tells me so much about Agon it makes me want to convert." And he and Jaldis crossed back over the street and went on their way. The priest and the two massive defenders of

Agon's doorstep remained where they stood to watch them out of sight.

For a long time, Jaldis did not speak. Only when they started up the last long cobbled rise to the palace gates, ablaze with torches and gay with the crimson tunics of the guards and the yellow and purple irises that decorated their helmets, did Jaldis say, "That is why we must find that world again, Rhion. That is why someone must go there."

Rhion shivered. Part of his mind reflected that the practical upshot of all this was that he'd be moving shelves out of the cellar in the morning to make room for the drawing of the Dark Well, but part of him knew that Jaldis was right. The priests of Agon saw in wizardry what the priests of all the cults of the gods saw: a body of men and women who did not need to petition the deities for assistance, a challenge to their authority, and a living question about the way they said the world worked.

But unlike most of the other cults, which were content to thunder and jeer, the priests of Agon, if they were to hear that it was possible to do something about this situation, would bend every effort to try.

Knowing this, however, did not lift from him the nagging tug of unreasoning dread which filled him as Jaldis spoke.

"At the summer solstice," the old man said softly, "I will weave another Dark Well. I have contacted Shavus the Archmage. He will be here, he says, to help me listen, to help me cast my power through the Void, seeking out the voices that cried. And then . . ." His voice sank still further, until it was little more than the crying of the crickets or the humming of the insects in the redolent night. "Then we will see."

ELEVEN

AS A RESULT OF THE FÊTE OF THE SUMMERFIRE, THE DUKE of Mere extended a formal offer to Jaldis the Blind of an apartment in the palace, along with his pupil and servant, Rhion, called the Brown.

And Jaldis, just as formally, thanked him and refused.

"But *why*?" Tally blurted, intercepting them in the great pillared hall of the palace as they emerged after the audience. "I know you said you were an old man, and unused to courts . . . But you can't be *that* unused to them if you knew about the silver-dust trick you used for the fête!"

And Jaldis smiled, pausing in his limping stride down the flight of shallow steps to the main floor of the long marble room, regarding her as he would have looked upon his own daughter while the next set of petitioners, like enormous butterflies in court dress of green and white, ascended past them to the bronze doors. "True, my child." His monstrous opal spectacles flashed in the diffuse light that came down through the traceried windows of marble and glass. "But I could not well have said that I declined because I knew courts too well to want to become a part of one again, not even his."

The girl, realizing she had blundered, flushed pink, a color which suited her, Rhion thought. Against the elaborate doublets and gowns of the courtiers, alive with featherwork, ribbons, and beads, the plain brown robes of the two wizards stood out like hens in a coopful of ornamental pheasants;

Tally's butter-yellow gown with its embroidery of carnelian and jet must have cost the price of a good horse. She stammered, "I only thought it would be more comfortable for you here. And safer."

"And so it would be." The old man propped his crutch beneath his arm and reached out to take her hand. Looking down the length of that high-ceilinged marble room, Rhion caught a glimpse of Esrex and Damson in the shadows of the pillared space beneath the musicians' gallery and felt the young man's pale impersonal gaze like the prick of a knife in his side.

"Your father is a true friend to me and a generous one," Jaldis went on, his sweet artificial voice blending into the underwhisper of viols and flutes from the gallery. "But did I live at court, I would be under an obligation to him—how could I not be, were he my host and protector? What I gave to him last week was a gift freely and joyfully given. Though I would never feel such gifts to be a duty, still I would hesitate to put myself in a position where either of us would ever feel that it was less than spontaneous. And you know that in the celebrations for the birth of your sister's son, or when your brother enters his first warrior lists as a man, or on the occasion of your lady mother's birthday, there will be those who will expect something equal . . . or greater."

Not to mention the fact, Rhion thought dryly, *that the last time you were a court wizard, you ended up getting arrested in your patron's downfall and losing your eyes and your tongue and the use of your legs into the bargain.*

"And it is a fact," Jaldis went on, as they continued their descent toward the groups of brightly clad courtiers gossiping in the pillared hall, "that many of the great feasts of the year—the Winterfeast, the Rites of Summer, the Festival of Masks in the spring—fall upon the solstice or equinox-tides, when certain spells are possible and certain powers available, as at no other time. I know your father would not see it as a conflict, but gossip would be inevitable.''

They passed beneath the shadows of the vestibule, and Esrex, rather pointedly, escorted Damson away from danger of contamination. Even upon court occasions, Rhion noticed, Damson had abandoned the corsetry that had always given her the look of a gem-encrusted sausage, and curiously the flowing eggplant-colored silk that she now wore bestowed upon her an infinitely greater dignity.

''As I told your father, my child, I hope sincerely that my choice will not make my welcome here any the poorer, or change his friendship toward us.''

''I don't think it will,'' Tally said frankly. ''Father is just and he likes you very much. I don't think he's ever—How do they phrase it? 'Ejected from his favor', I think the term is—anyone who disagreed with him. That would be like refusing to speak to someone who outran you in a race. And in any case,'' she added, as they came to a halt before the great outer doors, ''it won't change *my* feelings toward you.''

Jaldis inclined his white head, the sunlight streaming in from outside making hair and beard sparkle like snow. ''Then, my child, you have indeed relieved one of my fears.''

And as the red-cloaked guards in their bronze mail bowed them through, Rhion's eye met Tally's again.

As the weeks advanced toward midsummer, Rhion and Tally met more and more frequently. Sometimes Tally would angle to be seated near him when the Duke invited Jaldis to supper or find him working in the Duke's great library in the octagonal tower which overlooked the main palace square; sometimes they met when a hunting or hawking party of young courtiers would encounter the two wizards as they gathered herbs in the marsh.

Or, as often chanced, Tally would steal out of the palace at first light in the summer dawns to have breakfast with Rhion in the long adobe kitchen in Shuttlefly Court.

Those times were the best. With the deep warmth of summer evenings, Rhion would frequently stay up all night, reading or studying the plants he'd gathered, working on mathematics or sigil making, and sleep in the heat of the day. In the early mornings, when he suspected Tally might be coming to visit him, he'd call to his scrying-crystal the image of her mare; if the mare was contentedly dozing in her stall, he himself would go to bed or sally forth to do the early shopping while the teeming produce markets were still torch-lit and the vegetables in the barrows wet with dew. But at least once a week—which quickly became twice, and now and then thrice—the image in the crystal would be of the rangy bay hunter trotting quietly along the streets of the Upper Town, all the little glass chips that swung from her bridle flashing softly in the pearly light; or else he'd see her standing outside the Bakery of a Thousand Joyful Buns, which stood at the foot of the palace rise, while Tally bought hot rolls.

And they would talk: of magic, of dogs; of music and mathematics, for Tally, like many musicians, had a bent that way; or she would play her flute for him softly, so as not to wake Jaldis sleeping overhead.

And after she left, to return to her dancing lessons and music lessons and dress fittings at the palace, Rhion would tell himself that these meetings had to stop before the inevitable happened. But a few mornings later she'd be back.

"They want me to get married, you know," Tally said softly one morning as the two of them sat with their backs propped on either side of the kitchen doorjamb, consuming bread and coffee and listening to the water sellers' cries in the strange, breathing coolness of summer dawn. "Father needs the alliance. He doesn't trust the White Bragenmeres, who still keep their own men-at-arms, a private army, almost. They have support among the old land-barons, the ones Father took power from when he passed laws saying they couldn't punish their serfs at their whim. And some of the priesthoods are angry at him for entertaining wizards the way he does.''

Rhion said nothing. He had been awake all night; going up through the trapdoor to the flat, tiled roof, he had practiced the spells which summoned beasts by their true and secret names, calling and dismissing geckos and sand lizards and drawing down the bats which feasted on night-flying moths. Later, as the night deepened, he had slipped into long meditation, breathing the dark luminosity of the night until every whisper of sage scent from the looming mountains, every movement of the night winds, was as clear to him as song, and he could identify the position of every rat, every lizard, every chicken and pig, and every sleeper in the crowded courts that spread all around him like a lake of grubby humanity, by the colors of their dreams.

And all that calm, all that sense of wisdom and knowledge and peace that lay like shimmering light within his hand, was sponged away as if it had never been by the thought of Tally in some other man's arms.

She was tearing the roll she'd bought into smaller and smaller fragments, not eating any of it. He knew she never ate when she was upset. Trying to keep her voice steady, she went on, ''It was stupid of me to think it wouldn't happen— that I'd be able to stay here, to live at Father's court, the way Damson is doing because Esrex and his family live on Father's allowance, and to think I could go on just . . . just practicing my music, and training the dogs, and . . .'' She shook her head quickly and did not finish the thought.

Her voice shifted quickly over Damson's name. Rhion knew that Tally's relations with her sister had been strained since that night in the pavilion, and his altercation with Esrex had not helped matters. For many years, the younger girl had been the self-appointed protector of the older. But now that all Damson's will was bent upon Esrex—now that Tally was seeing a side of her she could not champion—she was left, Rhion guessed, feeling a little bereft.

"Every few weeks another nobleman from somewhere in the Forty Realms appears at court, and there are dances, maskings, new dresses to be fitted, the same tedious small-talk, and all my friends saying, 'Well, *he* isn't so bad.' And I can't get away. I can't think. I can't just . . . just be still. I used to be able to talk to Damson about it, but . . ." She turned her face to him, her gray eyes dry but desperately sad. "There are days when I wish I had never been born."

Don't take her in your arms, Rhion thought quite clearly, his concern for her sorrow, his helpless wish to make her life other than it was, almost drowned by the thought of that tall fragile body and the way those long limbs would fold against his. *If you take her in your arms, you're a dead man. If not now, soon . . . very soon.*

But her misery was more than he could bear.

"Father's being so good about it," she went on, her head pillowed on his shoulder and her hair a pearl-twisted smoky rope across his chest. "He doesn't want to rush me, but he truly needs a foreign alliance. And he's so . . . so *hopeful* . . . every time some good-looking peabrain or some muscle-bound martinet comes strutting around. I can just hear him thinking, *Well, is she going to like* this *one, finally?* And I just . . . I just *don't*. And Damson's worse, since she's been expecting. She keeps saying, 'Oh, when you bear your husband's child, you'll know what true happiness is . . .' until I want to slap her. I wish Jaldis had never made that silly tincture."

She wanted comfort, not love. So Rhion kissed her hair, and held her, and in time sent her on her way, then went back to his studies as well as he could.

Then in the second week of June, Shavus the Archmage came.

Rhion had been away—not with Tally, for once—most of

the day. He had wandered the olive groves beyond the city walls and climbed the dry sheep pastures and the rocky mountain beyond, drenched in the hot brightness of the sun. He had observed the swooping patterns of the swallows' flight, and marked which plants grew in the rock-tanks high up the sheeptrails; in the black pockets of cool pine woods on the mountain's flank he had observed the tracks of coyote, rabbit, and deer; high up, where the grass thinned over the earth's silvery bones, he had listened to the songs of the wind. Since his stay in the Drowned Lands, a love of wood-craft for its own sake had grown in him, and he explored, observed, and practiced stillness and silence, sinking his soul into the slow baking heat and the smells of sage and dust.

He returned to the city late, though the sun had only just set; above the Old Town's crowded courts, the sky still held a fragile and lingering light. In every court, the thick blue shadows were patched with primrose squares of lamplight: clear as amber in which men and women could be seen talking, eating, and making love; or else patterned and streaked with lattices or shutters, as strange a diversity, in their way, as the stones of the stream-beds or the plants that grew beside the tanks. Everyone in the city seemed to be abroad that evening, crowding porches and balconies with skirts hiked up or tunics off, throwing dice or watching the children who ran about like dusk-intoxicated puppies through the luminous blue of the narrow lanes.

Rhion could feel the whisper of magic in the air as he turned from Thimble Lane into the court.

He checked his steps, uncertain. Between the curious dis-orientation of returning to the city after a day in the hills and the deep, restless beauty of the night itself, it was for a mo-ment difficult to be sure it was magic being worked that he felt . . .

But a moment later he was sure. And looking across the

court at his door, he saw the green glow of witchlight through its many cracks.

Jaldis, he thought.

And then, *But Jaldis is blind.*

A skiff of children swirled by him, shrieking with excited laughter at their game. In the tavern at the corner of the square, someone plucked a mandolin and began to sing. With his mind Rhion reached out toward the two little rooms in the long bank of the adobe tenement, singling them from the quiet talk, the giggles, the rattling of dice, and the creak of bedropes on all sides, probing deep, listening, scenting . . .

A man in the kitchen downstairs. A smell of maleness— not young, he thought—road dirt, trace whiffs of incense and old blood, and the crackling whisper of pages turning.

Jaldis' books.

And below that was the muffled murmur of voices whispering beneath the ground.

Cautiously, Rhion approached the door.

''Come in,'' a deep voice said from inside, before he'd reached it. ''You must be Rhion the Brown.''

As he pushed open the door, a tall, thin, brown-faced man, head shining bald as an egg in the witchlight above the cowl of his black wool robe, rose from where he'd been sitting at the table and held out an emaciated hand. ''I am Gyzan the Archer, a friend of Shavus and, alas, not to be trusted in the same room as the magic-working below.''

Rhion dropped his satchel of herbs on the table and took his hand. A huge bow of black horn reinforced with steel stood unstrung beside the cellar's rude plank door and, with it, a quiver of arrows. The cellar door itself was shut, but through its cracks now and then flickered a ghostly, shifting light.

''What are they doing?''

''Weaving a Dark Well.'' He folded his arms, regarded Rhion with wise, ironic, gentle brown eyes.

Rhion had heard it said of Gyzan the Archer that if the Blood-Mages had possessed an Archmage, it would have been Gyzan. He studied him now, noting how the long brown hands were marked all over with scars like a Hand-Pricker's, the upper joints of both little fingers missing; his lips, too, and ear lobes were scarred where spell-cords had at one time been threaded through. But unlike the Hand-Prickers he was scrupulously clean, his head shaved—there were Hand-Prickers in the Lower Town that one couldn't get near for the smell of the old blood matted in their waist-length hair—and his nails cut short; unlike them, he seemed as sane as any wizard ever was.

"Shavus is going, then?" Rhion started to unpack his satchel and, as he did so, stole a glance at the cover of the book Gyzan had been reading—not one of Jaldis', after all, but a catalogue of star-spells he recognized from Shavus' library.

"So he says. Knotweed—very nice," he added, picking up a spiky stem from among the tangle of foliage. "Good for dysentery . . . And I'm going with him."

After the first moment of surprise that Shavus would have asked a non-Morkensik—even one who had been his lifelong friend—Rhion breathed a sigh of relief. He had once offered to accompany the Archwizard through the Void, but every instinct he possessed warned him that beyond it lay dangers with which he would be absolutely unable to cope.

"A curious thing, the Dark Well," the Blood-Mage went on, turning the herbs over in his scarred fingers, feeling the texture of root and blossom and leaf as he spoke. "Is it true that it shows other worlds, other universes, than our own?"

"I don't know," Rhion said warily. "I've only seen it once, and then it was quiescent, closed in on itself. But I don't know what else it could be." The Gray Lady had questioned him about it also, before they had left the Drowned

Lands, and he had his suspicions about why Jáldis had begun the rites of its making on a day when he, Rhion, was away— well-founded suspicions, when he thought about them. Both the Gray Lady and the Archer were far stronger mages than he, and he wasn't quite sure what he might be likely to tell them under the influence of a really heavy drug or spell.

The Archer shrugged, long lashes veiling his eyes. Like many Blood-Mages, he'd had the eyelids and the flesh around them tattooed, giving them a bruised and slightly ominous appearance. "A reflection—a projection—of the way his own mind conceives the shape of the universe," he guessed. "Or an illusion, perhaps, designed by spirits whose very nature we can only vaguely guess."

Rhion knew the Blood-Mages believed in such spirits, wholly unlike grims and faes and the other bodiless Children of the Dark Air, and attributed their own magic to communication with them. As far as he'd ever heard, every Order except the Blood-Mages themselves and a few of the less sane Hand-Prickers described this belief as balderdash.

"But if it is what he says it is," Gyzan went on, raising his glance once more, "I consider it rather foolish of him— of them—to keep the means of its making and use so deep a secret. What if Jaldis were to fall ill while Shavus and I are on the other side of this Void they speak of? There is an unsteadiness to the aura he carries about his body; I do fear for his health. He is a very old man."

"I'd be here," Rhion pointed out, a little miffed.

Gyzan set down the stem of dragon arum he'd been examining and studied him for a very long time. In their blue-black bands of shadow his brown eyes narrowed, limpid and beautiful as a woman's—Rhion remembered uneasily the rumors that the man had second sight. But he only said, "Well . . . perhaps."

"Nonsense," Shavus blustered later, when he and Jaldis had emerged from the tiny cellar, long after Gyzan had gone

up the ladder to the room above to sleep. "By looking into
the Void—by looking into the darkness *outside* our universe—the Dark Well may very likely contain the clues as to
what magic *is*. Its true essence, its reality. The Void seems
to be filled with a magic of its own, a dreadful and powerful
magic, and we'd be fools to let a Blood-Mage, or those Earth-
witches in Sligo, anywhere near it."

"They're not Earth-witches," Rhion pointed out, annoyed
at the Archmage's prejudice.

"Then they're the next thing to 'em, same way the Blood-
Mages are only Hand-Prickers who bathe." Shavus did not
bother to lower his voice. Presumably he did not express
sentiments behind his friend's back that he had not also said
to his face. His thick, gray hair was plastered with sweat to
his massive skull, and his broad face, usually clean-shaven
despite its scars, was gritty with stubble. Jaldis said nothing,
only sat, bent with exhaustion, his spectacles lying on the
table before him, massaging the bridge of his nose with one
crippled hand. He looked, as Gyzan had said, very old, and
rather unwell. Rhion came quietly around the table and
rubbed the old man's shoulders and back, feeling, not tension there, but a kind of dreadful limpness.

"Besides," the Archmage added, "who's to say one of
'em won't spread the knowledge to others, the Earth-witches
or some Bone-Thrower who chances by? The Gray Lady
didn't seem to have any qualms about *you* making free with
their library."

He tore off part of the loaf Rhion had set in front of the
two of them—it was well past midnight, the court outside
steeped in the silence of sleep—and sopped the bread in the
honey pot. "You ask Gyzan how willing he'd be to let me
have the spells to contact that 'familiar spirit' of his and see
what he'd say," he went on around a sticky mouthful. "Is
there a baths in this neighborhood that'd be open at this hour,
my little partridge? Ah, well—the Duke likes to pretend

his town's a cosmopolitan city, but when all's said you can tell you're not in Nerriok. We'll be at it again in a few hours . . .''

"Will you need my help?"

"In that gopher-hole? Only if you bring your own space with you."

Rhion found himself remembering again that Shavus knew he'd been the Gray Lady's lover and that he'd been up here fraternizing with Gyzan; he felt a kind of obscure anger stir in him. But Jaldis only reached up to grasp Rhion's hand in thanks.

Whatever Shavus' reasons, Rhion did not see the Dark Well until it was completed, two days later, the day before the summer solstice itself.

It was as he first remembered seeing it in the attic of the Black Pig. Hellishly complicated circles within circles, spirals leading out of spirals, the interlinking lines of fire-circle and water-circle, blood and smoke and silver, woven together with the intricate tracings of pure light that floated above the floor and seemed to lie, glowing, several inches beneath the surface of the hard-packed damp clay. Within those circles, like a dark and beating heart, lay the strange shuddering gate of colors, as though darkness, like light, had been refracted into a rainbow . . .

And within the colors was—nothing. Quiescent, closed upon itself, the darkness had a brownish cloudiness that reminded him of nothing so much as an eye shut in sleep. Standing between Jaldis and Shavus, with his back to the crude ladder upon which Gyzan was forced to perch, Rhion felt the sweat start on his face, not so much from the stifling heat of the cellar as from a deep, primordial fear that the eye would open, would look at him and know him . . .

"Tomorrow night." Jaldis' voice was so weak with weariness as to be barely intelligible, the crippled hand clinging to his arm for support. "Tomorrow night, when midnight tilts the Universe to its balance point and lets its powers be turned by humankind . . . Then the wizards in that other world will have the power to make their voices heard. Then *we* shall open the Well, and search within.''

''Ay,'' Shavus muttered, fingering the battered hilt of the sword at his waist. ''But what we'll find—now, that's another tale.''

Jaldis spent the rest of that day, and all of the one following, either sleeping or deep in meditation, gathering his strength for the night. Shavus and Gyzan, having a standing invitation to the Duke of Mere's palace from other years, went to pay their respects, and Rhion went with them. In part he only sought to avoid the uneasiness that whispered in the back of his mind whenever he thought about the Dark Well—the dread, not of the terrible unknown of that Void of chaos, but of something he sensed he had once known and then forgotten. It was a dread impossible to leave behind, exacerbated by his growing awareness of the pull of the suntide in his blood. But in addition to that, Tally's last visit had been four or five days ago, and he had begun to be concerned.

They found the palace in a flutter of excitement over the state visit by the Earl of the Purple Forest. This lord, who ruled the greatest of the In Islands and a whole archipelago of minor isles beyond it, was one of the most powerful in the Forty Realms: garlands were being strung in the gardens again, and among the pillars of the great entryhall. As the three wizards climbed the shallow steps and passed beneath the musicians' gallery they encountered squads of slaves with wicker tubs of flowers, trailing scent like rags of gauze in their wake, and the excited talk among the courtiers in the long pillared hall nearly drowned the floating sweetness of lyre and flute.

The Earl was seated in an ivory chair of honor beside the Duke when the three wizards were presented, a handsome, muscular man in his early forties, his red hair braided and crowned with jasmine, his mouth sensual, scornful, and hard when he forgot to smile. He expressed delight at meeting so notable a mage as Shavus Ciarnin, but, Rhion noticed, Gyzan was silent in his presence. The Duke invited them to keep the feast of solstice that night among his household. As Shavus declined gracefully, Rhion reflected again that Jaldis had been right: many of the great feasts did fall upon the occasions of solstice and equinox. Had Jaldis been a member of the Duke's suite, he could not always have had those occasions to himself.

It was only when they were descending the marbled spaces of the outer hall once more that Rhion overheard a woman saying, "Well, I'm sure he was worth waiting for—so handsome! I knew she could have no fault to find with *him* . . ."

And he realized what was going on.

The Earl of the Purple Forest had come to offer for Tally's hand.

And Tally, to judge by the Duke's relieved affability and the sheer magnificence of the decorations going up, must have accepted.

He felt as if his body were filled with broken glass. That he could not move—he could not breathe—without pain.

Why are you surprised? he thought, as the blue gloom of the vestibule closed around him like the darkness veiling the sun. *She said it, the first time you met . . . "So it isn't a question of what I want . . . just when. And who . . ."*

The red-cloaked guards opened the outer doors. Shavus and Gyzan descended the marble steps, brown robes and black like eagle and raven in the bright sun of summer, the bulky form and the gaunt. Rhion found he had stumbled to a halt among the pillars beneath the gallery, standing in the shadows like a milkweed-fae that fears the scorch of the sun.

Tally . . .

For an instant he was standing on the wharf, seeing the dust-brown hair haloed by the sunlight as the water widened between him and the ship that would take her away.

You should never have touched her. Never have taken her hand.

Of themselves his fingers had sought, in his pocket, the washed-leather bag where he kept his scrying-crystal—he let go of it in disgust. *Don't you hurt enough yet?*

The guards closed the doors, not noticing the plump, bearded little man with the flashing spectacles, who stood in the shadows of the vestibule. And he was, Rhion thought, withdrawing noiselessly to the huge square base of a drum-column where the diffuse light from the larger room behind could be caught in the crystal's facets, inconspicuous enough, and easy to overlook.

He sat on the column base and, taking the crystal from his pocket, angled its flat purple-gray surfaces to the light.

As if she sat in a room behind him he saw her, reflected in the crystal's heart. She sat on a bench of green porphyry and bronze, shawled in green-dappled light. Water flickered darkly in the shadows behind her. There was no expression on her face as she stared straight ahead of her, but the red-furred hunting dog lying at her feet twisted its head around to look up at her, and pawed anxiously at her skirts. Tears crept silently from her open eyes.

"Tally?"

He paused in the shadow margin between sunlight and gloom. The vines that curtained the little pavilion's entrance had not been cut this summer and covered the space between the slender pillars like a veil of petaled green silk. The buffets, the gazebos, and the stands for the musicians were all up by the long north front of the palace, on the other side of the network of canals and linden groves. Here it was silent. The heat, though strong on Rhion's back, lacked the dense oppressiveness it would have later in the summer; the grotto's dimness was almost chilly, the plashing of the fountain unnaturally loud.

Tally sat on the bench before it, bolt upright in her simple green dress. The silver and amber at her throat flashed softly as she turned her head.

For a moment she did not move, but he saw her shut her eyes and breathe once, a thick, dragging sigh.

Then without a word, as naturally as if she had known that he would come—and perhaps she had—as naturally as if they had been lovers for years, she got to her feet and walked into his arms.

Though it was the longest day of the year, still it was dark by the time Rhion got back to Shuttlefly Court.

The grotto faced east, designed to be a place of morning sunlight and silent coolness in the long summer afternoons. It was the dog who waked them, stealing quietly back in to lie across the feet of the sleeping lovers, though he would have barked, Rhion knew, at anyone's approach. Through the pillars and the gold-edged green of the vines, the hill's shadow stretched far out over the grass, rimmed by a line of burnished light. Against his shoulder, Tallisett's face was peaceful in sleep. It seemed to him that he had wondered half his life what her hair would feel like between his fingers. It was finer than it looked for its straight thickness, soft as a child's hair.

Dear God, what have I done?

But there was nothing he possessed, or ever had possessed, that he would not have traded for this time.

"Father needs the alliance," she said, quite some time after she woke up. "And I can't . . . I can't tell him I won't. Because there's no reason to—I mean, the Earl has never been anything but polite to me, courtly and gracious. But . . ." She hesitated, struggling with her fear that what she would say sounded silly. But at length she blurted out, "Rhion, his *dogs* are afraid of him! We all went hunting one morning—I could see. But he's never said a wrong word . . . Father likes him . . ."

And she clung to him again, as if he had saved her from drowning.

Still later she said, "I didn't want this to be something that had never happened."

Rhion nodded, his lips pressed to her hair. Their talk covered hours, a sentence or two at a time, and then long spaces where the only sound was the mingled sibilance of their breathing, the clucking of the fountain, and the occasional stir of breezes in the vines.

Gently, he pointed out, "He's going to know about it. At least, he'll know there was someone . . ."

"Do you really think he's going to give back the dowry over a little blood?"

Rhion remembered the Earl's sensual lips and cynical eye. "No," he said slowly, thinking how much of her naïveté Tally had lost even since he'd met her in the icy winter woods. To himself he added, *But he's going to hold it over you for as long as you live.*

"And so long as I'm not with child . . ."

"Don't worry." Rhion managed a faint grin. "That, at least, is something wizards know how to prevent."

"Oh, Rhion . . ."

He gathered her hands together in one of his, and held them against his chest. The dog padded over to the fountain's edge, sniffed about a little, and settled itself leggily down onto Rhion's crumpled brown robe. The rim of light on the grass drew farther and farther away, then began to fade.

It was two or three hours short of midnight when Rhion reached home, to find Shavus pacing angrily, muttering oaths, back and forth down the length of the narrow kitchen, while Jaldis sat very quiet in his chair near the cold hearth.

"God's teeth, boy, where were you?" the Archmage exploded when Rhion let himself in. "Bird-nesting? I haven't spent three days weaving spells in a hole in the ground to have you spoil things by not showing up in time!"

"But I am in time," Rhion pointed out. From long watching of the stars he knew subliminally to within a few moments when midnight was, even on ordinary nights, and Shavus knew he knew. And to a wizard, the night of the solstice was not even a matter of subconscious calculation. He could feel the tide of the sun and the stars turning, pulling at his blood and could feel the draw of magic flowing along every energy-path on the earth, in the grass, or in his body, in a glittering whisper of half-heard music in the sky.

All over the city, as he had made his way home, he had been conscious of the magic in the night. Most of the great cults were holding some kind of special rite on this, one of the major turning points of the year. He had passed procession after procession in the streets: the golden image of Darova in her glittering boat, surrounded by torchlit banners and by the shaking tinkle of sistrums; and the white-draped priestesses of Shilmarglinda with roses in their hair and their little boy dolls in their hands ready to be tossed onto the temple fires. Every tavern where the warriors who followed Kithrak forgathered blazed like a bonfire, and in even the windowless granite monolith of Agon's temple there had been the suggestion of hidden movement.

Every wizard in the city would be preparing some special ceremony, the charging of talismans or the deep scrying for some sort of knowledge, taking advantage of the additional power that moved in the air that night. Children raced excitedly about the streets, eyes bright under tousled hair, waving candy or flowers in their grubby fists. The very air seemed to crackle.

And Tally had come into his arms.

It took all Rhion's training, all the concentration disciplined into him by years of meditation, to tear his mind from the image of her rising from the bench in the grotto's darkness, walking to him . . . It took all his will not to return again and again to the memory of her lips first pressing his. Of her hair untangling from its pearled net beneath his fingers . . .

She was his.

Only for two months, part of his mind said. Only until the dowry negotiations are complete.

But a part of his soul knew that she would always be his.

And he was aware of Gyzan the Archer looking at him with a kind of pitying sadness as they descended the ladder to the black of the cellar below.

Through the odd clarity of deep meditation, Rhion watched Shavus step to the edge of the earth circle, where the great sun-cross of magic's eternal power had been drawn, and lift his scar-seamed hands. Within the woven circles, something seemed to shudder and move, the blackness deepening, clarifying, and breathing of matters unsuspected and better left unsuspected in the realms of mortal kind. Panic struggled to surface in Rhion's heart as he saw the Dark Well opening, the livid rainbow of refracted darkness parting, widening, like the opening heart of a black crystal rose. Darkness opened into greater darkness, abysses at whose bottom new abysses gaped. A dream . . .

Cold wind stroked his face, and he shut his eyes. Midnight was upon them, the power of it crying in his blood; all his will, all his strength, he concentrated into the rite of summoning that power, calling it from the bones of the earth, from the silver tracks of the leys, and from the shuddering air and the turning stars. From the four corners of the hollow earth the wizards called it, feeding it into the crippled old man who limped forward to the edge of the chasm, opal spectacles reflecting the hellish rainbow of darkness as he gazed within, listening, seeking . . .

But whether it was because Rhion's concentration was distracted by what had passed that afternoon or because Jaldis himself was exhausted by the three days of spellweaving which had gone before—or for some other cause that none of them knew—the power of the solstice midnight came and went. But in the Void there was only silence. No light, no movement stirred within that terrible chaos, to show them in which direction the universe without magic might lie.

TWELVE

"I DON'T UNDERSTAND." THE SLURRED DRAG OF THE VOICE-box was intelligible only by those who knew Jaldis well—to an outsider, Rhion thought, it would be only a seesaw of notes, like an expert musician playing a viol in an inflection to mimic human speech. The talismans of crystal and glass and the great gold sun-cross in their midst, flashed like the shattered fragments of a broken sun against the worn sheets and the hand that lay like bleached driftwood in their midst.

"They called out for help. I heard their voices at the Winterstead . . ." Jaldis sighed painfully and turned his face away. "I don't understand."

"The turn of winter was six months ago," Shavus replied, the roughness of his deep voice not quite successful in covering his concern for his friend. "God knows, a man's whole life can change in a week—in a day."

Silent at his elbow, Rhion had to agree.

"What makes you think any of them are still alive by this time?"

"If ever they existed at all," Gyzan murmured, from where he sat on the painted leather chest at the bed's foot.

"It exists." Jaldis stirred as if he would sit. Rhion, too unnerved by the grayness of his face and the ragged way he'd been breathing that morning to stand on ceremony, put out a hand and forced him gently down again.

"It exists," the old man insisted. "That I know. I heard them crying out . . ."

"I don't disbelieve you, old friend." The Archmage shook back his ragged hair, like tangled gray wool around his dark, scarred face. "But whether those people are still alive to call, let alone have enough power in 'em to reach out across the Void and guide us there . . ."

"I will find them," the old man said stubbornly. "I will. I must." And for all the weakness of his body, Rhion saw in that sunken face the indomitable determination of a dream.

"Can't you do anything for him?" he asked quietly, when he, the Archmage, and the Archer had climbed down the rough ladder to the kitchen. "Spells to give him strength, to steady his heart . . ."

"Something you can do as well as I." The big warrior grumbled the words over his shoulder as he rooted through the collection of fine porcelain bottles on the plank shelf—all gifts from the Duke—in search of brandy. Rhion picked up the nearly empty water jar and crossed the length of the kitchen to the door.

In the square outside the water seller whose beat covered this court was walking along the dense blue shade of the arcade, singing mournfully "Wa-a-a-a-ter, cool fresh wa-a-a-a-ter . . ." She eyed Rhion suspiciously but uncovered one of the buckets which dangled from her shoulder yoke and filled up his jar, then bit the halfpenny he gave her and made the little crossed square of Darova's Eye on it, in case he'd given her a pebble witched to look like a coin. Wizards were always being accused of doing that, though Rhion had never met anyone to whom it had actually happened.

"Don't be silly." He set the jar down again near the hearth in the kitchen's cool gloom. "Your spells . . ."

"My spells malarkey," Shavus retorted. "You know as well as I do, my partridge, that there's no spell can go against nature, not forever. What Jaldis needs isn't a spell, but to quit doing things like this to himself. Magic comes from the flesh as well as the will—I've seen you goin' after dates and honey and any sweet thing when you've done some bit of spell-weaving that's beyond you, same as I fall asleep like I'd been clubbed over the head, once the kick of the magic itself wears off. Jaldis can't keep goin' from spell to spell to keep himself on his feet any more than a man can keep himself goin' forever chewing cocoa leaves.''

He pulled the cork from the brandy bottle with his teeth and slopped one of the red-and-black cups half-full, while Rhion heaped a little handful of charcoal in the brazier and touched it with a fire-spell even as he worked the coffee mill.

They were all tired, for they had worked the rites of the summoning of power for an hour or two after midnight, trying to find some sign, some clue, in the darkness of the Well. After the shortest night of the year, dawn came far too soon.

In any case, Rhion had slept very little. Fatigued as he was by the calling down of power, no sooner had his head touched the pillow than the dream of Tally lay down beside him, hair like seed-brown embroidery silk and long cool limbs like ivory. In sleep he could have tasted her lips again, but sleep, like the coy girls he'd flirted with in his youth, had played hard to get.

It had been just as well. Waking with the first slits of light through the louvers, he had heard the stertorous rasp of Jaldis' breathing and had realized that the old man had suffered something akin to a mild stroke in his sleep.

''He uses too much power as it is,'' Shavus grumbled, pouring another generous dollop of brandy into his coffee and taking a handful of the cheese and dates Rhion had brought to the table. The dates were another gift from the Duke, like the coffee and the wine the three senior mages had drunk last night at dinner. The graceful clay bottle, stamped with the Duke's seals, still adorned the sideboard

and reminded Rhion that he had had no supper last night.
No wonder, he thought, he was starving. "Tampering with
that damn Well of his will be his death."

"Perhaps," Gyzan said, speaking for the first time, "death
is the inevitable conclusion of all dreams."

In the weeks that followed, Rhion visited the cellar seldom, though he was always conscious of the Well's presence
there, like something dark and terrible living in the ground
beneath his feet. Even after Shavus and Gyzan had returned
to Nerriok, between his own spells of healing and his pupil's,
Jaldis had rallied. For all his fragility there was an odd, stubborn toughness to him; he was on his feet within days, though
he moved more slowly than he had. Nevertheless Rhion was
uneasy. He knew that while he himself was gone, his master
would descend the perilous ladder to the cellar and open the
Well, sitting for hours before it, gazing into the enigma of
its abyss.

The Duke was deeply concerned to hear that his friend
was ill and would dispatch a sedan chair and four bearers to
Shuttlefly Court whenever he wanted the old man's company.
Betweentimes, his gifts multiplied: fruits, game birds, and
the light, pale wines of the high country. When Rhion came
to court without Jaldis, the Duke would invariably ask after
the old man and send back with Rhion some small token—a
book from the library or good quality soap from the palace
savonneries, or sometimes just summer flowers from the water gardens to brighten the little adobe rooms.

And Rhion was often at court. The Duke had offered both
him and Jaldis free use of his library, and it would be foolish,
Jaldis scolded, not to take advantage of this freedom to make
notes of anything of value he might find. Thus Rhion spent
much of the summer in those big marble rooms—three of
them, stacked one atop the other in the stumpy octagonal
tower—reading by the white, diffuse light that streamed in
through the high latticed windows or browsing through the

racks of ancient scrolls and shelves of books whose sheer numbers were famous throughout the Forty Realms as second only to the High King's library in Nerriok.

"And personally, I think ours is better," Tally remarked, one afternoon as she and Rhion, catalog and note tablets in hand, were engaged in one of their long paper chases through book after book, tracking down a reference by the rhetoritician Giltuus in his *Ninth Book of Analects* to spells by a wizard named Greigmeere. "The High King's library has been gone over a dozen times for orthodoxy by the priests of Darova. You can bet anything 'unfit' or 'unseemly in the sight of the gods' went for kindling years ago."

"And this hasn't?" Rhion balanced on a tall-legged stool to pull scrolls from the highest compartment of a rack between two windows: Greigmeere, according to Worgis' *Compendium*, had been a philosopher; though codex-type books had been in use for four hundred years, priests and philosophers still tended to regard them as newfangled and queer, making it far likelier that Greigmeere's writings, if they existed in the library, would be in the more ancient form. Tally, dressed in the plain green gown she wore when she was tending her dogs or hiding from court occasions, looked up at him where she held the stool steady as he sorted through the wax identification tags on the scrolls' ends.

"Well, more from pride than from intellectual merit, I think," she admitted. "I mean, the White Bragenmeres—Mother's family—always collected anything that came to hand and would never let anyone interfere with anything of theirs for whatever reason. I know Grandfather is supposed to have taken a whip to the Archimandrite of Darova when she came to him complaining his dog had bitten her—then turned around as soon as she had gone and beat the dog."

"Charming fellow." Rhion stretched out to the next compartment, nearly overbalancing himself in his effort to read the tags without climbing down and moving the stool. Tally laughed and put a hand on his calf to steady him, a touch that almost had the opposite effect; it was with great difficulty that he kept himself from springing down upon her then and there. He had found that sometimes, for hours at a time, they could be friends as they had been before, like two children playing in a garden—other moments he was consumed by consciousness of her, aware of every finger end, every pearl upon her headdress, and every eyelash, wanting nothing more from life than to crush her in his arms.

They had made love almost daily since midsummer after-noon: in the grotto at the end of the garden; in the hayloft above the Duke's stables; and in the little deserted pavilion with the painted rafters where Rhion and Jaldis had come to make spells for the saving of Damson's marriage. Of the love-philter and of Esrex and Damson, they did not speak.

Rhion was, in fact, about the court far more than anyone realized, coming silently under the cloudy aura of spells of Who-Me? and Look-Over-There. The places where he and Tally met, where they clung in passionate joy or lay drowsing in an aftermath sweet beyond words, were always hazed about by illusions which woke in chance passersby the dim sensa-tion that there was something urgent to be done *immediately* elsewhere in the palace. The vines which covered the front of the garden grotto grew long and untended as a beggar's hair; the pavilion by the postern gate acquired a neglected air that came of not having its steps washed or its windows cleaned.

Once, while Rhion hunted for milkwort in the wolf-yellow fields above the olive groves, he heard the horns of the hunt-ers ringing in the hills and caught a glimpse of the Duke, all in crimson, Tally in her familiar red riding dress with her dogs bounding about her, and the flame-haired Earl of the Purple Forest coursing after stag. Watching as the horses plunged out of sight into one of the thick knots of woodland that tangled these high gullies, it came over him in a sweeping rush of despair how terribly short time was. He could see, too, that Tally was right: the Earl's dogs, though too well-trained to shy when he came near, lowered their ears and moved restlessly when he was among them, cracking his whip against his boot.

Upon another occasion, he heard the horns ringing, very distantly, while he was in the Kairn Marshes, putting into practice the spells he had learned from Greigmeere's scrolls— a little-known cantrip to make a thing called a spiracle. Theoretically at least, a spiracle charged with the element of air would hold that element about it even when plunged into water; after a few tries, he found that he could, in fact, so imbue a spiracle that, with it bound around his brow, he could walk about and breathe at the bottom of the river, watching the fish slipping through the dark jungles of cattail roots. When he emerged from the water, his body dripping but his hair and beard and spectacles dry, he found Tally sitting on his clothes.

That was one of the best afternoons. The gnats, under the impression that the air was unaccountably filled with the smoke of lemon grass, hung in perplexed clouds upriver and down, the air clean of them in the thick yellow-green sunlight among the willow roots where Rhion and Tally lay. Afterward Tally insisted on trying the spiracle—a little iron circlet no bigger around than a child's bracelet, tied to a leather thong—and explored the murky greenish waters herself, breathing the bubble of trapped air which hovered around her head.

Later still, lying again on the spread-out bed of their clothing, she spoke of her upcoming marriage, the only time she had done so throughout that long summer.

"I'm saving times like this," she whispered, turning her head toward him, so that her long hair lay tangled over the worn brown robe beneath it. Out on the marsh, a fish leaped at a dragonfly, a silvery *plop* in the stillness; the air that moved above the water stirred the thick curly hair of Rhion's back and chest and thighs and murmured in the reeds which surrounded the lovers like a translucent green bed curtain, canopied with sky. "They're saying now it will be August, just before we leave for the summer palaces in the hills. Mother's been telling me to stay out of the sun so my skin will beautify and making me take baths in milk. They've been bleaching my hair and clarifying my complexion with distilled water of green pineapples, and Damson's been plying me with every kind of herb and tea and potion she knows to make me beautiful. And time is so short . . ."

She propped herself to her elbow and reached across to take his spectacles—all that he was wearing—from his face, then drew him to her, silken skin, bones like ivory spindles, beneath his hands. "This is my dowry," she murmured, holding fiercely to him, her face pressed to his shoulder. "When a noble woman marries, she has a jointure to live on, if worst comes to worst—these days are mine."

He gathered her to him, closer and closer still. His beard against her hair, he breathed. "Then we'd better make it a good one."

"I wish there was something I could do."

"Oh, Rhion." Jaldis sighed, and put his wine cup aside, to reach out and grasp his pupil's plump hand in his crippled one. The noise of the summer evening came dimly through the open door from the square: from both taverns, voices lifted in song, old ballads strangely sweet in the lapis dark and torchlight despite the rough voices that framed them. Children shrieked with laughter, whirling the big green-backed beetles they'd caught around their heads on strings to hear them buzz, and crickets creaked in the long weeds around the edge of the arcade. Two streets away the jarring rattle of the market carts rose like a clumsy staccato heartbeat to time the night's mingled sounds. On the rough wooden table between Jaldis and Rhion the supper dishes lay, and among them, like a nobleman gone slumming, stood the three-quarters-empty bottle of wine which the Duke's messenger had brought them that evening. Turning it in his hand, Rhion reflected that the Duke must have returned—he and his guest had been gone for two days, inspecting the summer-palace to which the whole court would soon move.

"I keep thinking . . ." He gestured helplessly across the ruined battlefield of plates. "I keep thinking about sailing across to Murik, the Island of the Purple Forest . . . about maybe settling there. But I don't want to leave you." It was the first time he had voiced such a choice aloud. "And I think, 'Well, he doesn't look like the kind of man who's going to get songs sung about his fidelity . . .' As long as I don't get her with child, why should he care? But *I* care. I hate the thought of her bearing his children. But that's why he's marrying her. I hate the thought of what he'll do to her."

"And what will he do to her?" his master asked softly. "She's the daughter of his ally. He can't very well take a whip to her."

Very quietly, Rhion said, "He'll make her unhappy."

Jaldis sighed and did not reply.

Rhion got to his feet and paced to the open door. For a time he stood looking out into the unearthly blue of the deepening night, his arms folded tight across his body as if to contain a bleeding wound. Above the mountains, a swollen cantaloupe-colored moon shed light brilliant enough to cast blurred shadows on every sage and juniper bush there, to silver every roof tile of the city beneath. In that drenched indigo world, the taverns stood out like tawdry carnivals; elsewhere in the square, two of the local prostitutes sat on their balcony, having a night off, their quiet-voiced conversation about hair styles and fashionable gamblers mingling with the smell of their perfume and the thick green scent of the marijuana they smoked. The day had been stifling, the last of July raging down like a furnace over the brown hills. Before the doors of their rooms, all round the arcade, men and women sat arm in arm in companionable silence, watching children playing in the dark.

Rhion whispered, "Dammit. Other people—people who aren't born to magic, who don't have it in their blood—think magic solves things. They come to us for potions, philters, talismans, amulets, and advice to solve some problem or other. But it doesn't, really. It doesn't change what we are. It doesn't change what we do."

"No," Jaldis said, from the soft glow of witchlight that haloed the table where he sat.

Rhion chuckled ironically. "Magic isn't . . . isn't magic. I keep telling myself every time I see her that it's just one more memory to hurt after she's gone. But I keep grabbing those moments, devouring them as I used to eat cookies . . . Damn, I make the best love-potions in the Forty Realms, but can I make one that'll fall me *out* of love?"

"Would you truly want to?"

His voice was nearly inaudible. "No." The witchlight flashed across the lenses of his spectacles as he turned back to the room. "No."

His hand unerring, Jaldis poured the remainder of the wine, dividing it between the two cups. Rhion shut the door, closing out the wild magic of the night, and returned to his master. As he picked up the cup, the touch of it, its graceful shape and glass-black glaze, brought back to him the still silences of the Drowned Lands, the flicker of fireflies across the blue marshes, and the marble faces dreaming in their winding sheets of vines. The Gray Lady's face came back to him, framed in the bones of the priestess' diadem and the pulse-beat tapping of the drums among the sacrificial stones. Magic.

The memories grounded him. Like *love*, *magic* was a word of many meanings: joyful or damning, hurtful or sweet, the same word describing a silly flirtation or a commitment that saved the soul.

"To magic," he said softly, raising his cup; as if he could see him do so, Jaldis returned the salute.

"To magic, then."

And draining the cup, the old man rose stiffly from his chair, collected his crutches, and limped off slowly to the ladder and so up to his bed.

Rhion gathered the dishes, dipped water from the jar, and washed them, reflecting with a twisting stab in his heart that, if the Duke had returned, it meant that the court would be getting ready to move up to the higher hills. Several of the wealthy merchants whose walled and decorated houses made up the Upper Town had left already; they would not be back until the minor festival of Shilmarglinda on the equinox of fall.

That thought brought others. He glanced across at the tiny plank door of the cellar, shut and bolted against intrusion, and wondered what Jaldis would learn at the turning of autumn when he again summoned the power of the heavens to listen into the Well. And listen he would, Rhion thought uneasily, at whatever cost to himself.

By the autumn equinox Tally will be married. This will all be over.

The autumn equinox, he realized, was less than sixty days away. It was as if something within him had been squeezed suddenly in a wire net.

And then, from upstairs, he heard the sudden, heavy crash of a stick pounding the floor. Summoning him, calling him urgently . . .

Jaldis.

He can't use the voice-box . . .

Rhion took two running strides toward the ladder and stopped, realizing belatedly that the witchlight that had illuminated the room had died. Being able to see in the dark, and being deeply preoccupied, he hadn't noticed . . .

But there was only a strange, leaden muzziness in the part of his mind that he would have used to summon the light back again. Like a limb that had been numbed, or the speech that eludes a drunkard . . .

And it came to him, whole, cold, terrifying, and with absolute clarity, what had happened and what was about to take place.

Pheelas root. In the wine.

The Duke never sent the wine.

The Duke is still out of town.

Behind him the door crashed open. Torchlight spilled into the long room like blood from a gutted beast, framing the crowding forms of men in the gray livery of the disgraced house of the White Bragenmeres—personal soldiers with weapons in their hands.

Before them, slim as a lily in unjeweled white, stood Esrex.

THIRTEEN

LATER RHION SUPPOSED HE COULD HAVE THROWN SOME-
thing—the tin basin of dishwater, a chair, anything—at Esrex's guards to slow them down. But at the moment, he didn't
think of it, and it probably would have done him more harm
than good. Smashing their way down the length of the room,
they caught him when he was three-quarters of the way up
the ladder to the room above, tearing his hands by main
force from the rungs and striking him with their spear
butts when he kicked at their faces. A blow caught him over
the kidneys, the pain stopping his breath; as he crumpled,
retching, to the stone floor he heard them in the room
above. "What the . . ." "Look under the beds . . ." "Try
the chest . . ." The sound of crashing furniture, the scrape
of a bedstead on the floor. Someone kicked him in the side.
The room around him was a fevered harlequin of torchlight
and clawing shadows. The clay earth smell of the floor choked
his nostrils, and the sweat-and-leather stink of the guards.

"Where is he?"

Rhion managed to shake his head. "He went up there . . .
if he's gone, I don't know . . ."

The guard kicked him again, sending him crashing against
the wall. The next second he was grabbed by the front of his
robe and hauled to his feet, pain stabbing him in the side so
sharply that for a moment he thought one of them had put a
dagger into him. The kick must have broken a rib. Two of

them dragged him to the hearth, where the remains of the small supper fire still smoldered. One held him by an arm twisted behind his back while the other pokered aside the layer of ash, exposing the glowing core of embers beneath. Rhion struggled desperately as they caught his hand, forced it toward the simmering heat. "Where is he . . . ?"

"Don't waste time." Esrex turned his head a little toward them, fragile profile stained amber by the sudden renewal of the flames. "Get out and search the area. The old man's a cripple; he can't have gone far. And in any case," he added maliciously, as the guards paused, holding Rhion's hand so close to the coals that the heat of them seared the hairs on his fingers, "we don't want to burn his *right* hand. He'll need that to sign his confession."

Even in that extremity, it flashed through Rhion's mind to mention to Esrex that he was left-handed, but that, he knew, would be asking for a shovelfull of coals in his palm. He was slammed back against the wall with another knife thrust of pain, but through a gray tide of sweating nausea he managed to gasp, "Confession of what?"

Guards were streaming out of the house, into the square, the alleyways around it, and across the roofs. *He's blind,* Rhion thought desperately. *Without magic to work the voice-box he's mute, a cripple* . . . A guardswoman came up from the cellar with surprising speed after she'd gone down. "No-body down there—nothing but witchery, some kind of demon-magic . . ."

The Well would be quiescent, Rhion thought blankly—a pity. One of them might have fallen into it . . .

And much as he hated the thing, he felt a pang at its destruction. All Jaldis' work . . .

Esrex paused directly in front of him, thin and incisive as broken glass. "The confession that's going to greet his Grace when he and the Earl of the Purple Forest return to Bragenmere late tonight,'' he said softly. ''The confession that the child my dear little cousin carries in her belly is yours.''

He was already cold with shock, but still he felt as if the floor had sunk away beneath his feet. ''That's impossible.''

''Oh, come . . .''

Rhion started to speak, then bit his tongue, realizing that his blurted protest would have been a confession. *I've been using spells of barrenness on her to prevent that, dammit!*

''Her chamberwoman is my fellow initiate in the rites of Agon, you see,'' Esrex went on, apparently absorbed in smoothing the pearl-stitched kid of his glove ever more closely over his thin-fingered, childlike hands, but watching Rhion from beneath colorless lashes as he spoke. ''The information one learns at the Temple is well worth what one gets under one's nails. There is no question that she has put horns on the Earl. That's all I really need to prevent that traitor Prinagos from allying himself with decent families, always supposing one could describe the Muriks as decent . . . But it will give me considerable pleasure,'' he went on, and looked up with a thin little smile, teeth small as rice grains in the parting of his fleshless lips, ''to see you, my arrogant little warlock, pay the fullest possible penalty for rape.''

Half the population of Shuttlefly Court was gathered around the door to watch Esrex's bravos manhandle Rhion out into the darkness. The torchlight showed him their faces— the tired, dirty, or unshaven faces of the weavers to whom he'd sold herbal simples, the painted faces of the whores who'd bought luck-charms and spells of barrenness from him and the snaggle-haired brown faces of the laundrywomen who'd come to him to have their fortunes read. The faces were blank and noncommittal, like the faces of people passing by a dog dying on the side of the road. Something struck his back and he heard a child's singsong giggle: ''Wi-zard, wi-zard, Turn you into a li-zard . . .'' and shrieks of nervous laughter from the other children in the square.

Another clear little treble crowed, ''Witch, witch, Give you the itch . . .'' and a rotting peach squished soggily against his sleeve. The two guards who weren't searching the neighborhood for Jaldis roped his wrists together and mounted their horses. Nobody even called out, *What'd he do?* They all knew what he'd probably done, having heard it traded back and forth in taverns all their lives: poisoned an old man to get his money, seduced an honest woman by means of spells, blackmailed a woman who came to him for help, and ruined someone—businessman, baker, farmer— by putting an Eye on their shop or stove or cattle . . .

Jaldis, dammit, get the hell out of town if you can . . . The men kicked their horses to a trot and he stumbled after them, grimly determined to keep up and wondering if he could. The pain in his side was unbelievable, turning him queasy and faint, but he knew if he fell there would be no getting up. As they disappeared around the corner into Thimble Lane he saw from the tail of his eye two of the local loiterers, pine-knot torches in hand, go curiously, cautiously into the house he and Jaldis had shared, looking to see what pickings they could find.

The horsemen avoided the main streets where farm carts would be clattering to the markets until dawn, taking instead the crisscrossing mazes of smaller alleys and back lanes, dark as pitch save for the light of the torches they bore. Rhion managed to stay on his feet through the dirt lanes of the Old Town, though the dust thrown up by the hooves nearly choked him and the pain in his side brought him close to fainting. He fell on the steep cobbled rise that led to the golden lamps and walled mansions of the Upper Town. Unable to get on his feet again, he concentrated what strength he had on keeping his head clear of the granite chunks that paved the street and not passing out. It wasn't far—at most a hundred feet—

but he was nearly unconscious when they came to a stop in a granite-paved court.

"Where's the other one?" a voice demanded, and Rhion moved his head groggily, trying to see where he was. It was useless. His spectacles had been knocked off somewhere during the journey, and all he had was a blurred impression of towering dark walls. But the smell of the place was enough to tell him. Not a tree, not a fountain, not a statue broke the dark monolithic walls around him—no smell on the turgid night of water, flowers, grass, or any of the things people paid for when they bought houses in the Upper Town . . . Only stone. And far-off, the mingled scents of incense and blood.

And terrible silence, the silence of the brooding god.

The Temple of Agon.

"Got out through a roof-trap," Esrex' light, steely voice said. A slim pillar of white in the flare of the torchlight, he stood surrounded by three or four—it was difficult to tell without spectacles—pillars of shrouded black. The pearls braided into his hair gleamed dimly as he turned his head. "He won't get far; anyway, this is the one we need."

Rhion barely heard the sound of footfalls as one black figure detached itself from the group and walked to where he lay, torn flesh bleeding through the tatters of his torn robe. Looking up he saw nothing, only the pale hands protruding from beneath the cloudy black layers of veiling. But he felt the eyes. The voice was high and epicene—it could have been male or female, chilled and frigid with self-righteous spite.

"I suspect the Duke will have a different opinion of wizardry when faced with a man who used those powers to seduce his daughter."

Rhion turned over, his body hurting as if he had been beaten with clubs, to look across at where Esrex still stood. "And what about a woman who used those powers to seduce her own husband?" he asked, fighting for breath, surprised at how changed his voice sounded in his own ears—slurred like a drunkard's. He tasted blood as he spoke. "Or did you think that fit of lust you had for Damson last spring was the result of some new perfume she wore?"

The priests of Agon looked at one another for a moment, and for that moment, Esrex did not move. Then, without hurry, he walked to the nearest doorway, where a painted clay lamp burned upon a stand. Taking it, he blew it out and came back to where Rhion lay. The priest standing near-by stepped aside, and Esrex removed the lamp's top and poured the oil deliberately down over Rhion's face, hair, and the front of his robe. Then he took a torch from the nearest guard.

"Repeat that lie again," he said quietly, "and you'll discover that there are worse things than the penalty for forcing a virgin to open her legs to you by means of your spells. For myself I don't care—a true man cannot be affected by such tricks—but you have slandered a good and loyal woman for whom my love has never wavered since first I saw her face. As she will attest." And he slashed down with the torch.

Rhion twisted aside as well as he could, covering his face with his oil-soaked arms and thinking, *Nice. Got any other clever ideas . . . ?* He felt the heat of the flames, flickering inches from his cheek, tried desperately not to think about what would happen next . . . Opening his eyes after a hideously long moment he could see Esrex' feet, close enough to his face to be more or less clear to him. With bizarre irony, he saw that Esrex still wore the long-toed shoes of embroidered ivory satin he'd had on the day of their confrontation in the grotto.

"Remember," Esrex' voice said above him, "that we don't really need you alive." He handed the torch back to the guard. "Now take him away."

They put him in a sort of watching room in the temple's vaults, tying his hands to an iron ring in the wall. Three or four men were on guard there, wearing the rough tunics and baggy trousers of laborers or slaves. Masks covered their faces, but Rhion guessed, looking near-sightedly at the hard-muscled brown arms and thighs, that two of them at least were "liverymen"—household guards—of noble or wealthy families, either freedmen or slaves on a night off doing service at the beck of the priests whose followers they were. Others might have been city ditch diggers, or chair bearers—the cult of Agon welcomed men and women, children, too, of all classes, anyone who could be of use. All of these, to judge by their conversation, were ignorant, foulmouthed, and delighted to have someone helpless and in their power.

It was a hellish night. The room was smotheringly hot, the smoldering torches set all around the walls not only adding to the accumulated heat of the day but contributing smoke as well. The men joked, diced, and passed a skin of cheap wine among themselves, but never took their eyes from their prisoner. The ring in the wall was just high enough that Rhion was unable to lie down. Though his wrists had stopped bleeding, the pain and cramps in his arms and shoulders grew steadily worse until he had to set his teeth to remain silent. The reek of the smoke, of the guards, of stale wine, and of the oil that still soaked his hair and beard and clothes turned him faint and sick, and he wondered if the priests of Darova were right and there was a hell, and he'd somehow ended up there without either dying or being judged . . .

The guards sprang to their feet, bowing in obeisance. Silent as the shadow of a crow, a black-veiled priest glided in. *They must train them to walk that way,* Rhion thought distractedly. The priest said no word, but, at a sign from him, two of the guards pulled Rhion to his feet and held his arms and his head while the priest drew from his robes a steel needle and a tiny vial of some liquid with which he coated the needle's tip before stabbing it, hard and accurately, into the big veins of Rhion's neck.

Then he left again, without speaking a word.

More pheelas, Rhion thought groggily, as he sank back to the floor. Did that mean Jaldis might, by this time, be regaining some of his power to use his spectacles—if he had his spectacles with him—or his voice-box? Or had they caught him already and kicked him to death against some alley wall like men *frugeing* a rat? And anyway, where could he go? Criminals frequently sought sanctuary in the temples, but no cult offered sanctuary to wizards. Wizardry was an offense to the power of all gods. There was not one, not even Mhorvianne the Merciful, who would let the mageborn hide in the smallest fold of their robes.

He thought about Jaldis, hauling himself painfully along the smelly back streets of Bragenmere, blind and voiceless, about the gangs of drunkards who prowled the streets on summer nights, beating up anyone they saw, and about the pickpockets and thieves who haunted the alleyways, who would kill a man for his boots . . .

And Tally? What the hell had happened to Tally?

Could she really be with child?

It had to be a trap, he thought frantically. Even if she had another lover besides himself—which he knew down to the marrow of his bones she had not—the spells by which he prevented her from conceiving would have worked, no matter who she lay with. *Dammit, I know I'm not that powerful a mage, but I can at least get that spell right. It's not as if she were using a counterspell against it . . .*

And then the warm sweetness of the marshes of the Kairn River came back to him, the green, musky smell of the reeds and the silken murmur of the water, striped sunlight playing over Tally's creamy skin. *Damson's been plying me with every kind of herb and tea and potion she knows . . .*

Damson.

. . . she keeps saying, 'Oh, when you bear your husband's child you'll know what true happiness is . . .'

He remembered how, long ago, Tally had come to him to buy a philter to make Damson's life better without her sister's knowledge. It would not have taken malice—only Damson's eager good will. The wedding coming up, Damson aglow in the joy of her own pregnancy . . . the tincture Jaldis had mixed for her in the candlelit dimness of that painted room . . .

"Hey!"

Rhion looked up, startled, as a rough hand seized his hair and cracked his head back against the stone wall behind him. One of his guards stood over him, a vast blur against the torchlight, cheap wine stinking in his sweat.

"You quit that, you hear?"

"Quit what?" Rhion demanded, too startled to realize that he should simply agree and profusely apologize.

The man kicked him. "You know what, you little witch-bitch. I haven't won a pot in fifty throws and I want you to quit witching the goddam dice or I'll light that goddam beard of yours on fire, and we'll see how fast you can witch it out."

Exasperated, Rhion snapped, "Look, moron, if I had the ability at the moment to work any magic at all, why the hell would I waste my time screwing up your dice game when I could use it instead to untie these festering ropes and get myself the hell out of this mess?"

The guard struck him, hard, across the face—*definitely a chair carrier,* Rhion thought, tasting the blood as the cuts on his mouth opened up again. "Don't you get smart with me, you little . . ."

"Hell . . ." Another guard came over, bored with dicing, not drunk enough to be careless, but drunk enough to have the wicked inventiveness of drunks. He took the nearest torch from the wall and brought it down close to Rhion's face. "Let's light his beard on fire anyway. We don't got any water down here, but we all been drinkin' that wine, and maybe if he begs us real pretty we could put out the fire by . . ."

"Heads up!" another by the door called, and the man with the torch turned swiftly, putting it back in its holder in the wall as a priest entered, black clouds of veils billowing eerily around him like the smoke of a fire without light.

"Bring him."

The cell they took him to was small, hotter if anything than the watching room. But if the priest who waited for him, sitting behind the single table of spare dark wood, felt any discomfort in his long robes of black wool and the veils that shrouded his face, he gave no sign of it. By the way the guards and the other priests bowed—by the height of the headdress that supported the cloudy frame of veils—Rhion guessed this must be Mijac, Agon's High Priest in Bragenmere, though it was impossible to be sure.

Was that, he wondered with exhausted detachment, one of the strengths of the cult? That its servants served in secret, even from one another? That the masks that covered the faces of the guards in the watchroom, the veils that hid the priests, concealed them, not only from outsiders, not only from each other's witnessing, but from themselves?

He looked up at the men beside him and behind him, whose strength, he suspected, was the only thing keeping him on his feet. They might be slaves of a man, of the city, or certainly of economic realities, but their wills had once been their own. Now they had given their wills to Agon, and it was Agon who acted through them—they could spy upon their benefactors, they could betray their friends, they could torture the weak, prostitute themselves, beat a helpless old cripple to death in an alleyway, and remain, in their hearts, good people, kindly people, men and women worthy of regard, because it was, after all, the Veiled God who was acting, not them.

They shoved him forward, and he had to catch the edge of the table in his bound hands, his legs shaking under him.

Without his spectacles, he wouldn't have been able to see the priest's face at this distance, anyway, but there was something unnerving about those blowing curtains of black, through which only a white blur was dimly visible, and the gleam of eyes.

A gloved black hand thrust a sheet of paper across the polished tabletop and offered him a quill. "Sign it."

He picked up the paper, his numb fingers barely able to close around the edge, and held it where he could read it, about a handbreadth from his nose. He caught the words, *by means of potions forced her to yield to my lusts* . . . before a guard ripped it from his grasp.

"He said sign it, not read it."

"It's lies," Rhion said quietly.

Mijac's voice, behind the veils, was startlingly deep, a beautiful bass, like the deep boom of distant thunder. "What does that have to do with it?"

"Oh, I forgot," Rhion said, still holding himself up by the edge of the table, blood, lamp-oil, and sweat dripping down his matted hair and onto the paper before him. "Lies are the common coin of Agon."

Mijac reached out and wiped the droplets carefully from the document with one gloved fingertip. "As they are of wizards," he returned calmly. The veils shuddered and moved as he leaned back in his chair again. "You are the architects of lies, the artists of illusion—the thieves of matters which should be left to the gods. When a man sees a monkey running about with a man's dagger in its hand, does he stop to inquire of the animal what it intends to do with the weapon? Of course not. And when other men begin to turn to that monkey in respect, bow to it with hand on brow and ask its advice . . . then it is time for sane men to step in and correct matters. Is it true that the Lady Damson used a love-philter to bring her husband to her bed last spring?"

Rhion's arms had begun to shake with fatigue—he stiffened them desperately, feeling darkness chew on the edges of his vision, a strange, detached numbness creeping over his chest. *Don't faint now, dammit.*

"Why don't you ask her husband?"

"Lord Esrex has his uses," the priest replied in a mild tone. "He and his wife are holding the Lady Tallisett now, awaiting his Grace's return. But knowledge is always a helpful thing to have."

"Provided you get your facts straight. Who told you I was supposed to be the girl's lover?"

"The girl herself," Mijac said. "And Jaldis confirmed it before he died."

Rhion looked up quickly, his face ashen.

"They found him in an alley behind the Temple of Darova. I had given them no specific instructions—perhaps the men thought it would be easier than carrying him here. The lower orders are lazy that way. Now sign."

Sickness and grief washed him like rising tide; even his blurred myopia was darkening. His voice sounded oddly distant through the ringing in his ears. "It's a lie." Tally would never have betrayed him . . . there was no way of telling whether anything Mijac said was the truth . . .

"What is not a lie," the priest's voice came from, it seemed, farther and farther away, "is that a man can live a long time while his bones are being broken and the splinters pulled out of his flesh, so I advise you to sign before you have cause to find out how much truth I can speak . . ."

"My lord!"

Rhion's hands slipped from the table, and he felt someone catch him, supporting him as the rising darkness closed over his head. Voices came from out of that darkness, dim and muffled, like words heard underwater. He struggled to surface again, to breathe . . .

"It's the Duke! He's at the gates . . ."

A chair scraped as it was pushed back. Dimly, Rhion reflected that it was the first sound of of agitated movement he'd heard from the priests of the Veiled God. "Right," Mijac said softly, and there was a momentary pause. Then, "There's no help for it. Finish him."

A huge hand gripped him under the chin and forced his head back.

"Not here, you fool—in the cellar where the blood can drain. And hurry . . ."

Rhion lashed out feebly with his bound hands, with some idea of struggling, fighting, delaying until the Duke could reach them, until he could tell him . . . Tell him what? That Tally had cuckolded his prospective ally?

But before he'd thought that far, something hard and heavy cracked over the back of his skull.

He came to lying on a stone floor, thinking, *Well, so much for that idea . . .*

Arthritis-twisted hands touched his face. In his dazed exhaustion the buzzing voice sounded no louder than a mosquito's hum. "Rhion? My son . . ."

And above him, as his mind slowly cleared and he thought, *He did lie . . .* he heard Mijac's deep, ringing tones. "We have broken no law, my lord."

Rhion opened his eyes. He was lying on the floor halfway down a dark stone hallway, through which he cloudily recalled passing on the way to Mijac's cell. A door at the far end had been opened—the movement of the tepid night air broke the stifling heat.

And surrounded by torchlight and soldiers in cloaks the color of new blood, the Duke stood framed against the heavy trapezoid of the opened doors, hands upon his hips and traveling clothes flashing with tiny mirrors and knots of gold.

"No," he said quietly. "You have broken no law, my lord Mijac. But you have disrupted my pleasure and you have done injury to my friends."

He walked forward, his gilded boots creaking faintly in

the absolute hush. The priests and the masked volunteers surrounding Rhion where he lay retreated a little, leaving only Jaldis and Mijac near him.

"I met him on the rise of land before the palace gates," Jaldis murmured swiftly, beneath the voices of Duke and High Priest. "I knew he must pass by there—I listened for the sound of many horses . . ." Even without his spectacles, Rhion saw how torn and filthy the old man's brown robe was, how gutter-slime smutched his face and beard and matted the ends of his thin white hair, as if he had fallen—or been kicked—over and over into the Old Town's garbage and dust. His hands were trembling as he pulled the bonds from Rhion's wrists, the dirty orange lamplight in the hall making a hundred juddering reflections in the crystal facets of his spectacle-lenses.

"Your *friends*?" Mijac's inflection twisted irony from the word like spilled wine wrung from a rag. "No more than they have done injury to you, Lord Duke." He stepped forward, holding out the yellow paper. "You see that it is signed."

The Duke took the confession and read it through. The priests and their followers murmured in the shadows at the inner end of the hall. Gently Jaldis helped Rhion to sit up. Marc of Erralswan, like a shining bronze god in his armor, made a move as if to assist and then seemed to think better of committing himself. At that distance, five or six feet, Rhion could not see Dinar of Mere's fleshy features well enough to judge his thoughts—only a stylized blocking of light and shadow, bronze and blue and black. *Of course Mijac would sign it himself*, he thought, with a resigned weariness that made him wonder objectively if he was going to faint again. He was only surprised they'd bothered to try forcing him actually to sign in the first place. As Esrex had said, they didn't really need him to.

Without speaking, the Duke came over to where the two

wizards sat, filthy, bloody, and ragged as beggars, on the polished floor, and it seemed to Rhion that Agon's faceless servants fell back a little further, leaving him and his master completely alone. For a time the Duke stood looking down on them, the old man he had befriended and to whom he had sent gifts and publicly shown his regard and the young one to whom he'd confidently given the freedom of his house. His eyes went from them to the confession in his hand, a confession of betrayal, cynicism, and rape. Then he reached down, took Rhion's left hand and turned it over in his, all streaked as it was with blood and sweat and lamp-oil. Straightening up, he looked again at the paper, clean and unstained from top to bottom. And, still without a word, he held the confession to the flame of the nearest torch.

"Bring him to the palace," he said quietly, after he had dropped the burning scrap to the floor and trodden it underfoot. "I think we need the truth."

The smell of smoke hung in the air behind them as they left the silent priests of shadow and went out into the night.

FOURTEEN

THE HORSES WERE WAITING FOR THEM IN THE STREET OUT-
side. "There is only one litter and two bearers," the Duke
said, nodding toward the curtained chair and its two muscular, fair-haired slaves. "Even with his crutches, Jaldis
could barely walk when he met us. Do you think you could
back a horse, Rhion?"

Rhion nodded, though he had private mental reservations
about his ability to get into a saddle unaided. "After being
dragged up here," he said, pushing back his blood-streaked
hair from his eyes, "believe me, if you just let me *walk* to
your gates at my own pace, I'd be glad."

The Duke's mouth hardened and he glanced back over his
shoulder at the featureless black doors which had swung shut,
silent and unnoticed, behind them. The torch-blown shadows of the guards jerked and lurched over the undressed
granite wall; bronze mail flickered darkly and voices rose,
relieved to be out of the Temple's oppressive gloom, as Jaldis
was helped into the litter. For the moment Rhion and the
Duke stood in a little island of stillness in the crowd.

Now, he thought, and his stomach curled into a tight, cold
ball within him. He swallowed hard.

"My lord." He reached out to touch the red leather sleeve,
and the Duke looked back down at him, hearing the change
in his voice.

231

"My lord," Rhion said, "thank you—thank you beyond words for saving us—for believing in us over Mijac . . ."

The big man sniffed. "I think I'd believe a gypsy horse coper over Mijac . . ."

Rhion shook his head, knowing there was no way out of what he had to say, and forced his eyes to meet the Duke's. "You shouldn't," he said quietly, his voice pitched low to exclude the guards. "That's what makes this all the worse. That confession is true."

The Duke regarded him in a silence which seemed to stretch out endlessly and seemed to drown even the restless snorting of the horses and the uneasy mutter of the guards. Rhion tried not to think of what the betrayal would do to this friend of Jaldis'—only what penalty Tally would have to pay for giving herself willingly to any man while her father was negotiating in good faith for her marriage.

At last he spoke. "All of it?" His voice was quiet, his face showing nothing.

"All of it," Rhion whispered, looking away. He had begun to shake all over, with exhaustion and dread and wretchedness—he had to force his voice steady. "Jaldis knew nothing. He warned me not to . . . not to betray you. Not to let my feelings for Tally get the better of me . . ."

They'll drown the child when it's born, he thought. He'd heard of that happening on those rare occasions when a woman did bear a wizard's offspring. Or Jaldis or Ranley, the court physician, could doubtless bring on a miscarriage . . .

He shut his eyes, unable to bear it, unable to bear the thought of what it would do to her.

His son. If it was Jaldis' tincture that was responsible for the failure of his spells, it would indeed be a son. Around them, the guards in their red-crested helmets fell quiet and glanced questioningly at one another, unable to hear what their master had to say to this battered and filthy little man, but aware of the forbidding stillness of the Duke's stance that kept even the stupidest of them from asking about the delay.

There was still no expression in the Duke's voice. "And is she with child?"

Still not looking up, Rhion nodded. "I think so. I don't see that Esrex could make a case for any of this if she were not." Keeping his voice level with an effort, he explained what he thought had happened, without mentioning how or from whom Damson had obtained the tincture—only that she had given it to Tally, meaning nothing more than a wedding night successful in Damson's own terms of motherhood and dynasty.

When Rhion finished, the silence was so deep he could hear a slave woman singing in the garden of some big walled house down the street and the endless rattling hum of the cicadas in the trees. He could not meet the Duke's eyes or look him in the face—even close as they stood he could have distinguished little but a blur in the fidgetting cresset glare. Overhead, the moon stood high, its whiteness shimmering on the curtains of Jaldis' litter as they stirred in a stray drift of wind.

The Duke folded his heavy arms. His voice was so quiet as to exclude even Marc or Erralswan, holding the two horses four feet away, but calm as if he were hearing the suits of strangers in his own law courts. "And you seduced her by means of a spell?"

Rhion nodded. "She . . ." he began, but could not go on. He was shivering, as if with bitterest cold.

"That is not," the Duke said, "what Jaldis told me."

Rhion looked up at him, the blood in his veins turning to dust.

"According to Jaldis," the Duke went on, "my daughter loves you very much. How much you love her I think you have just demonstrated by your willingness to shoulder the blame." And for all the quietness of his voice, his dark eyes were grim. "But half the scandals in the world are based upon sincere love, and it is scandal with which we now have to deal. Marc . . ."

At his gesture the young captain came forward with the horses.

"Come. Let's not keep Esrex waiting any longer than we have done."

Early summer dawn was just beginning to tint the sky as the cavalcade mounted the rise to the palace gates. The houses of the Upper Town crowded close here, not the villas of the rich—not on a street which bore so much traffic—but tall blocks of expensive flats owned by the wealthier civil servants or their mistresses, built over shops that sold jewelry, spices, and silk. The alley where Jaldis had waited for the Duke's approach could have been any of a dozen near here, Rhion thought, clinging to the saddlebow of his led horse— the alley where he'd waited, listening for just this clatter of hooves on the cobble, this creaking of leather and armor, this smell of torches made up with incense to keep mosquitoes at bay. Waited and, still blind, still mute, had dragged himself out on his crutches, with the terrible, broken groans of a mute which had not passed his throat in eleven years.

Waited to save him. To save them.

No servants were about in the great court yet, save the grooms who'd slept half the night in the shelter of the colonnade awaiting the Duke's arrival from the hills. Awakened an hour earlier by the advent of the Earl of the Purple Forest and the Duke's servants and baggage horses, they came running briskly as the gates were opened once again. Overhead, the sky was losing its darkness, the late moon huge and white, a solitary lily floating upon a still lake of lilac-gray.

"My lord!" Esrex came striding rapidly down the shadow-clotted length of the pillared hall as the door guards bowed the Duke in. Rhion noted that the young man had changed into a court suit of ash-colored velvet on which rubies gleamed like splashed blood. "I have been telling the Earl of the shocking crime which has been . . ." And he stopped, seeing Jaldis at the Duke's side, leaning on his crutches with his opal spectacles flickering eerily in the long, filthy frame of his white hair. Then his eyes went to Rhion, his torn robe stained with lamp oil and blood, standing at his other hand. Up at the other end of the hall, around the two or three bronze lampstands which remained lit, a handful of courtiers self-consciously tried to pretend that staying up until the bakers were taking the bread from the ovens was their usual prac-tice; but, in the sudden hush, the soft pat of a final card being turned was like the smack of a leather belt, and the clink of glass lace-spindles like the clatter of kitchen pans.

Lazily, the Earl of the Purple Forest rose from the pear-wood couch where he had been flirting with one of Damson's maids-of-honor. He, too, had changed out of his traveling dress, though his red hair was still braided back from the journey. Opal and sardonyx gleamed on the midnight velvet of his sleeves and breast. "Really, Dinar, I think you owe me some kind of explanation about what Lord Esrex has been saying."

"Even so," the Duke said. Neither his voice nor his de-meanor gave the smallest of his thoughts away. "Marc—fetch my daughter."

"She is with my wife, my lord," Esrex hastened to inform him with a mixture of officiousness and spite. His pale eyes darted uncertainly from Rhion's face to Jaldis' and back to the Duke's. "We thought it better to know where she was. If this man still holds her under his spells . . ."

"A matter you are most qualified to judge, of course," the Duke responded, and the young man's thin skin reddened with sudden anger. Then he turned and looked around him at the hall, and every head bowed quickly over fashionable

needlework, lace-making, or cards, and voices rose with exaggerated brightness.

"Oh, *pounds* thinner, darling, but the way she goes on
about eating vegetables, you'd think she invented them . . ."
". . . Everything—house, horses, lands, the town investments—on a single cut. The man has more guts than brains,
if you ask me . . ." ". . . horse couldn't run if you lit its
tail on fire . . ." A weary-looking corps of musicians in the
gallery, who had been frantically discussing what part of
their repertoire hadn't already been played four times since
the conclusion of supper, struck up a light air on viols and
flutes, as incongruous in that tense atmosphere as a fan
dancer at an auto-da-fé.

The Duke raised his voice, not much, but enough to carry
the length of the hall. "Good people, I bid you good night."

There was no mistaking the dismissal in his tone. The hall
was cleared in five minutes, and Rhion, leaning wearily
against the strapwork marble column that supported the gallery, half-smiled to himself. *If I could sell scrying-crystals
that worked for anyone,* he thought wryly, *I could retire tonight on the proceeds.*

Then he thought of Tally again, and his heart seemed to
die in his chest.

"Really," the Earl said, when the last reluctant gossip had
collected her feather tippet, her snoring lapdogs, and her
long yellow silk train and departed. "If the chit's pregnant,
as Esrex claims, I'm afraid our negotiations are going to have
to be . . . renegotiated. Not that I wish to spoil sport, but
there is the succession to be thought of."

"How did you know it was Esrex?" Rhion stepped back
to where Jaldis had unobtrusively sunk down on one of the
spindle-legged couches set among the pillars which flanked
the hall. In the smoky glare of a near-by lamp, the old man
looked drained and gray under the coating of grime. Rhion
sat down next to him, his legs still feeling weak. Between

lamp-oil, blood, and the miscellaneous sewage that covered both their robes, the servants would probably have to burn the cushions, but that was something they could take up with Esrex. "And how did you know what it was about?"

"I remained to listen, of course." Jaldis raised his head from his hands, making an effort to shake off the exhaustion that all but crushed him. "After getting out through the roof trap I hid for a few minutes near the door that leads out to the midden in the back. They were hunting for me across the roofs and down the alleys, not up next to the house itself."

Rhion was aghast. "You could have been . . . !"

"I knew we had been poisoned with *pheelas* root, of course," that soft, droning voice went on. "But it did not interfere with the senses of a mage. They waited, of course, for it to take effect before coming within the theoretical range of wizard's marks . . . As soon as I heard Esrex' voice, I guessed what it was about. If one is in the habit of storing grease beside the stove, one does not have to look far for a cause when the house catches fire."

Rhion bowed his head, grief and guilt washing back over him in a sickening wave. His passion for Tally—his yielding to hers for him—had brought ridicule and shame upon the man who had just saved his life, disgrace—almost certainly banishment—on Jaldis and probably Tally as well . . . He shied from thinking about what he had brought on himself. The Duke was a just man, but he had needed that alliance with the In Islands to guard against the White Bragenmere faction at home. He had saved Rhion from the priests of Agon, but, as he had observed, scandal was scandal.

Intent and terrible, the silence deepened in the room. For the first time, Rhion understood why the very rich, in palaces this size, maintained musicians to fill up the resounding hush. The guards had left, Esrex' liverymen as well as the Duke's mailed troopers, and the huge quiet seemed to echo with the breathing of those few who remained. Once Rhion looked up to see the Earl's dark eyes turned his way, though whether he was studying the man whom Esrex had described as his rival, or merely curious about the two grubby fugitives huddled together on the couch, his eyesight was not good enough to determine.

"What can be keeping them?" Esrex muttered through his teeth. The Duke, his arms folded and his face a careful blank, did not even look at him, but Rhion could almost feel the seethe of conjecture, of anger and disappointment, of possible salvage operations, options, scenarios, and covering lies that went on behind those dark eyes.

At length, Rhion's quick hearing detected the rustle of skirts in the stairway that led from the vestibule up to the palace's private suites and the firmer tread of Marc of Erralswan's gold-stamped military boots. All eyes in the room were on the archway as shadow played suddenly across its lamplit pillars. Then the pillars framed them: the tall Captain with his bronze armor and scarlet cloak, curly dark hair falling to his shoulders; Damson in plum-black velvet that flashed with jewels; and Tally like the flame of a candle, a blurred, slender column of dull gold.

She's with child, he thought again, and shivered with wonder and dread and grief. *My child. Her child.*

A wizard's child.

A child they won't allow to live.

Without his spectacles, her face was only a blur to him as she crossed the vestibule, to sink to her knees at her father's feet. Damson remained by the door, rigid and silent—one could only guess what had passed between the sisters in the hours since Esrex had ordered his wife to lock her one-time follower and champion in her room.

"Father, I'm sorry . . ." Tally whispered, holding out her hands. "So sorry. Please, I beg you . . ."

The Duke stepped forward and took her hands, raising her, his face suddenly strained. "My child . . ."

"No." Shaking her head she stepped back quickly, as if to study his face, and, by the flash of the jewels on her rings, Rhion saw she had squeezed his hands. Though her features were a blur to him, Rhion saw how tense she stood, like a warrior ready to go into a fight—a novice warrior, into her first fight, with no confidence of victory.

"How you can dare . . ." Esrex began, but a gesture from the Duke stilled him.

"Go ahead, daughter."

She swallowed. The huge amber beads around her throat gleamed softly in the lamplight as she turned to the Earl of the Purple Forest.

"My lord, I can only beg your pardon as well. They say you are a man who understands love and lovers . . ."

If you want to call it that, Rhion thought cynically, and saw the Earl's head tilt a little, with detached interest. Esrex drew in his breath, but, at a glance from the Duke, held his peace. Tally, it was clear, was going to be given her say.

"Your pardon also I ask, Rhion the Brown . . ." She gave him his formal title, setting distance between them ". . . for this shocking misunderstanding."

She turned back to the Duke. There was a small bunch of pheasant-plumes on the back of her bodice, the ribbons that hung down from it against her skirt tipped with a crystal set in gold. Rhion could see the facets of it flash with the trembling of her knees.

The hall was utterly silent.

"As usual Esrex was only half-right," she went on, her voice very clear and steady in the hush. "Father . . . and my lord . . ." She inclined her head toward the Earl, who was watching them with folded arms and an ironic gleam in his eye. "To my shame I admit it is true that I am with child. I beg your pardon, beg it abjectly, for having fallen in love with a man other than the one you, Father, would have chosen. But I have fallen in love."

Half-turning, she stretched out her hand . . .

. . . and with only the barest perceptible hesitation, Marc of Erralswan stepped forward, took it, and put a protective arm around her waist.

"My lord," he said to the Duke, bowing his handsome head. "It is I, too, who must beg your forgiveness."

Rhion, who had risen to his feet when Tally had briefly addressed him, had just enough sense to keep his mouth shut and his eyes straight ahead. But Esrex was far too stunned to look at him. *Tally* . . . Rhion thought despairingly, his hand groping for the support of the couch. *Oh, Tally, no* . . .

Stiffly, as if she spoke with a knife-point in her back, Damson stepped forward and said, "It's true, Father." She kept her eyes averted from her husband, whose dropped jaw and twitch of startled outrage were visible even to Rhion. Her high, childlike voice sounded strained but firm. "I learned of this two days ago. I would have spoken to you of it tomorrow. Esrex," she went on, her gaze fixed determinedly upon the gold ornamentation of her father's sleeve, "said that you must be told about Tally being with child, and so bade me lock her in her room tonight. But he never told me who he thought her lover was, nor what would be done to . . . to these innocent men."

"No wizard is innocent!" Esrex sputtered, completely losing his usual aplomb and looking suddenly many years younger, pale eyes blazing like a furious boy's. "And as for . . ."

"Esrex, *be silent!*" Damson's head snapped around and for a moment their eyes locked. Something in her look, either its urgency or its deadly venom, stopped his words as if with a garrote.

Rhion sank back to the couch, his legs suddenly weak. After the first stunned moment he could see the logic—and, in fact, the brilliance—of the solution. Esrex might or might not choose to believe that the story of the love-philter was a lie. But its corollary—that the tincture to make sure she conceived, the tincture that lay at the heart of this whole hellish night—was something whose existence Damson could never let him even suspect. It was perfectly possible that Esrex, to remain on terms with the cult of Agon, would repudiate a child so conceived; it was almost certain that he would repudiate Damson. But only if the matter became public knowledge.

Tally couldn't have known it would be Marc who would be sent to fetch her, Rhion thought, with a curious, despairing detachment. *The plan must have come to her when she saw him.* One had to admit that it cut through all the problems.

Except that Tally would now marry Marc.

It was fortunate that Esrex was still staring at his wife in stupefied rage as Rhion looked away, unable to endure the sight of that slim, dull-gold form in the brawny brown clasp of the young Captain's arm.

The Duke regarded his daughter for some moments in grave silence, seeing in the set ivory face, the desperate gray eyes, the mute plea for him to understand and to help. At her side, Marc was trying to appear noble, but had the air of one who has laid everything he owns on the table and awaits the cut of the cards. Rhion wondered distractedly how Tally had talked him into this. If he failed, he would surely be banished, though it was clear that the Duke was under no illusions about what was going on. But then, Rhion's impression of Marc had always been that he was rather easily led. She probably had not told him the name of the child's true father. If he succeeded . . .

"My children." The Duke held out his hands.

Rhion closed his eyes again, shaking all over with relief and grief. He was saved—Tally was saved—their son would be allowed to live. And if Esrex had thrust the torch into his oil-soaked robes in the courtyard of the Veiled God, he thought it would have been easier to stand than this.

The rest of the scene seemed to pass over his head, an exchange of voices at some huge distance, almost meaningless.

"It is not me that has been most wronged, but our cousin and friend, the Earl of the Purple Forest . . ."

"My lord . . ." Without opening his eyes, Rhion knew that Marc had gone to kneel at the Earl's feet. That was another thing rich young men or youths of noble family like Marc were taught—how to kneel with grace and when. "I can only beg of you as a lover that you release the girl I adore from her obligation to you . . ."

It was a comedy of manners, with all the stock characters present: the handsome but impecunious young lover; the stern father; and the glamorous roué with *noblesse oblige* and a heart of hidden gold. The Duke—and the Earl—must both have known from the start that any hope of an alliance was irreparably shattered. The rest of Marc's manly apology, of the Earl's gracious speech of agreement, of the ducal blessing upon the young lovers, and his gift to Marc of sufficient lands and estates to honor his soon-to-be-bride—undoubtedly why Marc, the son of penniless nobility, had agreed to the gamble in the first place—went unheard. Tally had seen a way out and had taken it, as she would have sprung from the roof of a burning building across a wide gap to safety.

But she would always now be another man's wife.

Of course, Rhion told himself, he had known from the start that this was how it must be. This grief he must have— he *had*—foreseen from the moment their eyes had met in the snowy, grim-haunted woods. There was no reason to feel this pain . . . no reason . . .

He lowered his head to his hand, his temples throbbing, feeling sick and cold and alone to the marrow of his bones.

After a time he felt Tally's hands on his shoulders, smelled the perfumes of her hair and gown, sweetgrass and dogs. He startled up. Esrex would see, would know . . .

But Esrex was gone.

The huge hall was empty save for Tally, Jaldis, the Duke, and himself. Gray light leaked through the window-lattices, making the whole gigantic space an echoing symphony of dove and pewter and white in which the few lamps still burning had a sleazy air. The Duke, his role in the comedy played, was regarding his daughter with grave respect tinged with deep sadness, fully aware of what she had done. Jaldis, at the other end of the couch, his head bowed upon his hands again, looked like something fished dead from a gutter.

Tally caught Rhion's face between her palms and knelt to kiss him. "Watch it . . ." He caught her wrists. "I'm covered with oil."

Something in that mundane remark served to shatter the brittle air of tragedy that hung between them. It came upon him that he really was alive, that they really were saved, that their son would be born, and that Tally's solution had been brilliant, decisive, and far better than he had ever expected. "To hell with it," he added, and crushed her tight to his chest.

It was only after a few minutes that he realized she was crying.

"Oh, Rhion, I'm sorry," she whispered, as their mouths finally parted. "I'm so sorry . . ."

"Ah!" Rhion cried, pressing a melodramatic hand to his brow. "I always knew you'd throw me over someday for some hunk of beef in a bronze breastplate . . ."

"You . . . !" She almost choked with laughter on top of her tears and, still laughing, pulled away and pummeled him on the shoulder, drawing a gasp of genuine pain . . . he'd forgotten the bruises that covered him.

"Oh!" she cried, horrified and contrite. "Oh, Rhion, I *am* sorry . . . !"

"You already said that."

And they both looked up, to see the Duke standing over them, his face grim, weary, and infinitely sad.

Hesitantly, Tally got to her feet, the front of her golden gown all blotched with grime. Her father caught her hand before she could sink once more to her knees. "No," he said gently, and touched her cheek.

She looked away from him, her eyes flooding again with tears of shame and remorse. In the heart of her deception, the show she was putting on for others, she had been brave. She whispered despairingly, "Father . . ."

He shook his head and removed with his thumb the tear that crept slowly over her cheekbone. "I can manage somehow without the alliance," he told her. "You haven't cost me my realm, you know. It will only mean . . . care and negotiation. And some plans which must now be postponed. The Earl is man of the world enough not to take personal offense, which is what I most greatly feared."

From what he had heard of the Earl, Rhion guessed his words had been, *Better learn now than later she's a slut,* accompanied by a casual shrug. But he kept his silence. Tally, who knew her suitor better than he, would have known perfectly well what he'd say.

The Duke's fingers moved to her lips as she began to apologize once more.

"That was very quick thinking," he went on, forcing cheer and comfort into his voice to cover his weariness and his anger at the miscarriage of all his carefully laid plans of alliance. "You forced my hand very nicely—no, I mean that as a compliment. Courage and resolution are the mark of a statesman, and the ability to use what the gods send. I'm only sorry it has to be Erralswan—not that he won't treat you well, but his family's a poor one and they have very little position . . ."

"It had to be someone," Tally said, her voice very small. "I mean, I had to find someone willing to say, *right then,* that he was my lover, that my child was his . . . And I could never . . .'' Her voice faltered. ''I knew I'd have to marry someone else and that I could never marry Rhion. And even without Esrex, I don't think I could have gone to the Earl pregnant by another man.''

''No,'' the Duke said quietly. ''Many women would have tried, but that he would never have forgiven.'' He sighed heavily, and by the expression in his eyes Rhion guessed his mind was already at work, re-shaping the possible concessions he'd have to make to the land-barons to salvage the wreck of his policies, now that he'd lost his chance of a foreign alliance.

''No,'' he went on. ''And I expect Erralswan jumped at the chance to improve his fortunes. But if I'd known that's the way out you were going to take,'' he finished, with forced lightness that almost succeeded in being genuine, ''believe me, I'd have sent someone of more fortune and better family up to fetch you.''

Tally laughed and gulped, trying to keep back tears of relief, and the Duke turned to Rhion, who got slowly to his feet to face him, teeth gritted against the agony of his broken ribs. Cold and frightened, Tally's fingers stole around Rhion's in the concealing folds of gown and robe.

''You'll have to go away, you know.''

''I know.'' Exhaustion, pain, and the aftermath of shock and grief were blurring into one vast, aching desolation of weariness. It would be enough, he thought, to know that his son was safe, no matter who the boy learned to call father. Enough to know that Tally was safe . . .

''I'll send you word,'' the Duke went on, ''when the child is near to being born. I think that will be long enough to quiet tongues. But even after that, it is probably best that you do not live in Bragenmere.''

It took Rhion a long moment of silence to realize that he was not being banished for good, but that he was being told that he could, eventually, re-enter the city gates. He started to speak, but the Duke raised his hand quickly, cutting off his words.

"Further than that I do not wish to know," he said. "And indeed, I cannot know. Not with what you are—not with most of the cults against such as you. I will not speak now of the decision that a scandal will force me to make, if one comes, but I warn you . . ." His eyes went from Rhion's face to his daughter's, the bitter grief in them the grief that only rulers bear. "I will make it."

Tally bowed her head, unable to meet his eye, but her hand tightened around Rhion's, and he felt it tremble.

"Until that day comes," the Duke went on, "you, Rhion, will be welcome in my city and under my roof. I trust you will remember." And before Rhion could speak he turned away; going to where Jaldis sat at the other end of the couch, he went to one knee and touched the crippled hand.

"Old friend," the Duke said softly, "half a dozen times I've offered you the hospitality of my household, to pursue your studies in quiet—and, I might add after tonight, in safety. I've banished Rhion for the time being—you understand that I had to banish him. But please understand that my offer to you—my affection for you, old friend—still stands as it has always stood. Will you come?"

Jaldis raised his head and, with the back of one twisted finger, adjusted the set of the heavy opal spectacles upon his face. He was thinking, Rhion guessed, of the elaborate preparations for the feast of Summerfire, and how they had taken him away from other matters dearer to his heart; of the constant small demands that drew energy from the great studies of magic; and of his days at the court of Lord Henak, and what had come of them.

Then he sighed, the brittle shoulders relaxing as he released what Rhion knew to be the last free years of his life. "I am an old man," he said, "and have been a wanderer for many years. Rhion my son . . ." Rhion released Tally's hand, limped stiffly to grasp the fingers his master held out to him. The surprising, powerful grip brought back to him the memories of the flight across the roofs of Felsplex, the rain in the Drowned Lands . . . a thousand memories, back to a bright morning heavy with the scent of flowers on the bridge of the City of Circles, a tall, straight old man and a young dandy in jeweled red velvet by the stalls that sold pieces of old books. *Are you hunting for secrets . . . ?*

He had certainly found them. One or two, he realized, he wished had remained beyond his ken.

"I'll be all right." He felt the old man's hand tighten over his. "I'll be back as soon as I can to see you . . ."

"And that will be soon," the Duke promised, his eyes traveling from Rhion's face to Jaldis' and on to his daughter's.

"Eleven years isn't long to study wizardry, you know," Jaldis said, straightening up a little as Tally flung herself convulsively into her father's arms. The talismans hanging from the voice-box made small, metallic music as he sat up, the golden sun-cross amulet catching a feeble glint of the dawn light. "But you have had a good start."

"Where will you go?" Tally broke away from the Duke's embrace as Rhion turned, stiff and aching—she had to catch his arm to keep him from falling when he tried to take a step. Every muscle in his body hurt without in the smallest measure detracting from the grinding pain in his side.

"First," he said a little shakily, "to have a bath. And then to get another pair of spectacles. And then," he said, sighing and putting an arm around her shoulders, "someplace where I'll never make another love-potion again as long as I live."

So it was that Rhion returned to the Drowned Lands of Sligo, to become the Scribe for the Ladies of the Moon.

And seven years slipped by with no more sound than sunlight makes upon the grass.

His son was born in April, a fat, robust baby named Kir. By that time Jaldis was settled comfortably in three small rooms on the top floor of the octagonal library tower and was looking better than Rhion had seen him in years. Of the few things stolen by neighbors from the house in Shuttlefly Court, nothing had been destroyed, and the Duke had managed to get everything back except the small quantities of gold and silver, which, to Jaldis, scarcely mattered. It was the books which had been his chief concern. Surprisingly, Prymannie the schoolmistress had kept them for him—perhaps out of gratitude for headaches cured or because, as a schoolmistress, she could not bear that books be destroyed; perhaps because, more intelligent than her neighbors, she had read the situation more clearly and was betting on a return to favor and a reward.

When Rhion saw Jaldis again, his brown robes were made of good-quality wool, warm against the sharp spring chill, his beard trimmed and his long white hair neatly cut.

"He misses you," Tally said, on one of the evenings when Rhion had come to sit beside her bed in the Erralswan apartments overlooking the palace garden, while the baby slept at her breast. "Father offered to give him a slave to look after him but he refused. He keeps house for himself well up there, but when I go up to talk to him, he usually talks about you."

"He hasn't . . . ." Rhion hesitated, troubled for a moment out of his delighted contemplation of the round pink cherub curled like a puppy in the linen nest of Tally's nightdress. "He hasn't talked about something called a Dark Well, has he? Or about a world without magic?"

Tally frowned, thinking back, and shook her head. "Not to me."

Rhion returned to Bragenmere fairly frequently after that, often four or five times in the course of a summer, before the snows and rains of winter closed the roads. Though Jaldis still sometimes instructed him and though they still spent nights until dawn, talking of new learning he had found, or old learning rediscovered, in the ancient books of the palace library, Rhion gradually came to think of himself as Jaldis' former pupil instead of Jaldis' student. Among the wizards and in the countryside between Imber and the Mountains of the Sun, he came to be known as Rhion of Sligo, Scribe of the Drowned Lands.

The living on the islands was not wealthy and in some ways it was painfully primitive, but he found to his surprise that it suited him. Among the crumbling pillars and morning-glory vines of the Island library, he studied the mysteries of healing handed down from the ancient priestesses of An. The Gray Lady, with whom he remained fast friends, though they never again became lovers, instructed him further in the lore of herbs and bonesetting; all his love of human beauty and all the understanding he had gained in the workings of the body and the mind when he had made love-spells for his living flowed into this new learning.

In time he came to have a reputation as a healer in the lands round about. Three or four times his visits to Bragen-mere were in response to urgent summonses from the Duke, for Damson's son Dinias, born four months before Kir, was a peaked and sickly child, unable to keep food down and susceptible to chest complaints. As for Damson herself, it appeared she had judged her husband rightly. Having broken the spiteful pride which had kept him from her, she knew indeed how to hold him at her side. Whether by obligation, by her father's wealth, by ambition, or some perverse under-standing of his body's needs—or who knew, perhaps even by love, Rhion could only guess . . . but the two infants she bore after Dinias died within days.

And time drifted by.

In the Drowned Lands, time was a deceptive matter at

best, the seasons passing like the slow stroke of a gigantic wing and leaving no shadow behind. In the summers Rhion studied the birds of the marshes, coots, herons, geese, and loons with their spotted backs and vacant laughter, watching their nesting and their mating and when they departed in fall. He harvested herbs, mallows, and lichens and experimented with their properties; he spent night after night with boat and lantern, watching grim and goblin and water-fae by the milky moonlight and made another spiracle charged with the element of air to wear around his head when he swam through the murky jungles of duckweed and cattail roots. He followed the goblins into their watery realms, but he never learned where they went. In the winters, he spent whole afternoons and nights listening to the whisper of the rain on the ivy that blanketed the library walls, reading the long, slow histories of the kings and priestesses of the realm of Sligo and the In Islands and the lore of the wizards who, throughout the Forty Realms, were popularly credited with the earthquake that brought its doom. He learned the deeper magics of the Ladies, and the effects of the moon's phases and the passage of certain stars upon spells and healing and the movements of birds; he learned small illusions to twist men's minds and strange little cantrips involving tangled string and braided straw.

And in the times of the spring equinox, he would sometimes preside over the rites at the half-drowned ring of stones, calling down the power of the turning stars to the victim who lay bleeding on the altar, feeling that power spread out to all corners of the earth.

They were days of peace. In his scrying-stone, almost nightly, he would summon Tally's image, or his son's—it was not the same as being with them, but at least he knew that they were happy and well. Going down to the noise and bustle of Bragenmere, visiting Shavus in his house in the Beldirac Wood, and listening to the arguments there about the latest enormities of the Selarnist or Ebiatic Orders or the insolence of the Blood-Mages and Earth-witches, he would return home to this ruinous, vine-cloaked silence, wondering if he wasn't beginning to comprehend for the first time what magic really was.

Then one winter morning in the library, while painstakingly translating an ancient scroll so black with age and decay that he had to lay spells on the crumbling linen in order to make the glyphs rise to visibility at all, he felt the scrying-crystal he carried calling to him.

Taking it from the inner pocket of his robe, he gathered his cumbrous woolen shawl about his shoulders and walked out onto the terrace, where the light would be better. It was only a few days after winter solstice and the chowder-thick fogs of the season lay like cotton wool over the estuary's watery mazes. The chipped balustrade seemed no more than a pale-gray frieze against a whitish wall, beyond which gulls could be heard dimly crying. Rhion's breath was a clouded puff of steam which fogged his spectacles in the raw cold, and the ends of his fingers, where they protruded from his woolen writing mitts, were red and numb.

"Jaldis?" He turned the faceted lump of raw amethyst over in his palm.

In the facets of the jewel, as if the old man stood behind him, reflected tiny in the smooth surface, he saw his master's face.

And he recoiled in shock. When wizards communicated by scrying-stone it was not the same as simply calling someone's image; there were differences between how a mage appeared in the lattices of the crystal and what he or she might look like in actual fact. But even so, Rhion could see that Jaldis was far from well. He seemed faded and wrung out, like a worn rag, his thin face sunken, fallen-looking behind the monstrous crystalline rounds of his spectacles. The heat of a midsummer morning years ago leaped vividly to Rhion's mind, Shavus digging through the bottles of brandy the Duke had sent them in that little kitchen on Shuttlefly Court, saying savagely, ''What Jaldis needs isn't a spell, but to quit doing things like this to himself . . .''

But through the exhaustion, the old man's spirit coruscated like a sunlit fountain of triumph.

''Rhion, I've done it!'' Even in his mind, now, Rhion heard the sweet, mechanical tones of the box—he could no longer bring back to mind what the old man's voice had been. ''I have opened the Dark Well with the turning of the solstice of winter. I reached in, as I have reached at every solstice-tide, at the midnight of every equinox, for seven years now . . .''

He was trembling with excitement, with vindication. It might have been a trick of the light where the old man was sitting, in the small and comfortable study in the octagonal tower, but his spectacle-lenses, even, seemed to blaze with a kaleidoscope of fire.

''I reached across the Void, seeking in the darkness for the universe without magic, calling out to them . . .

''And they answered me! At midnight of the night of the solstice, *they answered*!''

FIFTEEN

"I SPOKE TO THEM, RHION." THE MECHANICAL VOICE IN ITS rosewood box was steady, but Jaldis' crippled hands trembled where they rested on the arms of his chair. "I spoke to them, and they begged me for help. They said they had been seeking a way to project their minds into the Void for all the years since first we heard them . . ."

"Did they say what had happened to magic in their world?"

Outside, the wind groaned around the tower's eaves, driving hard little pellets of ice against the shutters. Stray drafts plucked at the lamp flames and made Jaldis' shadow tremble like a blown banner on the creamy plastered wall. For the last two days of his journey from Sligo, Rhion had been holding the storm at bay with spells, struggling over roads choked already with snow and mud and praying to Reliobag and Pnisarquas, those untrustworthy dilettante sons of the all-seeing Sky, that he could manage to keep the snow winds from blowing down the mountain passes long enough for him to reach Bragenmere's gates. It had been exactly eight years since he'd had to travel in the dead of winter, and, as he recalled, he hadn't liked it then either.

"He—Eric—his name is Eric—He said he did not know."

On the hearth, the hanging kettle boiled with a small rumbling like the purring of a cat. Tally rose soundlessly to her feet, raked the fire a little to one side, and tipped the water into a teapot, the fragrance of brewing herbs rising in summery sweetness among the room's winter smells of lamp oil and damp wool.

"That magic once existed in their world there is no question, no doubt, he says. Document after document attests its presence and its strength. Three hundred years ago there was a period of unrest, of anger, and many mages and many books were burned, both by civil authority and by angry mobs. Then two hundred years ago . . ." The old man shook his head. "Eric says he does not know what happened, why, or whether it was a single act, or an accumulation of unknowable events, chance, or the moving courses of the universe. He knows only this: that no documents of magic can be authenticated later than two hundred years ago. And beginning in that time, magic has been regarded as no more than silliness, superstition, the games of children, or the delusions of madmen."

"All over the world?" Rhion tried to picture it, to grasp that deathly silence, and failed. But the thought of it turned his heart sick.

Jaldis nodded. His twisted hands gently cradled the blue porcelain cup Tally had set before him, seeking the warmth of the clear green liquid inside.

"So he has said. He said that in place of magic there is a thing called 'science' . . ." He used an alien word for it, the Spell of Tongues carrying the term to Rhion's mind as meaning simply 'knowledge,' but with curious connotations of exactness and close-mindedness and other things besides.

"By this science," Jaldis went on, "they have done many things in these two hundred years: the wagons which travel without beasts to draw them, by the burning of an inflammable liquid; the winged ships which journey through the air; something called a telephone, by which they speak over vast distances—anyone, not just mages; and artificial light, which glows without burning anything but which is the product of . . . of creating lightning at their will. But whether this 'science,' or some element of it, arose only after magic's disappearance, or whether magic's failure was somehow connected to its arising, Eric cannot be sure. No one can be sure.''

The old man leaned forward, his pale face hollowed and gray looking in the scrim of steam curling from the cup between his hands. ''But whatever the cause, they have become a world of mechanists, of bureaucrats, of slaves, working each for his own living and not looking farther than the filling of his belly every day. It is a world where magic is not only despised, but hated. There is only one ruler now in whose realm mages—those who study magic though they can no longer work it, those who seek the true secrets that lie at the heart of the universe—are honored. And against this ruler, a coalition of these other monarchs, petty and corrupt bureaucrats, ruled by wealthy merchants and narrow of soul, is gathering for war. If they succeed—if they win—then even the memory of magic will die. And then the darkness will truly triumph.''

''And they want help?''

Jaldis nodded. ''I have contacted Shavus,'' he said. ''Shortly before the equinox of spring he and Gyzan will come here. They have long been preparing for this, knowing that one day I would find this world, these mages, again. Your help, too, I will need, my son. It is perilous and needs magic on both sides—the less is there, the greater it must be here, to protect them as they cross.''

''But if there's no magic there at all,'' Tally said doubtfully, perching beside Rhion on the sheepskin-covered bench, ''how can they reach out to guide our men?''

''There's magic and magic,'' Rhion explained quietly. ''Even someone who isn't mageborn can use a scrying-crystal after a fashion, under the influence of the proper drugs. But to reach out across the Void . . . I still don't see how . . .''

"Only with the power of the solstice-tide, the sun-tide, or to a lesser extent with the momentum of the equinox's balance," the old man said, pulling one corner of the fur he wore about his shoulders more firmly around his arms. *He's too old for this,* Rhion thought, watching the careful way he moved, seeing how thin those blue-veined wrists were in the gap between gloves and soft-knitted arm warmers. *So old . . .*

"Even so it will be a great gamble, my daughter," the blind mage went on. "But it is one we must take. Shavus, Gyzan, myself . . . all of us. Or else all of this . . ." His stiff hand, its fingers barely mobile now at all, moved to take in the scrupulous neatness of the study, with its potted herbs, its small shelf of books—even, Rhion noticed with a faint smile, its tremendously expensive, half-grown crocodile drying in a glass case near the fire : . . "All that we have lived for and have accumulated over the centuries will be for nothing. It will be in danger of vanishing like frost upon the grass with the sun's rising, and our world will be left with nothing but the might of the strong against the strong, the unscrupulousness of those both clever and wicked, and the demagogues who lead the mobs."

"You don't think it's an illusion of some kind, do you?" Tally asked softly, as she and Rhion descended the narrow stair that led from Jaldis' rooms down to a discreet door hidden away in a corner of the topmost chamber of the library. "Something he's convinced himself he's heard because he's hunted so long or because he wants it so badly?"

Rhion considered this as he worked the bolt on the other side of the heavy oak door back into place with a spell. "I don't think so," he said at length. "I've dealt with people whose illnesses stemmed from that kind of self-delusion . . . he's obsessed, but he doesn't have that air."

They crossed through the high-ceilinged marble chamber with its shelves of books and racks of scrolls, the floating ball of blue witchlight over Rhion's head making the gilt bindings wink and the shadows dart and play among the lightless pendules of the hanging lamp.

"A trick, maybe, or a trap . . . ?"

"Set by whom?" Rhion asked sensibly. "And for what purpose?"

Tally shrugged, uneasy at the thought herself, and pulled closer around her shoulders the thick robe of red wool and fur which covered her court-dress of green and white—the Erralswan colors.

"You hear about the—the Great Evils, the priests of Agon call them—spirits who try to lure people into danger and wickedness, the same way grims try to lure you into getting lost in the woods." She glanced sidelong at him as they descended the wide terrazzo stairs to the floors below, as if not sure how he'd react.

"Maybe they do exist," Rhion said. "Only everyone who's been out in wild country at night has seen grims for themselves, and knows how they act. From what I understand only the priests of Agon claim to have seen the Great Evils, and then they pretty much seem to be whatever will fit Agon's purposes at the time."

Tally chuckled her agreement. "You do have a point," she said. "On the other hand, everyone has seen wizards— and still believe the lies that are told about them. And that's illusion, if you will—the altering of perception. And people don't even need magic to do it."

Rhion, wrapped against the December cold in the black cloak of the Morkensik Order, with a plaid shawl the Gray Lady had given him over that, shivered. He had passed the Temple of the Eclipsed Sun on the way up from the city gates and had seen for himself the great new hall of sable pillars that spoke of the cult's increasing riches and power. The sight of it had brought back to him, with terrifying clarity, the cold self-assurance of the High Priest Mijac's voice from behind the veils, the hideous sense he had had of seeing men who had been released from responsibility for their deeds. Artists of illusion, Mijac had called wizards . . .

And yet he sensed that his growing dread stemmed from something deeper, some rotted ghost of memory connected somehow with the Dark Well, a memory that still stirred now and then in his dreams.

They passed down through the lower two rooms of the library, each larger than the one above, and through the vast, echoing spaces of the empty scriptorium below that, and so to the library's anteroom on the ground floor of the tower, and through the great bronze doors into the colonnade that embraced the palace's vast central court. Even in its pillared shelter, gusts of wind clutched at Rhion's mantle and Tally's long fur robe, and the driven snow, scudding before the wind across the granite paving blocks of the court, swirled between the columns and wet their feet.

Sheltered by a numinous aura of Who-Me? they passed through the vestibule of the palace's marble hall. There, under the shadows of the musicians' gallery, only a few lamps burned on the clustering pillars, but beyond, a hundred lights on tall bronze stands filled the hall with silky primrose radiance, warming the tucked and pearled velvets, the shimmering featherwork and ribbons, of the courtiers' clothing to a moving rainbow of crimson, blue, and green. Pausing in the shadowy doorway that led up to the private apartments, Rhion wiped the mist from his spectacle lenses, then looked out into the hall, automatically picking out those he knew.

The Duke—and in any room he'd ever been in all eyes still went first to the Duke—looked a little older, a little more tired, than a man of fifty should. Even his son's death in a practice joust—preparing for his first tournament three years ago on the eve of what would have been his seventeenth birthday— hadn't affected Dinar of Prinagos as badly as had his wife's last summer of a fever no one had thought much of until it was too late. The big man still had his old air of power, his easy movements which dominated everyone around him, but streaks of gray had begun to appear in his thickly curled black hair under its after supper crown of hothouse roses. Damson sat beside him, corseted cruelly into a gown whose entire front seemed to be an iridescent armor of pearls, her plump, jeweled fingers nimbly flicking at the glass spindles of a lace-making pillow.

Perhaps it was losing Tally's friendship, Rhion thought, or perhaps it was her obsession with Esrex—but it seemed to him that over the years the steely quality of a single-mindedness in her had grown. Lines of will and watchfulness carved deep in the suety face now, aging it under its heavy paint. Despite her ladylike occupation, her shrewd gray eyes traveled over the room, missing nothing of what they saw.

She was currently watching Marc of Erralswan with considerable disapproval. Dressed in a very short blue velvet tunic with elaborately padded sleeves, he was flirting with one of her maids-in-waiting, their teasing intimacy telling its own tale. Rhion sighed and gritted his teeth. Marc had never, even on the night of his wedding to Tally, laid a hand on his bride of convenience; it was not to be expected that he remain celibate. *But,* Rhion thought, illogically angry for Tally's sake, *does he have to be so goddam blatant about it?* As the Duke's son-in-law and the holder of considerable wealth and estates—not to mention as a beefy champion of the tilt-yards—he found his scope had considerably widened from the days when he was the captain of the ducal guard, and his hunting field hadn't been exactly narrow then.

Rhion glanced sideways at Tally and saw her face set in an attempt at unconcern. She shook her head comically and sighed, ''That's our Marc . . .'' But Rhion knew that it hurt her when the court ladies giggled about her behind their feathered fans.

And Esrex . . .

Esrex was almost invisible, half concealed in the shadow of a pillar, talking to someone who would have been hidden by still deeper shadows from any but mageborn eyes.

Rhion shivered. He was talking with a priest of Agon.

"Are there many of them at Court these days?" Rhion asked softly, as he and Tally moved through the small door and up the stairs. Their hands sought one another automatically—he had not seen her for nearly three months, since his last visit to Bragenmere in September. Even had he lived with her daily, he suspected he would have craved her touch. "Priests of Agon?"

"Was that who Esrex was talking to? I'm afraid so." Tally, like the rest of her family, had changed, her coltish skinniness maturing into spear-straight, graceful strength, her long features settling into serene beauty. Rhion knew that, over the years, Tally had patched up a working relationship with Damson—as two ladies of the same court must—but that never again had the sisters been friends. The isolation and the caution of leading a double life had left their mark on her—a kind of measured steadiness, sadness tinged with golden strength.

"Since the High Queen has had a shrine built to the Eclipsed Sun in the palace at Nerriok you see them more and more," she went on somberly. "Esrex is supposed to be very high in their hierarchy, though of course no one knows. And Father . . . he's had to be more careful with the cults, as you know."

That, Rhion also knew, had been the fruit of the aborted alliance with the Earl of the Purple Forest. The death of the Duke's son had destroyed the last chance of union with one of the other great Realms. With only a minor nobleman for a son-in-law Dinar of Mere had to take support where it could be found.

"With most of the priesthoods, it doesn't matter." Bars of tawny light from below crossed Tally's face as they climbed through the shadows of the columns, like two shadows themselves in the dim upper reaches of the great stair. "But they're not the same, are they?"

"No." Rhion remembered the masked men in the watchroom of the Temple, the words of the priest on the threshold: *As for lepers, and beggars, and slaves, Agon has a welcome for them, as he has for all who serve him* . . . And how many served him, he wondered, for the sake of that welcome, which relieved them of responsibility for what they did? He didn't know.

No one knew.

But he suspected that Esrex was not that kind of servant. With the lies of Agon's priests as his main source of information—lies, perhaps, that he wanted badly to believe—it might well be that Esrex was not aware of being a servant at all.

Glancing back down through an opening in the wall, he could see the ivory-fair head—losing, he could also see, its hairline's long struggle with destiny. Esrex' face, too, was prematurely lined, with petty stubbornness and will, and his eyes had a kind of restless glitter to them. Rhion knew that Esrex took drugs upon occasion, either on his own or as part of his involvement with the priests of the Eclipsed Sun, who gave them to their chosen followers; Rhion wondered what his consumption was up to these days.

"No, I'm afraid they're not."

Halfway down the gallery were the doors to the nursery wing, clear-grained red wood inlaid with patterns of silver wrought into intricate protective seals. The window shutters, Rhion knew, were silver, also—Damson had had them made—though it had been fifty years since there'd been a case of grim harrowing in Bragenmere. There were some these days who believed that silver was proof against a wizard's spells as well, but Rhion had no trouble reaching with his mind into the locks and shifting the silver pins.

A sentry dozed in the anteroom, and Rhion imperceptibly deepened the man's sleep with a whispered charm. From around the shut door of the room where the sickly Dinias slept came the drift of eucalyptus steam and the snores of a nurse. Elucida, at the age of eleven the biggest matrimonial catch in the Forty Realms, had her own suite and her own chaperon and maid. But the two sons of the Duke's younger daughter shared a smaller chamber, and there was no nurse whose dreams needed thickening as Rhion and Tally ghosted inside.

Brenat had been born when Kir was three—"Jaldis makes a good potion," Rhion had joked at the time. Standing in the doorway of the dark chamber and looking at the night-lamp's fretted red glow playing across those two double handfuls of brown curls, he felt a curious sense of unalloyed delight in these sons of his, a desire to whoop and shout, an almost uncontrollable yearning to touch . . . though he knew, as he had known the first time he had taken Tally in his arms, that it was madness.

The problem was that he could not now imagine a world that did not include his sons.

Kir's hand, clutching the hilt of the toy sword he'd fought tooth and nail to take to bed with him, was big in spite of its childish chubbiness. He would have the Duke's height when he grew up, as well as Tally's long, delicate features and gray eyes. That, Rhion thought in his moments of cynical despair, was fortunate—Marc was tall, too. Brenat's eyes were also gray. Tally, who adored the boys, sometimes spoke of another child, but they both knew they had been fools to have these.

"Will you be here to see them tomorrow?" Tally asked quietly, stepping closer to Rhion as he put his arm around her waist. She still had to bend her head just a little for him to kiss her temple.

"Oh, yes—till the storm lets up, in fact. That should be

sometime tomorrow." The wind groaned along the gallery as they stepped out again, closing the door behind them. The quilted red hangings which kept the chill from the walls in winter rippled uneasily with the scurrying draughts, as if bodiless monsters raced behind them to some unknown goal.

"I'm glad. They ask after you when you're not here, you know."

In spite of himself Rhion smiled. He'd seen his boys with Marc, polite and respectful and in awe of their putative father, but on his last visit in September Kir had said something to him about, "Father chasing lightskirts all around the court," with a disapproving look in his gray eyes.

"Well," Rhion had said at the time, "it probably wouldn't do to say that to him."

Kir's mouth had hardened. "But it's wrong. He's married to Mother. And it makes her sad when the other ladies laugh. You're a wizard, Rhion. Can't you make him stop?"

Rhion had groaned. "What, you, too?" This conversation had taken place in the mews, where Rhion had gone to help Tally doctor a sick goshawk and the boys had tagged along to see what trouble they could get into in the room where the varvels and jesses were stored and the lures repaired. "Look, Kir, you might as well find out early that magic can't make people do things differently than they do. It can't change what people are like."

"Dinias says it can." The boy had picked up a long tail-feather from the floor, where Brenat sat placidly arranging straws in order of their length, and dug among the leather-scraps near the workbench for a thong to wind around it like a simple lure. "Dinias says that a wizard can cast a spell on a man that will take away his brains and make him cut up his own wife with an ax, and when he wakes up in the morning he won't remember what he did, but they'll hang him anyway." He looked hopefully up into Rhion's face for corroboration of this gory program.

" 'Fraid not." Rhion sighed, realizing that it was a tale every child in the city heard as soon as they reached school.

Kir's face fell. "Oh. Dinias said you were a wizard and didn't have a soul, but I beat him up."

"Thus changing his opinion of me and endearing yourself to his father in one—er—blow."

And Kir had said, "Hunh?" and had looked at him with the baffled exasperation of a child confronted by adult nonsense.

Thinking back on the scene Rhion sighed again, and shook his head. Tally looked at him inquiringly, the glow of the small votive-light near the nursery-door turning her lashes to ginger and leaving her eyes in shadow.

"It's just—they grow so fast," he said softly. "And I envy you the time you have with them."

She reached over and gently scratched his beard, then drew his mouth to hers. "If I were anyone else," she murmured, "I would envy myself."

But much later, as he was dressing again by the low throb of ember light that glowed from the hearth in her room, he returned to the earlier topic—something they did with subjects discussed hours, weeks, or even months previously. Wind still savaged the window shutters behind their quilted hangings, its howling sounding louder now that the small noises of servants passing in the corridors had dwindled.

"It should be quieting down by noon," Rhion said, struggling into his shabby brown robes. "Then we should have nearly a week's clear weather, enough for me to get back to the Drowned Lands before the next big storm."

She held out his spectacles to him. Without them, kneeling among the sheets, he saw her only as an upright column of shadowy gold in the firelight, wreathed in points of light—her jewels, all that she now wore. "Will the Gray Lady be angry, if you leave at the equinox?"

"Not angry," Rhion said quietly, carefully hooking the

metal frames over his ears. "She'll understand. But the rites need a lot of power. If I'm not presiding, they get Cuffy Rifkin, an Earth-witch from up the marshes, to do it, and his strength isn't as great even as mine, which is only average. It puts the victim's life at greater risk. But the Gray Lady knows what I owe to Jaldis. Even at midnight of the equinox, getting Shavus and Gyzan across the Void is going to take more power than he should be trying to use these days. Maybe more than he has."

"He was very ill, the day after Winterstead." Behind the tawny halo of her hair the emblems of the house of Erralswan gleamed on the bed hangings amid a thicket of heraldic gingerbread, as if Marc's name and station covered the lovers literally as well as metaphorically. "I was afraid he'd had a stroke, or his heart had failed him. But he said no, it was only that he'd overtaxed himself . . ."

"I'll look in on him again tonight," Rhion said quietly, more worried than he cared to admit. He slung his cloak around his shoulders and the Gray Lady's plaid on top of that. "And he still won't have a slave to look after him?"

Tally shook her head. "And do you know," she said after a moment, "with what they say about the cult of Agon— about not knowing who is in it, who their spies are— sometimes I think that's just as well."

The palace bulked dark and silent as Rhion stepped out onto the ice-slick terrace, a sleeping beast with all its hues of terra cotta and peach and gold, its bronzes and its porcelains and its columns of porphyry and marble, drowned in the depths of night. Even so, Rhion chose to take the long way around from Tally's rooms, moving in silence through the barren, wind-lashed garden and surrounded once more in a cloudy haze of spells. What Damson and Esrex had had to say to one another on the day after his brush with the priests of Agon he had never found out, but he knew Esrex still sought proof that he was the father of Tally's children—

sought revenge for the fool he had made of himself before the court and the priests that day. And in spite of the Duke's deep friendship for Jaldis, his fondness for Rhion and his love for his younger daughter's children, Rhion never felt quite safe in Bragenmere.

In his rooms in the octagonal tower, Jaldis was asleep. Standing in the curtained door arch of the old man's chamber, Rhion listened to the soft hiss of his breathing and reflected that he'd heard that sound almost nightly for eleven years of sharing quarters in some of the worst accommodations in the Forty Realms. And looking around at the tidy cubicle, with its warm fire and fur robes, its books neatly shelved—two more had returned to Jaldis only last year, brought by travelers who'd found them in middens or estate sales, men who'd known the Duke was a collector—its small jars of herbs, crystals, and silver powder, he felt a vast relief that the old man had found shelter at last. The years had been hard on him. He had a fragile air these days that Rhion did not like.

The thought stirred in his mind, an uneasy whisper in the darkness.

Moving soundlessly, Rhion let the thick wool curtain fall and went into the tiny study. It was pitch dark there and cold—he moved easily through it, smelling the new-cured parchment, seeing, in the dark, how every crystal, every inkpot, and every piece of chalk and wax was in place and ready for Jaldis' hands. In the far corner a ladder led to the attic above, waste space under the tower's conical roof cap. As his hand touched the rungs a hideous sense of danger seized him, the sudden, overpowering conviction that Tally and his sons were in peril, immediate and terrible, from which only he could save them and only if he got there in time . . .

It was a spell, of course. And the fact that even here, in

the heart of his own rooms, Jaldis would feel such a spell was necessary troubled him deeply.

Brushing aside the phantom dreads, he ascended the ladder and opened the trap door.

It was bolted from the other side, of course—there were even spells on the bolt. Rhion remembered Jaldis' warnings, when the Gray Lady had sought to probe the secrets of the making of the Well. *The key to what magic is,* he had said. Something indeed to be protected at any cost, even at the cost of losing it entirely.

Then he stood in the dark of the loft, looking into the Well itself. It was quiet now, closed, a vague whisper of brownish shadow, a column of darkness within the scribbled circles of silver, blood, and light unpierceable even by mageborn eyes, a hidden whisper of primordial fear.

The attic had been closed for a week and, huge as it was, it smelled stuffy and cold, lingering traces of dust and incense clinging to the great wheel of the rafters overhead. Even the heat that rose from the rooms below did not warm it, and thin drafts worked bony fingers through the folds of Rhion's cloak and the robe beneath.

A world without magic, he thought. A world where all things were mechanical, sterile, even those which sounded most fantastic, like the wagons which traveled without beasts to draw them and the artificial lightning, or the flying machines. A world where beauty had been forgotten, and where the men and women born with wizardry in their blood and the gnawing conviction that other possibilities existed beyond the invisible curtain of dreams were unable to put their hand through that curtain to touch what lay on the other side.

A world that had begged for help.

A world of Jaldis' children, as Rhion was his child—a world to whom to pass his power, as he had passed it to Rhion. He would not turn aside from it.

Fear of the Dark Well—fear of what he half-remembered,

of what he half-guessed—was growing in Rhion, but he forced himself to remain where he was, gazing into that darkness as Jaldis had gazed for seven years now, seeking what lay beyond.

But the Dark Well held its secrets. And in time his fear overcame him, as he felt the refracted blackness of the rainbow abyss drawing him into itself. He backed to the trap door and climbed down the ladder, bolting the door behind him.

But the thought of it pursued him into his sleep, and troubled his dreams.

SIXTEEN

IT WAS CARNIVAL WHEN RHION CAME NEXT TO BRAGENMERE,
the Feast of Mhorvianne. Ribbons and bunting decorated the
tenement balconies of the Lower Town, yellow and red and
green, lining the route of what had obviously been a procession. Garlands of roses, hyacinth, and cyclamen still twisted
round the porch pillars of the temples in the squares and the
pediments of the public baths. The remains of pink and white
petals could be discerned, trampled in the muck of the brim-
ming gutters, and the public fountains of the markets still
smelled faintly of the more inexpensive varieties of wine.

"You could have knocked me over with a feather," Tally
said, after their first kisses had been exchanged in the deserted shadows of the library vestibule, where even on the
gray spring afternoon the slaves had already kindled the
lamps. It was coming on to rain again—Rhion wondered
whether Jaldis had been asked to keep the skies clear for the
procession. Tally wore an unlikely geranium-hued gown
whose hanging clusters of ribbons were tipped with bells,
haloing her every movement in a starry glister of sound.
"Father's getting married again."

"Getting married?" Rhion paused, startled and amused,
in the act of cleaning his spectacle-lenses, which had gotten
rather smudged in their initial embrace.

"Yes. To the heiress of Varle, who's about as old as I am.
Esrex is *furious*."

"What business is it of his?" Hand in hand they ascended the long curve of the library stairs, surrounded by what Rhion—in reminiscence of a joke as old as the hills—thought of as the Nobody-Here-But-Us-Chickens Spell. Rhion had guessed from the bustle in the palace courtyard below that the library would be deserted; their footfalls echoed with small, sharp music in the tall vaults of the marble ceilings. "I mean, except that it's finally the foreign alliance he's been after all these years . . ."

"Poor father." She half-laughed at the irony of it—two marriageable daughters, each determined to have the man she wanted and not the alliance their father craved. "But it's more than that. Since Syron's death . . ." Her voice still flawed a little on the name of the young brother she had loved, "I think Esrex has gotten used to the idea that Dinias would naturally be Father's heir. And with offers coming in from all sides for Elucida's hand . . . Did you know the High Queen even sent her astrologer to take the aspects of her birth and cast a horoscope?"

"You mean, to marry Elucida to the little Prince?" Rhion's eyebrows tweaked upward—quite a fate, he thought, for that tiny fair-skinned child, sleeping in a hollow log where the grims had abandoned her. "Esrex better not count on that one. Shavus tells me the boy's sickly and suffers from convulsions. Besides, I thought the High Queen was one of Agon's initiates and didn't hold with astrologers."

"Well," Tally said, "when it comes down to it, *nobody's* supposed to go to astrologers and necromancers and people who make love-potions . . ."

"Don't look at me; I've retired."

"But all that will change," she finished simply, "if Elucida is no longer going to be sister to the Duke of Mere one day. Not to mention the White Bragenmeres being cut out of the succession entirely."

Rhion was silent, remembering Esrex' overwhelming, bitter pride. Upon occasion, he wondered whether what really angered that young scion was the suspicion that any kinswoman of his had mingled her blood, not with a wizard, but with a banker's son.

Jaldis rose from his chair as they entered his study and hobbled to greet them, the huge, opal rounds of his spectacle-lenses flashing strangely in the witchlight that burned like marshfire above his head. Rhion frowned, seeing how bent and frail the old man looked, and wondered if he'd been working with the Dark Well since the winter solstice, probing at its shadowy secrets with whatever power of his own he could raise.

Or was it merely, he thought, that he was getting old?

"Have Shavus and Gyzan come?"

Jaldis shook his head. "They will be here late tonight." The fox-fur wrap which covered his shoulders and chest slightly muffled the voice of the box. The chamber was warm, but still the old man clung to it, and now and then Rhion saw him shiver. "Shavus said that with things as they have been, it was best . . ."

"Things?" Rhion's frown deepened. "What things?"

"You have not seen these, then?" The old man turned and limped back to the table. From the side of his eye, Rhion saw Tally's somber face and realized that the sheet of cheap yellow paper which the old man held out was not news to her.

It was a crudely block-printed handbill, labeled, *The God of Wizards*. It depicted a grossly goat-headed man in a wizard's long robe—in the print there was no attempt to show what color, or what Order, only that it was hung all over with sun-crosses, gods-eyes, and other symbols of magic—copulating with a naked woman whose mouth was open in a protesting scream. A dead baby, its throat slit, sprawled beside them.

"According to Shavus, these have been appearing in the streets of Nerriok for weeks."

Rhion's hand was shaking with anger as he set the leaflet down. *Artists of illusion* . . . "Did Shavus say anything else?"

"Only that he would speak to me more of it when he arrives tonight." The blind wizard removed his spectacles, laying them down upon the desk. Beside the leaflet, Rhion saw a scrap of paper bearing a few lines of the Archmage's explanatory scrawl. He glimpsed Gyzan's name and remembered that the Blood-Mage had his house on one of the capital's outlying islets. The leaflet could very well have been found shoved under his door.

"Have you shown the Duke?"

"It only arrived today." Jaldis hobbled to the hearth and stood there, holding out his crooked hands to the coals. "I fear it may mean they shall have to cut short their visit to the other world . . ."

"Cut short?" Rhion stared at him, shocked to realize the extent of Jaldis' obsession with the project. "What makes you think he'll be willing to go at all?"

Jaldis turned back; by the startled ascent of his white eyebrows, Rhion realized the old man was equally shocked that the question would even have been raised. "Cancel our plans? I have sought them—Eric and Paul, his helper and fellow student—for seven years. I am not going to put the matter off over a few pieces of paper."

"It's not a few pieces of paper. It could be preparation for something, some major stroke . . ."

"Indeed it could." Jaldis limped back to him and took his arm, his thin face in its frame of white hair as grave, as earnest as Rhion had ever seen it. "Don't you see? It is because of this that he *must* go. The enemies of magic are moving, my son. And what happened in one universe could just as easily happen here."

But Rhion was uneasy as, unseen in the gallery's shadows, he watched the feasting in the palace's great hall that night.

The Duke, when he had seen him before dinner, had apologized for not asking Rhion or his master to the feast or the masking afterward. It was a state occasion, and the priests of all the Great Cults would be there. As Tally had said, since losing the possibility of foreign marriage alliances the Duke had become more careful of the opinions of the cults.

They were all present, seated in places of honor, from Darova's gold-robed Archimandrite and the red-gowned Archpriestess of Mhorvianne down to the local Solarist Holy Woman in unadorned white who regarded the whole scene with the polite interest of an adult at a children's party. It was not lost on Rhion that Esrex, costumed for the masking in the simple black pantaloon and white mask of a juggler, was sitting next to Mijac.

His eye traveled as it had three months ago to others he knew around the board and to the Duke, recognizable despite his red leather huntsman's costume and spiked black-and-gold mask. The way he moved, the warm charm of his manner, as much as the broad shoulders and strongly curled black hair, would have identified him had he been in rags. At his side was his new bride, blond and pretty and, as Tally had said, younger than the Duke's own daughters, costumed in a pearl-sewn gown supposed to represent a shepherdess. The plump little lady in the improbable goddess robes beside her, being gracious and kind and welcoming, was unmistakably Damson. On the Duke's other side sat Dinias, a thin pale boy in scarlet who looked as if his chest was hurting him again, and, gowned as a woman for the first time in jewel-plastered brocade and clearly embarrassed about the visible expanses of flat white chest, Elucida, promoted to womanhood on this, the feast of the Goddess of Love. As usual when she was nervous Elucida was taking refuge in her formidable erudition, and arguing theology with the Archimandrite, at whose left hand she sat.

The tables had been set in a big U around the sides of the

hall to accommodate courtiers, merchants, and nobles of town and country; Rhion scanned the gaily costumed figures around them for a glimpse of Tally. She had told him Ranley the physician was coming as the God of Ocean complete with the Ocean's Twelve Daughters, and Rhion wondered where they'd found eleven other girls of Tally's height and build. They had, however—all were moving about the hall, up and down the tables as they were cleared after the final course, flirting with this man or that, absurdly gowned in identical pearls and green silk, with long green wigs like braided seaweed hanging down their backs. Rhion smiled, trying to guess which one of them was Tally.

Then his eyes passed over Esrex again, and his smile faded. Esrex, too, was watching, clearly trying to determine the same thing.

Overhead in the musician's gallery, a trumpet shrilled. A procession of young men trooped into the hall, clothed in the fantasy regalia of barbarian knights, dancing in time to the martial music and swinging their gold-hilted swords. Among them Rhion recognized his son Kir, garbed as a chieftain's squire, flourishing his weapon with a firm adeptness well beyond his years. He'd seen Brenat earlier, costumed as a baby sprite and sound asleep on what appeared to be Kithrak the war-god's cloak—at least, he thought with wry amusement, there was no doubt about *his* paternity. Where Kir got his streak of ferocity he couldn't imagine.

But looking at the boy, solemn and blazing with controlled excitement among the tall mock-warriors around him, Rhion felt the stirring of pride in his heart, a delight in his son's perfection, even at something as incomprehensible as weaponry . . .

Raising his eyes, he saw Esrex' son Dinias again, slouched at the High Table, watching with sweetmeats clutched in his sticky hand.

And it came to Rhion for the first time that Esrex sought to expose Tally's iniquity, not out of revenge for past slights or hatred for him as a wizard, but in order to discredit the boys whom the Duke favored far above his unprepossessing heir.

Better, maybe, he thought with a chill, that the Duke marry again, to father another son and put both his grandsons out of the running . . .

A hand touched his arm. He spun around, startled, and found himself looking up into the face of one of the Ocean's Twelve Daughters, whose gray eyes laughed at him from behind an explosion of green feathers. "I had to look for you five or six times before I saw you standing here," she said softly, leading him through the half-hidden doorway and toward the dark of the stair. They paused to kiss in the shadows, the down of the mask trim tickling his nose, and all considerations of the Duke and Shavus and Esrex—of wizardry and danger and the perils of the Dark Well—slipped for a time into insignificance.

"Come," she breathed. "I think by this time everyone's lost track of whether there are eleven Daughters of Ocean out there or twelve."

The last of the fireworks were blossoming like chrysanthemums against the tar-black sky when Rhion again reached the library tower. He'd left Tally sleeping, and the sight of her closed eyelids, her face in the braid-crimped swatches of her hair relaxed as a child's, had filled him with both tenderness and guilt. *I shouldn't have left her alone in this place,* he thought, drawing his knitted pullover on over his head. And then, *Don't be absurd. Her father's the Duke, for gods' sake—Marc may be a casual husband but he wouldn't let anything happen to her, or to the children . . .*

The smell of coming rain was thick in the air—the rockets cast red and gold flares against the louring bellies of the clouds. The fragile sweetness of spring, of new grass and damp earth, breathed about him as he made his way through the darkness of the gardens, conscious of soft giggles and silken rustlings in grove and thicket as couples celebrated the coming of spring in the age-old fashion. Between the Carnival of Masks and the celebrations of the Duke's new wedding, the courtiers had already had a week and a half of continuous feasting and dancing, to culminate in tomorrow night's procession to Mhorvianne's shrine on the edge of Lake Pelter—Rhion could only shake his head wonderingly at their stamina.

And tomorrow night, he thought, climbing the curving marble stairs—when the Sea Lady's worshipers knelt masked in her precinct, to be cleansed of their sins so that crops could grow again in the lands and when the Gray Lady's husband stretched himself on the granite altar to receive both the knife and the power of the stars—the Dark Well would open. And Shavus and Gyzan would step into the abyss.

And after that . . .

He opened the small door in the topmost of the library's rooms, and ascended the winding little stair. But even as he climbed he knew something was wrong.

No sound met his ears from the room above. No hospitable thread of firelight rimmed the tiny upper door. And as he came closer, he heard the thin drone of Jaldis' voice scraping like a cricket at the syllables of Shavus' name.

Goddess, no. He can't stand another failure—another three months of searching, of waiting . . .

And who knew what would happen in those three months?

Alone in the dark of the workroom, Jaldis sat with his brownish crystal cradled in his hand. A wan feather of blue witchlight flashing off the scrying-stone's facets prickled the rounds of his spectacles with tiny fire. Rocking back and forth with concentration he crooned, "Shavus . . . Shavus Ciarnin, Archmage . . ." over and over as he channeled all his will, all his strength, into reaching out to his friend's mind and getting him to look into his own crystal, wherever he might be.

"What happened?" Quietly Rhion brought up the other chair.

Raising his head tetchily, Jaldis snapped, "If I knew do you think I'd be doing this? I'm sorry," he added immediately, and stretched out his hand in apology. "I have been seeking word since before midnight. I scried the road between Nerriok and Bragenmere, even tried to scry Gyzan's house . . . and saw no closer than three streets away from it as usual, I might add."

"Dammit!" Rhion whispered. "It's been raining on and off, yes—the roads are muddy and the creeks swollen. But I'd have thought Shavus would have left enough time . . ."

"No," Jaldis corrected him softly. "No. When I said that I had scried that road, I mean that I have scried, to the best of my knowledge, every mile of it. And everywhere it appears passable. It is not a question of . . . simple delay."

He set down his crystal. Up until a year or so ago his hands had had enough mobility for him to cut his own fingernails— latterly Rhion or Tally had done it, but one or two of them still had the look of claws in the wavery magelight.

Rhion was silent as the implications of his words sank in. The memory returned to him, like a haunting thread of music, of the poster of the God of Wizards, and his uneasy conviction that something else was afoot. "It might still be something simple," he said hesitantly. "Illness or something that has nothing to do with . . . with their being wizards. They could have met bandits. A horse could have gone lame . . ." His voice trailed off. All those things sounded weak and unlikely. Such things happened—but they seldom happened to the Archmage of the Morkensiks or to the Blood-Mage Gyzan.

"Look," he went on after a moment. "We'll speak to the

Duke, first thing in the morning. He can have men out on the road . . .''

"Indeed." With the fumbling care of the old, Jaldis removed his spectacles and laid them beside the scrying-crystal, then bowed his head so that the bridge of his nose rested against the hooked edge of his fingers. "Indeed, that . . . that is what he must do. Surely he will find them by nightfall . . .''

"Or the following day," Rhion agreed. "In rains like we've been having it takes four days, easy, to get to Nerriok. Seven or eight from the forest of Beldirac, if that's where Shavus was. If one of the bridges washed out . . .''

Without raising his head, the blind mage said, "It cannot wait four days." He spoke as simply, as steadily, as if the subject under discussion were some cantrip for his patron's entertainment, some magical toy of fires and smokes. "If he has not come by the stroke of midnight, then I must go myself."

For one long beat Rhion was silent, though it would not have been true to say that he was shocked or surprised. But it took a moment, before he could speak.

"The hell you will!"

The old man raised his head and seemed to regard him from the collapsed ruin of his eyes. "Of course I will go. Rhion, I have waited seven years to find them again. Searched seven years, solstice after solstice, equinox after equinox. The last time I waited they were gone from me, vanished . . . There is no question of waiting another three months."

Rhion was on his feet now, cold with a panic that was partly anger, partly something he did not want to look at too closely just yet. "As far as I'm concerned, there's no question of *not* waiting another three months, or six months, or as long as it takes to locate Shavus and Gyzan! You see by magic, you speak by magic . . .''

"I've told you before that it should make no difference."

"And what if it does?" He was shouting now, his quick

anger covering the terrible chill of fear; the fear for Jaldis covering that other fear that his mind turned away from, refused to see even in itself . . .

If he goes you'll have to go with him.

"Holy gods, with the amount of power it takes to cross the Void, the crossing itself might kill you! You damn near had a stroke once, just working with that thing . . ."

"I will be well." The quiet serenity of his voice was unshakable, the depth of his dedication—his obsession—like a stone foundation unmovable even by the earthquake that had drowned Sligo. "I must go, Rhion. To help them, and to . . ."

"No."

The old man simply faced him, his scarred mouth with its set, drooping line as stubborn as a child's.

"And if I have to go up to that loft with a scrub-brush and wipe out the circles that are holding the Dark Well open to keep you from stepping into it and killing yourself, I'll do it."

Still Jaldis said nothing. The huge crystal spectacles on the table by his elbow seemed to stare up at Rhion's face in defiant silence.

There was something so childlike in that silence, so sure of itself, that fear-born anger swept over Rhion like a wave. "Right," he gritted between his teeth, knowing that nothing would shake Jaldis from his resolve. Turning away he picked up the broom from the corner and started for the ladder that led up to the attic trap.

From the tail of his eye, he saw Jaldis move one crippled hand.

The shock-wave that struck him took his breath away, knocking him almost off his feet and wrenching the broom from his hands. It crashed against the wall and fell clattering, its shaft snapped in two pieces. The next instant pain hit him, his vision dissolving in a swirl of grayness and flakes of falling fire. Agony clamped his head and twisted his guts like a wrenching hand. His knees turned to water and he fell, pressure crushing his chest, smothering him like burning stones. In the roaring of his ears, he thought he heard the thunder of power, the scream of black rage, blind and mute for years, a sightless revenge tearing his flesh to pieces, darkening his eyes . . .

Then he could breathe again. As he lay gasping, he was dimly conscious of the sound of something falling, the scrabble of something crawling desperately to him across the wooden floor. Crippled hands shook as they turned him over, touched his face, the bent fingers absorbing back the last of the pain while a sweet, buzzing voice said "Rhion! Oh, Rhion, forgive me . . . !"

He opened his eyes. His head still throbbed with the echo of what had felt like a vise about to split his skull and his stomach flinched with nausea. Smeared and blurred by the floor dirt on his spectacles, he saw Jaldis crouching beside him, anxiety twisting his ashen face. The horrifying vision that for a moment had flashed through his mind, the terrible sight of some nightmare entity, blind and crippled and tongueless for years of resentful inner fury, retreated into a shadow and left him feeling, not frightened of the old man who had done such a thing to him, but overwhelmed with pity. Tears tracked down from beneath the scarred eyelids, the jeweled artificial eyes, glistening in the witchlight.

"Rhion, I am sorry! So terribly sorry. I don't know what came over me . . ."

Rhion laughed shakily, knowing perfectly well that Jaldis did know, and was scorched with shame to the bottom of his soul. He closed his plump hand on the crippled one. "Not so sorry you wouldn't do that to me again if I tried to stop you, I bet."

"Rhion . . ." There was pleading in his voice. Rhion sat up, all his joints tingling with the backwash of the fevered pain, and hugged the old man close. It was like embracing a bag of sticks. Past his shoulder, he saw Jaldis' crutches lying on the floor near the table. The old man had tried to run to him, forgetting them, and falling, had crawled.

"Rhion," Jaldis said softly after a few more moments. "You may come with me—indeed, I pray that you will. But it is your own choice. The peril of crossing the Void will be great, maybe greater than either of us can survive. Eric and his friends may not be able to raise sufficient power there, even with the equinox, to guide us across. But I beg you, do not try to stop me. If I must, I will sit up guarding the Dark Well—guarding you—for the next twenty-four hours. But to be ready for the crossing, I will need rest, need sleep. Swear to me, please swear to me, that you will not try."

"Of course I swear it, Jaldis," Rhion said, deeply distressed that the old man would beg him thus—in spite of the fact, he thought wryly the next moment, that he'd just demonstrated the need for such an oath.

"If you do not choose to come, I hold you in no blame," the old man went on rapidly, his hands closing hard around Rhion's, as if willing him to understand his obsession, his need. "Truly, I leave you with my blessing. Only guard my books while I am gone, do not let strangers or curiosity seekers like the Gray Lady or Gyzan touch them . . ."

"Don't be silly," Rhion said. "I'm not letting you go without me." It was as if he had meant to say it all along.

Jaldis embraced him again, his arms surprisingly strong but his body and his narrow skull with its long streamers of white hair, fragile and delicate as a bird's against Rhion's sturdy shoulder. "My son . . ."

"Look." Rhion took off his filthy spectacles, pulled a cotton kerchief from the pocket of his robe, and wiped at the glass, peering across at his master as he did so. "It's still almost twenty-four hours until the equinox. Shavus and Gyzan could walk through that door any minute, covered with mud and cussing out their horses. Whether we're going to another universe or staying in this one . . ." He forced lightness into his voice. ". . . we're both going to need a lot of rest between now and then."

The blind man nodded. His face in the blue glow of the witchlight was wax and ashes. The magic of ill had taken from him strength he could not well spare. Rhion had forgotten, over the years, the old man's terrible power, which Jaldis had so seldom used, and had forgotten how strong the bond between master and pupil could be, and the dreadful hold of a master-spell over the student's mind. Jaldis knew, no one better, every vein and muscle and nerve of him, had seen how the fibers of his mind wove together and how memory and spirit and soul informed his flesh. His whole body hurt, and deep in his heart, buried and deliberately unseen, was the whispered knowledge that it could have been far worse.

"Sleep . . . yes," Jaldis murmured. "To rest . . . to meditate . . . Rhion, I'm trusting you not to try to stop me. I'm trusting you not to . . . to damage the Dark Well, or try to, while I sleep. I need to sleep, will need it so badly. I trust you, my son."

Trust me, Rhion thought a little bitterly, when fifteen minutes later he stood looking down at Jaldis' slumbering form, like a paralytic child's among the dark quilts of his bed. *Trust me to stand back and let you walk into danger. Trust me to enable you to get yourself killed in pursuit of your dream.*

Jaldis, he remembered, had once done the same to him. When it would have been far more sensible for him to have remained home and learned accounting from his father, Jaldis had taught him, even in pain and disorientation and new mourning for sight and voice and freedom; had helped him to pursue his own perilous dreams.

Maybe all dreams end in death, Gyzan had said.

That was the worst thing about being a wizard, he thought, as he moved around the little rooms, tidying them from habit, exhausted but unable to sleep yet, washing the supper dishes and setting the books to rights in the places where he knew Jaldis always kept them. Eventually, one saw too much. One knew too many things, and no decision was ever clear anymore.

No wonder some wizards went a little mad.

He looked across the room at the ladder which led up to the attic. His eyes strayed to the broom, its shattered pieces still lying where they had been flung by the force of Jaldis' rage. The handle was charred and splintered, but the business end could still be used. It took at least three days to weave a Dark Well's outer circles, to create that terrible flaw in the fabric of the Universe through which its dark interstices could be seen. If anything happened to it now, Jaldis would be crushed with grief, shattered with anxiety and sorrow for those young men whose voices he had heard in the Void . . .

But Jaldis would be alive.

Yet Rhion had sworn. Jaldis trusted him. And there was always the chance that Shavus would, in fact, show up at the last minute, as he had shown up so many times before.

Rhion opened the window shutters and stood looking out over the sleeping palace below him and the city—its mazes of roof tiles and arcades, balconies and squares and pillared temples—lying huddled under the scudding grimness of charcoal clouds. Deep in his bones he could feel the stirring of the equinox's approach, as he could sometimes in meditation feel the pull of the moon.

And as strong, as deep, as silent as that awareness, was the knowledge in his blood that Shavus would not come, that come tomorrow's midnight, he and Jaldis would face the darkness of the Void themselves.

SEVENTEEN

IT RAINED THE FOLLOWING DAY. AFTER A FEW HOURS OF troubled dreams Rhion walked out through the Lower Town, where he and Tally had used to go, past the Temple of Agon with its windowless granite walls, and out to the marshes, like beaten steel under a flat silver sheet of sky. There was a shrine there, to some forgotten god, crumbled almost back to its native stones now, but built upon the invisible quicksilver track of a ley. In a corner of its old sanctuary, Rhion angled the facets of his scrying-crystal to the thin, cool light, and concentrated all his power and everything he could draw up from the ley and down from the first-stirrings of the equinox-tide into the calling of Shavus' name.

While gray rain whispered in the hollows of the broken floor and the wild herons rose crying from the reeds, he summoned every foot of the road between Nerriok and Bragenmere into the crystalline lattices of the stone's heart, scrying every footbridge, every gully, every curve of the mountain track where the rain sometimes washed stones down to block the way.

But he saw no sign of the Archmage. And the light grew broad in the sky.

All over the Forty Civilized Realms, men and women would be drawing and heating water for ritual baths, shaking out the soot-colored cloaks of penitence, preparing to go masked to the shrines of Mhorvianne to ask that bright-haired

Lady's forgiveness for the sins of a year. The Solarists, of course, serenely confident that there was no other god than the Sun in Mid-Heaven, would undoubtedly stay home tonight and play cards; the priests of Agon, behind their windowless walls, would hold their own smoky and terrible rites. In the Drowned Lands of Sligo the ancient rituals of the Moon would go forward, as they had gone forward for three thousand years, treading out the Maze in a shifting aura of blood and starlight.

And in the octagonal tower at Bragenmere . . .

Rhion shivered and blew on his cold-reddened fingers, though he knew it was not the cold that touched his flesh.

Before leaving the tower, he had made another effort to talk Jaldis out of his resolve, hoping against hope that the light of day might make the old man more amenable. Obsession, he well knew, like many things, worsens with the night.

But Jaldis had only shaken his head. "When I spoke to them—to Eric and to Paul—" And the voice of the box slid and gritted over the alien names. "—at the Solstice, I told them how to create a Dark Well, that they may see into it, and guide us through. Even that will cost them all they can raise. I cannot abandon them."

Rhion took a deep breath, knowing the words he had to say and fearing them as he had not feared the faceless soldiers of Agon. "All right," he said shakily. "I agree that someone has to go. But it doesn't have to be both of us."

Rain had wept against the shutters, the wind groaning in the rafters, hair-raisingly like the voice of something coming from the Dark Well itself. Jaldis had sat for a long time, his untouched bread and coffee before him, looking up with sightless eyes into the face of the young man who had followed him, had cared for him, and had learned from him all that he had to teach. His hand found Rhion's unerringly, as it had always done. "My son . . ." the voice of the box began, the voice that could embody no emotion, none of the feeling that tugged at the muscles of his face. Then, for a long moment, a pause.

"My son," he said again, more steadily. "Thank you—for I know how little you want to undertake this quest at all. But it cannot be. A cook knows by the smell of the broth what herbs are lacking. A farrier can tell what ails a horse by a glance at the stable muck. I have studied the nature of the Universe, the structure of magic, for sixty-five years, and Shavus has for thirty-five, even though for part of that time he was not aware what it was he learned. Even Gyzan, or the other great ones of our own order—Nessa the Serpentlady of Dun, or Erigalt of Pelter—might stare at the solution in that other universe and not realize that it was anything which pertained to magic at all. My son . . ."

His grip tightened, like a hard-polished root over the younger man's soft palm and pudgy fingers. "My son, I love you, and no more now than when you have offered to go in my stead. But yours is not a powerful enough wizardry to do what needs to be done. Maybe not even to cross the Void alive. A strange and terrible magic fills that darkness, and I do not know its strength. You simply have not the experience."

Quietly, Rhion said, "I don't want you to die."

The old man smiled. "Then I may not. It is only an hour past sunrise—there is an entire day for Shavus to reach us. And then all our fears, all our endeavors on this subject, will be for naught, and we'll laugh about them over the steam of tomorrow's coffee. But thank you. I will never forget."

Listening to the thrumming of the rain on the tower's sand-colored walls, Rhion had felt only a sinking darkness of despair. If Shavus had been delayed, the rain would delay him further. It had been too late even then to do much in the way of turning the storm aside.

And now, huddled in the sheltered corner of the old shrine

under what was left of its crumbling tile roof, that despair returned, bringing panic and a hundred imagined scenarios of disaster like camp followers in its train.

Toward noon, before he left the shrine, Rhion called to the Gray Lady through the crystal and, after a few moments, saw her face in its facets, more beautiful, more ageless than in true flesh, like a crystal herself filled with hidden light.

"I don't know what I can do," Rhion concluded, having told her of Shavus' nonappearance and Jaldis' resolve to cross the Void, come what may, that night. "I can't let him go alone. He says he'll be all right, that Eric and Paul—the two wizards on the other side—will take care of him. But I can't know that."

"No," the Lady said softly. Her hazel eyes clouded, and Rhion felt a stab of guilt for laying upon her a new trouble, when, with the difference his absence could make to the power of the rites, she had sufficient worries already. "No— I understand your fears. But Jaldis is right in saying that Shavus may yet appear. He's a wily old man, and very powerful, trained in the skills of war. Neither is Gyzan to be reckoned lightly. They both know your master's resolve. If they could not come, Shavus would contrive to send word."

"To what purpose?" Rhion sighed and straightened his water-flecked spectacles with one plump forefinger. "If he tells Jaldis not to undertake the quest to this other world— which he will if he sends word at all—Jaldis will only ignore it. He is—obsessed."

"Then you must make your choice," the Lady said, and there was sadness in her eyes. "But Rhion, if you both go . . . What will become of Jaldis' books?"

"Ah . . ." Rhion looked away, unable to meet her eyes even through the crystal's tiny image. Away across the marsh, hunting horns were ringing through the drizzly mist as a party of young nobles splashed their horses through puddles, their dogs bounding happily in their wake. Rhion thought he recognized Marc of Erralswan's bright-green doublet, close beside a lady in a yellow gown with long cascades of raven curls. He did not want to lie to the Gray Lady, but Jaldis had ordered him strictly to say that he did not know.

"Rhion," she said sharply, calling his gaze back to hers. "This is not a trick. Does he think I will wait until his back is turned and then come to steal them?"

It was, in fact, exactly what Jaldis thought, and something Rhion himself would not quite put past the Lady, much as he cared for her. So he only said, "He's made provision for them. They'll be safe—Shavus or any of the Morkensiks, will be able to get to them."

"But not corrupt and superstitious Earth-witches, not Bone-Casters who weave little spell-dollies in straw and divine the future from the flight of ducks. I must go," she said, exasperation at the opinion of her fading from her face, leaving it weary and sad. "It is noon. I must rest, and prepare. And so must you, if you will do this thing tonight."

Rhion nodded. Indeed, he thought, if the victim of the spring rite were to survive, the Lady would need all her power—even as he would need all of his, such as it was, to see the other side of the Void alive. He felt spent already from long scrying. The slow stirring of the sun-tide was rising in his veins, like the pull of the tide in his blood.

"I pray the Goddess will keep you safe."

Her image faded. Rhion got to his feet, chilled and slightly nauseated, though, as usual, the nausea changed to an overwhelming craving for sweets before he was halfway up the muddy road to the town gates. He bought half a dozen balls of steamed sweet dough wrapped in greased paper in the Old Town market, enough for himself and his sons; the rain had eased by this time, and the steam from the vendor's cart blew in soft white clouds, like rags of fog in the gray air. Most of the market stands were shutting down, farmers and their wives folding up the bright-colored awnings of orange and blue, to return to their homes to prepare for the procession tonight. Not only in his own blood could Rhion feel the coming of the equinox. It was implicit in every closed shop, in every home-hurrying slave, in the steam that leaked from every window he passed on his way back to the palace. The city and all who worshipped the orthodox gods had lapsed into the time of preparation, the time of acknowledgment of their sins from whose consequences only the gods could save them. But for the mageborn there was no salvation. As he walked by the Bull and Ring Tavern in Market Lane, a glimpse of something yellow caught his eye—he saw it was the poster of the "God of Wizards" crudely pasted to the wall beside the door.

In the rooms above the library tower, he found Jaldis asleep and no sign yet of Shavus' coming. Jaldis' books, he noticed, were gone, entrusted already under every seal of protection the blind mage could devise to the Duke's care. The old man must have told him that he was going away for a time, though of course not how or where. The secret of the Dark Well was too deep, too dangerous, to be shared, even with one whose lack of ability or thaumaturgical training would have made his knowledge harmless.

The afternoon passed like the slow gray wheel that crushes out the grain. Rhion knew he should sleep, should rest and meditate, but sought out Tally and his sons, instead. The boys were far too absorbed in the excitement of trying on their masks to have much attention to spare even for their favorite of their mother's friends. It was said to be bad luck to try on one's mask before the procession, but the boys were doing exactly what Rhion and his friends had done at their age—holding the masks to their faces with meticulous care not to touch the flesh and seeing how close they could come. In the secrecy of a loft above the mews, Rhion and Tally made love, feverishly clinging to one another amid the smells of sawdust and leather and the cinnamon of Tally's perfume, and lay locked in one anothers' arms in the huddle of cloaks and horse blankets until nearly dark.

The dark fell early, overcast and grim. After a final, inconclusive attempt to argue Jaldis out of his resolve, Rhion tried to sleep, but the slow fever of the spring-tide was flowing too strongly in him now, the awareness of the heavens' turning towards their balance point . . . and the awareness of how increasingly unlikely it was that Shavus would arrive in time.

"You are fretted," the old man said comfortingly and patted Rhion's arm. He seemed rested, stronger and livelier and with the quiet serenity of one whose mind is made up. "That is understandable . . ."

"*Fretted* is *not* how I'd describe my reaction to the prospect of throwing myself into an infinity of chaos, with nothing reaching out toward me from the other side but a bunch of half-trained wizards who can't even work magic!"

Jaldis smiled. "All will be well," he said softly. "They need my help, Rhion, if they are to defeat the enemies of magic in their world—if they are to return their world to the true paths of power. I cannot turn my back."

"We can't leave this way!" he pleaded. "Shavus could be in trouble! We have no idea what's going on in Nerriok, in Felsplex, or anywhere . . ." He thought of Esrex again and of Tally and his children—a wizard's children—floating like chips in a tailrace on the deep intrigues of court.

Jaldis' face contracted for one moment with concern, anxiety for his friend and for all the possible permutations of what would happen in this world after they left it . . . then he shook his head. "We cannot think of that," he said, and his lined face was deadly grave. "Truly, truly, we cannot. Not if we are going to call forth our entire strength, our entire concentration, to make the leap across the abysses of the Void. We can think of neither the future that we go to nor the past that we leave behind."

From the massed shadows of the pillars of the library porch Rhion watched the Procession of Masks assemble in torch smoke and drizzle. The stone-gray cloaks of the penitents gave them a look of fantastic ghosts, the cressets' glare picking out here the blue mask of a grim, there a lion head's serene golden eyes. Horns, jewels, feathered dragon manes . . . men and women alike, no matter what god or gods they worshipped. Rhion suspected that the crowd numbered a sprinkling of Solarists—certainly he thought he had seen Esrex and Damson, discreetly masked from the eyes of other gods than Mhorvianne.

"They won't miss me," Tallisett murmured, standing in the darkness at his side. On either side of the bland silver face of a marsh-fae her unbound hair hung in curtains of bronze-gold silk, darkened with the rain and the bath. "The boys are with Dinias, his nurse is looking after them all."

Rhion trusted the furtive and sickly heir no more than he trusted Esrex, but there was no time to think of more elaborate arrangements. Dread and tension were making it difficult for him to think at all; added to those, were his growing guilt at leaving Tally and his sons unprotected and the black premonition of disaster which had settled on his heart. "Tally . . ." he began desperately, but she touched his arm and shook her head.

Together, beneath the cloudy cloak of his spells, they made their way to the massive bronze doors, where Jaldis waited. The smoky torchlight from the court, flaring and dying between the arcade's shadows, caught in the huge rounds of his spectacles; the voice-box with its clinking talismans seemed about to overset his fragile form, like a too-heavy yoke bound upon too young a child. Propping one crutch in the hollow of his armpit he held out his hand, and said, "My son . . . daughter."

Tally pushed up her mask, stepped forward swiftly and

hugged him. She had, Rhion realized, been much closer to
Jaldis these last seven years than he had, looking after him
and making sure he was not lonely in his little attic rooms.
Then, turning, she placed her hands on Rhion's shoulders,
and all he could remember were all those afternoons when
she'd play her flute for him in the grotto at the end of the
gardens, and the hazy glimmer of firelight in her hair.

Clutching at any straw of hope, he whispered, "Keep
watch for Shavus," in a voice very unlike his own. "If he
comes, send him up, please, fast . . ."

Somewhere above them, the palace clocks struck eleven,
the heavy bronze note sounding leaden and dead.

"I will." She took his face between her palms and their
mouths met desperately. "I love you." Her hands traveled
down his shoulders, his arms, his back, as if to memorize
the shape of muscle and flesh. "Always . . ."

"I'll come back . . ."

She nodded convulsively, and he knew she didn't believe
him. Then she was gone, walking swiftly through the blowing curtains of rainy mist to the dark of the palace gates.

In the black loft above Jaldis' quarters, they made the conjuration, waking the Dark Well from its shadowy quiescence,
watching it deepen and clear until it stretched before their
feet in an abyss of sightless chaos. Past the shuddering dark
rainbow of unnamable colors, Rhion sensed things about the
Void which terrified him, and it took all the discipline of
seventeen years to keep his concentration unwavering upon
the spells they wove in concert. For Jaldis was right: they
could afford to think neither of the future nor the past, neither
of what strange world they would find nor of what would
befall those they loved once they had stepped through the
shifting colors of that dreadful gate. He became only the
spells that he worked, summoning power from air and earth
and aether, watching the darkness before him deepen to

blackness and to something else far beyond that, something that swallowed all matter, all light, all time.

Deep in that bottomless infinity, Rhion saw a shining pin-prick of gold.

He knew instinctively that what he saw was ten or twenty times as far away as it seemed, that the flickering glimmer, the tiny sun-cross shining like a star in the blackness, had been blown huge so that they could see it at all.

And he understood that, delayed by the gods only knew what, Shavus was not going to arrive to save him from having to do this thing.

Midnight was upon them. He felt it through the shining tracks of energy which webbed the earth and carried magic forward and back to the world's farthest corners, the balance point swinging like the fulcrum of some huge beam above their heads. Beside him, Jaldis' face was untroubled, the withered lips and throat twitching in subconscious echo of the voice that spoke the words of power, the words that would open the Void itself, from the box upon his chest.

He held out a hand and Rhion took it, his own palm icy as death. The arthritic fingers gave his a quick squeeze of thanks, the only human thought they could spare, then trans-ferred their astonishing grip to his forearm. Rhion focused his mind away from his terror—for his life, for his past, for the nightmare dreams of the future—and formed of it a cut-ting crystal lightblade of concentration. Together, the two men stepped into the Dark Well.

And fell. Fell into infinity.

Later Rhion remembered very little of it except the terror, and the cold that drank at his life in a single greedy draught. Jaldis' mind and soul closed around his, a blazing column of strength that had nothing to do with the old man's frail body— the splendid obverse of the strength that had swept him aside in anger when Rhion had tried to part him from his dream.

It was only that, Rhion understood even then, which kept him from dying or worse than dying. He could see the tiny red beacon of the far-off sun-cross; but, as he had feared from the start, there was nothing there to touch, no magic in it, no power to draw them through.

The drag of the abyss pulled them, the black current which had never heard the name of life, and swept them away.

Then the fragile spark seemed to gleam brighter, a flare like a tiny starburst. Something, tenuous and silvery, like a single glowing spider-strand of magic came drifting towards them across the flooding spate of darkness . . .

He was lying on something hard. His fingers moved and felt damp stone which would have been cold had there been any warmth left in his body. A confusion of voices drifted in and out of the exhausted darkness of his brain, voices crying ''Eric . . . *Eric* . . . !'', shouting things he didn't understand.

Eric, he thought. The wizard born to magic in a world without it—the wizard who had summoned them, brought them here.

They'd made it. They were in this world where magic no longer existed.

And, more surprisingly, he was still alive.

He was too weary for joy or exultation, almost too weary for surprise or thought of any kind. It occurred to him that he really hadn't expected to make it here.

But where and what was ''here''? Unbidden, there crossed his mind, like the fragment of remembered magic, something—a dream?—some dread connected with this world, some terrible premonition that made him wonder suddenly what this world was, that they had come to . . .

Jaldis had said, *We can think neither of the future, nor of the past we leave behind* . . .

The stench of blood and incense filled his nostrils, dark

forms bending over him out of darkness. He heard someone
say Jaldis' name. Then he passed out.

Book II of Barbara Hambly's SUN-CROSS will reveal what world
it was that Rhion found—the world of unknown and impossible
danger and the tangled quest for power which led to true wizardry
. . . and beyond.